The Apocalypse Revenge
The Undead World Novel 9
A Zombie Tale by Peter Meredith

Fictional works by Peter Meredith:

Chapter 1

Jillybean

Ipes the zebra, Jillybean's best friend in all the world, was buried in a cake box next to the Neosho River in Northern Oklahoma. Jillybean went out alone the day before Christmas, taking her usual assortment of weapons, a Hello Kitty backpack filled with a wide range of what she considered necessary items, and a modified Jeep Rubicon.

The Jeep resembled a small tank and had been through so many changes that it was nearly as dangerous as one.

Using her new self-taught welding skills, Jillybean had added layers of sheet metal and Kevlar around the entire structure and a triple layer chain skirt to protect the tires. It was, in essence, utterly bullet proof. Since this reduced visibility to zero, she had installed miniature cameras which led to her having to mount monitors within the vehicle so that the driver's seat looked like the cockpit of a low-budget spaceship.

Besides the armor, she had added a number of weapons including a wire-guided, M249 Squad Assault Weapon set on a track, allowing it to swivel left and right. Jillybean had implanted the monitor for the infrared camera-mounted weapon in the steering wheel, where the airbag had once sat, and with a push of a button she could rattle off two hundred rounds a minute.

For tougher than average foes, she had also added a device that released homemade pipe bombs from beneath the Jeep. Each of the bombs was on a three second fuse and each had approximately the power of two hand grenades.

In the event that the machine gun and the bombs proved inadequate, she installed a smoke generator that combined potassium chlorate, baking powder and malt. It operated using the heat generated by the exhaust pipe and could produce enough smoke in seconds to hide her, the Jeep and forty elephants if needed.

And lastly, she welded aluminum struts to the gas and brake pedals so that her feet could reach them without a problem. Needless to say, her driving was much improved especially as she had "wasted" gas practicing driving on the football field of Vinita High.

Granny Annie had thought it all a sad waste of resources and never failed to natter on when Jillybean would leave to test her inventions. "Please, we don't have a lot to waste on all of that nonsense. You're safe here, my dear."

Not for a moment did the little girl believe that. The only slight bit of safety in the world lay in the twin sciences of preparation and constant vigilance. Granny Annie was fine with preparation; she had laid aside quite a bit for the coming winter, and Jillybean had augmented that with daily forages out into the wilds of Oklahoma. Already she had thoroughly ransacked the towns of Bushyhead, Adair, Clairmore, and had even gone as far away as Tulsa.

The winter would not be a problem when it came to supplies. It would be a problem, however, when it came to vigilance and common sense. Granny Annie had been lucky so far. In the year and a half since the start of the apocalypse, no one had bothered her. In fact, almost no one even knew there was a town called Vinita and even fewer knew she lived in the heart of it. This was not due to any precautions taken on her part.

In broad daylight, she ambled around town with her squeaky cart and rarely saw a living soul and when she did catch someone passing through, she was generally pitied and given very favorable trades. It was only through luck that she had yet to have a run-in with slavers and bandits, not that anyone would try to enslave her; that was preposterous even to Jillybean, but they would take her belongings. That was a given. They would leave her with absolutely nothing and if she gave them lip, they'd kill her without batting an eye.

Despite Jillybean's stories about the evil in the world, Granny Annie refused to believe it and acquiesced to some of the little girl's demands only after she threatened to leave.

"Please stay, oh please, please," Granny Annie had begged, her gnarled fingers clutching at Jillybean's pink sweater—it had not yet been December when this conversation had taken place and Jillybean was still wearing mostly pink. It wasn't until the second week of the month that she had traded out her favorite color of pink for reds and greens as was only appropriate for the holiday.

"Okay, but you have to do some things for me," Jillybean had answered. "Really, it's for both of us; to keep us safe." In truth, the little girl had no intention of leaving Granny Annie. For one, she had nowhere else to go. The world had turned against her in as complete a fashion as she could imagine. Although she had always tried to be a good person, it just never turned out like she planned and everywhere she had been, she had left bodies and blood and enemies in her wake. Even the people of the Estes Valley, the very people she had saved from the Azael and an army of monsters, had been turned against her.

The second reason that she didn't want to leave was that she loved the humpbacked old woman. Yes, she wasn't exactly pleasant to look upon and she was plodding and set in her ways, but she was also sweet and loving and treated Jillybean like a real person, something she hadn't experienced since her father had died.

Jillybean's precautions were simple enough: no fires in the daytime—the smoke would be a beacon visible from miles away; supplies were to be divided up into two equal parts and hidden around town; the house was to be booby-trapped at night and emergency hiding places prepared.

She even tried to get Granny Annie to run evacuation drills, but gave up after three tries. No force on earth could get the old woman to move at more than a snail's pace.

A tornado could, a voice said, speaking directly into Jillybean's ear. Quick as lightning, she spun on her heel, her .38 caliber police special suddenly in her hand. It was Christmas Eve and she was standing by the river where the water flowed calmly by and the air was still. She would have known if someone had snuck up on her, and yet, the voice had been so clear…so real that her hand shook as her eyes darted about.

"You aren't real," she said, slowly spinning in place. Nothing moved in the clearing and little moved beyond it save for a crow gliding off in the distance just above the trees. Jillybean waited, listening, her head tilted as her heart thrummed in her chest. "The voice wasn't real," she said when her pulse finally slowed. "None of them are ever real."

She slid the gun back in her pocket and glanced down at the cake box where Ipes laid, snuggled in a square of white silk that she had found in a woman's clothing store in Tulsa. Like a perfectly framed picture, she could see him through the clear plastic and with the gaping hole in his belly hidden by the silk, he looked to be sleeping.

Who sleeps with their eyes open?

Jillybean's hand was in her coat and back on the grip of the .38 so fast that she almost shot a hole through the pocket. A second later, she realized that it was the voice in her head again. She forced her hand off the grip. "It's not real!" she hissed.

I'm as real as Ipes was. Hell, I'm more real because I'm an actual person. I'm your fath...

Before the voice could finish, Jillybean's hand, flat and hard, swung through the air and smacked her own left cheek. There was a crack like thunder, her head shot back and her eyes crossed for a brief moment.

Jillybean! What are you do...

The hand came again, hitting the little girl so hard that she reeled and her knees buckled. She fell to the cold earth, a rock biting into her left palm, while her right felt as though it were on fire. She raised it again, waiting for the voice to dare speak again.

The voices weren't real because she wouldn't let them be. It was a conscious decision on her part not to be crazy and she had vowed not to be crazy even if she had to kill herself. For the most part, her attempt to force sanity had been working. The voices in her head came only when she was stressed or afraid... or sad. And, just then, her heart was heavy with sadness.

The cake box with the dead zebra had fallen to the earth and now there was dirt on the side of it. She licked her thumb and cleaned it, forgetting that she had been about to bury it.

"It should be clean," she said to herself. "Ipes would have wanted it clean." In truth Ipes would have been afraid to be put in the dirt forever. Jillybean knew this and it was why the box had been in her room at Granny Annie's for so long. And, if she hadn't caught the slightest twinkle in Ipes' eye the day before, it would still be there.

Had the twinkle been real? Or had it just been a trick of the light? Or was it a trick of her broken mind? She didn't know and she wasn't going to take any chances with her craziness, not even for Ipes. She had decided right then that it was time to bury him before he started talking again.

With one last look around, Jillybean placed the box on the ground and removed a gardening shovel from her backpack. The dark earth came up easily and, although she could have dug very deep, she only cleared enough room to fit the box. "So he won't be that afraid," she said, not realizing that she was developing a bad habit of talking to herself—and answering herself.

When the box was snugged into its hole, Jillybean said a prayer in a hitching voice, cried so many tears her jacket sleeve became a boogery, wet mess, and then covered up the box with indecent haste. For a second, as she wiped her sleeve across her face to catch all the tears, she was sure she had seen something move within the cake box.

Had it been a monster version of Ipes coming back to life, she could have handled it. After all, the monsters were usually slow and Ipes had been slow back when he was alive. He'd be like a turtle, now, or a sloth. And he didn't really have any teeth or claws or anything that could hurt her, and even if he did, she was well armed with both guns and bombs.

The real reason she had covered him so fast was the idea that it was actually Ipes moving around in the box. The real Ipes, alive like he used to be, despite the huge hole in him. He would make a funny comment and ask to go home with her and that was an altogether scarier thought than any monster version of Ipes.

"It would mean I'm still crazy." And there was nothing worse than that in her world. She stood when the box was covered in a mound and watched the loose dirt to make sure that it remained still.

After half a minute, she breathed out a sigh of relief and said, "Good. Ipes, I love you, but please rest in peace. That's what means go to heaven and wait for me there. Okay? Good." She made it to the Jeep before she remembered something and hurried back. "I almost forgot to say Merry Christmas. That cookie in your box is from me. Granny Annie helped me make them, but I did all the work. Oh, I forgot to tell you: I can cook stuff now. I hope you like it."

With a final goodbye and her usual, cautious look around, she climbed into the Jeep. "Let's go home, Jessica," she said. No one replied and it would have been very odd if they had. Jessica was the name she had given to the Jeep and everyone knew that Jeeps couldn't talk.

She left the Neosho River behind and drove along the back roads until she came to the edge of Vinita where the houses were worn and dusty-looking. All the homes on the edge of town had the same flat-earth weathered look, and it was no wonder since they took the brunt of the wind that howled through the state, sometimes day and night.

The wind had blown itself into Texas the night before and so Jillybean could see the smoke rising in the center of the town just as plain as day—of course it meant that if there was anyone within ten miles they'd also be able to see it.

"Oh, for all darn it," she cursed her heaviest curse as she gunned the Jeep down the street, using the front camera to weave in and out of the monsters. As always, Jillybean drove to the street that ran parallel to Granny Annie's and parked in the garage of a house that was two doors down and one back.

When she slipped out of the garage on foot, she hunkered down next to a bush that had spent the last year and a half growing out of control and looked like a thousand-armed stick monster. With her ears pricked, she listened for the sound of a car's engine and when she heard none, she focused on the moans of the monsters to see if they were more excited than usual. They weren't.

Still, Jillybean proceeded with caution, easing through the shrubbery and then through a gap in the loose boards in Grannie Annie's back fence. She paused once to glare at the smoke drifting up from her chimney. It was a black feather rising a hundred feet into the sky before it dissipated into nothing.

With an irritated air about her, she came at the house from an angle that would minimize exposure until she stood in the shadow of the eaves, listening to Granny Annie sing Christmas carols in her wheezy voice. She was alone and safe. *But for how long?* Jillybean wondered as she slipped in through the back door leaving tiny wet tracks behind her.

"What did I say about the fire?" Jillybean asked, her arms folded across her skinny torso. She seemed more like the adult in the room than the wrinkled and weathered granny.

"But it's Christmas, silly. Even bad guys celebrate Christmas. And besides, I have a surprise. I know you've been very mopey in the last couple of days and so I started the pies early. I've got apple and pecan going."

It was true that with the coming of the holidays and with Ipes' funeral, Jillybean hadn't been herself. She had been dour and sad. Pies would certainly help that. *I'll let it go, just this once*, she said to herself.

"A nut pie?" she asked, coming around to look at the uncooked pie covered in what looked like split nuts. She'd never had pecan pie before. "It sounds crunchy." Actually, it sounded strange, dry and a little icky.

"Oh, you will love it," Granny Annie assured, and she was right. Jillybean had two servings of both and discovered that pecan pie was her favorite pie of all time.

The next day was Christmas and Jillybean said nothing as Granny Annie made another daytime fire. Her cooking was really extraordinary and Jillybean couldn't wait to taste the stewed rabbit. The two of them had a fine division of labor going: Jillybean would hunt the various critters, usually rabbit, squirrel, or pheasant, and Granny Annie would do the cooking and the cleaning.

That night the little girl fell asleep with her tummy bursting. She dreamed vibrantly and in depth, but not of pies. She saw herself on the Colonel's Island leading a string of men who were horsing heavy boxes on their shoulders. One of the men was the Colonel himself, looking nervous. He kept licking his lips and darting his eyes around at the dark. A part of her enjoyed his discomfort.

As dreams always seemed to, the scene shifted erratically. Now they were on the pontoon she had stolen. Neil stood over three bound men holding a tall axe. The men blabbered and blubbered and suddenly she was behind one of them holding her police special. When she pulled the trigger, it was oddly muffled. "Haigh," she whispered in her sleep.

Haigh spasmed and fell straight into the river to float among the monsters. In that slow-motion way of dreams, she turned to the other two men on the boat. They tried to run, but the edges of the boat seemed to hold them on board and they only went in circles. She shot them over and over, but they wouldn't die.

Flush with guilt, Jillybean tossed and turned as the night wore on and she dreamed of murder and death and executions until her body glistened with sweat. Lastly, she dreamt of her father. Just as tall and handsome as ever, he walked through Granny Annie's front door and strode down the hall until he stood in Jillybean's bedroom.

"You've forgotten something important," he whispered. "You have to go back before it's too late." As he spoke those few short words, his face grew grey and his body twisted and a scream of agony erupted from somewhere around him.

It was the scream that finally woke her.

"What did I forget?" she asked, sitting up, still partially in her dream. For a few seconds, she waited for an answer, but when it came, she didn't want to hear it.

Hello Jilly, her father's voice spoke into her ear.

"No!" she cried, jumping out of bed and staring around, her heart racing. She couldn't see her father, but she could feel his presence. A year ago, she would have burst out in tears over the warm feeling of having him so near.

That was then. She raised her right hand, stared for a second at it and then slapped herself in the face so hard that it spun her around.

Jilly! Stop! You have to hear this.

"No," she said and struck herself again. Now, her ears rang and there were orange blooms in her vision as she hit herself repeatedly, until Granny Annie, wearing a flowered muumuu, bustled in and grabbed her hands.

"It's just a dream, dear. It's just a dream," she said, cuddling Jillybean to her bosom.

That's what Jillybean tried to tell herself, however a part of her knew that there was more to it than just a dream. Her subconscious was trying to tell her something very important. Unfortunately, it was trying to do it using the outmoded vehicle of her insanity.

Jillybean couldn't have that and she wasn't going to give in no matter what. Even if it ended up killing her.

Chapter 2

Jillybean

The day after Christmas, a cold front rolled in and, where before the days were brisk, now Jillybean could see her breath plume up out of her like little clouds. She was prepared for the cold just as she was prepared for the possibility that the day would warm. Although each layer of clothing draped upon her appeared ratty and torn, they were actually quite snug and could be removed without attracting much attention from the monsters moaning up and down the street.

Supposedly, she was outside that morning making her usual rounds, when in truth she was doing her best to keep busy to take her mind off of Ipes and the terrible dreams she'd had.

Lucky for her there was plenty to keep her going: checking her traps and snares, replacing the batteries in certain devices and, since there had been the lightest dusting of snow, cleaning off a dozen or so solar panels.

The traps and snares were small and thus not meant for humans or monsters. They were for food. The solar panels, or rather what they were connected to, were, however.

Jillybean had, long before, decided that the town of Vinita was indefensible. Other than two shallow creeks, it had no natural barriers and the way into town lay wide open, especially down the main thoroughfares of Route 2 and Route 66, which cut the town into three sections.

The only place in town that would have been a suitable place to defend was the Craig County Juvenile Detention Center. With its heavy fencing and sharp barbed wire, it might have been ideal for a community of a few hundred survivors, but with just Granny Annie as a companion it was nothing but an unsprung trap simply waiting on a few bad guys to lock them in where there would be no escape.

Besides, the detention center was too spooky to live in. Jillybean had been in it twice to scavenge and had found it, with its echoey corridors and dark basements, to be one of the scariest places she had ever been. This, coming from a girl who had almost been traded as a child-bride to the evil prophet of New Eden, and who had been in the prisons of both the River King and the Azael, who had swum in a river of death with ten thousand monsters, was saying something.

Jillybean preferred a fluid defense based on camouflage, subterfuge and above all, options. She liked to be able to move freely and to be able to strike back at the time and moment of her choosing, something that wasn't possible with the stagnant defense of walls and fences.

The key component of her defenses lay in the fifteen video cameras she had set up around the town. Each was slaved to her iPad and she could flick from feed to feed with just a swish of her finger. She also had seven bombs prepared, ten smoke generators, and eight previously sighted weapons points.

On that morning, she checked everything. Her mind wanted to hold on to her dream and the newly awakened memory of killing…no, executing the Colonel and his men. Thankfully, the memory had been eroded by time. The blood was dull and dark. The flash of the gun, dim. The panicked pleading of her victims, muted.

Still, it was enough to make her tummy feel icky and so she busied herself over-preparing for a battle that wasn't likely to happen.

Jillybean had just climbed into a tree overlooking Route 66 where she had a Winchester 30.06 slid between two steadying branches, aimed at a tarped trailer that she had set on the side of the road. The empty boxes inside made it appear filled with untouched goods.

Before the little girl set her eye to the scope she saw something that made her groan: smoke trickling up from within the neighborhood to the east. It could only be coming from Granny Annie's house.

"Oh, Ipes, I can't believe how silly she…" Jillybean stopped herself when she realized that she was alone in the tree. Even though it had been six weeks since the little zebra had been killed, she still caught herself starting conversations with him. "It's just grief," she said, the corners of her lips pulled down. "Mister Neil said we all deal with grief differently and that's what means I can make mistakes."

With a sigh, she put her eye to the scope and swiveled it towards Granny Annie's house. It was mostly hidden by the tops of trees, and so she pulled out her iPad and scanned the four different views of the house and the streets around it. There was nothing showing on the screens except a few dozen monsters roaming around in their usual dull manner.

"Okay good," she said, of the monsters. She hadn't feared the monsters in months, not since her old, and now dead, friend Ram had taught her how to blend in with them.

"But that's getting tougher and tougher," Jillybean murmured as she re-sighted on the trailer. She was in the process of doing an independent study on the unprecedented physical growth of the monsters, something she had only theorized about before. It was now becoming conclusive.

She had three of them trapped in an empty pool three blocks from Granny Annie's home. They had been there for almost a month and every day, as part of her regular routine, she would swing by, drop ten pounds of moldy hay into the pool and measure how high they could reach when trying to rip her into shreds. Each could reach at least a half inch further than on the first day of their internment and bigger monsters meant she would stand out. The creatures wouldn't notice, but any human nearby would.

On that day, with the cold being so harsh, the three monsters seemed a touch stuporous and were slow to attack when she threw the hay down. "Interesting," she said and made a note of that in her iPad, marking the time, the day and the temperature.

Although she could have dawdled outside for half the day, she felt a pull to get home again before anyone saw the smoke. As always, she approached the house from a different angle than the one she had left from and, again as always, she paused at the front door.

Normally, she paused to listen, this time she paused to steel herself. Granny Annie was a sweet woman but was set in her ways. Unfortunately, those ways were very dangerous, not just to the old woman but to Jillybean as well. She would have to be scolded.

The house was warm to the point of being hot and still smelled of cinnamon and stewed rabbit from the Christmas feast. In fact, the smell was stronger than when she had left that morning.

Granny Annie was cooking again, which meant a surprise for Jillybean, which meant that it was going to be very difficult for the little girl to admonish the old woman. And when her tummy growled, she knew it was going to be next to impossible.

"What is that smell?" she asked, stepping into the kitchen and shedding clothes one layer at a time.

"Oh just something I whipped up that I thought you might like. It's a rabbit bolognese with homemade noodles and you get to help make the noodles! Have you ever made noodles from scratch?" The little girl shook her head, not quite understanding the term scratch. "Then you're in for a treat. But first you need to go wash up. You smell like gun oil."

Excited, Jillybean started for the door, but then paused with her hand on the frame. As much as homemade noodles sounded fun and delicious, Jilly still had to confront the old woman. After taking another deep breath, she said: "Miss Granny Annie, ma'am? I'm sure the rabbit bolo-knees will be great, but is there some reason it couldn't have been made tonight? Amember, I talked to you about the need to only cook at night?"

Granny Annie's face fell. "But it's Christmas. The day after is still Christmas and not just for me, but for everyone. Didn't you still have that Christmas feel the day after, back when you were growing up?"

"Yes, but…"

"No buts. You did before and you do, now. And I'm sure that all those bad guys out there are still in bed hungover from all their merrymaking."

She was probably correct, and yet, if Jillybean had been a bad guy, she would have been out marauding, hoping that her prey was relaxing just as Granny Annie was. "I suppose it's possible," the little girl allowed. It was true that, in her experience, bad guys were frequently lazy guys. "But tomorrow we have to go back to being as careful as…" She was about to say: "rabbits" but as she had just captured two and there were three in the pot, she changed her words to "Careful as cats."

Annie agreed and for the next month she cooked only in the evening and during the day kept the coals banked in the side of the fireplace, where they smoldered, keeping the house pleasantly warm. In that month, they had two scares from scavenging humans.

The first came a week after the rabbit bolognese had been eaten. Twenty men, leading four chained women by the throat came walking into town at a frantic clip. They were desperate for food and fuel, though they seemed to have an endless supply of bullets and shot a thousand monsters in a running battle as they hurriedly ransacked every home sitting off of Route 66.

When preparing her caches of supplies, Jillybean had expected exactly this kind of behavior so none of their hidden

15

goods was ever touched. It was a relief that Granny Annie was nervous over all the shooting and didn't like the way they treated their women and decided against going out to haggle for goods with the men.

Thirteen days later, the town was visited by a second group. This one consisted of only men. There were eleven of them in two banged about trucks. They were an ugly lot, scruffy to the point of being shaggy. Jillybean, who had a vision in her head of what good people looked like—and they didn't look like this—was wary, and counseled that they should remain hidden, while Granny Annie thought otherwise.

The old woman couldn't be swayed and in minutes of hearing their trucks rumble into town, she had her cart and was squeaking out towards the men. Jillybean went out the back door and into a grey day, overhung with threatening clouds. She hurried to one of her secret weapons caches, guessing where the two parties would intersect and knowing she would have time.

It had become a standard practice for most people to lure the monsters to one end of a town with blaring car horns before rushing past them to scrounge in relative safety.

Jillybean got to her position, and after wiping away the snow from the rifle, she quickly slipped off the protective caps from both ends of the scope. With the safety still on, she peered across two hundred and fifty yards at Granny Annie huffing and puffing towards the trucks, though why she bothered, Jillybean didn't know; they were heading right for her.

Just as Jillybean had when she had first met her, the men mistook the old woman for a monster. Even with the cart she pushed, the lead driver's face showed shock as he brought the truck to a shuddering halt. The driver and the old woman exchanged words, but what they were Jillybean couldn't tell.

After a minute of this, the driver and another man got out of the truck and glanced in at the cart as Granny Annie continued to speak. Unexpectedly, the driver pushed the cart over, picked up the back end and dumped everything out. When Annie stepped forward, he shoved her down and pointed a black pistol at her midsection.

"Oh, for all darn it!" Jillybean cried, switching the Winchester to fire and leaning her head once more over the stock. The weapon was far too big with far too powerful of a kick for the fifty-one pound girl to even try firing it as an adult would. She had it set up on a tripod with a big foam cushion glued against the butt to absorb the shock.

The driver looked back at the man who had stepped out of the truck with him. They spoke for a minute and then Granny Annie started gesticulating angrily. She said something to provoke the driver and now the gun in his hands was aimed with a bit more authority.

"What do I do?" Jillybean asked. "Do I shoot? Do I wait?" She feared that if she killed the driver, one of the other men would kill Granny Annie. And, of course, she feared that if she didn't shoot, the driver would kill her anyway. "What do I do? Oh, I wish Ipes were here."

She was sure the little zebra would have helped her… somehow. "Yes, he was always somewhat of a chicken, but he was a good counterbalance and now I don't have any balance at all."

Just saying his name seemed to bring a crowded buzz into her head as if there were a thousand beings in between her ears demanding to get out. She raised her hand, threatening to lash her own face with it and hissed: "No!" They backed down and yet she was still without an inkling of what to do.

"Think…think…do I shoot? Or do I don't shoot?" She became paralyzed by indecision, which led to her not shooting, which led to Granny Annie not dying that day. The bandits, and it became obvious in seconds that they were indeed bandits, started throwing the cans and candles and the odd items that Granny Annie had been hoping to trade, into the back of one of the trucks.

The old woman only lay in the street crying, something Jillybean would have cautioned against. Sometimes tears made bandits wiggy and there was no telling how they would react.

In this case they ignored her and once they were done stealing everything worth stealing, there was a brief discussion with much gesturing and pointing. Then, just like that, the bandits got back into their banged-about trucks and left town the way they had come.

Jillybean watched them go, switching from the rifle to her camera feeds to make sure they were truly gone and not trying to trick the old woman in some sense. Once they faded from view, Jillybean hurried down to see if Granny Annie was alright.

"This is all my fault," the old woman said, through tears. "They took everything and it's all my fault."

Had Ipes been there he would have agreed with her, making some sarcastic remark in the process. Jillybean would have shushed him or told him to behave. Now, without the expected remark, she didn't know what to say. Yes, it had been her fault for not listening to Jillybean, but what good would come from saying so? And yet to disagree would be a lie. Jillybean took a neutral stance, giving her a shrug and a pained, sympathetic smile.

Granny Annie went on: "They wanted everything but I told them they could kill me if they wanted to, but I wasn't going to tell them where we lived."

"That was brave," Jillybean said, trying to bolster the old woman, who hadn't made any move to get up. It was making her nervous being out in the open for so long and in such an obvious way.

"It was stupid and I was stupid. Look at the predicament we're in, now. That was over forty cans of food."

Jillybean knew exactly how much food had been stolen: twenty-eight days' worth. It put them in a dangerous position if the winter ran long. "We'll find more," she assured Granny Annie. "I'll go to Tulsa tonight. That place is huge and I haven't even seen five percent of it. It'll be okay."

"And what if it snows? Those are snow clouds, Jillybean. You'll be trapped and hungry and…and I have to forbid it." Granny Annie started weeping again.

"No, I have the Jeep. It's a good car. It'll be fine." This was a bit of a lie. Yes, the Jeep was a good vehicle, and yes she had made plenty of trips alone in it, however if snow came in any significant quantity she would be in deep trouble. Oklahoma's driving winds could pile the snow into banks higher than the Jeep's hood, making roads impassable even in four-wheel drive.

If the snow came while she was driving, she'd likely freeze to death on the lonely and mostly barren roads. If it came while she was in the city, she'd be stuck with little in the way of rations and less in the way of warmth. She would have to take dangerous chances just to survive.

"But that's not going to happen," she murmured, as she got Granny Annie to her feet and began the slow trip back to the house. "Who says it's gonna even snow?" she asked, glancing up at the ominous clouds.

Jillybean was turning over the different scenarios she would likely confront on a trip to Tulsa and was somewhat lost in thought when the voice in her head came back: *You've forgotten something very important.*

"Have not, now shut up, or else." Her hand was raised.

Fine, I'll be quiet once I've said one word.

Jillybean was just about to slap her own cheek, uncaring whether or not Granny Annie saw, however the idea that one word would shut down the voice in her head caused her to hesitate. "What word is that?"

Revenge, the voice said, in a ghostly whisper.

It was a most curious word and she dwelt upon it all during the walk home and during the bleak and windy afternoon she spent preparing for her trip into Tulsa. As she turned the word over and over in her mind, she could feel the owner of the voice looking over her shoulder, patiently waiting for her to ask what it meant.

She refused to ask.

There were so many people who wanted revenge on her that it was somewhat of a joke. Of course, the voice could have been referring to the people she wanted to have revenge on. Most were already dead, executed by her own hand: the royal family of the Azael, the Colonel, the River King, all the slavers and bandits and pirates and the bounty hunters who had ever tried to kill her...and who could forget Eve.

"Eve is dead. Mister Neil killed her. So, who am I forgetting? Not Yuri, I'd never forget him." Of all the people who deserved to die, Yuri Petrovich was at the top of her list. He had killed Ram, whom Jillybean had loved, and he had tried to kill Neil Martin, who was her adopted father, and he had sold the baby Eve to Abraham, the evil prophet of New Eden, and he had a bounty out on Jillybean's sister, Sadie.

But of course any voice in Jillybean's head would know that. And it would also know that Jillybean had no intention of going to New York and exacting revenge. The idea repulsed her. In fact, any killing repulsed her. Yuri might deserve to die but that didn't mean she had to be the one to kill him. And if it wasn't Yuri that the voice in her head was referring to, then who did that leave?

After two hours of trying to come up with a name, she gave up. It was a maddening puzzle and one she didn't have the energy for. She had to save her energy so that she could worry over the clouds. She also had to try to soothe Granny Annie, who also worried over the clouds, but with much more volume.

19

Jillybean left Vinita just as the sun began to set. She drove without lights and so it was slow going. On long open stretches, she was able to safely creep the Jeep up to fifteen miles an hour, but otherwise she put-putted along closer to ten, passing quietly through the dark night as just a shadow.

At that dull speed, it was a six hour trip and the snow didn't come until that sixth hour. "Oh boy, here we go," she said, sitting up higher on the pillows stacked under her bottom and gripping the wheel even harder than usual. The snow came down like sifted flour and her initial fear of slipping all over the road was unfounded and so too was her secondary fear of white-out conditions.

The fifth fear on her big list of fears did come true: as she drove, she left blatantly obvious tracks ranging behind her. "But what can I do about them?" she asked herself. There was nothing she could do but find a home to act as a base of operations as soon as possible.

It was midnight before she found what she assumed would be a perfect spot. It was an area, dense with houses that was separated from the rest of the city by two highways, a fenced off strip of land with train tracks running through it, and a meandering river with steep banks. Jillybean guessed that very few scavengers had ever taken the time to figure out a way into the area.

Satisfied with her choice, she parked in a cul-de-sac and stepped out of the Jeep, pausing to listen. Normally, listening was the key sense she used on a dark night such as this, however this time it was her nose that alerted her—there were people nearby. The scent of a wood fire came to her and it was strong and it was very close.

Chapter 3

Jillybean

The little girl with the fly-away hair tucked up under a white
ski hat that sprouted a silly red pompom from the top, spun
slowly about, her nose sniffing the air like a bloodhound. She
had parked at the bag end of a cul-de-sac and was just about to
choose which house to hole up in when she noticed the smell of
a wood burning fire.

Before she was halfway around, she saw that one of the
houses was occupied. The curtains on it were drawn and it
looked darker than the others around her. It seemed to have a
sensation of evil hanging over it, almost as if the house had eyes
and a black heart.

When the first gunshot rang out, she decided that it was
more than a feeling. The bullet passed just under her right
earlobe, tickling the downy blonde hairs that had been there
since birth. The next bullet missed by two feet as Jillybean
dropped to the ground using the open and heavily armored door
of her Jeep for cover.

From the black house, a number of people began yelling in
confusion, but not in fear. That, even more than the bullets,
spiked sudden terror in Jillybean's gut. Only people who were
used to causing fear wouldn't be afraid when a strange car pulled
up in front of their house in the middle of a snowy night and
gunshots started ringing out.

Jillybean didn't want to be anywhere near those kind of
people. With bullets whining off the armored Jeep, she dove in
and keyed the ignition. In a state of barely controlled panic, she
waited for the iPads to boot up and the cameras to sync. Without
them, she was blind. In the ten seconds it took before she could
see out of the Jeep, she couldn't count the number of bullets
striking the Jeep as a second gun joined the first.

Finally, the rear camera came on line and she pounded the
gas, sending the Jeep spinning back as she cranked the wheel
around. Her lack of experience driving in the snow showed as
she spun too far. Now the bullets were hitting the driver's side
door squarely. It sounded as though a dozen men were beating
the Jeep with hammers.

Pulling the wheel back around, she went lighter on the gas
and the Jeep responded properly, heading straight out of the cul-

de-sac the way it had come. As she got to the intersection, she slowed long enough to let off a few rounds from her rear-facing M249. She didn't even aim, she just wanted to give them something to think about.

There was plenty for her to think about: monsters poured out from the neighboring houses and rushed into the road, as the Jeep suddenly felt mushy under her controls as if one of the bullets had hit something vital in the steering column. To make matters worse, the rear camera blared white as headlights suddenly flicked on from back in the cul-de-sac, while the front camera was a blur as snow began to build up on it.

She was blundering down the road, going too fast for the conditions, when she saw a stop sign at an intersecting street. Beyond that, the road ended at an embankment—she had a quarter of a second to decide between right and left. She chose left because taking lefts had always been easier for her, however the Jeep had other ideas.

It ignored the turning wheel and the little foot stamping the brake. It even ignored the girl's scream as it slid right on through the intersection. Jillybean wasn't sure what she screamed, but with the crash and the ear-grinding screeches as she tore down a chainlink fence, it didn't really matter what came out of her mouth.

The Jeep ran up the embankment almost to the top, threatened to get hung up on the first line of railroad tracks and then went sliding back down. With its wheels still pointed left, it turned awkwardly and ended up facing in the wrong direction.

Jillybean had no time to try to correct her direction—an SUV had turned out of the cul-de-sac and was roaring down the road straight toward her. "Oh, jeeze!" she cried and forced the Jeep out of the tangle of fence and back onto the road. Next, she flicked on her lights; the time for secrecy was long past. What she needed now was precision and timing and something to make the people chasing her go away.

She decided to use a bomb instead of the M249 because for her, making bombs was easier than finding bullets. And she hoped that one well-timed explosion, whether completely successful or not, would turn the bad guys away. But it wouldn't be easy.

During her practice "bombing runs" she had used a towed dummy car on dry pavement at a speed of thirty miles an hour. In those runs, under those precise conditions, a following distance of eighty feet had resulted in eleven out of twelve direct hits. What she hadn't tried was a night run in snow with her rear end swishing all over the place, against an opponent who wouldn't come on slow and stupid.

Still, there were things she could extrapolate from her training: a slower speed on her part, combined with the friction of the snow slowing the bomb, which normally bounced along for about thirty-eight feet before it blew, meant that an early release time relative to the SUV's speed would be necessary.

With one eye on the forward screen and another on the rear screen, she yelled: "Bombs away!" and hit the eject button just as someone in the SUV started shooting. Again she screamed, hunching down in her chair. It wasn't easy for her to trust her own metal creation seeing as the structure had only been tested by two separate weapons and there was no knowing what calibers the bad guys were using. The bullets sure sounded big, whapping into the back of the Jeep.

Two thoughts went through her head just before the bomb exploded: she should either add angled rear armor or up-armor her chair. The chair seemed like a less weighty alternative, which would help with fuel consump...

The bomb's detonation, a heavy boom that pulsed the air within the Jeep, brought her around. The rear camera bloomed an intense white and by the time the camera's lens adjusted, the SUV was already in a death roll, sending glass, metal and at least one body flying. The SUV tumbled twice, crashing through a fence and ended up on its roof, its tires spinning and its engine whining.

Jillybean had to drag her eyes from the screen and by the time she turned to the front camera, the Jeep was barreling into a half-dozen monsters. She plowed through and over them, making the vehicle swerve and buck. This she handled with amazing calmness, however when the front screen went suddenly black, she screamed for the third time.

She mashed the brake, throwing a monster from the hood, and clearing the camera except for a brown blur that was probably blood or something equally icky.

Once more she rumbled the Jeep forward, bouncing over the still squirming bodies of the undead. She drove three blocks, took a left, drove another three blocks and took a right. Ten blocks after, with one eye on the rear camera and one on the front, she went through a series of turns, basically going in circles so that her tire tracks went in every direction at every intersection until she was lost.

In truth, she wasn't hopelessly lost. She was only somewhat lost. After all, she knew that Vinita lay north-east of Tulsa and she still knew which way that was. Still, she had no idea where she was in relation to the bad guys she had left behind, nor did she know where she was going.

After twenty minutes, she found a mall with an immense but empty parking lot where she stopped and got out of the Jeep to inspect it. The first thing she noticed was the sharp smell of gasoline.

"Oh jeeze," she whispered and went to the rear of the vehicle, fearing that the tank had been punctured. Before she could get her tools out, she noticed something glistening on the armor. The gas was leaking from one of the reserve jerrycans she had tied to the roof rack.

"Thank goodness it didn't blow up, right Ipe..." She bit off the question and then rephrased it as a statement: "Thank goodness it didn't blow up." After finding the holed can and breathing a sigh of relief that the bullet had struck near the top, she stuffed the hole with a shorn-off piece of her monster outerwear and then climbed back down to inspect the Jeep.

It had taken a beating and was no longer as "pretty" as it had been. She had painstakingly painted it in swirls of greens to maximize its camouflage. Now the paint was chipped and pitted. The steel showed through in a hundred places and the armor was no longer smooth and "cool" as it had been.

She made a face at it and grunted: "Humph." On one level, she was proud that her personal tank had stood up to its first test, but on another she was tired from her long trip and lack of sleep, and she was stressed to know there were bad guys so close. It would make scrounging that much harder.

"At least we know they're here. We won't be taken by surprise again." Jillybean said, patting the Jeep's door before climbing back in.

The little girl drove into the nearest neighborhood and drove in more convoluted circles before choosing a quiet street and a house on a hill to make camp for the remainder of the night. Yawning, she explored the home, set up cameras, alarms and bombs, and then went to sleep in the Jeep, which had just fit into the garage.

Sleeping in the Jeep was perfect for her. She was small enough to be comfortable, while the heat given off by a single candle was enough to keep her pleasantly warm. She also felt what could only be described as amniotic tranquility, cozied by so much armor.

In the morning, she watched her video feeds while heating up her breakfast of stew, using a can of homemade sterno. She had created the sterno from the simplest of ingredients: a coiled strip of cardboard set into a tuna fish can which was then filled with melted, left over candle wax. She liked it over other, alcohol and propane based sterno attempts she had concocted since it burned slower and gave off a pleasant smell, usually strawberries or cinnamon depending on what candles had been used by Granny Annie.

The feeds from the various cameras she had set up showed nothing but a few ambling monsters and some birds rooting about in the snow for food. There was no sign of trucks or SUVs.

Satisfied that she hadn't been followed, she thoroughly explored the house the garage was attached to, finding little of use other than a few batteries and a hidden stash of candy in a little boy's room. Despite it having been ransacked some time before, it was a nice house with many family touches that Jillybean appreciated: pictures on the walls and mantle, photo albums sitting out on the living room coffee table and a snugly den where the family of four had watched TV in the evenings cuddled on a large and comfortable sofa.

Jillybean lingered over the house, picturing happiness and smiles, picturing her own face in with the others. Eventually, she turned from the imagined warmth and looked out a second floor window at the falling snow. It was still so fine that it didn't amount to much. Fine but dangerous. The snow would show the tracks of her Jeep.

"I'll have to go scavenging on foot then," she said with a sigh. There were things she had to do before she left, however. Going back to the Jeep, she rummaged in the back for another pipe bomb to replace the one she had used the night before.

Without a touch of fear, she crawled up under the Jeep and opened the first of three bomb compartments and inspected a four-foot length of string. One end was tied to the Jeep's rear axle and the other end had a tiny sliver of plastic attached to it. It appeared undamaged and so she wrapped the new bomb with the

25

string and slid the plastic into a small opening in the back of the pipe. The plastic cut the circuit leading from the batteries she was about to put into the bomb, to the fuse on the blasting cap.

The premise was simple enough. When she keyed the bomb's compartment, its door fell open, dropping the bomb, which rolled, unraveling the string as it went. In half a second, the string would play out and yank the tiny slip of plastic from the slot, thus completing the circuit and initiating the fuse which was on a three second delay—and then: *bam-o!*

Once the bomb was set, she replaced the used section of the ammo belt feeding the M249, and finally, she topped off the gas tank, making sure to use the damaged jerry can first.

All of this should have been done the night before. "Ipes woulda called me lazy," she said, when she was done. After this pronouncement, the house seemed extra quiet. It made her want to zip her lip and that was just fine. "Talking to yourself is what means crazy." And she didn't want that.

To fight the possibility of crazy, she kept busy. Snow was gathered in pots because everyone knew that snow and rain were always clean to drink. Next, she investigated the other houses on the block, moving slowly in the snow, dressed as a monster. In one house, in boxes marked "Christmas Decorations" she found a dozen red candles. In another, among the camping supplies, she found two small propane tanks and flashlights with batteries. She tossed away the flashlights and kept the batteries.

When it came to food, she found almost nothing. Next to a fireplace on the last house on the block where there sat the ash of a months' old fire, she discovered the jelly packet from an MRE. In another home, beneath the lip of a stove, was a can of tuna. In that same home, sitting in the official "junk drawer" were eight packets of ketchup, three of soy sauce and five fortune cookies. This was enough to keep her going for two days if needed.

Scavenging alone like this was slow and dangerous. It was a laborious time-consuming process and monsters tended to get in the way. Twice she had monsters rush at her as she was busy nosing through drawers in an obviously human manner. Both times the snow and the deep carpeting in the houses masked the noise the monsters made.

"This will never get me anywhere," she groused, after the second attack. She had managed to lock the monster in a back bedroom by running around a queen-sized bed, scampering over it and then rushing out the door before the stupid beast knew what was going on.

The smart way to scavenge was to reconnoiter neighborhoods first, only with bad guys prowling around Tulsa, reconnoitering was impossible…unless you had a drone or two.

After a light lunch of ketchup and fortune cookies, Jillybean went to the Jeep and brought out one of her two heli-drones. It was a Phantom 4, remote-controlled quadcopter with a built in HD Camera RTF 4 Channel 2.4GHz 6-Gyro Headless System with a modified flight time of thirty-six minutes. The batteries were checked and the camera was synched to her iPad before she sent it aloft.

The first step she took was to find out where she was in Tulsa. She had a map, but as all the street signs were filmed with snow, it hadn't done her much good. She sent the drone straight up and at five hundred feet, she was able to compare enough landmarks to pinpoint her location: the subdivision of Lortondale, two miles from where she had been shot at the night before. It was so close that she sent the drone towards it, running up the same road on which she had exploded the SUV.

Morbidly, she brought the heli-drone down closer to inspect the crash. Thankfully, if there had been any bodies, they had been removed and, for the most part, the blood had been covered by the steadily falling snow. She went over the dead SUV as best as she could with the drone's camera but could learn nothing more of the people who had chased her.

Had they really been bad guys? It was possible that they had mistaken her for someone else. Maybe they had thought she was the bad guy. Or maybe she had stumbled into the middle of a war; it wouldn't be the first time.

To help settle the matter, she sent the drone to the cul-de-sac where she had been attacked. From above, all she could see was snow-covered roofs and so she settled the drone on the top of a parked car that sat at the corner. From there she had a perfect angle to view the house but other than smoke drifting from the chimney, and some tire tracks in the snow, there was really nothing to see.

She gazed at the unmoving image on the iPad for a few minutes before hitting the record button and going to fetch her second drone. Once more she went through battery and camera checks. As she did, she sang *White Christmas* even though Christmas was long over with.

She sent this drone along a different path. She was, after all, there looking for food, not looking for trouble. North and slightly to the east, the drone buzzed over the University of Tulsa. There was a football field and a basketball stadium and the actual campus with dormitories and buildings where the kids actually learned abo…

Her mind stopped describing what she was seeing as it latched onto a vision of what the campus must have been like a year and half before when the monsters first started appearing on the east coast and the population of America went from disbelief to nervous denial to panic in the space of two weeks.

What did the children at the school do during this time? Did they wait around for the monsters to surge inland as their numbers doubled every twelve hours, so that by the tenth day there were fifty million of the creatures? Jillybean didn't think so. The empty parking lots suggested that the school was abandoned very early on as the students and the teachers rushed home.

Things had to have been left behind. Not a lot, mind you. College kids were notoriously poor, but at the same time they were notorious eaters. There would be food in those dorm rooms…or there had been food there, but surely someone else had thought of this.

Jillybean second-guessed herself for so long that the battery on the drone began to run down. Quickly, she set it down on the corner of Harvard and Route 66. "I can't lose that," she said, hurrying to the garage and pulling the door up. It had just rattled loudly to the ceiling when she realized she hadn't checked for monsters or bad guys outside her own door!

Luckily, the coast was clear and she backed the Jeep down into the street. Gathering her wits, she made a number of convoluted turns so that her tracks couldn't be easily retraced. It meant more time out in the open where any bad guy could see her, however after the events of the night before she wasn't all that afraid. More than likely, the bad guys would turn tail the moment they saw the tank-like Jeep.

It took her a half hour to get to the intersection and the drone was none the worse for the wait. She scooped it up, replaced the battery and immediately launched it to see if anyone was following her. Ipes would have called her paranoid but that was only because no one was following her. If she had been followed, he would have scolded her for not being paranoid enough.

"There's no winning with you is there?" she asked, only to be greeted by the same heavy silence that had been with her since the trip started.

You can fix that, a voice said, speaking into her ear. She swatted at the side of her head as if a wasp had buzzed there, tickling her exposed flesh with its nasty stinger.

"No. We'll have none of that." She glared around, daring any voice to make another appearance, so to speak. When none came, she began to sing *White Christmas* again in order to ward off the crazy effect the silence seemed to have on her. As she sang she retrieved the heli-drone and drove to the nearest dorms, where she was greeted by a storm of monsters.

"This bodes well," she said, rushing around the side of the nearest building and dropping one of her monster distraction devices behind her. In this case, it was a Bumble Ball that she had taken from the nursery of a home back in Vinita. The child's toy bounced around, its led lights flashing through all of the prime colors.

As expected, the beasts were properly mesmerized which allowed Jillybean to slip into the building. There were other monsters here, wandering through the dark corridors, but she had no fear of them. In her rags and perfected "monster mask" she appeared exactly like a smaller version of them and they walked on by her.

The only time she was in any danger was in opening doors. It was a tricky operation since only humans opened doors, however the laser pointer she carried was usually enough to distract the closer monsters.

The first dorm room she entered was surprisingly small and surprisingly messy. At first Jillybean thought that it had already been ransacked. The drawers to the under-bed dressers were all open with clothes hanging out of them, and the two desks were littered with papers and books and trash, and the floor wasn't much better; she had to be careful where she stepped if she didn't want to turn an ankle.

Despairing that she had been too late, she went to the first desk, opened the top drawer and right away found an opened package of Twizzlers—really, at this point it was an open package of green and black mold, but it was something and she went through the drawers with growing eagerness.

In that first room, she found candles, lighters, batteries, what appeared to be old oregano in a baggy, orange Tic Tacs, and thirteen individually wrapped, bite-sized Snicker's bars sitting in a plastic pumpkin. For one room, it was a pleasant haul. She stashed it in her backpack and went on to the next room, which was very similar to the first.

Two hours later, she waddled over to her Jeep, feeling a bit like a reverse Santa Claus. Her backpack was stuffed and very heavy. This was her third trip and, needless to say, the dormitory had been a fantastic success. All told, she had discovered eighty-four packages of Top Ramen, thirty-nine cans of different soups, mostly chicken noodle, forty-four cans of tuna, three large tubs of muscle building protein powder, a hundred and twelve packets of Weight Watchers shake mix, two trash bags worth of assorted junk food and about three pounds of the strange smelling oregano.

She figured that it had gone bad, but there was no telling what Granny Annie could do with the stuff.

There was little room in the Jeep now, so Jillybean decided to go back to "her" house where she would arrange her treasures and wait for night to make her way back to Vinita. There were many more dormitories to explore, but not only had she found enough, she didn't like the idea of leaving Granny Annie for so long.

Once more she took a very convoluted route back to the house, weaving over her own tracks time and again until she had to send up the drone just to figure out where she was.

She also sent it ahead to make sure the route home was secure. It seemed clear and she was able to make it back to the house without incident. Once there she ate until she was full, made a little nest of blankets and fell asleep, forgetting for the moment the first drone she had sent to spy on the bad guys. It was only when she woke around four that afternoon that she remembered it.

Turning on the iPad, she watched a fast-forwarded version of the video feed. The only thing that seemed to change during the first fifteen minutes was the very light shadows cast by the trees. Like a sundial, the shadows swung slowly across the yard until suddenly, at the 3:16 mark, a group of people rushed out of the house in a blur.

"Whoa, hold on," she whispered, hitting the rewind button. The people had been standing in a crowd and now she watched them move backwards to the house. Wanting to get an accurate count, she rewound until everyone was inside once more. Only then did she hit play.

Three men led the way out into the snowy afternoon. The one in front pointed to the expanse of white that represented the lawn and another group: two men and a woman stepped forward. The woman was thrown into the snow. She knelt there, looking at it as if she'd been drugged. She had no expression on her face despite the cold.

More people came out of house and stood around the woman. Altogether there were fourteen men and four women. There was a span of thirty seconds where one of the men spoke and gestured angrily, and then, out of the blue, all of the men began pulling off their belts.

Jillybean thought that they were going to use the bathroom right there in the snow, but they beat the lone woman instead. Each of them smacked her with their belts until her shirt was in tatters and her blood was sprayed about in the snow.

Out of the blue, she heard the crazy voice inside her say: *You've forgotten something very important.*

Jillybean growled, her lips were drawn back in a feral grimace: "I haven't forgotten a thing. And don't say revenge. I know all about it."

Don't fool yourself. You're only a child. You don't know what true revenge is.

"We'll see about that," she whispered as she watched the men kick the woman back into the house.

31

Chapter 4

Jillybean

The little girl burned with a righteous anger, one that couldn't be quenched or disregarded. "It's not revenge," she told herself. "It's justice." A year and a half ago, she would have shied away from anything even resembling danger. Back then she had sat in her house, slowly dying of malnutrition, staving it off by sucking on acorns and drinking pine-needle soup.

Fear had caused that. Now, fear played second-fiddle to the fiery anger as a cause for her actions. Of course, neither could hold a candle to love. She would burn down the world for someone she loved, but Jillybean didn't love these poor women. She pitied them and that tempered the fire in her somewhat.

She gazed over her map of Tulsa, trying to pinpoint the perfect spot for her ambush. Planning the attack was easier now that Ipes wasn't around to point out the terrible odds arrayed against her. Fourteen to one—that is fourteen adult males against one fifty-one pound seven-year-old—seemed pretty bad, but she wasn't fazed; she had faced worse and in less ideal conditions.

He would have also asked: *Why was she doing this?* That was an easy one to answer: because Captain Grey would have done the same thing and so would Neil and Sadie. They had always done the right thing no matter the odds.

"And really, the odds aren't all that bad," she said as if Ipes were sitting on the dashboard of the Jeep. "They just look bad because there's so many of them and only one of me."

She had definite advantages. Surprise for one, but there was also the snow and the cold, which played into her hands. They were her friends when she had no other, besides her bombs that is and her M79 grenade launcher, which was out of ammo and her .38 caliber police special. She also had an M4 but preferred not to use it if at all possible.

"This should be easy enough if the RadioShack on Harvard hasn't been completely picked over." The plan was taking shape in her mind and she went out into the cold hoping to find a radio scanner which would allow her to listen in on conversations, forewarning her about her enemy's actions.

She parked in back and crept inside, gun in one hand, Bumble Ball in the other. Her precautions were unneeded; there were no monsters in the store and looked as if there never had been. The shelves, other than batteries, were very well stocked with everything *besides* scanners. She took a two-way radio and had to hope that the "bad guys" as she thought of the unknown men, had a scanner of their own and would hone in on her plaintive, pleading voice when the time came.

Once she had the radio, she exploded in a flurry of activity preparing everything she would need for a desperate fight: batteries were charged, the Jeep was topped off, *smokers*, as she called her handcrafted smoke bombs, were made and a reciprocating gas powered saw was located.

Then it was just a matter of picking her location. Everything depended on restricting vehicle access to the target location. She only had a limited number of bombs—four to be precise, and that included the ones under the Jeep. With the snow still falling and the wind picking up, using a bomb-laden drone wasn't going to be an option to begin the battle. She would have to use a planted mine and thus she had to know exactly which road the bad guys would be driving on.

The only problem, and it was a big one, the city was a maze of roads, all going in every direction.

Making a cranky noise in her throat, she squinted down at the map and began tracing the lines that represented the different streets. Logic dictated that she would be able to pinpoint the exact route the bad guys would take, however that presupposed the bad guys would use either logic or common sense in their approach to the trap Jillybean was preparing, something that experience had taught her not to trust.

"What I need is a gated community with one way in or out." Her map didn't show her anything like that, at least not in a three mile radius and so she was forced to send up her drone to find something that would work. The first four flights out into the darkness were a bust. The snow played havoc with her controls and reduced visibility.

Time seemed to be getting away from her and as the evening slipped into a dismal night, the stress on her shoulders increased. *You're forgetting something important*, the voice said for what felt like the hundredth time. She had just been fitting a newly charged battery into the drone she had named Matilda and the voice made her jump.

"Stop it! I'm not forgetting anything. The plan is good. It's solid. You should know that better than me. Wait, leave me alone. I'm not talking to you, remember? I'm doing this on my own."

Despite her words, she revisited the plan step by step, looking for the weak spots, looking for something she had overlooked—not forgotten, just overlooked. "There's nothing. I don't know what that guy's talking about. I got this." Only she still didn't have a location for the ambush. In the countryside where there were only a few narrow roads, these sorts of things were a little more simple. In the city, not knowing was more than just problematic, it was deadly.

Her plan was to use her radio to send out a false cry of distress; she was sure that a lonely little girl on her own would bring them running. Using their scanner, they would hone in on her voice and bam-o! they would fall into her trap. Except the use of a scanner wasn't an exact science. They would have to move about to triangulate her location and could come at her from any direction.

"For all darn it!" she hissed. "I'm not forgetting anything it's just I don't know where they'll be…" She stopped suddenly as a thought—her own thought—came to her. *I am forgetting something.*

What she had forgotten in her anger was that there was no real reason for her to rush through this at all. "It has to be a clean operation and if that takes more than a single night to make happen then it takes more than a night."

She sat back, her frenzied mind calming, realizing for the first time that her fingers were numb with cold. She blew on them and groused: "And I can't even start a fire." She stood to fetch some of the candles she had found at the dorm when the same thought from earlier struck her again: *I am forgetting something.*

"That's it! I can't start a fire or the bad guys will know and they'll come after me! They'll come *straight* for me. Okay, what I need is my own cul-de-sac, preferably a long one. Or a dead end street and there are plenty of those." It took less than a minute to find a dead end street a mile from where the bad guys were holed up.

As quickly as she could, she gathered her belongings and placed them in the Jeep. She then went around the house, taking down the cameras and the alarms and the traps. Next, she drove through the gloom, her eyes flicking from monitor to monitor, equally prepared for either fight or flight.

There was no cause for either. The bad guys were nowhere to be seen, not even on the monitor synched to the drone she had set to keep watch on them. It had long before been covered by snow and now its battery life was at eleven percent. She would need it and since it was too weak to lift off, she would have to retrieve it by hand, which meant another stop and a trip out into the cold.

She parked three blocks away from the bad guys and slowly trudged through six inches of fine snow. Her monster outfit kept out *most* of the cold and yet since she had to, out of necessity, plod along, by the time she reached the cul-de-sac she was shivering and her shoulders were drawn in and her feet in her light Keds were like blocks of ice.

Jillybean was miserable and her body ached and yet when she once more caught the scent of wood burning, she breathed a sigh. It was a smell that she loved and for a moment she thought about abandoning her plan to free the women. She wanted to go home, back to Granny Annie's place, and sit by the fire where the heat would defrost her frozen toes. Annie would make her soup or stew or maybe even a pie and then she would tuck Jillybean into bed, but not without a bedtime story.

There was nothing that Jillybean loved more than a bedtime story when she was cuddled in clean sheets and warm blankets on a cold night.

You're forgetting something.

Jillybean jerked, upsetting the mantle of snow that had fallen on her shoulders. "I am not forgetting any…" Movement to her right caught her attention and she froze both literally and figuratively. She *had* forgotten something. She had forgotten to be vigilant and something resembling a yeti was now shuffling towards her. It was a snow-monster, huge and wild looking. It was covered in matted hair, which was, in turn covered in ice. It had to be at least seven feet tall, still, Jillybean wasn't afraid.

The feeling that best described her emotional state was annoyance. Irked to be pulled out of a wonderful daydream, she aimed her laser pointer at the snow to the creature's right. It immediately turned and stared down at the red dot that zigged back and forth. Gradually, she led it away with the pointer before turning back to her task of retrieving the drone.

Carefully it went into her backpack where it clicked against her odds and ends as she made her way back to the Jeep. She wasn't nearly as careful as she could have been and the giant ice monster was back again, following her. "What a pain," she complained and zipped the laser pointer once more at its feet until the thing turned in a circle and fell over.

"How anyone can really be afraid of these things is beyond me," she whispered, heading back to the Jeep and climbing in, happy to get it started and even happier to get the heat going.

She drove in the dark, going slowly because she couldn't chance a light. Every few minutes, she would yawn and soon her eyes were dripping with sleepiness. She fought the exhaustion building up inside of her and even went so far as to roll down her window so that the stinging cold air rushed in. Even that only staved off sleep for a few minutes. She tried singing next, belting out more Christmas carols, messing up the lyrics, sometimes sticking the words to *Silent Night* in with *Frosty the Snowman*.

When she finally got to the street she wanted to use as the ambush site, she had reached her breaking point. The previous two days had drained her of her energy and with not a single nod to security, she climbed into the back of the Jeep and fell asleep.

The snow stopped at midnight as a sharp wind swept the clouds to the southeast. Although the wind howled, Jillybean was rocked by it and she never came out of a much needed REM sleep.

As it was dark in the Jeep, she slept until eight in the morning and, strangely, it was hunger that woke her. She hadn't really been hungry in ages, however she had eaten so well the day before that her stomach was expecting the same treatment and began a ravenous growl as soon as her eyes clicked partially open. "One second," she said, sliding into the front seat and checking the monitors for danger.

Everything was white and bright, even the monsters that had come out of the houses to nose around under the pine trees were soon covered in snow as they dug for needles to eat. The trees were so laden down with snow that their boughs dipped almost to the ground.

While they were busy feeding, Jillybean climbed out of the Jeep and stood in the middle of the street, trying to picture how the fight would go down. "It all depends how many of them come. Will they leave the women behind and, if so, how many will stay to guard them? One would be sufficient, but they'll probably leave at least two."

If twelve men came, that would mean at least three vehicles which would be hard to deal with. It would mean three separate bombs planted in the street. Which was best to blow first? Did she go with the lead vehicle or the last vehicle? What would their reactions be?

"They might think they're trapped if I blow the last first... and don't tell me I'm forgetting something, cuz I'm not." What would a trapped person do? Turn around? Blast through in the hope of escape? What would the following cars do if the lead exploded? They'd go from feeling like the hunter to the hunted in a flash.

Chances were they would turn around. "Unless they were trained. Captain Grey wouldn't turn around in the middle of a kill zone. He would fight his way out and then turn on his attackers. Which leaves me, where?"

It left her guessing. She had four bombs; four chances to end the first part of the fight in seconds. That was important because there was no way to know what sort of firepower these bad guys possessed. Did they have grenades? Did they have rockets? Did they have .50 caliber machine guns that would turn her armored Jeep into Swiss cheese?

In the end, she decided to hedge her bets. She would take out the lead vehicle and assume that the next two would turn around, but just in case, she would plant the fourth bomb further up the dead end street. The first three bombs, she buried in the snow at sixty foot intervals. The fourth was seventy yards up the road sitting between a pair of trucks which were parked across from each other, narrowing the lane.

Since she was out of remote control detonators, she had to run wires from the bombs to a row of tall bushes that mostly hid the Jeep which she had parked in someone's driveway just up from where she hoped to initiate her one-girl ambush.

Next, she tramped down the road almost to where it dead ended. As they all had chimneys jutting up from their roofs, she picked a house at random and went inside. It was large and pleasant appearing, however an all-pervading smell of decay had seeped into its bones. There was a dead body somewhere in the house. Normally she would have searched for it, hoping for a suicide, which usually meant there'd be ammo with it.

"I don't have time," she whispered to herself and went straight away to the back of the house where the chimney ran down into a family room fireplace. "Lucky, lucky," she said.

Next to the fireplace was a neat mound of wood. She started a good roaring blaze going and then went to the garage.

She was out of luck when it came to gas, however there were two quarts of oil sitting out for anyone to take. She grabbed one, broke the seal as she went back to the family room and tossed it into the flames. An ugly black smoke rose up. Against the pale blue sky, it would be seen for miles.

But, just in case the bad guys were lazy dullards, she also keyed the radio and said: "Mom this is…" She almost gave her own name! "This is Sarah. I just wanted to let you know that Chelsea isn't feeling well. Can you get some Pepto for her, too? Hello, mom?"

As if she didn't have a care in the world, Jillybean went on nattering like that as she went to the head of the street and set up a security camera that would cover the intersection.

On the way back to the Jeep, she allowed fear to creep into her voice as she called, over and over again for "mom."

Twenty minutes went by before she heard the first engine and when she did, her stomach coiled in on itself. "Mom? I hear engines. Is that you? Mommy, why aren't you responding?" She opened the Jeep's passenger door and took hold of the iPad and as she did the voice spoke again: *You've forgotten something*, and this time she agreed. "Yeah, earplugs. Why don't I ever remember earplugs?"

She hated how her head rang and her ears ached after an explosion. There was no stopping things now for her to look for earplugs. On the video feed, a Suburban was just nosing up to the dead end street.

Jillybean carried the iPad around the front of the Jeep and went to where the detonators were laid on the ground, each numbered and laid in order. She picked up the detonators marked 1 and 2 and peered through the run of bushes. "When the Suburban gets to that tree…"

She could hear the engines clearer, they were coming closer, moving slowly. The feed from the iPad showed that there were indeed three vehicles coming: the suburban and two white trucks. Jillybean's stomach was turning flips. There was nowhere to run now. She had to fight.

If she froze and failed to set off the bombs, they'd see the Jeep and, even if it wasn't recognized from the night before, there was no mistaking it for just a run of the mill Jeep and they would come and investigate.

"So, we blow the bombs," she said, except there was no "we" it was just Jillybean all alone and feeling suddenly vulnerable with just a few twigs and some old leaves to stop whatever hell the bad guys were going to throw her way if they caught sight of her.

She wanted to hunker down, but she had to be able to see— there, the Suburban! It was coming up the road at a cautious ten miles an hour…and now it was at the tree. "Fire in the hole," she whispered and hit the detonator.

Chapter 5

Jillybean

The pipe-bomb, filled with a pound of C4, detonated under the front right tire in a blinding flash and an ear-shattering roar. The driver's side of the Suburban lifted up eight feet in the air and then came crashing down in almost the same exact position that it had started, with the only difference being that it was now engulfed in flame and smoke.

Fifty feet away, Jillybean felt the air sucked from her lungs. It was a gentle tug that was returned a thousand times over as she was blasted by a blistering rush of scalding air. The explosion, seen and felt without any barriers, was far larger than she had expected and with a cry, she ducked down low as shrapnel tinged off the houses and broke windows up and down the block.

The following two trucks stopped at the explosion and there was a second where both drivers seemed too stunned for thought, but then both reacted at the same time and in the same way. They both turned sharply to their left, ran up into the snow-covered yards on the side of the road and peeled out of there as best as they could under the slippery conditions.

At least one person in the trucks rolled down his window and began firing an M16. He had no clue where Jillybean was and his bullets raked a two-story home next door, shattering every window and punching holes in the siding.

Jillybean hopped up with detonator number 2 in her hand, her head poking into the bushes, her eyes at squints. The next bomb in line was directly across from a light post and from where she stood, it was hard to see exactly when the truck would pass over it. She had to guess.

When she thumbed the detonator, the bomb went off right next to the truck blowing in the windows and killing two men in a blink. The truck turned sharply to the left, its engine screaming as if in pain, flames engulfing the bed. It rammed a parked car, silencing the engine so that that the crackle of flame and the echoes of the bomb blasts could be heard. Jillybean guessed that the fuel tank had been ruptured and now the vehicle was an inferno.

The driver bailed out, complicating Jillybean's plan; she had no idea what she was going to do with him, especially since the driver of the last truck wasn't cooperating with her plan, either. She had hoped that he would try to escape around the burning wreckage and she was all ready to go with the detonator marked number 3.

What she hadn't expected was for the driver of the last truck to abandon the road and the truck altogether. He must have been terrified. With vehicles burning both in front and behind, he plowed the truck into a hedge and while Jillybean was gaping in confusion, three men jumped out and dove behind it.

Suddenly bullets were ranging up and down the block and once more Jillybean ducked down. She wasn't being targeted, but that didn't mean a stray bullet couldn't get her.

"Now what?" she asked. The last thing she had expected was for the men to get out of their vehicles and she wasn't sure how to deal with it. She had her armored Jeep, but her very assault had shown her what she already knew: just because she had added some metal didn't mean that the Jeep was necessarily impervious to attack. One grenade would knock her right out.

She needed some way to kill the men without exposing herself or her Jeep. She had two drones, but no bombs, or rather no bombs which she could reach. There was no way she was going to run all the way up the street and back again with people shooting. She'd be dead in a second.

"Oh, Ipes, why'd you have to die?" she asked, in desperation. He would have known what to do. Sure, he might have told her to run away, but that was something, at least. With her plan in shambles, she didn't know whether to run or stay or hide or fight.

"I need another bomb, that's what I really need." Moving in a crouch, she went back to the Jeep and climbed in where it was reasonably safe and where she could have a moment to think. "What am I missing?" she asked, looking at the odds and ends she had amassed. "And don't say I'm forgetting something," she said cocking her eyes up, "cuz I'm not. I just need to build another bomb, real quick…but how and with what?"

*You've forgotten someth…*the voice began, making Jillybean grind her teeth in frustration. Thankfully a bullet struck the Jeep with a heavy smack and the voice ceased in mid-sentence.

"Thank goodness," Jillybean whispered. She didn't need that voice replaying in her head over and over. She knew that it wasn't talking about her present situation. It was talking about something deeper, something from her past, but whatever it was, she was sure it was bad and she had more important things to worry about.

The bad guys were yelling back and forth to each other, trying to figure out what was going on. It wouldn't be long before they crept out from behind the thick hedge and went in search of her. Once they spread out, stopping them would become that much harder.

"I guess I could use the M249," she said, glancing back at the butt end of the machine gun, jutting into the cargo area of the Jeep. To use it, she would have to drive out into the street and face away from her enemies, relying on the barrel-mounted camera to pinpoint them. It was a crappy idea.

Feeling time compress, her eyes flicked around the interior of the Jeep with growing frustration. There was nothing in the vehicle that she could use as a bomb. The only real materials lay under a few inches of snow out in the middle of the street. She was about to despair when she saw one of her drones sitting among the packages of Top Ramen. "If I had a claw, I could fly the drone over and pick up one of the bombs," she said, picturing the claw lifting the bomb and running it over to the hedge, its long wire trailing behind. She didn't have a claw, however. "What about glue? Hmmm." She had tape and a small tube of Super-glue.

"But the snow would mess up the stickiness. For all darn it," she whispered. She liked the idea of the claw. It was very neat. She thought furiously of different ways of making one in the seconds she had left, only nothing would come to her frazzled mind.

Finally, she had to give up and sighed at the dull plan that took its place: she would blow both mines in place and then race by in the Jeep while the men were still wondering what was going on. Once she was beyond the truck, she would shoot it up with the M249.

This would leave the men free to either travel on foot the mile back to the cul-de-sac or to use the battery from the truck, if it was still in one piece, to start a different vehicle. Either way, Jillybean would be pressed for time in trying to free the women from whatever force had been left to guard them.

"And they're already warned, what with all the 'splosions and gun-shootings." When her stomach rolled this time, it did so with a painful clinch—her fear was ramping up.

Still, she had no other plan, and so she slid out of the truck and hurried to where she had left the final two detonators. She picked them up and was just about to set the bombs off when she saw something so obvious that she called herself a fool: the detonators were attached to rubber-coated wires which were attached to the bombs themselves.

"I'm so stupid!" she groused and quickly began pulling on the wire connected to the fourth bomb. Like some mechanical creature, it popped up out of the snow and began crabbing towards the Jeep as Jillybean reeled it in. Once it was close, she fetched the nearest drone, slapped the bomb on it with tape and used the remote to set it hovering.

She didn't even wait to set up the iPad. The hedge the bad guys were hiding behind was all of forty yards away and she was able to direct it visually. Her enemies were slow to spot the whirring device and by the time they did it was almost over them.

Judging by the fact that they took the time to shoot it down, they must have assumed that it was for surveillance only. At least one bullet clipped it and it fell into the hedge almost right on top of them. As fast as she could, Jillybean thumbed the detonator and once more the early morning was rocked by a thunderous explosion.

Quick as a wink, Jillybean hopped into the Jeep, slamming the door behind her and even before the last echoes died down, she was racing down the driveway and out into the street.

The front camera showed a road littered with burning trucks, pieces of metal and glass, bodies and parts of bodies. She had to drive carefully but as she didn't know if all her enemies were dead, she couldn't dawdle either. She wove in and out of the debris and then used her rear camera to line up a shot with the M249.

She thumbed the fire button and raked the last truck until it too was on fire. In fact the smoke seemed exceedingly close, so close that a grey haze drifted across her view, appearing to *fall* over the lens. That made no sense to her and neither did the sudden stench of gasoline enveloping the Jeep.

The smell was so strong that she could only conclude that her vehicle was also on fire and this didn't make a lick of sense either. When she had topped off, she had used up all the fuel in the jerry cans. There was no gas on top of her vehicle, unless…

43

The tiny seven-year-old turned to the side view cameras just as a man leapt up from behind a parked car on the right side of the road. In his hand was a bottle, the top third of which appeared to be sprouting flames. It was the driver of the Suburban, whom she had totally forgotten about, and in his hand was a Molotov cocktail.

Too late she stomped on the elevated gas pedal and now that her machine gun wasn't running, she could both feel and hear the glass break and the gas ignite with a loud *foomp!* noise. Her Jeep was on fire and only the perfection of the welds in her armor had kept the flaming gas from leaking down and setting her on fire, as well. But it wouldn't be long before the fire ate up her oxygen or cooked her alive.

The smart thing to do would have been to abandon the vehicle in the few seconds she had left. Jillybean, however, was sixty I.Q. points above what was considered smart.

All of the trees along the street were laden down with snow, their boughs hanging so low she could've reached up and touched them. She aimed the Jeep off the road and onto the sidewalk and as she drove, the steering wheel rocked and shuddered as she smashed into branch after branch.

In seconds the front camera was covered in snow but she refused to stop. There was no way for her to know if the fire was out or if the bad guy was coming with another fire-bomb. She drove, but she didn't drive blind. She used the rear camera to correct her progress. It wasn't a perfect system and in eighteen seconds she hit the trunk of a tree and although it was a glancing blow, she was thrown forward.

Now, all the cameras were covered in snow and the monitors only showed a steady white nothing.

Groaning, Jillybean picked herself up and set her pillows back in place. Fearlessly, she had driven with her Jeep covered in flames, but now doubt crept in. She was altogether blind and there was no way to know where the bad guy was or if she was still on fire except to open her door, and there was no way to clear the front camera except to get out where bullets could get her.

But it had to be done and the sooner the better. She cracked the door and despite her genius, she yelped when snow poured through the crack. For a split second, she imagined she had somehow driven straight into the side of a glacier.

The snow ceased falling and a piercing light caused her to recoil and squint. Everything was white—which was a good thing. No black smoke meant no fire. Above her came a sizzling and popping sound, like bacon frying. *Ipes would have had something to say about that*, she thought, realizing that one of her problems had been taken care of: the fire was out.

"Now, about that guy." From where she was, she couldn't tell if he was coming and so she decided to let him know she was still alive and still full of fight. Leaning over, she thumbed the "fire" button for the M249. The Jeep thrummed as thirty spinning hunks of lead blasted up the sidewalk, hitting who knew what.

Quick as a rabbit, she jumped out into the snow and ran to the front. The Jeep had hit an elm and the armor was crumpled in on one side. She made a face, knowing it was going to be a pain to fix, but she didn't stop to examine the damage: the bad guy was shooting at her. Bullets were skipping off the Jeep.

She squatted, hooked snow away from the camera she had welded into place in the grill and then ran to the passenger side door and climbed in that way. In seconds, she was zipping away from the scene of the battle, leaving fire and death in her wake. There was no reason to look back when ahead of her was more of the same.

Chapter 6

Jillybean

Did they have radios? Did they know she was coming? How many of them were still at the house? And how many had she left alive? And would they be coming for her? And…and…

Jillybean was suddenly so flooded with questions, concerns, and fears that she had to pull over. Her insides were shaking, making her tummy feel like the inside of a blender, and soon the shaking spread to her arms and hands. Her chest grew tight, making it hard to breathe and, in a panic, she pushed open the door and rushed out into the bright morning.

She was four blocks from the battle and safe for the moment, or so she told herself as she leaned against the Jeep. It was in sorry shape: banged up and scratched and pitted and scorched. And it was ugly. It was still running, however.

"Good job, Jessica," she said, patting its side. For some reason, seeing the damage the Jeep had absorbed had a strangely calming effect on her tummy. She walked around it, leaving little impressions in the snow, her right hand running over the "wounds" as she thought of the damage.

When she got back to the driver's side, she looked in at the items she had prepared for the next part of the fight: Matilda the drone, the smoke bombs, the gas operated saw, the keys to a standard set of handcuffs, the thermal rifle scope, a gas mask, the M4, and her pistol. She had been hoping to have at least one of the real bombs with her.

"If there's only two bad guys, I can do this. And no, I'm not forgetting anything, so don't say so. By the way, it's getting annoying hearing that all the time," she cranked, as she climbed into the Jeep and headed, not for the cul-de-sac where the women were being kept, but for the street behind the cul-de-sac. She was going to sneak up on them, or so she hoped, and towards that end she parked on Tuliver Lane, a hundred yards from the bad guy's house.

Once more, when she stepped out she smelled the wood fire going. This time there wasn't a smidge of nostalgia in her. She was there to kill. Nostalgia really had no place inside of her when death was on her mind. And neither did doubt about the righteousness of her cause. She was in too deep to even consider weighing right and wrong.

She slung her bulky pack across her back, shouldered her rifle that was nearly as tall as she was, and wrapped a length of bungee cord around her wrist. The other end of the cord was attached to the reciprocating saw, which she dragged behind her. The darn thing was just too heavy for her to carry at least for very far.

With her back bent, she started trudging down the street through nearly eight inches of snow. It was hard going for someone so small, but she persevered, thankful that the shooting and the explosions had pulled the monsters away and that she was alone on the street. They would have added another dimension of difficulty that she didn't need. Assaulting a home where the occupants were alert was hard enough as it was.

But, as always, she had a plan. It started with her taking up a position behind the house. The property that abutted the cul-de-sac had a peaked roof sitting on two levels and seemed very tall as Jillybean straggled up to it. She cleared a spot in the snow for her last heli-drone.

"They better not shoot you down, Matilda. That would be mean, cuz you never did anything to anyone." On its first run, Matilda, the drone, went up with only its camera. She was careful to approach the house at an angle, not that there was much to see. Almost all of the windows were covered in blankets which was as she expected.

When she brought the drone back, she loaded up the first smoke bomb and carried Matilda into the house. The front door had been kicked in long before and the place was a shambles. She didn't even notice. Her focus was on finding the stairs. Once on the second floor, she went to the master bedroom, slid open one of the windows, and used the butt end of her M4 to knock out the screen.

"Here goes nothing," she said, lighting the fuse on the bomb before spinning up the drone. It whirred gently, wafting smoke down in intricate curls as she sent it floating out the window. The first drop point was on the porch two feet from a sliding glass door.

The bomb was already emitting such a cloud that Jillybean accidentally thudded it against the glass. "No problem, no problem," she whispered and thumbed the release button. The smoke bomb dropped perfectly into position and before Matilda was even halfway back, the rear of the house across from her was nearly completely obscured.

She attached the next bomb as fast as she could. There were shouts coming from the house—some angry, some afraid. She counted three voices.

"It'll be okay," she said, sending Matilda out once more, smoke trailing in a long grey tail. This bomb was destined to go into the house and, since there wasn't a way into the house, Jillybean had to make one. As Matilda floated in midair, hidden in a cloud of its own making, the little girl hauled the M4 to her shoulder. Its barrel rested on the window frame as she aimed. She was so close that the fancy scope really wasn't needed.

She fired five times at an upper floor window, which disintegrated in a shower of glass.

Quickly, the little girl ducked away and took up her iPad and the controller for the drone. She sent it zipping into the house just as a chaotic gun battle began. It was an entirely one-sided affair. She had no idea what the bad guys were shooting at, and they probably didn't either. For the most part they shot willy-nilly into the smoke as if it were alive and bullets could kill it. Overall, it was a pointless waste of ammo, however on the off chance someone got lucky, she kept low as she directed the drone through the house using its belly camera.

The room she entered was a guest bedroom which led to a hall. She turned Matilda to the left as the picture went grey from the smoke. Speed was her only option and she buzzed out of the cloud, bounced off a wall and then spun so fast everything was a blur and she had to try once more.

The smoke was too much and the picture nothing but swirling madness. She dropped Matilda down and started spurting in different directions. The first two attempts only resulted in the drone smacking into walls. On the third, she found the stairs and slipped down them, descending into an open area.

Once more, as she turned the drone around, the smoke belching from the bomb was too much. She tried jettisoning the smoke bomb, only the room was too filled with clouds to make sense of anything. She flew Matilda about blindly for half a minute before she had to give up; Matilda was lost and there was no more time to save her. The controls and iPad went into her backpack as the little girl picked up the M4.

At thirty inches in length, with a loaded weight of seven and a half pounds, and hardly any kick, the M4 seemed to have been designed as the perfect assault weapon for a child. The littlest warrior once more set the barrel on the window frame and peered through the dense smoke with the thermal scope, finding a target in seconds: a man crouched by the sliding glass door.

He appeared as a light grey, human shape with white eyes. Jillybean centered her crosshairs and fired a three-round burst and hit with all three bullets. The man pitched over and lay still.

Although small, the gun was painfully loud and both of her ears felt as if someone had spiked them with an icepick, and yet she didn't even blink. She was in the zone. Yes, she was killing out of necessity, but that didn't change the fact that she was exceptionally gifted at taking lives. With amazing serenity, she shifted the barrel, picking up a new target: another person hunkering low near an open window.

This was a harder shot as she could see only about four inches of the person's shoulder and two inches of the side of their head. At fifty yards, this would have been a tough shot for a trained soldier. If she had time, she would have waited for the man to shift positions or glance out, but time was against her.

It wasn't just that her super-smoke bombs would burn themselves out in a minute or two, there was also no telling if the survivors from the first part of the battle, and there was at least one, would come rushing to take part in the second. She doubted they would, but to be on the safe side, she took the shot and missed. The man disappeared and the little girl had to search for a new target, but in vain.

"Oh, for all darn it," she whispered, and crawled backwards from the window. When she got to the door, she raced down the hall and then took the stairs two at a time—the worst case scenario at this point was that the remaining bad guys would grab the women, run out the front door, jump in whatever car remained to them and escape.

To prevent that possibility, she had to close the distance quickly. She went out the front door where the saw and bungee cord awaited her. It was a twenty pound tool that she barely felt as she dragged it around the side of the house. Adrenaline was coursing through her arteries and she felt as though she had the strength of an eleven-year-old.

This strength carried her to the back fence where she hooked the free end of the bungee cord to her waistband and began to mount the fence. Like most kids her age, she was a natural climber and she monkeyed right to the top. She paused to slide her rifle from her shoulder and aim it through the smoke. It

49

was exceedingly dangerous to sit there exposed. Any devil-borne gust of wind would leave her a sitting duck and any stray bullet could plunk her from her perch like a plastic duck at a carnival shooting gallery.

But she had to drag the saw up and it made sense to check for bad guys. It scared her that there were none to be seen even with her fancy scope. She slung it once more and, as the boards bit into her skinny rear end, she hauled up the saw, pulled it over the top of the fence and let out the slack until it was sitting in the snow-covered backyard.

She followed after, dropping into a hunch, her M4 up once more, and once more, there wasn't anything to be seen. "Poopy," she whispered.

Now came the most dangerous part of the mission. Closing to within knife-fighting distance with full grown men. Still hunched and dragging the saw, she scurried to the corner of the house, where she could hear one person shooting, one man yelling, and the low babble of frightened women.

"I got the front!" the yelling man cried.

One guy in the front and one in the back. If she picked a side window to enter from, they would be separated and easier to kill—or they would be able to converge on her and catch her in a crossfire. If she went to the front and tried to kill the man watching there, she could be shot from behind by one of the bad guys from the earlier fight. Or she could try to take out the man in the back, only this was the direction they were expecting the attack to come from.

There was no good choice left to her. "No perfect choice," she corrected the inner workings of her mind. With so much left to chance, each choice could only be considered good or bad as judged by the outcome.

As she was pressed for time, it made sense for her to act as soon as possible. She dropped down and pulled the last smoke bomb from her backpack. When she lit it, it went up as if someone had condensed and packaged a small volcano and she had to step back.

"Holy-moly," she said, cringing away from the bomb. The moment she moved, there was a rattle of gunfire and breaking glass and something whickered the air next to her cheek.

In a flash, she pinned herself against the wall and sucked in her breath as more bullets zipped past. Only the fantastic cloud that had enveloped the entire side of the house was keeping her alive, however the stray bullets were going everywhere and it was only a matter of time before one found her.

The cloud was less dense near the ground and Jillybean saw, four feet to her left, a basement window well. Acting without hesitation she stepped away from the wall and fired off three bursts from her M4, shattering the window and causing the screams and gunfire from the house to increase.

From somewhere above her, bullets were now being sprayed like water from a hose. With them slicing through the cloud all around her, she dropped into the well and without bothering to knock out the remaining glass, she threw herself into the window with her M4 raised in front of her face.

Her cold weather clothes combined with the monster outfit she wore over the top of that kept her whole as she landed in a darkened basement. It was unfinished and wide open save for a few support beams running from the cold concrete floor to the ceiling joists.

A few feet away and cringing in fear were the four women she had seen the day before. They were chained by the neck to the closest support beam. Three of the women stared in amazement at Jillybean as if this tiny girl in her shredded clothing, with her wild hair and even wilder eyes, was the last thing on earth they expected to see drop down into their dungeon.

The fourth woman didn't seem to see Jillybean at all. She lay on the ground just inches from the little girl, clutching her stomach, her wide eyes staring up at the exposed joists. It was a second before Jillybean saw the blood and when she did, she didn't understand it, figuring that flying glass had cut her.

Jillybean turned around and yanked the reciprocating saw out of the well. "Here, get up," she said to the woman on the ground, holding the heavy saw out to her. "Cut yourselves free. Just click the "start" button and then pull the handle thing."

One of the women grabbed her. "You shot Sylvia," she accused.

"No, I didn't," Jillybean answered, pulling away. Of course she didn't shoot anyone, except bad guys, that is. Or so she thought. When she glanced back down at Sylvia, a small, thin woman with hollow brown eyes, she noticed there was more blood than before. More than any flying glass would produce. And there was more coming up through her fingers.

Jillybean stared in growing horror as more guns were being fired and more shouts came from above. Someone was staggering around the house on the first floor, knocking into furniture and walls as he went. The sound barely registered. The little girl's mind was in a twirl. It felt disconnected from the rest of her body. It felt as it was about to dissolve and reform and when it did, she didn't know if she would be Jillybean anymore.

Shooting people is what Eve used to do. *She* was the evil one. *She* was the bad guy, not Jillybean.

"I shot her?" she asked, in a quiet voice.

Before the first woman could answer, another of them pushed forward, reaching out with ragged fingernails that reminded Jillybean of monster claws. She flinched back, however the woman didn't care about her, she was after the saw. "Gimme that," she demanded.

Witless, Jillybean held out the end of the bungee cord, which was ignored as the woman went for the saw itself. Two of the women looked it over while the third looked upon Jillybean with hunger. The girl didn't notice. Her whole world was centered on Sylvia.

There was much more than pain in Sylvia's brown eyes, there was fear. It ran deep and it was no wonder. Where in all this horrible, monster-filled land was there a doctor? Where was there a working hospital with an emergency room and nurses with blue masks and gloved hands?

The closest that Jillybean knew of was in the Estes Valley, seven hundred miles away. And what would they think if she brought in a gunshot victim? They would blame her and this time they'd be right to.

"I didn't mean it." Her voice was now so quiet that it couldn't be heard. It didn't really matter one way or the other, no one was listening. One of the women was yanking back on the pull-starter of the saw as the other stood as far back as she could. They were all chained one to another in a line with Sylvia closest to the pole.

The next closest was a woman who was so beaten that it was hard to tell she was Asian. This was the woman who'd been attacked. The belt marks were hideous. She oozed puss from fifty wounds. Jillybean was aghast at the wounds on the woman and dazed by what she had done to Sylvia, and was not prepared when the Asian woman launched herself right at her.

The attack was the only thing that could have gotten Jillybean moving. The snarling woman, raking with her claws, broke the miasma engulfing Jillybean's mind and she reacted with just enough speed to leap back out of range. She held the gun on the woman, her finger all over the trigger.

Like a dog, the woman went to the end of her leash and snarled: "Gimme the gun! Gimme the gun, damn it! You're just a kid."

The saw started and it was loud. Jillybean had to shout to be heard: "No! Cut yourselves free and don't leave without me." She switched out her magazine for a fresh one and headed for the stairs that lead to the first floor. It would normally be the worst move possible, only just then smoke was creeping through the cracks from top to bottom; she would be invisible and would have the advantage.

Already she knew the approximate location of one of the bad guys: she could hear him coughing. He was approximately ten feet to the right of the door and, judging by the plumbing coming down from the ceiling, he was in a bathroom. She could picture him in her mind's eye with uncanny precision.

Slowly, carefully, she opened the door and was immediately engulfed in a foul grey bank of smoke. Holding her breath to keep from coughing and giving away her position, she slid the M4 out into the hall and leaned out after it.

The bad guy showed up perfectly in the smoke. He had his shirt pulled up over his nose and mouth and stared around with wide, frightened eyes. They were white eyes and he resembled a ghost, which made killing him much easier for Jillybean. She fired one three-round burst straight into his chest, tearing out his heart in a blink as he pitched backwards, his gun firing once into the ceiling.

By her reckoning, there was only one other bad guy out there. She paused to listen for him, but couldn't stay in place for more than a few seconds because of the smoke. Ducking back into the basement, she fished out her gas mask. It was an ugly, bulky thing that she had taken from the corpse of a soldier a few weeks before. With it on, her vision was limited and her ability to shoot was impaired.

Still, she could breathe without coughing. It meant she could ghost around the house with only the slight patter of her tiny Keds giving her away.

The first floor of the house was filled with smoke from ceiling to floor and yet Jillybean was not lost or confused about her whereabouts in the least. The open floor plan of the basement, the positioning of the water pipes, the sewage pipes and the gas lines combined with what she had discerned through the windows gave her the entire layout of the first floor, down to the last square foot.

She turned to the left towards the front of the house, holding the M4 up to her masked face. The image in the thermal scope showed nothing but layers of grey, even when she made it to the living room—there was no one there. To the right was a sitting room, but it was empty as well.

No one guarding the front? she thought. *How strange.* As she headed towards the kitchen at the rear of the house she considered what the last bad guy was likely thinking.

With the explosions and the earlier battle, he probably thought that his crew had run into a bigger and better armed party than they had expected. Then, his own home had been attacked in a most bewildering fashion. Gunshots and smoke bombs on the outside were easy to explain, but when they came from the inside as well, it had probably sent the bad guys into a panic.

But nobody had run away out the front as far Jillybean could tell. Had they feared an ambush? It was the only explanation that made any sen...

Just then the saw in the basement stopped and there came an air of expectation that made Jillybean suddenly very nervous. The saw shouldn't have stopped. There were four chains that had to be cut, not one. She spun in place as a new sound reached her: the tinkle of glass falling. They were going out the window!

It was one thing to calmly walk through a house filled with smoke, navigating by counting steps, it was another to try to run in that same darkness. She hit a wall after five steps and then a chair that she fell over, losing her sense of direction but not realizing it.

She reached out, one-handed, found the wall and retraced her steps, going as fast as she dared, but then her hand ran up on cloth. She was at a window. Quickly, she brushed the cloth back and then the drapes and then she was staring outside. She was in the dining room and the view outside was mostly obscured by the smoke of the last bomb she had deployed.

In the smoke were ghostly shapes. Three of the women were escaping. They had cut themselves free of Sylvia, but were still chained together, running for the backyard where there was a cloud of smoke stretching from fence to fence.

The three women were slow and stumbling. The last woman on the chain held the saw. It was heavy and ungainly and she was weak after so long living at the end of a chain. It swung like a pendulum changing her course slightly, leading her and the other two women on a curving route into the smoke. They were still visible when the first shot rang out.

Jillybean saw the woman's face clearly: the shock written in the long lines that ran from her temple to her jaw, then the grief in her eyes. If there was pain, it was far down the list and she was dead before it showed.

She fell and dragged the others down with her where they were pinned to the cold earth place by a hail of bullets.

Chapter 7

Jillybean

Someone on the floor above her emptied a magazine into three defenseless women, turning the snow red, turning Jillybean's soul black. Once more, she found her mind slipping away, this time into a realm of rage and hate. It was very familiar, like walking on a well-worn path, one that was easy, one that seemed to rise up and greet her feet.

She could lose herself going down that path; she had done so before with terrifying results. A part of her wanted to resist. On the other hand, a much larger, much stronger part wanted to give in to the anger. There was safety in it, but also there was a vacation from her big brain within it. That brain thought too much. It dwelled on sad things, such as the fact that because of her, three innocent women were dead—and Sylvia was as good as dead. In her rage, there was no sense pretending otherwise.

And there were also the bad guys whom she had slaughtered…maybe they hadn't all been bad. Maybe there had been fear in the group, maybe some had given in to peer pressure and had gone along with the others in order…

"Shut it," Jillybean growled, speaking to her silly, endless thoughts. She was too upset for such wishy-washy thinkings. The bad guys were bad, pure and simple. They had beaten those women, they had killed those women. And they deserved to die.

That thought echoed in her head, bouncing off her skull, driving her through the billowing clouds of her own creation, her gun in hand. The anger and mental pain were such that she no longer thought of it as an M4 and she no longer counted her steps and imagined the interior of the house as a perfectly laid out, and to-scale, blueprint.

Everything inside her had become guttural and base, emanating from some little squiggle of brain that hadn't evolved in two million years. She raced through the house on instinct alone, listening as some evil fiend dropped a magazine to the floor and slapped in a second one. She honed in on that sound as her feet found the stairs and raced up them.

The bad guy was in an upstairs bedroom. Despite her anger, when she pictured the room, it wasn't a flat, two-dimensional map, clean and neat; she pictured it complete: a little boy's room with blocks on the floor, plastic cars sitting with their unmoving wheels pointing at the ceiling and a half-finished game of Candyland laid out. The board game, with its colorful winding trail and its Gum Drop Mountains, was like a small world of its own.

All the pleasantness of the image was quashed by the shade of evil that hunkered by the window with the gun in its hand. That evil was a magnet for her and she set her legs pumping as she mounted the stairs. In no time, she was three risers from the top and that was when she was stopped by the now familiar and very hated voice. It was back, echoing in her head: *You've forgotten something important.*

Her feet stopped, one in midair, as her free hand gripped the soft polished pine of the banister, her nails cutting tiny grooves across it. She growled in frustration because *now* was definitely not the time for that damned voice! She was utterly furious and the growl was loud. It came right up out of her throat, pushed through the filters of her bug-eyed mask to gently part the clouds.

The growl was not a second from her throat when a gunshot cracked the air and a bullet ripped so close to her head that it parted the wisps of her flyaway brown hair as neatly as a greased comb. She dropped low as the shock of adrenaline crashing into her system drowned out the mindless hate that had filled her and suddenly her frontal lobe was engaged once again, clicking out the facts presented to her like a stock-ticker.

In an immeasurable fraction of a second, she was able to calculate the distance and direction of where the shooter sat in ambush. Yes, she had forgotten something very important: her mind, genius though it was, was not infallible. She had misjudged the number of bad guys in the house. She had thought there was only one left, but there were at least two. If there were more than that she would die. That was a fact that was just as cold as the three dead women lying out in the snow.

"Did you get him?" This came from the bad guy who had killed the women. He was up and to the right and he was afraid, Jillybean could hear it in his voice. The man who had shot at her was straight down the hall that led from the top of the stairs—this man kept silent. He knew he had missed and he probably knew he was in deep trouble.

Slowly, Jillybean eased upwards, the M4 at her shoulder, her masked eye peering through the thermal scope. She stopped when she was inches above the level of the floor and at first she saw nothing. There were four bedrooms on the second floor; the one at the end of the hall was where the shooter was hiding.

He wouldn't hide for long. He would pop out and shoot any moment, and she was ready with her gun sighted and her finger on the trigger.

But she wasn't ready when he stuck only his rifle around the corner and started shooting without aiming. It seemed like cheating to her. She ducked back down as bullets went everywhere, hitting everything, except her. As he wasted his ammo, she wasn't idle. She slid her pack from her shoulders and let it drop behind her.

It thudded and clanked and jingled down the stairs, and to that sound, she added a groan in the deepest voice she could manage. The shooting stopped and, as she had hoped, the bad guy peeked around the corner. Like the others, he had some article of clothing wrapped around his head and his glowing eyes were at squints. Jillybean had him dead to rights. She took in a breath, held it and squeezed off a three-round burst, destroying his face, turning it into raw chuck.

"Hal?" asked the man to her right.

Jillybean answered for Hal, once more speaking as deeply as she could: "He is dead." She already had her gun trained on the bedroom door, hoping that this last bad guy would be as foolish as Hal and take a look into the hall.

Seconds went by and she could practically hear him thinking: *I'm trapped!* Where would he turn? Where would he run? What desperate plan was in his head? She expected some sort of spastic shooting followed by begging.

She decided to reason with him. "Drop your gun and come out. I won't hurt you." She planned on shooting him in the head; there was very little pain to it as far as she knew.

"You're a girl?" he asked.

The hate in her wanted to cry out: *I am Jillybean, destroyer of worlds!* Instead she bit it back and went with: "*We* have you surrounded. Do as I say, or else."

More silence followed. He was probably now trying to factor her sex and youth into whatever survival equation was going on in his mind. She wished she could save him the effort. His equation was unbalanced. He was going to die and the world would be better for it.

"I'm going to set the house on fire," she told him. "Come out before I do or else." Lighting the house on fire was a last resort; she wanted the house intact. There had to be food and weapons and possibly goodies such as Doritos or flour or...

Her thoughts were interrupted by a thud and a grunt. After that came the unmistakable sound of boots scraping against siding. *He's going out the window!* The thought struck her hard. She couldn't let him escape. The idea sent her running into the bedroom, which was nothing like she had imagined. With the window open, the smoke was only a thin haze and she could see without the fancy scope.

What toys there were in the room had been shoved into a corner to make room for the belongings of one of the bad guys. There were two backpacks on the floor that were bursting at the seams with what looked like military paraphernalia.

She couldn't spare a second to give the items more than a passing peripheral glance as she threw off the gas mask on the way to the window. A man was on the grass eighteen feet below her. From above she couldn't tell much about him beyond the fact that he was losing his sandy brown hair and already had a patch on the top of his head that was so thin she could see his scalp plain as day.

Eighteen feet was so close that when she stuck the scope to her eye, the man's back seemed to be the size of an elephant—she couldn't miss him as he struggled to his feet and began limping away, passing within an arm's reach of the dead women he had killed. They were the evidence of his guilt and she was his judge, jury and executioner. In a blink, she found him guilty of murder, and sentenced him to death.

Her heart was racing, her desire for revenge like a fire inside of her, her need to kill was primal. She was the predator and he was the prey. Even if he hadn't been guilty of murder, she had an instinctual need to kill that was inflamed by his odious fear and his wounded flight.

One thought stopped her: had he felt this same intense desire when he had seen the chained women running away. Hadn't they been afraid? Hadn't their flight been just as pathetic? Hadn't they been an affront to the Darwinist principle of survival of the fittest?

She could picture the man standing at the window, wreathed in smoke, sweat beading on his lip and running in his thin hair, his heart going a mile a minute, his reactions keyed to the slightest movement. Had he been able to stop himself? Had he

59

blazed away and then stared down in horror at the corpses he had created?

Is that how she would feel when the smoke cleared? Jillybean's finger came off the trigger. And as it did, her body began to shake worse than the Bumble Balls she set off to distract the monsters. Her hands were shaking so badly that she had to put down the gun and watch as the balding man tried to mount the fence with a leg that didn't look like it could bear even a fraction of his weight. He was whimpering like a frightened child.

"Run away," she said to him, speaking normally, neither yelling nor whispering. The world was quiet and had been since the monsters came. Her little voice carried easily. "I can kill you, you know. But I'm going to let you go. You better run, though. Run far away and don't look back because I will kill you if you do. Do you believe me?"

He was at the top of the fence leading into the neighbor's yard and he chanced a look back. She saw the fear stamped on his face. He was pale as the snow around him and his thin lips were drawn back across mangled yellowed teeth. Jillybean was a tiny girl and yet, from his angle, she had to seem bigger than she was and more frightening, with her hair mussed by the gas mask into a wild mane and her eyes were piercingly blue and dreadfully cold.

She was letting him live, but only as an act of willpower and he seemed to know it. He nodded, his mouth bouncing up and down, his eyes wide and terrified. With a last whining noise, he dropped over the other side of the fence. She could hear him hobbling through the snow. With a sigh, she stepped back from the window.

The house was quiet save for the steady hiss of her smoke bombs as they vented great billowing clouds. To be on the safe side, she listened for over a minute, but there was nothing in the house save for the dead and the dying. "Sylvia," she whispered. A wild thought struck her: *Leave her. Walk away and don't look back.*

Oh, how easy that would be. And wouldn't it be nice if she could hide this memory from herself? Wouldn't it be just swell to walk away thinking she was still a good little girl?

"But she would suffer," Jillybean said, her face drooping. "Because of me." That wasn't good. "Of course, she's gonna suffer no matter what." That really wasn't good. What made the most sense was to go down there and do the right thing: she should kill Sylvia.

"It's not evil," she insisted, as she changed out magazines. "She's gonna die anyway."

You're forgetting something that is very important.

"Oh jeeze! I'm not." Except, maybe she was. Hadn't she read all those anatomy books for a reason? Didn't she want to be a healer? "Yeah, but I can't start with this. It's too much." Yes, it was too much, but that didn't stop her mind from running down what she would need to do, what she needed to learn and what she needed to get.

"Maybe," she whispered, as she saw the possibilities. The gas mask was on the floor, sitting like a black, disembodied head, its buggy lenses watching her…maybe even judging her. She snatched it up, stuck it on and went in search of the smoke bomb she had set off in the house.

It was so hot that it was scorching the flooring. She had to use oven mitts to carry it outside. Next, she went around the houses, opening windows. After that she checked on the dead to make sure they were in fact dead. They all were. It was distressing going from body to body and nudging them with her foot. What was more distressing was going down into the basement. She dreaded each step and as she went, she ardently wished that Sylvia was already dead. It would make everything simpler.

But Sylvia was alive, lying in a puddle of her own blood, staring up at Jillybean with dulled eyes. The fear had been replaced by pain and that was quickly being replaced by the onset of shock.

"Hi," Jillybean said, waving one small hand. She had stopped one step up from the cement floor and was nervous about committing to the last step.

"Hi," Sylvia replied after swallowing.

Silence held sway as the two only stared at each other. Sylvia appeared content to let it spin out until the last drop of blood trickled out of her. When Jillybean couldn't take it anymore she said: "I'm sorry. I didn't know you were right there." Sylvia shrugged as far as she was able, but didn't say anything.

"My name is Jillybean. I know your name is Sylvia and… what? What are you looking at?"

Sylvia's eyes had come open with a bit more life in them. "I know you. I—I heard about you. They...they say you blew up the River King's bridge. And they say y-you killed the Colonel." She paused to catch her breath. Those few words had taken much of her energy.

The memories of the bridge coming down and of the Colonel flopping forward like a dead fish flashed through her mind and in the background she heard the voice moan: *You've forgotten something...*

"Yes," Jillybean said, quickly. "That was me, but I had to do those things. My friends were gonna be sold in New York, and the Colonel knew who we were and he would have...Oh, Miss Sylvia, ma'am I really didn't mean to hurt you. I'm sorry. I really am."

"What's done is done," she answered slowly. "I was getting tired of it all, anyway. You know what I mean? This world is no good anymore."

"I guess I know that, a little. But there is some good things left. In Colorado there's some good people and it's pretty there. And in Vinita there's this lady named Granny Annie and she might be able to help you." This was a bit of a lie. Granny Annie had never displayed any medical ability or knowledge beyond the simplest bandaid. Jillybean wanted to give Sylvia some hope.

Sylvia had been fading, but now she started blinking. "She has a medical background?"

"She knows a lot, that's for sure," Jillybean assured. "First we have to get you stabilified and that's what means that you don't die. Isn't that good?" Jillybean thought that would be the best. It sure would help her guilt, which was like an anchor weighing down the filmy nothingness of her soul.

"I guess," Sylvia answered and then coughed. The smoke was lighter in the house but with the basement door open, some was filtering down.

Alarmed that a coughing fit would kill Sylvia, Jillybean ran back to the first floor to shut the door. "Hey, I'll be right back, k? I got a few things in the Jeep that could help you a lot."

As she hadn't expected to run into trouble of this magnitude, she only had so much in the way of supplies. Altogether she had one IV bag, a few bandages and some pills. It was enough to start with but she would need more.

Although she had rushed up the stairs, from there she began to creep, careful as always. She moved through the clouds like a stalking ghost until she came to the fence. Unencumbered, she went right up and leapt down on the other side. When she got to the Jeep, she was able to throw pretense to the wind and revved it around the side of the house.

The Jeep made short work of the fence, sending boards flying in a spectacular manner; on the monitor inside, however, it was very humdrum. She pulled right up to the back of the house and, grabbing the medbag, she rushed back down, this time *afraid* that Sylvia had died. Jillybean was hanging a lot on the idea of being able to save the woman.

She would go from murderer to healer in a flash.

Down the stairs she went. "Oh good, you're still alive. Can you swallow pills? I got some for pain. Sorry that they're so big."

Sylvia was able to down two of them, though they didn't seem to work. She groaned and cried even more as Jillybean inspected her wound. There was a hole just to the left of her belly button from which blood ran at an alarming rate.

"Bandage first," Jillybean whispered to herself. She had seen her share of wounds and the first thing everyone ever did was try to stop the bleeding. She pulled out all the gauze she had and pressed it into the wound. "Sorry, Miss Sylvia, ma'am. Can you hold that right there and press down as hard as you can?"

"It hurts," Sylvia said, in a whisper.

"Yeah, sorry. But you're gonna have to hold it while I get the IV ready." IVs were nothing for the little girl and in no time, she had one lodged into the crook of Sylvia's arm. Like the bandage, which was soaked with blood, and the pills, the IV didn't appear to have helped.

Jillybean stood and gazed around. "We need to get you out of here. Can you walk?" Sylvia tried, but couldn't even sit up without screaming in pain.

"No...and I'm too heavy to carry," she said, her voice high and breathy. "I'm going to die down here, I know it. Maybe... maybe you should use the gun."

Jillybean stepped back and saw the obstacles in her way, not the least of which was the fact that she was only fifty-one pounds and Sylvia was over twice her size. Uncowed by this, she shook her head. "No, we don't need a gun. I can get you out of here, easy. Just wait here and keep pressure on your wound."

It seemed like a waste of time. The gauze was soaked through and Sylvia was too weak to press down hard enough to make a difference.

"That's got to be first," Jillybean said to herself as she ran upstairs. On the first floor landing, she paused again to scan and measure and plan. "I'll need towels and sheets." The little girl zipped upstairs to "the hall closet." Every house had one and they were always well stocked with sheet and towels. She laid down one sheet and piled the rest on top until the mound was nearly as big as she was.

It was bulky but not terribly heavy and in one trip she was able to pull everything she needed down into the basement. She went back to the living room where there stood a tall bookshelf made of cherry wood. She pushed it straight over and cringed as it boomed like a cannon when it crashed to the floor.

Pulling her prybar from her bag, she went at the now ruined bookshelf until she was able to get one of the long side panels off. Taking three of the heaviest books, she put them on the nearly six foot long panel and dragged it to the basement.

The panel would be her sled to carry Sylvia to the car. The books would provide sufficient weight on her wound to slow the bleeding. The sheets were quickly torn in long strips, each four inches wide. Two of these were entwined to make an eight foot length of rope—she made nine of them and tied them together in one long run. Normal rope would have been better but where would she find sixty feet of it on such short notice?

In twenty minutes, she had Sylvia strapped to the panel, which was tied to one end of her homemade rope. The other end was tied to the Jeep's bumper. Towels were rolled into compact bundles and set on each of the stairs so that the ride up would be smooth. Two hand towels had replaced the red dripping gauze and the books were bungee corded to her belly.

Sylvia watched Jillybean working with slowly dulling eyes. She needed more IV fluids. Blood or plasma would have been ideal, however there was simply none to be had.

"I'm gonna get you out of here now, so don't worry," Jillybean said to Sylvia and then left to pace out the length of the basement and then the stairs. Afterwards, she went to the front bumper of the Jeep and paced out the same length and made a mark in the snow.

"Gentle now," she whispered once she was inside the Jeep and had the engine turning. Gradually, she released the brake.

She didn't need to give the vehicle any gas; it slowly eased forward until the bumper was at the mark. Jillybean put on the parking brake and ran inside, following the now taut run of entwined sheets.

The panel, with Sylvia still on it, was all the way up the stairs, but canted upward at an angle that was causing Sylvia to cry. Quickly Jillybean hauled down on the high end and pulled back with all her might. She was just barely strong enough to get the panel flattened and far enough into the hall so that it wouldn't slide back down the stairs.

She made a few more calculations and then ran back to the Jeep to drive it forward exactly twenty-two feet. Now the panel was at the kitchen door but stuck against the jam—just as Jillybean had figured, she took the prybar out and used it to push the panel away. One more trip got the panel right to the sliding glass doors.

"I just have to do some things real quick," Jillybean said to Sylvia. The Jeep had to be emptied and the seats folded down before she could get the panel inside. Jillybean also had to ransack the house of everything valuable; in this world of scarcity, to leave valuable items behind was unthinkable.

Luggage was found in the basement and all the guns and food and odds and ends were put into the luggage, which went onto the roof rack and was strapped in place. She used her homemade rope and the branch of a looming tree to pulley everything into place.

She would have to do the same thing with Sylvia, but that would be easier since she would only have to get the woman to the height of the Jeep's cargo area. The kitchen table was the right height and so she dragged it out using the Jeep as muscle.

Once it was in place, she pulled Sylvia out the same way and pulleyed her into the air. She whimpered, not in pain but in fear of being dropped. Jillybean did her best to soothe her but Sylvia wouldn't stop until she was safely in the Jeep.

"What is this thing?" she asked, panting and staring at the blocky machine and its strange dark interior.

"It's a Jeep is all. I made some modifications and that's what means it's safer than a normal Jeep." Without bombs, it was only a little safer, but Jillybean was not going to say that. She climbed in and, after glancing at each of the screens, she moved through the hole in the fence she had made earlier.

Until they were back on the road, it was a bumpy ride and Sylvia cried out a number of times. After each, Jillybean would mumble: "Sorry." But she didn't stop and when she got on the snow-covered streets, she didn't slow. Sylvia was desperately in need of more fluids to replace the blood she had lost.

Thankfully, medical supplies weren't difficult to find. Hospitals had been ransacked for food and recreational drugs, but there were plenty of other items, suture kits, gauze, bandages and the like, just sitting around for the taking.

The little girl found everything she needed at St John's Medical Center. She came out dragging a box filled with stuff. "We'll get you fixed right up," she said to Sylvia as she hung another IV bag.

"You mean this Granny person will," Sylvia replied. She was pale, even her lips were just the slightest bit pink.

"Yes." The lie came easily. It was a white sort of lie designed to make Sylvia feel better and there was nothing wrong with that as far as Jillybean knew. The only thing that really made Sylvia feel better was when Jillybean gave her Duramorph, a liquid version of morphine, that had been overlooked by earlier looters. Sylvia passed out seconds after it hit her system and Jillybean didn't know if that was a good thing or a bad thing.

Regardless, she drove on, knowing that she had to get Sylvia stabilized as quickly as possible, and that meant getting her to Granny Annie's. Traveling in the daylight was dangerous, but she had to risk it and, thankfully, nothing bad happened as she blazed a trail through the untouched snow, heading northeast.

It was a four hour trip and during that time, she changed out three IV bags and gave Sylvia two more ampules of Duramorph.

Then they were on the outskirts of Vinita and the very first thing that Jillybean saw was a trail of smoke running up into the sky. "Oh no. Why would she have a fire going? She should know better."

Jillybean had been planning on going straight to the house but with the smoke acting as a beacon, she did a wide circuit, first of the town and then of their neighborhood, looking for tracks in the snow. Only when she was satisfied that they were safe did she head to the house.

"I'll be right back," she told Sylvia and hurried inside the little cottage to douse the fire. The first thing she noticed was how dreadfully hot and dark it was inside. Jillybean stopped in the doorway, knowing right away that something was wrong.

"Granny? Miss Granny Annie, ma'am?" Her hand stole into her pocket where she kept the .38. "Are you home?"

"Shut the damned door!" a voice croaked. Granny Annie sat in a corner of the room covered practically head to toe in blankets. The blankets made no sense, however the sweat running down her craggy face did: it was hot, of course she was sweating.

But why were her eyes so balefully red? And why did she look so crazy? The answer stopped Jillybean in her wet tracks.

"You've been bitted, haven't you?" Jillybean asked, taking a step back and pulling the gun.

Chapter 8

Jillybean

Granny Annie didn't answer right away. Her red eyes were angry and filmy as if the grey muck that covered the eyes of the monsters was very close to encasing hers.

Eventually, she hissed: "Shut the door! The light burns. And the cold…it's so cold out. I don't think I'll ever get warm."

"When did it happen?" Jillybean asked. She shut the door but kept near it. As well she kept the gun out, though out of respect, she had it pointed at the floor.

Annie breathed a sigh of relief when the room was shrouded again in darkness. "It was this morning when I got up to get some snow to melt." She pointed at the half-filled water pail next to the fireplace. "I didn't do anything, but that Rhonda from across the way came out of nowhere and tried to get me. Oh, my head. Jillybean, I need something for my head. It aches so much. You need to fix this. You need to fix all of this. Do you hear me, Jillybean?"

She nodded, but she didn't mean anything by the move. It was involuntary. Just at that moment, the little girl was crushed under the weight of guilt and responsibility. Her day had been long and difficult and filled with blood and death. She had been hoping to come home and have a grown up finally be in charge of her so that she didn't have to do all the thinking and all the work and all the killings.

The sad truth was that she was going to have to kill Granny Annie, one of the sweetest, most harmless people she had ever known. She didn't want to, and a part of her, the part that was still just seven years old, wanted to stamp her feet and say: NO! That part wanted her to run away and not come back.

The voice in her head spoke again, repeating the same tired sentence and to it she mumbled: "I don't care." The voice wanted her not just to remember, oh, she was sure of that. It would want her to do something once she had. And Jillybean would bet dollars to doughnuts that whatever it was would be big and it would be scary and the world would look to her to fix all their problems.

And she was tired of doing that sort of thing. She was hiding in Vinita, Oklahoma to get away from responsibility, to get away from the endless killings.

"Please, Jillybean," Granny Annie begged. "Help me." Isn't that what they all begged for? And where were they when Jillybean needed help? She needed help right then, but who would come to rescue her? No one.

"I have a shot that'll help you," she finally said, "but you have to promise to sit on your hands."

In the Jeep was a weighty book: the Physician's Desk Reference. It held information on every drug known to man. She had seen one before and had smartly picked it up back in St. John's. She had also taken an entire bin's worth of Duramorph. For someone Annie's weight and age, thirty milliliters was considered a heavy dose. Jillybean sucked ninety into her syringe, which would do a lot more than ease her pain. The Duramorph section of the PDR had listed off the bad things that could happen when taking the drug and death from respiratory failure was high on the list.

"And that's what means you stop breathing." As she said this, she glanced at Sylvia's skinny body strapped to a flat panel of cherry. The woman was still passed out...and still breathing. How much easier on Jillybean would it be to give her some "extra" Duramorph as well? Then it would be just a matter of burying them—but could she bury her guilt along with the bodies?

"I can't," she whispered, taking only the one syringe. Just like the stupid voice in her head, the guilt would haunt her, perhaps for all time. Her only hope was to try her best to save Sylvia, even though she had no idea how. Bodies were not like machines. Parts couldn't be switched out and welds couldn't be slapped on when needed. They operated on a far more advanced level than the fulcrum, the electric motor or the nuclear reactor.

It was a frightening thing to even consider and when she got out of the Jeep, she just stood there, already emotionally spent. She had to drag her feet back into the blistering hot house where disease shimmered in the air. The monster disease did not worry her overly much. First, she knew you had to be bitten or scratched and second if she ever got bitten or scratched, she would suicide herself because nothing else made sense.

For her that was logic and she kept that logic squarely in the front of her mind as she advanced on Granny Annie, who was whimpering in the corner closest to the fire. She was now so hunched that she looked like a giant toad and there was such an evil glint in her eyes that Jillybean hesitated a few feet from the woman.

Strangely, it wasn't Ipes whom she wished was there with her to buoy her spirit and tell her that this was all for the best; she wished Eve was there. Eve was a monster. She would have made short work of the old lady…and Sylvia as well. If Eve had been there, Jillybean could have been sitting with her feet by the wire, nibbling on Doritos, with in fifteen minutes.

If there was one thing that Eve could be counted on, it was the fact that she didn't draw unpleasant things out with useless worry and guilt.

With a sigh, Jillybean told Annie: "Sit on your hands, okay?"

"Why?" Annie demanded, her red eyes filled with angry suspicion.

"So I don't slip. Shots aren't the best you know. I remember when I was really little I used to cry because I thought they felt like a bee stinging me. So yeah, I guess that's why. Now sit on your hands." The real reason was that she had the sinking suspicion that Annie would lash out at her.

"Okay, but hurry. My head feels like it's about to split open." Jillybean guessed that stuff in her head would be black and icky and she didn't want to see that, no way. She went to stand partially behind Annie just in case the old woman did get edgy, and in a swift move, she jabbed the needle into the woman's arm right through the two sweaters she wore.

Far from reacting in a violent manner, Annie only turned her feverish gaze on Jillybean and whispered: "Thanks."

"Y-You're welcome," Jillybean said, still pressing the amber liquid into the old woman's flesh. She could feel the end of the needle grinding on bone and it turned her stomach.

When the syringe was empty, she stepped back, expecting to see Granny Annie topple right over, however it was a gradual death and a peaceful one. The old woman's eyes began a slow blinking and then her head slumped onto her bosom, which rose and fell slower and slower until at last it stopped.

Jillybean waited for a few minutes, wondering if she would turn into a monster or just stay dead. To be on the safe side and because it wouldn't be good for Sylvia to see a corpse in the living room, Jillybean got two sheets from the closet, spread them one on top of the other and toppled the woman onto them.

She used the first to wrap Granny Annie in and the second was used to drag her out into the backyard. It wasn't easy for the little girl, however it was expedient. Sylvia was still alive and in Jillybean's book the living had precedent over the dead.

There were, of course hurdles to moving Sylvia but these were overcome readily enough using applied engineering, and soon the woman was resting on a mattress next to the fire. She had only woken for a few minutes during the move from the Jeep and her state of consciousness could not be described as coherent. She gazed around blearily with washed out, uncomprehending eyes.

With her respirations so low, Jillybean was afraid to give her more of the Duramorph and decided that as long as Sylvia was sleeping she wouldn't give her anything more.

"Okay, what do I do first? And don't say that I've forgotten something because I don't know enough to have forgotten anything important." The voice in her head remained silent. Thankful for that at least, Jillybean bent over Sylvia to inspect the wound. There wasn't much to see. Her stomach was covered in layers of congealed blood. It was black at the edges and a dark, ugly brown in the middle. Brighter red blood bubbled up from the interior.

She was going to have to clean all that off to see what she was getting into. But she wouldn't do it just yet. The blood loss had slowed to a trickle and any messing around would get it going again. Jillybean wanted to be ready before doing anything invasive.

The only problem was that there was so much to do and learn and so little time; Sylvia didn't look like she would last through the night. The task Jillybean had set for herself was so overwhelming that she was at a loss and beginning to panic. She knew the basics. She had personally witnessed Captain Grey perform surgery on Nico's arm.

"What had Grey started with?" Sterile water to clean the wound. Next, he used a scalpel to open the wound and cut out the dead flesh. He used clamps to cut off bleeders and sutures to tie up the muscle and skin.

This would be the same, but only in the concept. In reality, everything about it would be a hundred times more difficult.

"I need to practice," she decided. Thankfully, there were plenty of subjects available for her to practice on. There hadn't been many monsters about earlier; banging some pots around did the trick and a dozen came around. Once more, Jillybean was amazed at the size of the beasts. She chose the smallest to single out. It had the remains of a bow in its draggle of hair. It had been girl, but was now a broad shouldered monster that was nearly six feet in height.

It was a ratty, ragged thing that was missing great chunks of hair and half its face. Its one remaining eye followed Jillybean's laser pointer right into the garage, where it stood staring stupidly at the wall, not noticing the plastic drop cloth beneath its feet.

The little girl shut the door with a loud, rattling thump and quick as a wink, it spun around, a growl in its throat. Using her . 38, Jillybean shot it in the forehead from five feet away. Its one remaining eye seemed surprised as it collapsed, its knees coming unlocked. The monster was dead before it hit the plastic, which made shooting it in the guts as simple as pulling the trigger.

Jillybean didn't waste a moment. She kicked on the gas-powered generator and brought lamps into the garage. Next, she gathered her surgical supplies, though she wasn't going to waste sterile water on a monster. On the other hand she used two pairs of gloves.

The monster wore rags, which Jillybean cut away. Beneath that it was covered in feces, mud and blood, both old and new; Jillybean washed the area until the flesh looked almost human. Using the scalpel, she opened the monster's belly.

"Oh gross!" The smell coming from the corpse brought up a burning hunk of something nasty in the back of Jillybean's throat. She had to lean back for a minute and catch her breath before she bent back over the dead monster.

"I guess that's why those surgeoners wear masks. Hmm? This isn't all that bad, considering." She had been afraid that the insides of the monster would look like spaghetti made from the tentacles of an alien creature. At first there was a lot of green stuff and dark red blood, looking like an evil soup, but after she had doused it with water and mopped it up with paper towels she could see everything there was to see well enough.

"There's the small intestine and the big colon…" She ran her fingers through the guts, finding the holes made by the passage of the bullet. They were easy to find since they oozed green gunk. After a ten minute search, she found the bullet lodged in a muscle in the monster's back between the lowest two ribs. Using a pair of forceps, she fished it out and gave it a look, amazed at how warped it had become smashing into the soft guts of a dead monster.

She tossed it onto the monster's chest and decided: "Okay, I can do this." So far it hadn't been bad, besides the stink, that is. Now, she just had to teach herself how to sew a human back together. "It's all about tying knots." Her first few tries at suturing were laughable and looked childish, which was no real surprise seeing as she was a child. But she worked diligently at the slippery stuff, reconnecting the perforated colon until she felt she had the hang of it.

After throwing all of her used supplies into the open cavity in the monster and wrapping her up in the plastic tarp, Jillybean cleaned herself up and went into the living room to find Sylvia awake and staring at her. She was slack-jawed and pale. "I thought you left me," she said.

"No, I wouldn't do that. I was getting things ready. It's…it's going to be okay. I have everything we need."

"And where's this person. This lady who knows medicine?"

Jillybean hesitated before glancing out to the backyard where Granny Annie lay wrapped in her sheet in the snow. "She's resting. She's old so she needs to rest before she does her surgeoning." Resting is what Jillybean wished she could be doing. Bombs and fighting and all that had taken their toll and she was plum worn out.

The little girl went back and forth from the garage carrying lamps and boxes as Sylvia watched. "I heard gunshots before," she said. "Who'd you kill?"

"Just a monster that got into the garage. Don't worry, it was a small one," she said and then held up a syringe. "This stuff is what's called Ketamine and Propofol and that's whats means the medicine that makes you go to sleep."

Sylvia didn't question that a girl was shooting medicine into the port of her IV. She lacked the energy to, or so it seemed. Jillybean pushed in a quarter of the mixed dose and asked: "Tell me if you start to feel sleepy or…" Before she could finish her sentence, the woman's eyes were drooping. Seconds later, they were closed.

What the PDR had failed to mention was how long the medicine would last. Jillybean quickly put on her gloves and began cleaning the wound—she'd been right, it began to bleed once more, but not as badly as she had guessed. When Sylvia's abdomen was clean, Jillybean open a sterilized package that held a new scalpel.

"Miss Sylvia, ma'am?" she asked. The lady didn't respond, so Jillybean, very gently, gave her a poke with the scalpel to see if she would jump. She remained entirely inert. "Okay, here goes. I open her up, fix a few holes, take out the bullet and put her back together. No problem."

Despite saying that it was no problem, her hands shook as she made her first incision. With the guts being so squiggly and the holes in them so tiny, Jillybean made the cut big enough for her to be able to really get in and see what was going on.

Right away things went to hell. The incision had not been any bigger or deeper than the one she had made in the monster and yet the amount of blood pooling in the wound was frightening. It just kept coming and coming. She went through all of her remaining gauze trying to soak it up and all she had to show for it was a red mound on the floor next to her leg.

She got up and ran for the closet, not caring that the hand towels weren't sterile. She thrust one into the wound and held it there until it too was soaked. When she pulled the towel away, she had a clear shot at the wound track and went right to work on the first length of intestine with the suturing needle.

In thirty seconds, the blood had seeped back thicker than before. She grabbed another towel. And so it went with growing fear and frustration gripping the little girl. Jillybean had forgotten something important. When she had operated on the monster it had been dead, meaning that its heart was no longer pushing blood through its arteries.

Sylvia was alive and bleeding from something worse than a few holes in her intestine. Jillybean had to find the bleeder and tie it off before the woman bled out completely. The only problem was that the pierced artery was deep—too deep for a hand towel to be useful.

Soon Jillybean was digging in what was basically a bowl of intestines and blood soup. She couldn't see what was what. Everything was red gore and pale intestine that went on and on as though the slick tube was part of a magician's act. The idea of pulling it all out and just heaping it onto Sylvia's chest struck her, only she was sure that she would never get it all back in place correctly, or she would knot it by accident.

There didn't seem to be any other option but to keep digging in her belly. It was miserable and soul damning.

Uncontrollable tears sprang up clouding her vision, blurring it, and her chest began to hitch and she blubbered into the hole she had made in Sylvia.

It was a few minutes before she cried herself out and she was able to pull herself together. Exhausted, she put a gloved hand to the carpet to push herself straight again, only to jerk her hand back when the carpet made a "squishy" noise.

"Oh no. Oh, my god." She saw that she was kneeling in a pool of blood; the carpet was soaked and the red stain was spreading outwards.

Quickly, she put her hand back inside the body, feeling for Sylvia's pulse. It had been there thrumming away, going faster and faster. Now the blood in her guts felt cool and heavy. It was congealing.

"Sylvia? Sylvia? Hey, hey, Sylvia?" There was no answer from the pale lips. The woman was dead and growing stiff. Jillybean had killed her. To the little girl, it felt as though she had killed her twice over and the guilt that hit her was almost too much for her seven-year-old soul.

Tears poured out of her, wetting the blue surgical gown she had put on over her clothes, until she had nothing left inside to cry and she only sat there staring at Sylvia. The woman's eyes had fallen slightly open and they seemed to be glaring at Jillybean with more than a hint of anger.

"I didn't mean it," Jillybean whispered. She had seen people close the eyes of the dead, only she couldn't bring herself to touch the body again. It was like returning to the scene of the crime. "But it was an accident and that's what means I didn't mean it." There was no answer to this, not even by the voice in her head.

The silence felt like an accusation in itself and for once she wanted to hear that voice or any voice, any voice other than Sylvia's...and Granny Annie's. "Sorry. I really am sorry."

The apology felt unaccepted as the silence grew until the air was heavy with it. When she couldn't stand it anymore she pushed herself up and turned her eyes from the body. It was dark out and she was so bone tired that she had trouble holding her lids open, and yet, there was no way she was going to share the house with Sylvia's corpse.

What would happen if it came alive? Not like one of the monsters, but like a ghoul bent on revenge. The thought gave her the shivers and the impetus to move. She wrapped Sylvia's body in a new sheet and dragged her out into the snow. Without her blood in her, she was remarkably light and Jillybean didn't have to resort to using her mind, which was good, she was tired of her mind. She was tired of thinking and worrying and she was tired of guilt, but she had one more task before she could throw herself into her bed.

She had to pray for the souls of the two women. They had been good people. The only problem was that no prayer would come to her except the one her mommy and daddy would say to her before bed: "Now I lay me down to sleep. I pray the Lord my soul to keep. If I die before I wake, I pray the Lord my soul to take."

It felt like a strange prayer to say over the dead, but nothing else would come from her lips except endless apologies and she was tired of those. They were utterly worthless. With a final sigh, she went inside where the living room looked like a crime scene.

Someone with a less fragile psyche might have left the cleanup until morning. Jillybean feared the dreams that would come if she fell asleep with the gory mess just outside her door. For the time being, the mattress and the red towels went into the garage. She even cut a big square out of the carpet and shoved that out too, locking the door behind her as she came back in.

That night she dreamed of the Colonel. She saw the attack on his fortress on Rock Island as if she were a bird. Neil being captured, the exploding fuel tanks, stealing the pontoon, racing down the river, stopping when the booby trapped barges went up like a fireworks display, lighting the night. She even saw herself execute the Colonel.

But that wasn't enough and the voice came back, only this time it was a howl: *You've forgotten something very important!*

"I haven't! I remember all of it, so leave me alone!" she yelled back. She remembered it like a fading dream and it was enough, or so she thought.

Chapter 9

Jillybean

Unlike every other dream she'd ever had, the dream of the Colonel and the assault on Rock Island did not fade from her memory. This didn't make much sense to the logically driven girl.

The attack had been in vain and people had died for nothing…how many people, she didn't know. The memory, like the dream, was a hazy string of pictures. A part of her had blocked it out as a way of coping with all the death and pain she had been surrounded with for so long.

Now, the memory had crept back in, though why, she didn't know. Supposedly, it was "important."

"If it's all that important, why don't I remember the whole thing?" The memory was mostly intact except for little splotches here and there. She remembered being on the roof of a building watching Neil through a scope, but she didn't remember getting up or down it. She remembered having a claymore mine strapped to her chest, but not where it went after that. She remembered being in a building filled with bombs and bullets, but she didn't remember leaving.

"Did I blow that place up?" If so she was a little disappointed that she hadn't remembered, it would have made a hell of a show.

She went about that morning cleaning Granny Annie's house and garage, using enough bleach to give her a thumping bad headache. She was so thorough, that by lunch, a detective would have been hard pressed to find a single shred of evidence that two people had died in the home the day before.

The last of the evidence, the two bodies in the back yard was harder to hide. The frozen ground was like granite. She tried using a shovel but it bit into her hands so cruelly every time it *clinked* into the dirt that she gave up the idea and went with something more primal: fire.

For the rest of the afternoon, she worked at building a funeral pyre for the two women. Since there would be smoke, she put the bodies into the back of the Jeep and drove out to a lonely farm west of Vinita that she'd been to once before. It was where she had picked up the moldy hay that she fed to the three monsters trapped in the pool.

On the property was a rickety barn with peeling paint and a hundred loose boards that probably would have gone up in flames with only a quick dousing of gasoline. Had Jillybean been pressed for time she could have simply used that, however her subconscious wouldn't allow it. Using the barn was too easy. There was no sweat and toil and blood in something so easy. There was no true penance in lighting a match and walking away.

She pried away board after board until the barn was a strange looking top-heavy skeleton of a building that would certainly come down during the next big gale. Using the boards and the rectangles of hay, the girl built a pyramid whose pinnacle stood fifty feet in the air.

It was an arduous task and one that she couldn't have stopped even if she wanted to do. She was driven to it by an acid combination of guilt, sorrow and loneliness. Every time she took more of a break than a simple breather, the three forces threatened to overwhelm her and she found herself, not just crying, but sobbing.

She lost herself in the work of building the funeral pyre and when it was done the setting sun threw a shadow of it a half mile long. Still, she waited to light it. Night seemed the most appropriate time.

As her knowledge of pyres was mostly theoretical, she had set the two bodies on the fourth layer of the pyramid, what she considered the exact center, and had covered them over with three more tiers of wood and hay. While at the very top she had set a symbol of each woman: a cookie for Granny Annie and a child's doll for Sylvia.

When the stars were sharp and bright above, Jillybean said the same prayer as she had the night before and then set the primitive edifice alight.

For an hour, the little girl stared at the flames and breathed in the smoke. She thought it would smell like burning bodies, but it didn't. It had its own earthy aroma that was pleasing and she found herself saying: "If Ipes were here, he'd want to toast marshmallows…but that would be wrong."

The idea and the smell made her hungry and after the pyramid had settled into a roaring mound of flame, she felt that her penance had been completed and her guilt satisfied. She drove back to the house using a meandering, unpredictable course and helped herself to a bowl of Top Ramen and fell asleep next to the fire.

That night she wasn't haunted by dreams and the same was true for the next two weeks as a bitter January gave way to a dreary February. She had enough food to last her a year and her supply of ammo was great indeed, ever since she had begun hunting monsters in uniform. They almost always had a magazine or two stashed in the remnants of their BDUs or in the chest rigs that hung off them.

In February, the dreams of Rock Island started up again. Sometimes they would run all night long and she would wake in the middle of the assault on The River King's base. Once she woke after eight in the morning, which was astonishing in itself. That dream had been so far advanced that in it she was riding on the mammoth truck of the traders with Sadie. In the west, there was smoke from the last truck. They had won the battle and she hadn't yet found out that Ipes was dead.

It was a joyous moment, tempered, not by the voice telling her that she had forgotten something, but by her own subconscious. She felt a single moment of unease that had her smile faltering.

When she woke up she had that same feeling and this time she listened to it. There had to have been something she had forgotten. On the truck, it had been a minor feeling, now it seemed to be growing in importance, and was tantalizingly close, like a forgotten word that sat just on the tip of her tongue.

"Does it getting warmer out have anything to do with anything? That's the only change that's occurred in the last few months. And the voice also mentioned revenge before, which doesn't make any sense...unless I left enemies in my wake, which I'm sure I did. So, that means...what?"

Jillybean looked up at the ceiling of Granny Annie's house and asked: "Well? I'm ready to talk."

She had been dying to talk to someone. It had been over five weeks since Sylvia's last words and, more and more, Jillybean had caught herself talking to *things*. Usually she spoke to herself or the mirror, but sometimes it was to her food or the fire or the monsters that came near the house.

She was especially anxious when she caught herself talking to her toys. In the last month, she had collected many toys: Barbie dolls, chess sets, remote controlled planes/helicopters/

cars, Game Boys, tea sets, marbles, sling shots, coloring books, and doll houses. Pretty much anything that caught her eye.

The house had been transformed into something that looked like the aftermath of an earthquake in a toy store, except it was missing something obvious: stuffed animals. Jillybean was afraid of them, or more exactly, she was afraid of what she would be like around them. She was afraid to be crazy again.

But here she was talking to the air and fully expecting an answer. It was something of a disappointment when she wasn't given one. A minute passed in silence. Finally, she said: "Hello? I've forgotten something *very* important, would you care to tell me what?"

More silence followed and when it had spun out too long, Jillybean lashed out with one of her Keds and kicked a game called Stratego, sending blue and red pieces flying. She didn't much care. It hadn't been a game that was easily played alone. None of them were. She picked them up, brought them home, played with them once or twice and then set them aside where they collected dust.

In the last five weeks, she had tried hard to be "normal" but it hadn't been easy. She had read a lot. During the day, she went through what she called learning books. These all concerned science, math or "How to" books. At night, she allowed herself to rest with entertaining reading such as Harry Potter or Little House on the Prairie.

To stave off the silence that seemed particularly heavy in Oklahoma, she tried to keep herself occupied in other ways as well. Early on she decided that she was too skinny. Stepping out of the bath on the day after lighting the funeral pyre, she stared at herself in the mirror and thought for a moment that her bones had grown but her flesh had shrunk. Even after Granny Annie's pampering she could count her ribs, and her legs were those of a grasshopper's.

On her next trip to the Vinita Town Library, she went into the sports and fitness section and spent an hour going through the dozens of books. For her they were relatively simplistic and equated to: a protein heavy diet combined with exercise would equate to bigger muscles and more strength.

From that day on, she went to Vinita high school, home of the Hornets, where there was a gymnasium to work out in. She did wind sprints every single day until it felt as though her lungs were on fire. And there was a weight room that, even after a year, smelled strongly of stinky boys. Straining, she dragged the weights out into the main gym where everything was brighter and more open.

There, she followed the instructions in her books and pumped "iron," starting with tiny two-pound dumbbells for curls and five-pounders for the bench and military press. She did box jumps and lunges and all sorts of wearing exercises. Since her readings insisted that she keep her workouts "fun," she made sure to play games as well.

She jumped rope and laid out a hundred and ninety foot hopscotch course that ran around the room. On the second day she tried basketball only the hoops were very high and amounted to frustration. She liked tennis, though she didn't much care for the rules and so she pounded the balls against the cement walls, hitting them in whatever direction she wanted.

When she wasn't reading, eating and exercising, she filled in the quiet time by creating more bombs, and more drones. She repaired the Jeep and added secondary cameras to the front and rear.

Keeping busy was all she had. Every minute that went by in utter silence, where her mind could wander, was one spent in fear. She was afraid of the return of her craziness and the fact that she was talking to an empty room was a bad sign.

"I just have to hold on for a little longer."

It would be March soon and a person could travel in March. Yes, late snows came, but on the wide plains they were generally short lived, messy things that were more of an inconvenience than a real threat.

"I'll leave on March tenth. That should be plenty late enough. Maybe even too late. Hmmm, that is true. Everyone will be moving again in March. All the traders and the bandits and the people who have barely scraped by this past winter. There'll be a lot of them. They'll be getting desperate and…"

She stopped, realizing that she was talking to herself again. "March tenth," she murmured, finalizing her decision. Whether she left earlier or later hardly mattered, she would have to be careful one way or another.

There was no question where her destination was. Her heart had been begging to go to the Estes Valley, only they weren't ready for her just yet. To them she was still a monster, a murderer, a psychopath. "And that's what means a crazy person." She was hated there and feared. The last time she had gone to the valley, a mob had sprung up to run her out of town and only Neil Martin had kept her safe.

No, she couldn't go to the Estes Valley just yet. She was going to Scottsbluff, Nebraska to find a woman named Lauren and her daughter Tristyn. Lauren had a second daughter, only Jillybean didn't know her name. "Jacquelyn, maybe?" The father's name had been Jack, so it seemed to match in Jillybean's mind.

Although she had never met any of them, she felt a connection to the family that was based solely on hope. The year before, she had chanced upon the home in a moment of desperation and it had given her everything she had needed, including a short moment in time where she was able to walk into the past when the world wasn't yet overcome by monsters.

The house had been perfect except for two things: there was no one home and sitting on the kitchen table had been the saddest of letters:

Dear Jack,

We're going to my mom's place. I'm sorry, but we waited as long as we could, and the girls are getting scared, and so am I. The army isn't telling us where you are or what's happening at all. This is the third time I've written this letter. I don't want to leave, but we can hear the guns now and I don't want to wait until the last minute. That'll be worse.

If the army lets you go, get up to Scottsbluff as fast as you can.

I love you, Jack, always,

Lauren

The letter had sat in that perfect house for over a year before Jillybean had read it and now four months later, Lauren had to have figured out that Jack wasn't ever going to make it to Scottsbluff and yet Jillybean still felt the need to make the trip, to tell her in person that she had been the only one to have read the letter.

Lauren would cry and Tristyn would also. It would be sad, but it would also mean closure for the family.

"But what if they blame me?" Jillybean asked the empty room. "What if they get mad that I took some of their stuff? What if they don't like me?" People only seemed to like her for a little while. It wasn't ever long before they would whisper things like: *She creeps the bejesus out of me.*

There was no dictionary reference to something called a "bejesus," but she got the gist nonetheless. "Maybe I can act like someone else." She hadn't wanted to be Jillybean anymore for some time, but her sister Sadie had talked her into keeping the name. "I could call myself Jillian, which was aposed to be my real name anyways, but that sounds too much like Jillybean. Maybe I could call myself Jill. It wouldn't be like a lie since it could be a nickname. And I wouldn't act like myself neither. I wouldn't be smart or nothing."

The idea didn't sit well and she wore an odd look on her face as she headed out to the garage to where her patient lay trussed to a steel bed frame. She had a monster chained there, hand and foot. It growled and snapped its teeth as they always did.

"Oh hush," Jillybean said, slipping a surgical mask over her face and sliding on two pairs of rubber gloves. Her hands were so small that she had to add a rubber band to keep them from getting too loose. Next to the monster was her "practice" surgical kit.

It had everything she needed to operate on a person…or in this case, a monster. Step one was to shut it up. It already had an IV running into the fat vein in the crook of its arm. Through the IV's port, she gave it a heavy dose of ketamine—more than any human could survive—and it slowly fell asleep.

As Jillybean waited for it to go fully under, she asked herself: "But how can I not be smart and be a surgeoner at the same time? Everyone knows doctors are smart."

Her dream of being a healer had not died with Sylvia. Although her attempt had been a horrible fiasco, she had decided that it had been the right thing to do and that, given similar circumstances, she would do it again. And that is why she trapped the monster and practiced on them.

The one sleeping on her table was the fifth one she had gone through. Unlike Jessica Jeep or Matilda the drone, it wasn't given a name. Naming things and then shooting them wasn't exactly a nice thing to do.

This one had lived through two surgeries so far, and it wasn't looking good, which is saying something when it came to a monster. They were usually quite horrible to start with.

It looked dreadfully thin and wasted except for its left thigh, which was swollen. She had shot it there the day before and had spent an hour fishing out the bullet and sewing muscles back into place. The swelling could have come from a nicked artery or a bleeder she had missed or just plain infection. Had it been a person she would have had them on some stiff antibiotics to begin with. She wasn't going to waste those sorts of drugs on a monster.

If it died, then it died and no great loss. She would drag it out, using the Jeep and get a new one.

When her gear was ready—reused instruments that had soaked in Jonny Walker Black all night—she stepped back and shot the beast in its other thigh, using her police special.

She then went to the record player in the corner, switched it on and carefully set the needle in the first groove. Although she had come across many record collections, most of the albums were not what she considered "good" music. She had listened to The Doors, Jethro Tull, Blue Oyster Cult and many others with her lip curled in disgust.

Of the eight records, only two were rock and roll and these were only just barely, the Beatles *Yellow Submarine* and the Beach Boys *Greatest Hits*, the rest were oriented towards kids with her favorite and the one spinning in perfect circles on the player: *A Chipmunk Christmas*.

"Christmas, Christmas don't be late…" she sang as she went to work, opening up the wound and clamping the edges back so she could see. To her instruments she had added a suction machine to clear away the pooling blood and a cauterizer to zap the smaller bleeders so things didn't get so messy. Arteries were clamped off so the beast wouldn't bleed out, and in no time, she had found the bullet.

Now came the trickiest part: sewing the monster's leg back together without scratching herself. Just in case it did happen, she had a sterile scalpel and a bowl of alcohol sitting out. She would open the wound and dunk it in the alcohol if anything happened.

As she was very careful, the closing went without mishap and in her fastest time she had the monster almost as good as, well, almost as good as when she had walked in.

She practiced her surgery five days a week and was getting good, though she would be the first to admit there were huge lapses in her knowledge. Still, she knew what ability she had would be questioned the moment she tried to use it. How could she try to blend in with Lauren and Tristyn and explain her skills?

"I could say it's a hobby, or, or maybe I could say it was what my daddy used to do and he sort of taught me before he died." Her daddy had done something with computers back in the before, but no one would know that.

"Lying is bad, only this is one of those white-colored lies and it'll be okay, 'specially if I save someone's life. Then everyone will cheer." She was still daydreaming about being on a parade when she glanced over and saw that monster number five was dead.

She gazed at it a long time before deciding to do a postmortem on it. She had shot it five times and she opened up each of the previous surgery sites to see what had happened. The one leg stank like spoiled meat. "Infection might have killed the thing."

The two belly wounds were also infected, but not to the extent that the leg was. However, it was in the one shoulder wound where she felt she had found the cause of death. The bullet had fragmented and she had missed it. There was a wound track that branched off the main one that ended in the right lung which was now nothing more than a bag of pus and blood.

"Oh boy, that's not good. I guess this shows that I'm not quite ready to..." She stopped, once more realizing she was talking to herself. *Two more weeks*, she said to herself as she unchained the corpse and wrapped it in its plastic death shroud.

Chapter 10

Jillybean

Fourteen days and three dead monsters later, Jillybean climbed into Jessica Jeep, just as the sun set on a wet and lonely Oklahoma evening. A line of gold on the western horizon marked the only color in the sky, besides grey, that she had seen in a week of miserable, wet weather that marked the transition from winter to spring in this part of the country.

She wasn't going to miss it. Not that sloppy Philadelphian late winters had been any better, but at least after the winter there came a real spring where she would be able to enjoy a thousand types of flowers blooming and lush green grass and pink cherry trees exploding in color. In Oklahoma, there would be a brief flash of green and then months of dull browns turning duller still as the months wore on under a crushing sun. She was sure there were parts of the state that were prettier than Vinita coming out of a harsh winter, but she had yet to see them and she turned her back on the state without reservation.

Although the Jeep was piled high and stuffed to overflowing with all the items she had been able to stockpile, it plowed easily through the mud in the front yard and pushed through a throng of monsters that had been crowding around a now inert Bumble Ball.

Once on the road, she struck west on Route 60 and was amazed at the condition of the highway. This had been the second winter since the beginning of the apocalypse and the damage was beginning to mount. In places, mud two feet deep covered the road while in others, there wasn't any road at all. Rivers and flash floods had just swept it away.

Potholes were no longer a nuisance, they were now dangerous. After Jillybean hit one that was so deep that the impact knocked one of her front cameras off, she had to slow down even more until the Jeep was crawling along at eight miles an hour.

The dreadful pace and the dull nighttime scenery were enough to put her to sleep, literally. To fight sleep, she listened to books on tape or put on CDs and sang along to her favorites.

At midnight, she ran into her first horde and had her first scare. With the dark, the horde's size could not be measured.

There was just an endless ocean of grey faces with eerie white eyes. They all turned to stare at the Jeep, but they didn't attack.

With its blocky armor and lack of windows, there was nothing very human about it; in truth, it didn't look much like any vehicle ever made. For the most part the monsters just gazed stupidly at it as she pushed forward into them at a gentle two miles an hour. Some punched the metal, which came across as a soft thud and wasn't unnerving in the least. Others fell in front and were crushed and mutilated.

Although she had no fear of the beasts, she had a healthy respect for what a big enough pothole would do and so she stayed calm and pushed on. There were so many of the monsters that she grew bored and sleepy again, however something on the side of the road caused her to instantly come awake.

At first, she thought it was a house, it was so big, but then the low-light camera caught a flare of white that lasted only a couple of seconds. It could only have been a match.

"Oh jeeze," she whispered, bending in close so that her pert little nose was only an inch from the screen. What she saw caught the breath in her throat. Ahead of her were four of the massive trader trucks—basically castles on wheels, complete with dungeons.

If they knew that there was only one little girl in the armored vehicle, they would very likely try something. "They might anyways," she whispered, easing the Jeep to the right, moving *closer* to the traders. It would seem counterintuitive to get closer, only Jillybean knew that their main armament were the .50 caliber machine guns set on the top of the machines.

These sat in armored turrets and because of the high angle, it made them useless at ranges closer than sixty feet. Of course, Jillybean knew she'd be vulnerable once she was past them but there was nothing she could do about that except to hope that the intervening monsters would absorb the rounds.

As she slowly passed, Jillybean watched the starboard side monitor with her breath held, one finger poised over the smoke machine, and her right foot hovering over the gas, ready to stomp down.

There was an air of tense, fearful expectation in the Jeep, while in the trucks there was curiosity. The trucks possessed loopholes from which the traders could shoot. They could look out as well and she could see bright faces at each of the openings.

"Faces are better than guns," she reasoned.

Ten agonizing minutes later, she was beyond them and running down the dead, the Jeep bouncing over bodies, her possessions jingling and rattling. She went faster and faster until she hit a pothole with such a tremendous bang and rending of metal that she was thrown forward, bouncing off the steering wheel.

Panic seized her as the Jeep was pointed nose down with the front monitor showing nothing but black and the rear giving her an excellent view of the dark sky. She was sure she had driven the Jeep into a sink hole and would never get it out again, however a glance at the side monitors showed that it wasn't a sink hole but a normal hole and her position wasn't nearly as bad as she thought.

The rear end of the Jeep had come to rest on a mound of squiggling monsters and even as she watched the monitor, the angle grew less severe as some slithered their broken bodies out from beneath. When her heart slowed, she worked the Jeep free and continued on, going even slower than before.

Eventually, she left the horde behind. She got off the highway as soon as she could. Route 60 hadn't been the biggest of roads, only two lanes with the occasional suicide lane thrown in when it cut through the middle of some dinky town, and yet it proved big enough for the trader trucks.

She took to the tiny back roads that would go from being paved, to dirt and back again without rhyme or reason. When daybreak came and the sky held hues of pink and blue that reminded Jillybean of the "baby wards" at hospitals, she was forty miles away from the trucks and searching for a place to hide for the day.

The land, being so flat and open, limited her choices. She gazed fondly at a far off barn, remembering that her adopted father, Neil Martin, had always loved using them to keep out of sight—they were too obvious. She also considered a grain silo staring with squinty eyes, remembering New Eden and how the Believers had used silos as watch towers.

In the end, she saw a line of trees curving through the land and knew that a stream had cut its way into the earth. It wouldn't be a perfect place to hide for the day, there weren't many perfect places left anymore. The stream bed fell into the "good enough" category.

She cut across country and drove alongside the gulch until she found a way down that wouldn't tip the machine over. With everything so open, she couldn't set out her customary traps and alarms, which didn't sit well with her as she folded down the driver's seat and snuggled into her blanket and comforter.

Instead of going straight to sleep, she let her mind wander over the idea of a sound-generated alarm. Of course, there were movement sensors in every RadioShack in the country; the only problem with using them was the hundreds of millions of monsters roaming everywhere. They rarely stopped moving and would set off the alarms on a constant basis.

What made more sense to her was a sound sensor set to the low rumbly frequency of a car's engine. She could set one out in a tree and on a calm day, she would know if a car came within a mile of her. Sleep stole up on her while she was planning out the particulars. She was out until a heavy rain began to beat on the fuel cans strapped to the roof rack.

The cans sounded like steel drums being poorly played by a deaf man with a dozen arms. After a light meal, she resumed her trek, spending most of that night slogging through the rain heading either north or west. Her speed never crept above ten miles an hour, which, coupled with the fact that she saw no one and nothing, made the night drag on.

She slipped across the Kansas border just before dawn. It was just as flat and dreary as Oklahoma had been and with red-rimmed eyes, she began to look for a place to sleep for the day. She was so tired from the long hours of sitting behind the wheel that she nearly missed the trail of smoke in the sky. It was a thin, brown ribbon centered over the town of Kiowa. It hung there for a while and then trailed away to nothing the moment the sun was a finger's length over the horizon.

"People," Jillybean said, feeling a demand to find out exactly what sort of people they were. "Bad guys, probably." That was true. There did seem to be a lot of bad people left in the world, but what if they were good?

She really didn't know the answer to that because what if they were good but weak? What if they were good but stupid? Did she want to get mixed up in that sort of trouble? It would mean putting her life on the line for them over and over again just to hear them eventually say: *You creep the bejesus out of me.*

Still, there was no denying that she was drawn to the town. "Like a moth to a flame. That's what Ipes would have said. He would have said it was too dangerous to go and too dangerous to be alone." Despite his generally poor advice, she missed his companionship.

In the end, her terrible loneliness was the deciding factor.

Dressed like the tiniest monster, she tottered her way to the town which, at a half mile in length and width, was dinky by any standard. It made finding the humans an easy thing.

They were holed up in the local elementary school that was constructed mostly of brick and thus a good enough spot to defend. They were somewhat careless in their attitude towards safety, at least in her opinion, and made frequent trips out of doors.

The men, a rough and hairy lot, killed the stray monsters hanging around, while the women, also rough but far less hairy, went to fetch rain water from the many buckets that had been set outside the front doors.

All told, Jillybean, using a fancy set of high-powered binoculars, counted twenty-two men and sixteen women, none of whom looked abused in the slightest. The little girl proclaimed that as: "Good," though she didn't make any move towards the group. Evil took more forms than the abuse of women, and besides, she had already classified them as both weak and stupid.

Their weakness lay in their lack of numbers and their stupidity was evidenced by their overall attitude towards safety. It was too dangerous of a world to rely on army camouflage against the monsters. It was too dangerous of a world to be so complacent with their defenses.

Jillybean could have destroyed the building and all of them in it with ease if she had wanted to, and she was just a little girl. Where were the lookouts? Where were the alarms? Where were the designated fields of fire? Why was there still so much vegetation around the school? Jillybean sat in a clump of bushes half a block away, invisible to all of them.

Still, she didn't hurry away. She missed people and so she watched them as they pulled chairs out into the morning and sat around, some talking, some doing chores. Two of the women fascinated Jillybean. They were pregnant. One had a belly that was the size of a beach ball, while the other's was much smaller, barely a lump, which didn't stop her from caressing it almost nonstop. The two held a special place in the group. Seats were given to them without hesitation and they received smiles from everyone who stopped by.

Jillybean could guess that the others asked them about the babies growing in them or asked if anything was needed by them. "I'll have some tea and cookies, thank you," Jillybean said, dipping her head. "And the baby is fine 'cept she's gonna be a soccer player when she grows up on account of all the kicking she's doing."

"A tea party sounds nice. I haven't had..." A huge yawn gaped her mouth and reminded her that she had been up all night. Beat, the seven-year-old went back to her Jeep, which she had parked in a stand of trees a mile outside of town. Once more she made her bed inside the vehicle and slept until the sun had crossed over to the other side of the sky.

It was four in the afternoon when she woke and six when she decided to continue her journey. "I can always come back," she said to herself, as she struck north on a dirt road that had seen better days.

In the next five days, she saw three more people: one was a crazy man who was so vile in appearance that Jillybean didn't see him mixed in with the monsters. He started raving and beating on the Jeep, which had no effect whatsoever because of the armor. However when he started to climb up to get at the supplies lashed on top, she was forced to do something and spurted the Jeep suddenly forward, knocking him off and leaving him crying in the dirt.

The next person she saw was a woman wearing what looked like a sheet draped across her. She had been at a river crossing and because of the water hadn't heard the Jeep's approach. Like a child, she tried to hide in a run of low bushes, but the sheet was white and she stuck out.

As she was alone and unarmed, Jillybean tried to talk to her: "Hi...hi...hey you in the bushes. Hi, my name is Jillybean. I won't hurt you." Despite saying this, Jillybean had her hand on the .38 in her pocket.

The woman said nothing until Jillybean got out of the Jeep and approached. "Uh, do you have any gas to trade? I've got all sorts of stuff, but my gas is getting a little low." She had enough to get to Scottsbluff, however she had seen the size of the town on the map and because it was so small, she decided that it would be smart to collect what she could before she got there on the off chance that it was deserted.

"I can't talk to you," the woman said. "It's not allowed."

This declaration had Jillybean backing away, glancing up at the bank of the river and now the gun was out. "Who won't let you?"

She expected a man's name or something generic like *them*, however the woman looked straight up into the sky and said: "God won't let me."

"Oh, God, right. That's…that's right I forgot. Sorry." Jillybean turned and ran for the Jeep. The lady was part of another doomsday cult and little scared Jillybean more than them. Today's evil sprang from selfishness and fear, and could be understood on some level by the little girl. The evil cults, however thrived on blind fanaticism. It was a frightening force that could override love and even the sense of self-preservation.

Although it was light out, Jillybean drove hard for another thirty miles before she pulled over in a state of utter exhaustion.

It was nearly a day later in a town in Nebraska call North Platte which, oddly in Jillybean's eyes sat just north of the South Platte River, that she saw the last person before she got to Scottsbluff.

After a not-so-restful day of tossing and turning in the Jeep, she had gone out scrounging for fuel using a battery-powered drill to bore her way into the gas tanks of the cars parked along a quiet street. In four hand-numbing hours, she had filled three five-gallon jerry cans, one plastic water bottle at a time, which she kept hidden beneath her monster clothes as she made her way back and forth from the cars to the hidden jerry cans. Fifteen gallons was barely enough to get to Scottsbluff and back, not that she had any intention of coming back through North Platte.

There was so little to the town that it didn't feel worth it. If Scottsbluff was empty, she would go on to Wyoming, either north west to Casper on her way to the Pacific, or south west to Cheyenne if she felt like slipping into the Estes Valley. She hadn't decided and was mulling over the possibilities as she monstered her way back to the hidden Jeep when movement caught her eye.

It was only a blink of what looked like a face, then there was a flash of brown before it was gone behind one of the houses.

Jillybean staggered on, only now her chin was tucked down and her eyes were crooked to the right as far as she could get them without appearing to be staring over her shoulder. *That was a boy!* her mind screamed.

It hadn't been a man or a monster. Yes, there was a chance that it could have been a young woman however the way he had moved reminded Jillybean of the little boys she had known: all wild legs and unholy speed.

Gradually, Jillybean the monster girl, turned to the side and crossed into the backyard of an ugly A-frame home where old weeds were plastered over after a long winter. She slunk down, creeping around the house, moving with all the guile and stealth she could muster. Her sharp eyes studied every window in every house and every shadow beneath every eave as she moved— there was nothing to see.

When she came to the house she'd seen the boy dash behind, she took extra care, all in vain. He had so completely disappeared that she began to doubt her senses, which was a nice way to say she began to worry about the crazies coming back. A pent-up breath blew out of her when she finally saw that the boy had left behind a single print in the mud. She measured it against her own sneaker; it was significantly bigger but still within the dimensions that fit what she considered child size.

"Which makes him how old?" she murmured. The only boy she had known in the last year was Joe Gates, a boy who had been twice orphaned, once when Jillybean had found out that his mother was a traitor and a second time when his aunt and uncle had died within days of each other during the war with the Azael.

"And that wasn't my fault…not completely." She had not planned the escape from the Duke's lair and because of that people had died. She had not planned it because she had been crazy at the time. "And that wasn't my fault…not completely. And that's not here or there or anywhere, not just now. That print is the same size as Joe's, or at least the same size that Joe's had been. He's older now, probably eleven."

Although the boy had been slick in his escape, she knew that, with patience, she would be able to discover the hiding place of his group, but that was only if she wanted to, which she wasn't sure she did. The town was small and its resources limited. She hadn't seen any sign of a fortified structure and the Jeep's tracks had been the only ones that had been through the place in at least a week.

This suggested that the group had set down roots in North Platte and that suggested a serious weakness in leadership. They would survive, only they would do so living like rats, digging in the corpse of a dead town. They needed help, the sort of help that Jillybean could have provided if she wasn't on a mission already, and if she wasn't haunted by a voice echoing in her head.

"They need to get to Estes," she said. "But that doesn't mean I gotta take them." She thought for a while and then grinned as an elegant solution struck her. "I could leave them a map."

Once Jillybean got back to Jessica Jeep, she dug through her belongings for a piece of paper and then, after consulting her road atlas, she wrote out detailed instructions to get to Estes and added the words: *Where it's safe!*

After picking up her three hidden jerry cans, she drove to the center of town, honking her horn and flashing her lights. There was a city hall that seemed like the only proper place to set her map. As there were monsters converging, she drove over the curb, up the sidewalk and right up to the tall wooden doors, where she got out of the Jeep just long enough to stick the map there using one of her knives to pin it in place.

It never occurred to her that she had seen the only occupant of the town. There was no chance that a boy of ten would be alone in the world, after all it was an unquestionable fact that boys weren't smarter than girls. Sure, they could catch up as adults but at ten they *liked* to play in the mud for goodness sakes!

"And comic books. Don't get me started on comic books," she said as she drove away. "Talk about dumb!" And yet, he had given her the slip. "Which makes him fast, but nothing more. I bet he...I'm talking to myself again, for all darn it. But it won't be for long. I'll find Lauren and Tristyn soon."

The last hundred miles were the quickest yet, and at dawn she stood on a rise staring at the quietest town in America. Other than the monsters, Scottsbluff was utterly devoid of life.

Chapter 11

Chris Turner

The rat had died even before the freighter left the harbor in Alexandria, Egypt a year and half before Jillybean stood staring at the ruins of Scottsbluff. It had crawled out of the blistering sun and into the dank hold, spitting and gnashing its teeth in the ugly way rabid rats could get, and yet it wasn't rabid. The disease eating up its tiny brain was far worse, far more deadly.

The disease brought a fever with it that burned out the neurons in its brain, leaving nothing but a raw, grinding hate for anything with a pulse, no matter how big. When the first pallet was lowered down into the cargo hold of the freighter, the rat had glared up at it, the feeble light glimmering off its dim grey eyes. It tried to stand on its hindquarters to reach the pallet, but in a previous moment of rage and hunger, it had eaten half of its own leg, which sat in its shrunken belly in a stew of acid that kept boiling up its throat.

The rat could do nothing but hiss in rage as the pallet crushed it. And there it sat in the hold, decomposing and festering, the virus still alive and going strong, multiplying, breeding death.

The freighter was at sea for ten days and sat in the port of Norfolk, Virginia for another three before the load was checked by a bored customs agent. There was nothing special about this particular load—meaning there wasn't anything illegal or pseudo illegal and thus nothing that would garner a bribe.

The agent, a fellow named Arnie Franks owned two cars: the eight year old KIA Sedona with the stale french fries strewn like spilt matches around the driver's seat that he took to work every day and the new Corvette that had less than three thousand miles on it, which he only used to drive out to the shady honkytonks on the south side of town where the women might not have all their teeth, but were properly appreciative of a man with a fancy car, regardless of his receding hairline and the potbelly he sported.

The Sedona still had two years left on the loan, while the Corvette had been paid for with the cash that was slipped to him whenever someone needed an "irregularity" overlooked on one of the loads.

Franks made a very good living with the illicit side money because he had a very good nose for trouble. On that particular freighter, the smell of trouble struck him as soon as he stepped through the cargo door—literally.

The stench of rotting meat was sharp and he immediately began considering how to pry a little something extra out of the freighter's loadmaster. He made a show of it, wrinkling his nose and waving a hand in front of his face like a southern belle about to get a case of the vapors.

"Just some stagnant bilge, nothing to worry about," the loadmaster said in answer. He was a big, beefy man with a gut that hung over his belt by a foot and a half. He knew how the game was played and he tried to push on through into the hold, but Franks grabbed his arm.

"Bilge water? Oh, I really doubt that. That's something expired. That's something looooong expired."

The loadmaster could smell the rancid meat as well, there was no mistaking it for anything else. "Okay, prolly a rat. Look at your sheet. We aren't carrying anything that would make that smell, spoiled or no. Not even the olive oil. You ever smell olive oil that's gone over? It's not like this. This is too…tangy. Oil is sharper." It was an ugly word to use in conjunction with the smell and Franks, who had smelled all sorts of unfortunate aromas in his time, only gave the loadmaster a queasy smile.

"I don't know," Franks said, sadly, his face long, as if the smell of the dead rat had struck him emotionally as well as physically. "It's too bad, we might have to break down a few of these containers." This was Franks' only real threat—his only real way of getting a bribe on a load like this. Normally, he would only open each container and give the contents a quick once over. It would take a couple of hours but that was to be expected.

It could take up to ten times as long if he opened each of the seventy containers and spread everything onto the pier in haphazard piles, leaving it to the crew to figure out how everything went back into each of the 2,400 cubic foot containers. The cost in overtime and dock fees would be outrageous.

The loadmaster rolled his eyes. "Just stop. It's a rat or it's stagnant bilge water. Half of the containers have nothing in them that can possibly spoil and the other half is either bottled or canned. Everything has been checked already, twice…no three times. I forgot the Egyptian container seal team. Their signatures are on each invoice. Trust me, the containers have all been inspected and sealed according to every law known to man."

"Then account for that smell," Franks said and then waited with an officious eyebrow raised. When the brow came down, it would land with the full weight of the United States government and that was a ton of shit that no one wanted to deal with.

The loadmaster knew this as well as anyone. "It's a rat, jeeze." He freaking hoped that it was a rat. Bilge water had its own particular, eye-watering stench and this wasn't it. He walked away from the loadmaster, his eyes scanning back and forth, knowing that he'd find a rat. Years of experience told him what the smell was, though in this case it was particularly rancid and he wouldn't be surprised if he found a dozen of them rotting away.

He honed in on it like a bloodhound and when he saw the decomposed body, his grin stretched from ear to ear. "Just like I thought." He'd crossed the Atlantic twice a month for the last twenty-seven years and knew the smell of decomposed rat. He reached down and yanked the thing out from beneath the pallet getting a single heavy splinter in the process.

The rat came apart as though it were a slow-roasted pig.

The smell had Franks stepping back, as well as conceding the point. He did so with magnanimity. There would be other ships and other chances to make a buck.

The loadmaster pretended as though the dead rat was just like all the other rats he had chucked overboard in his time. His smile remained fixed as he kicked the mess aside and walked Franks through the freighter. Now that the governmental threat was gone, he chatted amiably and yet all he could think about was washing his hands.

He had never before felt a slimier carcass in his life and the smile hid a queasiness that kept creeping up the back of his throat. It threatened to turn into a "chunky burp," and who knew what would come up next.

Thankfully, Franks went about the freighter in a perfunctory manner after the rat incident and left two hours later. Right away, the loadmaster, a man named Roy Hapson, rushed to the nearest sink and washed his hands in the hottest water he could stand— but by then it was too late; the splinter had introduced the disease into Roy and he was officially the first person in America infected.

The super-soldier virus was already replicating by the thousands and the hundreds of thousands and then by the millions, coating him in an invisible film, and racing through his bloodstream. Two hours later, as he sat in the bridge watching the wharf cranes haul out the containers one by one, his head began to pound something fierce. And, at first, he thought nothing of it.

Crossings weren't easy and the process of unloading was stressful and the custom agents were annoying and that rat had been disgusting. The headache had almost been expected. He popped four extra-strength Advils, slugging the pills back with some potent Irish coffee, and went back to work.

The whiskey and the pills barely dented the pain in his head and thirty minutes later he was back for more. This time he didn't bother with the coffee and didn't give one thought to what his breath smelled like.

He staggered back out to the deck, worked for all of an hour until the headache became blinding and the fever that came with it was enough to actually frighten him. He had never been this sick in his life.

"I gotta go," he said, in a whisper to his assistant, his eyes barely cracked. "Sick. Migraine. Just finish and send me an email with the signatures." He stumbled away to the gangplank, which looked to be a thousand feet long and if it hadn't been for the railings, he would have fallen into the trash-strewn bay.

The walk to his truck was an ordeal, one he couldn't have made a second time and, with a pathetic whimpering on his part, he rumbled the engine into life.

Half-way to his home, he pulled over, his head roaring so badly he couldn't see straight. It thudded horribly as he fished under his seat for his emergency bottle of whiskey. He told people that he was only a "social" drinker, however he downed the bottle as if it were water. It did very little to help the pain.

"Oh, crap," he whined, with his teary eyes half-closed. The afternoon sun, blaring and loud was too much for him. It made him want to scream and vomit and hide deep underground where it would be cool and silent, and where if he died nobody would know or care.

He felt as though his brain was roasting inside in his skull. The pain grew and grew, becoming so horrible that his one wish was for his heart to give out and yet, through a tremendous effort, he made it home, staggering inside and going straight for the liquor cabinet where he drank a quart of booze, and even if his life had depended on it he wouldn't have been able to tell what it was.

Pills by the handful came next and again, he didn't know exactly what he was taking. His eyes couldn't focus through the tears, but what did it matter? Pills were pills.

They didn't work. Nothing worked and by the time his wife came home, he was too far gone for pills anyways. He sat in the furthest corner of the basement drinking in the dark and hating everything other than that dark.

His wife Sabrina was a small woman, but her steps on the floor overhead made it seem as though she had ballooned to the size of an elephant, and her voice, normally sweet and soft, had become the screech of a hag's.

"Roy! Roy! Where are you?"

He cringed, while the hate coursed along his nerves. The feeling reached a crescendo when the boys started running around. They weren't his kids. They were nobody's. They were foster kids that Roy normally could only just tolerate when he was in port and he did so because he knew how much they meant to Sabrina.

Her womb was, and had always been, a useless hole stuck up inside her. It was a lifeless desert—and thus, the stupid foster kids that were changed out every few months. The current pair, Chris and…what's his name, Roy couldn't remember what, were as different as night and day: one quiet and sad, new to the loss of his parents and the other, Chris had been on his own for years, bouncing around from home to home, always at the whim of the system.

At the moment, Roy wanted to strangle Chris. He wanted to beat his head in and tear out his guts. The strange desire, so foreign to his usual calm state didn't even cause him to blink. He stomped upstairs, completely out of control, his heavy, angry steps thudding so loudly that it stopped all activity.

Roy slammed open the basement door and stood breathing like a bull, spittle bubbling at his lips.

Sabrina froze, her mouth open in mid-call. The no-name kid was caught in a strange contortion, trying to twist his school bag from his back, while Chris had just tossed a football into the air. It seemed to hang there suspended for a second that stretched out and out.

The moment it landed in his hands seemed to trigger an explosion of activity. Roy felt like a lion among sheep, each so innocent and tasty. He roared into them, his long arms outstretched, catching the no-name kid but missing Chris who spun out of reach.

Roy bit the no-name kid in the neck. It was entirely instinctive, and yet it was no instinct that he had ever felt in his life. He was just *hungry*. The blood rushed into his mouth, metallic and hot. He sucked it down in one great pull and then tossed the body aside.

Sabrina was next. She hadn't moved. She had only stood there with her mouth hanging open and her eyes wide and wet as peeled grapes. Roy leapt on her and threw her down, and was just about to feed a second time when his mouth bit down on metal. Chris, fast as an adder had snatched a knife from the rack and plunged it up to the handle into Roy's throat.

Roy didn't feel the knife, except for a strange tickle and an inability to swallow, neither of which stopped him from attacking Chris. He leapt up, growling around the blade, and flung himself at Chris, who was cornered between the dishwasher and the dining room wall. It should have been nothing for him to corral the kid, only Chris's eight hard years of life had prepared him for exactly this moment.

His father had died when he was four and his mother had not done well for herself or her son ever since. A string of abusive boyfriends had taught Chris quickness so that when Roy came at him, Chris was able to react as if this was just another drunk asshole. He feinted one way and went the other, heading for the front door with Roy lumbering at his heels.

Chris was plenty scared. After all, the man was running after him with a knife sticking out of his throat, and yet this wasn't the first man who had chased him with murder in his heart. Chris knew he had to get outside where the world would see and judge—that had stopped four of the last five men who had thought they were going to use Chris Turner as a human punching bag.

It didn't work with Roy. He kept coming, never slowing. The streets were empty and no one came to the boy's rescue, he wasn't all that surprised. People were weak. They didn't like trouble.

With Roy reaching out bloody fingers to catch Chris's shoulder length dark hair, the boy suddenly changed directions, jigging left, he ran at a four foot high chain link fence that came up to his chin. He was over it in a blink.

"People are calling the cops, Mister Hapson. You better stop." Chris backed away from the fence as he said this. Roy wasn't listening, he was slowly climbing, what to him was a relatively short fence. When Chris saw that he wouldn't stop, he looked around, finding himself in someone's front yard.

By the relative perfection and the strange decorations, he guessed that it was an "old" person's yard. Anyone over forty was old in his book, though in this case the owner of the home was a seventy-three year old widow who was even then hurrying to her front door to bark at the boy trampling in her flower bed.

It was poor timing on her part. Her screeching voice drilled into Roy's ears and without thought, he turned on her the second he cleared the fence. When the owner of the house saw him, her screech of fussy anger turned to terror. Too late and too slowly, she tried to run back into her house. He was on her before she could take two steps, rending and tearing away her sensible cardigan to get at the wrinkly flesh below.

Chris stopped him. The only weapons in reach was a family of clay garden gnomes. Chris went through three of the bizarre decorations, crashing them down on the back of Roy's head with all his might, before the man slumped down on top of the old woman, who was weeping and babbling about that in "her day" men were so much kinder.

She never thanked Chris for saving her life and, in truth, he hadn't. She had been scratched by Roy and in six hours she went on to bite and scratch two EMTs, a nurse, and a doctor before she was finally restrained. Those four would go on to infect over a dozen people before they were killed by police in four separate shootings.

Within a day of Roy's death, those dozen would infect a hundred people and from that point on the spread of the disease would be unstoppable and Chris was in the thick of it—an eight-year-old boy, who had already spent half his short life alone, would see the city of Norfolk dissolve around him.

Chris Turner was not special in an obvious way. If a comparison was made, it would seem as though he did not have Jillybean's natural genius, or Neil Martin's inherent luck or Sadie's speed or Captain Grey's rugged durability. They epitomized these traits while he, on the other hand rather blended them. He wasn't a genius, but he was highly intelligent with a sharp eye. He didn't have world class speed but he was very fast and, more importantly, his reactions were shockingly quick. He didn't have the endurance of a trained Navy Seal, but at eight, he was already tough and resilient.

Where he differed in the greatest respect was that he had never, not for even a single moment in his life, been lucky. Every group he had joined after the apocalypse had been destroyed, enslaved or disbanded. Every friend had been killed, infected, enslaved or had turned on him. Every hiding place he had perfected had been found and every stash had been looted.

And yet he thrived where others had died, or had given up or were driven insane. Unlike Jillybean, he was just fine being alone. In three years of being in the foster care system, he had lived in eleven separate homes and had gone to eleven separate schools. He was always the new kid in old hand-me-downs that were, as a rule, either too big and had to be cinched with a belt, or too small and ran high up his ankle. As far back as he could remember, he had been alone. In a way, it made him sensitive— he knew when people were near.

The Jeep and the little girl had intrigued him, greatly. A person dressing up as a zombie had been a first for him. Jillybean's disguise had fooled him to such an extent that he had almost slipped up, only one false move...one human move, that is, had given her away.

The little zombie had scratched her nose. Zombies yawned and burped and farted, but they did not scratch. So, when the zombie reached up through the wild thicket of hair covering her face to scratch her nose, Chris jerked in surprise. He also slunk low, suddenly anxious.

If this girl was a fake, wouldn't it make sense that some of the other zombies were fakes as well? From deep inside the living room of a crumbling ranch house whose ceiling had long before fallen in, he watched the girl and the other zombies that wandered here and there. The others seemed real enough, which only made him more nervous.

Somewhat hypocritically, he thought that there was no way she was traveling alone. The girl was tiny, skinny as a twig, and she was young. Judging by her size, he thought she was probably not older than six, and who had ever heard of a six-year-old on their own in a zombie world?

Although Chris had been eight when he had fought and killed the first zombie on American soil, he was now a scrappy nine years old, his muscles were lean and ropey, his feet agile, his temperament one of survival first. He was also a chauvinist in the way that young boys were.

"There had to be people with her," he whispered. Unlike Jillybean, he talked to himself all the time and thought nothing of it.

When she disappeared around the side of a house down the block, he felt that she was about to give away the position of her friends and he slipped forward from house to house, but was utterly shocked when he caught her heading towards him! He was utterly baffled. When had she spotted him? And why on earth would she be trying to get closer? Shouldn't she be running away?

"She must have a gun," he decided. It was either that or her friends were closer than he realized. Quickly, he slipped out of sight, hunkering down next to some overgrown bushes as she stalked past, brave but foolish in his eyes. Everyone had a gun these days. They were the great equalizers in a world where might made right.

He watched her head straight to the house he'd been in and he watched her search the ground and knew right away that he had left a print. "Balls," he cursed. That he had left even a single print wasn't acceptable; he prided himself on being a ghost in a world filled with bad guys and monsters.

He figured she would go tell her friends that there was a kid around somewhere and that they would begin the hunt. Grinning, he moved into a better position, heading back to the half-destroyed ranch house where he had a choice of places to hide in. If they came for him, he'd take them out one by one. He had a .44 caliber magnum, a triple length of rope he used as a belt, and an appetite for fun. The idea of a hunt thrilled him.

But he was disappointed as he watched the girl playact back down the block, where a minute later a strange, windowless Jeep pulled out from beneath a low-hanging willow. It made a production of heading into the center of town and then left.

It was such a production, with the horn going and the lights blinking, that Chris felt as though he would be a fool to run out and investigate what had been stuck to the doors of the city hall building. He had not lived through a hundred different adventures by rushing out of hiding the moment everything *seemed* safe. That's how you got killed.

Patience wasn't exactly his strong suit, however he had learned to embrace it over the past year and a half. Two hours went by as he sat, waiting and watching, his keen ears cocked. The only time he moved was to shift his position once and urinate against the side of a bookcase.

Finally, he decided to move down to the city hall building. That took him another two hours, flitting from shadow to shadow, listening with every fiber of his being, ready to blaze away at the first sign of trouble. Trouble did not come.

Satisfied that there wasn't a trap, he took down the note and read the instructions and the words: *Where It's Safe!*

"Yeah right." He balled the paper and tossed it aside, thinking that he was being asked by the lion to step into its den.

Chapter 12

Jillybean

Nothing moved in Scottsbluff, not birds or squirrels or anything, not even monsters. She drove through the town and knew in her heart that she was too late to find Lauren and Tristyn. Was she a month too late, or a year? It was impossible to tell given the limited facts before her. She just knew that it seemed as though she was the only thing alive in Scottsbluff.

Depression wanted to sink deep into her bones, so she forced a smile onto her face. "You're with me, right Jessica?" For just a split second, she feared that the Jeep would actually say something and when she didn't, Jillybean breathed a sigh of relief.

"We don't want to start that nonsense all over again. Okay Lauren, you left a note and came here to be with your mom. Did you write another note before you left Scottsbluff? I say we go... I mean, I say *I* work on the premise that she has. So, I just need to find Lauren's mom's house."

Scottsbluff wasn't the biggest town on the map, still it had a pre-apocalypse population of fifteen thousand people. That was a lot of people which meant that there were a lot of houses to explore. Without a first or last name, or any other information besides being "Lauren's mom," trying to find the right house would be an arduous task, possibly weeks of work for someone who wasn't a genius. For Jillybean it took twenty-two minutes.

"Scottsbluff is an old town," she said, trying to picture what it was like two years before. Had the tired-looking buildings along Broadway been as grim? Had they been vibrant with busy people bustling in and out, smiling and waving to one another, saying: *Good day!* and *How are you, Lauren?*

"That is a good question. Had Lauren lived here? Was this the sort of town that Lauren had moved away from?" The answer was a firm: "Probably. And since Lauren was young, we...I can assume she went to high school here."

She was at Scottsbluff Senior High in five minutes where she quickly found the office. Proudly displayed along one wall were dozens of old yearbooks. Jillybean picked out one from twelve years before and a second from fourteen years.

There were seven hundred names with seven hundred pictures to run down in the first book, but she only got into the three hundreds before she found Lauren Burle with a picture that was very close to one Jillybean had seen in that perfect home back in Missouri.

Although she wanted to go through the book page by page looking for pictures of Lauren playing softball or having lunch or laughing in a chemistry classroom, Jillybean forced the desire away and dug around in the gloomy office for a phone book. There were six people in the town with that last name and only two of them were women. Jillybean chose Rhonda Burle as the most likely since there wasn't a man's name associated with the address. Lauren had written: *My mom's house in Scottsbluff.* She hadn't written: *My parents' house.*

Taking both the phonebook and the yearbook, she drove to the address and, although every house in town looked to have been broken into, Jillybean felt herself tearing up to see the front door of Rhonda's L-shaped ranch house had been kicked in.

With a lump in her throat, Jillybean went in, fearing to find bodies, but there were neither corpses nor bloodstains. It was definitely Lauren's childhood home, the pictures on the walls showed the woman in a strange state of regression. As Jillybean slowly made her way to the back rooms, the pictures showed her at different stages of her life, getting younger and younger, until she came to the last picture at the end of the hallway. It was of Lauren in a highchair with a smushed and mostly demolished birthday cake in front of her. Icing covered her bald head and on her face was the happiest smile in the world.

Jillybean grinned for a moment at the goofy picture, imagining herself with Lauren in the kitchen thirty-three years before. "The cake must have been vanilla…or lemon, I guess. And it got everywhere and everyone was laughing." Slowly, the grin faded as she sighed, feeling drained after her long journey and not knowing what to do, exactly.

Lauren and the girls hadn't made it back. Parts of the house were in a state of odd disarray. It had been ransacked by someone hungry and desperate. In the bedrooms, the drawers of the dressers hung open making them look like multi-mouthed wooden beasts, while all around on the floor were piles of musty smelling clothes. The kitchen was strewn with utensils and plates and shattered glass. The cabinet doors sat back on their hinges, showing nothing inside but empty shelves.

The rest of the house was tidy and perfect in a way that only lonely people who were perpetually hoping for guests maintained things. The perfection suggested that no child had graced the halls for years. Children and messes went hand in hand.

Lauren and the girls had not made it to Nebraska. If they had gotten to Scottsbluff and found the home empty, Lauren would have left a second note for Jack. There wasn't a note. It hadn't been read by the person who had ransacked the home and then cast aside. It wasn't sitting on the credenza near the front door or on the kitchen table or stuck to the fridge with a magnet.

It wasn't balled in the trash. It had never been written. "Had they been stopped in Wichita?" On the way north, Jillybean had come across the remains of a traffic jam that had stretched for twenty miles.

There hadn't been bodies in or around the cars, which was a blessing and yet the long line of abandoned cars had depressed her as she had driven along the shoulder, passing them. They emanated fear and desperation as if there were ghost families still in them sitting, crammed among their belongings, staring out the window with empty eyes and wondering where they would end up and what they would do once they got there.

Jillybean had made it a point not to look through the side monitors, afraid she would actually see a ghost.

"Either way, they're not here and that's what means I wasted my time." She turned to leave, but stopped at the front door. Another sigh slipped out. "There's always a chance."

Lauren's mom had a desk in the living room where Jillybean knew there would be paper and pens. She found dun-colored stationary that had a beach motif in the corners: a child's shovel and bucket, starfish on a sandy background, a colorful umbrella planted over a chair.

Using the blocky and lopsided lettering of a second grader, she wrote a brief note to Jack and Lauren detailing who she was, where she had been and what she knew about the house in Missouri. She didn't know much and what she did know wasn't all that helpful or even hopeful. Still, if she were either Jack or Lauren, or any of their children, she would want whatever information she could get her hands on.

When she was done, she cleared off the refrigerator of its pictures and its many magnets and stuck the note there, square in the middle where it couldn't be missed.

After that Jillybean went back to her life in the apocalypse. She found a wooded lot, where she hid the Jeep. She set her traps and alarms before lying down in a strange bed in a strange house, in a town that echoed with silent loneliness.

Sleep wouldn't come and she tossed about in the bed until she decided what she needed to do was to come to a decision about what she was going to do next and where she was going. As she was considered something of a criminal in a dozen states, she didn't have a lot of choices left to her. Once she ruled out Canada on account of the cold and Mexico because she didn't speak Spanish, she was left with working her way either northwest to the Pacific or southwest to the Estes Valley.

She was starting a mental pros and cons list of both when the voice inside of her reminded her, yet again, that she had forgotten something. "Yeah, I forgot to hit myself over the head with a mallet. Sheesh, what could I have possibly forgotten that was so important?"

You've forgotten something very important, it repeated.

"You said that already!" Jillybean yelled, thumping her little fist on the nightstand next to the bed, causing the lamp on it to jump and tilt crazily before she caught it and straightened it out. "How about you tell me if I'm getting warmer or colder? Is it a person? Did I forget a person?"

She paused, her head cocked waiting to hear the ghostly voice. When it didn't answer, she asked: "Is it a place? Did I forget there was a land of chocolate and bunnies?" She kind of wished that was it, but knew better. "Ok, is it a thing? A stash of gas or a big pile of bullets? Or food? Is it food?" Although she had plenty of food, she could always use more.

The voice remained quiet and Jillybean went on: "Is it someone I killed? Cuz if so, I don't want to know. What would be the point?" She couldn't come up with a salient reason why any part of her subconscious would want her to remember another murder on her part and so she decided to rule it out. The voice wasn't just repetitive and annoying, it was earnest. She had forgotten something that needed to be remembered.

"But when and where and what?" Again, no answers. Her subconscious was hiding something from her. "Why would it do that? Because it's afraid of me? Is that it? It's afraid of what I'll do…there was the word revenge thrown in there before."

Jillybean didn't want revenge on anyone and she wondered who could want revenge on her. True revenge wasn't a simple concept. It demanded a poisonous concoction of love and hate.

Who truly loved the Colonel or the River King enough to stoke a burning hate for Jillybean?

No one she could think of. Certainly not a woman. The Colonel had treated women like slaves and the River King had treated them like whores. The only child that was known to have been produced by either man was Sadie, and she had spat: "Good riddance," when she heard about the death of her father.

"I'm too tired to figure this out and I don't know if I want to. If I put all of the Rocky Mountains between me and whatever this is, then what could it do to me? Nothing, I bet."

That idea held strong appeal. So far, her pro-list for going to the pacific northwest had been sparse: it rained a lot, so fresh water wouldn't be a problem, it was pretty with all the green forests, there were fish in the rivers and she liked salmons, and lastly and most importantly, no one would know who she was. At first it had been a shock when Sylvia had recognized her name, however on further reflection it made sense.

Without television or movies or adequate light to read by most of the time, what was there to entertain people but gossip and outlandish tales, and who was more outlandish than her? "Nobody, that's who," she said, lifting her chin defiantly

She fell asleep thinking about the coast and the giant trees and the soft rain falling, but this wasn't what she dreamed about. In a gauzy dream where everything was misty and indistinct at the edges, she found herself behind the wheel of Jessica Jeep, only there wasn't any armor on her and Jillybean had an excellent view of mountain roads, narrow and twisting as an endless snake. The road was bound by walls of rock and cliffs of ice on one side and a fall into a black unknown on the other.

It's a trap, someone said from the seat next to her.

She knew the voice. "Ipes!" she cried in sudden happiness, turning. It was her little friend, however he wasn't his usual animated self. He just sat there on the seat, half flopped over, his beady black eyes looking at her knee.

Don't go, he said.

"Why not?" Her cons list was even shorter than her pros list: It was far away, was all she had on it.

In answer, he pointed at the road ahead where it curved around a mountainside. She watched in horror as the road beneath her tires began to crumble away in a slow motion avalanche. With a cry, she fought the Jeep onto the shoulder of the road but soon that too was falling away into the black depths.

With no choice, she shifted to 4-wheel low and ran up the mountain itself, sending rocks and ice cascading down behind her until it seemed as if the entire mountain was going to come apart and fall into hell.

The ordeal went on and on and the Jeep was screaming out a roar that echoed for miles and miles, causing all the monsters to turn and come for her. But then, magically, she was up and over the peak where everything was bright and sunny again and the ground was solid beneath her feet.

"That was close, Ipes," she said, laughing as she raced down the slope, aiming for where the road had curved back towards her.

Your con list is right. It's a long way. A long dangerous way. She bounced back onto the road and at first it seemed smooth and perfect, but she was afraid and slowed down, wondering what danger Ipes was warning her about. At first everything seemed proper, but then she saw the gaping black maw of a tunnel entrance bored into the side of the mountain.

If ever there was a perfect place for a trap, it was in that tunnel. She turned the Jeep around in a sharp turn only to find that the road behind her had disappeared into a darkness that was deep and deadly. She reached for the switch for the headlights, but Ipes warned: *You'll be seen. You'll be caught.*

Normally, the darkness was her ally but there were eyes staring out from the depths. She could feel them on her, waiting for her to venture forward where the shadows were all but impenetrable. Again, she spun the Jeep in a tight circle, thumbing the red button on the dash. In seconds the smoke machine was pumping out a heavy cloud so that the darkness swirled and eddied behind her as she raced from one danger to another.

"Ipes, should I drop one of the bom…" She stopped in mid-sentence. Ipes was gone and suddenly the cab of the Jeep was filled with a blaring noise, jolting her awake—it was one of her alarms! Blinking, she slithered out of the bed in a pitiful state: her heart racing, her face aglaze, her hair plastered to her forehead.

The .38 was already in her hand. Now was not the time for subtlety. Seconds were essential. Keeping low, she zipped to the window and stared out into the late afternoon where the shadows of the houses on the block were deep and long, reminding her of her dream. There were eyes in the shadows as well, only she did not fear these eyes knowing they belonged to the monsters in the street.

Jillybean breathed a sigh of relief as she saw that they were gathered around one of her noise makers. "Okay, just some stupid monsters."

She watched them for a while, not wanting to hurry back into the sweat-drenched bed, fearing what her subconscious would feed into her dreams next. If it wanted to give her a nightmare about the Estes Valley, it had ample ammunition, enough to drive her back to Crazy-ville.

"I get it. I forgot something back east and you want me to go find out what. Fine, I'll go." She was sure that her brain didn't mean right that second, but she didn't have anything better to do. Her journey to Scottsbluff had ended in failure. Lauren and Jack and Tristyn were all dead or blown to the four corners of the earth by the winds of fate.

There was nothing more she could do in the town except stock up on fuel, if there was any to be had.

In the two hours before dark, she went from car to car, drilling out a Jerry can's worth of rusty gas, which immediately went into the Jeep's tank. And then she was headed back the way she had come—in fact, she was speeding back the way she had come. She was supposed to be on some sort of adventure to discover a hidden mystery within her, but that didn't mean she had to go alone. She was making for North Platte. The pain at finding Scottsbluff empty had probably triggered her dream and, forgotten something or not, she was still lonely and needed people.

Having just traveled up I-26 the night before, she was pretty familiar with its dangers and was able to "zip" along at a plucky eighteen miles an hour. This meant that her attention had to be hyper-focused and she was red-eyed by the time she coasted down from the hills surrounding North Platte with the engine only purring beneath the heavy armor and the front camera growing hazy from a soft misty rain that wasn't exactly falling; it just seemed to hang in the air.

Not wanting to spook any of the people, she stopped north of town where two railroad tracks suddenly split, and then split some more, becoming fifty tracks looping here and there. She figured the trains used to come here to spend the night or make way for speedier trains. Not that she cared all that much or wasted any of her mega-watt mind power trying to divine the purpose of the tracks. All she cared about was hiding the Jeep in one of the warehouses and finding the people in the town before she fell asleep on her feet.

The night's drive had tuckered her out and it was all she could do to concentrate on the task of finding what she assumed to be the group hiding out in North Platte, before they found her. It made sense to figure out if they were good or bad, or just normal before approaching them.

Right away, she came across a major issue with her search: the town felt just as dead as Scottsbluff had been. There weren't any of the normal signs that suggested there were people in the town. There wasn't any smoke from cooking fires, or tire tracks in the mud, and there weren't the usual semi-secretive noises that people made: low, echoing laughter or the clang of metal being dropped or even a soft cough.

Another key indicator that the place was empty was in the way the monsters behaved. They grazed placidly or went about slowly, clearly not agitated by the presence of humans. Even groups of humans who were smart and careful to stay hidden during the day got the monsters riled, although how Jillybean didn't know. She guessed it was a scent thing, but had no evidence of this.

When humans were hiding nearby, the monsters were slightly more alert, and slightly more growly, and they usually congregated in clumps nearby. The ones in North Platte were all over the place, moving slowly as if without a care in the world. "For all darn it, they must have left," she whispered, trying to stifle a yawn. Slowly—as slowly as the rest of the monsters, which was an agonizing pace for the energetic little girl—she retreated into a house. Right there in the hall she broke out a tremendous yawn that made her eyes water.

Pulling off her monster coat, she unslung the heavy pack from her back, rummaged in it until she found the pair of maps she had stashed earlier. One was of south-central Nebraska and the other was specific to the North Platte area. "Where did you guys go? Omaha? Kansas City? Denver?"

The morning was grey and the light had all the strength of old dishwater; she moved from the living room to the kitchen, which faced east and had marginally better lighting. Spreading the larger map on the table, she gazed at it. "80 east or 80 west seem to be the only choices. Unless they took one these back roads, then we have I-83 and Route 30 as options. Which actually helps…"

She froze suddenly, her heart seizing in her chest and her breath catching in her throat—there was someone in the room with her. A shadow had moved, one that was very close, just to her right. The shadow moved with utter silence until it fell across her maps.

The shadow and the person making it had come from a short hallway that led from the garage and now whoever it was stood poised just over her shoulder. Quick as a wink, Jillybean went for her gun, only to realize that her .38 was in her coat, which was in the living room!

Cold metal touched the back of her neck. "Don't move," a voice said.

Chapter 13

Jillybean

Nothing could have prepared Jillybean for the sight of Chris Turner or the gigantic pistol in his hands. He stood only a head taller than her and yet he seemed to tower over her like some primitive beast. His hair was very dark, almost black, and it was wild as a lion's mane and just as long. His eyes were the color of the forest, a beguiling mixture of green and brown.

At first, he seemed oddly large and bulky, to Jillybean, but then she noticed that he had on at least two sets of clothing. The top layer of clothing was what she considered a childish attempt to dress as one of the monsters: the shirt had been cut with a pair of scissors in long, obvious lines, while the pants were only trimmed below the knee. It was likely that a monster would have no idea what to make of such a person dressed like this, but a human would pick him out of a crowd with ease.

And yet, Jillybean had not seen him and had certainly not heard him.

"I'm not gonna move so you can point that silly gun away. Was that your only choice for a gun? I only ask cuz it's all way too big for your hand. That must mess up your aim awful bad."

His lip curled as he replied: "My aim is fine. Actually, you know what? I have real good aim and you know what else? I happen to like this gun, a lot. People are afraid of it like they should, and they're afraid of me when I have it, so no, it's not silly."

Jillybean didn't believe him concerning his aim, but it wasn't really a point worth arguing over. "So, where are your people? I didn't see much evidence of them…evidence is what means clues, if you know what I mean?"

His face had screwed up in puzzlement for a moment when she mentioned evidence, though now his dark brows came down. "I know what evidence is, duh. Everybody does. And I don't have people. The last person with me got bit and turned into one of *them*. What about you? Who was driving that car?"

"Me, I was."

He laughed and as he did, he finally lowered the huge pistol. It made his arm swing like a pendulum. "You drove it? Yeah, right. Now, tell me who drove it or else." He lifted the gun, but didn't aim it.

"For reals, I drove it. And I'm not with anyone, either. The same thing happened to me. The lady I was with, Granny Annie, she got bitted and...and she died." She had almost opened a can of worms that would have spooked this boy right away. "My name is Jilly...ah, I mean it's Jill. My name is Jill."

Once more she had almost made a huge mistake. As long as she was on this side of the Rockies, the name Jillybean couldn't be spoken and, what was more, if she wanted to be just a normal girl, she had to hide her intellect.

"What's your name?" she asked, to cover up the slip.

He had noted the stumble on her name. "I wonder if I should tell you mine," he said. "I read a book once that said there is power in names. It said that demons never tell their real names. It was a scary book. Probably the scariest book ever written."

Now it was her turn to be skeptical. "Your parents let you read a scary book? That doesn't seem right."

He looked down his nose at her. "I don't have parents. I never did. Well, I had a mom. Everyone has a mom, only mine really sucked. She always had these real bad dudes over and they would hit her and they'd hit me and then someone would call social services and they'd take me away. You know how it is."

Jillybean did not know at all. Her family life had been such an idyllic arrangement that, before the apocalypse, child abuse was only a vague sort of unhappiness that happened in far off places and the term social services had no meaning to her at all, however the thought of being pulled from her parents' home was horrifying.

"It sounds awful."

He shrugged. "Yeah, I guess. It was worse before. You know, before all the zombies. But now everyone is an orphan and I don't stick out any more like I used to. So, that's good."

In Jillybean's mind there had been nothing good about the apocalypse and the very idea grated on her nerves. "Tell me about this scary book," she said to change the subject. "What's it called? Or is it not allowed to have a name, either, ha-ha."

"I didn't say you weren't allowed to have a name, you're just not supposed to reveal it or the person who hears it has power over you. Weren't you listening?"

Of course she had been listening, and she still was—realizing, suddenly how the book wasn't wrong. Her own name was a dangerous thing, and the person who knew it could wield more power than they knew. "Yes, I'm sorry, go on. You were going to tell me the name of the book."

"I don't remember. Something Hell-fire. Either way, it was a real book…it was an adult book. They used to say I read on sixth grade level which is funny because I never even graduated from the third grade!"

"You didn't? How old are you?" Having no idea that she read at a college level, she had been very impressed concerning his boast, however that was tempered by the fact that he hadn't gotten past the third grade. That suggested he was straight up dumb, an infliction in others which she had never been able to cope with as well as she would have liked.

The idea that she thought he was stupid must have been imprinted on her face because he sneered and snapped: "Don't look at me like that. I told you they took me out of my house, well they also took me out of my school, and they kept moving me back and forth and all around. It got so confusing that I never knew what anyone was doing and so they held me back. That wasn't my fault, you know."

Properly shamed, she gave him a mumbled apology to which he waved his hand, good-naturedly. "It's okay. It all worked out. I didn't like school and I always wished that it would burn down and guess what? It did! With a little help."

"What? You burned it down?"

He waved at her again. "Not with anyone in it. I'm not crazy. Though there's a lot of crazies running around these days. Am I right?"

"Yes," she answered, hoping her grin wasn't too terribly fake. Once more she had to change the subject. "You never told me how old you are. I'm seven going on eight. I'm a May-flower; that's what means I was born in May. And you never said your name. Hey, you know what? I could call you Kid-X on account of the unknown, right? It's like the algebraic variable that you have to solve for in…uh, I mean it sounds cool."

He seemed to miss Jillybean's cerebral lapse. "Yeah, it does sound cool. Kid-X. I like it, but really it doesn't matter what you call me because I'm not going to have a kid hanging around me. Sorry."

"A kid? Why are you calling me a kid? How much older are you? Are you even fifteen?"

A loud laugh barked out of him. "What are you stupid? I'm nine and a half. Sheesh! You don't know anything. That's why I don't want you hanging around me. You'll say something stupid or you'll do something stupid and get me killed."

"Me? Stupid?" Jillybean was stunned by the very notion. Forgetting that she was *trying* to appear stupid, she lashed out: "Look at your monster outfit for all goodness sakes. That won't fool anyone. Does it even fool the monsters? Have you seen them? Do any of them look like that? Jeeze. You know what? Maybe I don't want you to hang around with me. Oh, and by the way, you don't smell all that good, neither."

He smelled like a boy…an angry boy. His hazel eyes went hard as he snarled: "You think I smell? How do you think I found you? I just followed the stink." He stomped away to the front door but didn't open it right away. The monsters had sensed them and were congregating outside the house.

A grown up curse escaped him, making Jillybean's eyes widen. "That's a bad word."

"Do you think I don't know that? Sheesh." He breezed past her, heading towards the garage, but stopped in the hall. "What's wrong with my outfit? It looks just like yours."

She almost answered as herself, but held off using words like angular and symmetrical. "It doesn't really look the same. Sure, its cut up but the cuts are…too regular. They're all the same. And the coat looks new. None of the monsters wear new clothes. And, uh, I'm sorry I called you stinky. I was just mad that you called me stupid, which I am a little, I guess."

"And is your hair part of the disguise?"

Her hair seemed to be ungovernable by existing technology. It might have helped with her monster outfit, but it also made her self-conscious. Afraid that it was worse than usual, she touched her hair, the first wisps of which stood out eight inches from her head. "Yes, I guess so. The entire purpose behind the disguise is to hide your human-ness. Humans have nice hair and new clothes and they carry things and they look around a lot. You have be the opposite of all that."

"That's pretty smart except the carrying stuff part. You got to have a gun on you. Look at you. I caught you no problem because you don't have a gun. Are you afraid of guns?"

"I have one, it's in my coat." She pointed at the garment which looked as though she had found it in a gutter somewhere. He made a grunting noise and then there came an awkward silence during which Jillybean grew steadily more nervous though she couldn't pinpoint exactly why. Finally, she stammered: "W-Would you l-like to have breakfast w-with me? I have Doritos."

He appraised the little girl through narrow eyes. "Maybe. But you know what they say: never trust a gift horse. You never did tell me who was driving your car."

"Sure I did. It was me. The gas and brake pedals are modified. I—I, uh the person who had it before me made some changes because she was...she was a midget. That's what means someone who has a condition for shortness."

"Oh yeah? And you just happen to find it? Out of all the cars in America you find one that someone made to fit a seven-year-old? I don't believe you."

She jerked her thumb towards the door: "That's okay. If you want, I can show you the Jeep. It's really pretty cool. It's got a smoke machine and bombs and a rear gun and all sorts of stuff." Her sudden desire to impress Chris had overcome her common sense.

He blew out a dismissive breath. "Who are you trying to fool? You talk like that thing is the Bat Mobile and there's no such thing."

"Bat Mo-what? No, it's a Jeep that I up-armored in order...I mean, uh, it has armor so you don't get shot. How about I show you. Come on." She reached for her coat, but he was quicker, grabbing her stick-thin arm with a grip as strong as a man's.

"Not so fast. Didn't you just tell me you had a gun?" He fished around until he came out with the police special. "Cute," he snorted and stuck it in his pocket. "Look, Jill, no offense, but your story is dumb. It's fake and we both know it. You're with someone and if you don't tell me who, there's gonna be trouble."

He held up his gigantic pistol again. She was unafraid of it and him. "Why are you being like this? It's very mean, you know. I am alone; that's the truth. And I was nice enough to invite you to breakfast when I didn't need to. Would a bad guy do that?"

He laughed at the question. "Yes, all the time. Didn't they always warn you not to take candy from strangers? There's a reason why and it's because you aren't supposed to trust something that's too good to be true. That's only smart. Now turn around so I can tie you up."

"What? No. That's not right. I'm being nice and friendly and you're a kid just like me."

"Yeah, I'm a kid, but that doesn't mean I'm stupid. Turn around or I'll smack you one, first." She could tell by the look in his eye that he wasn't joking, he really would hit her. Slowly, she turned around and put her hands behind her back. He tied her up, cinching her hands tight, but not painfully so.

Taking her by the shoulder, he walked her to the couch and sat her down. "Wanna tell me who's in the Jeep, now? You could be saving their lives by telling me." He said this, once more showing her the gun.

"What are you going to do if you go there and find the Jeep empty? Are you gonna take my stuff?"

A shrug. "Maybe. I got stuff of my own, but I'll see what there is first. And really, we both know that won't be the case. A kid like you couldn't make it on her own, so that means someone is there. I'm not an idiot. You're the bait for the trap. You walk around all cute just as plain as day and then bammo, the trap closes."

"You think I'm cute?" This left her quite stunned.

"Cute? No. I meant like a little kid." He shook his head in disbelief. "Gawd, you better not be getting a crush on me. That's the last thing I need."

She knew what crushes were; her friend Janice back in first grade had a crush on Ronnie Tibits, who was a zany kid who could be dared to do anything. For a first grader, Ronnie had a big personality and seemed to take all the air out of any room he was in—sort of like this tall boy.

Jillybean had never had a crush before that she knew of and yet, she found herself staring closely at the boy, noting his white teeth and thin nose and pointy chin. Although she didn't care for his cocky manner or the heavy sweat aroma that surrounded him, she was intrigued with his grace and the quiet manner in which he moved. He had snuck up on her, something she didn't think was possible.

But a crush? "No way…whatever your name is. I don't have a crush on you. I barely know you and what I do know isn't all that good. You're too afraid to tell me your name. And you tied me up and you're gonna steal my stuff and that's what means you're evil. Only bad guys are stealers. Everyone knows that."

"I didn't say I was going to steal your stuff. I said maybe. It depends on if you're lying to me." She insisted that she wasn't, but he only said: "We'll see."

He left her then, slipping out the back door, moving like a stalking lion. Jillybean watched him as far as she could, leaning forward on the couch. She tried to tell herself that she was only interested in how he could move so stealthily and yet her eyes lingered on him in a way that added nothing to her knowledge base.

"I don't have a crush on him," she insisted. "I'm way too young for crushes. Janice was too young and that was for certain. Remember, how everyone made fun of her? You know what?" she asked the empty room, "I think I'm just lonely. That's what it is."

It had been a long lonely time since Granny Annie had died and it was no lie that she craved human interaction. "But with this boy? I don't know. Ipes wouldn't have cared for him. I know that for certain. And what if he steals some of my stuff?"

The Jeep was locked, so most of the "good" stuff was inaccessible to him...unless he could pick a lock. "Oh boy," she whispered, picturing what would happen if he managed to get inside. If he pressed the red bomb-release button, he could be dead in moments.

"But could he pick a lock?" He hadn't struck her as exceptionally smart, though to be fair they had only spoken for five minutes. "I can't chance it," she said, squirming on the couch. Seven seconds later, her clever little fingers had freed the razor blade she kept hidden on the inside of the canvas belt she always wore. The blade slid in and out of a special little notch she had sown there. It sat next to the silver key that could open a standard set of handcuffs.

Seconds later she stood, letting the severed rope fall and giving her arms a little stretch. She then slithered into her monster coat and hurried out the door. Hurrying anywhere was dangerous, everyone knew that. Monsters simply did not hurry unless there was something to eat or destroy, but she had to make up time.

The boy was not normal. She had noted that when she had come through the town the first time. He could move among the monsters quicker than anyone she had ever seen, and so it was not outside the realm of possibility that he was already nearing the warehouse where she had hidden the Jeep.

Would he be cautious or wary? Would he slink around looking for traps or go right in with that big gun of his, ready to shoot the first thing that moved? Normally, she relied on logic to set the range of possible human reactions in any given situation, so far the boy had defied logic and she was forced to envision the worst case scenario.

In it, he would sense the utter emptiness of the warehouse. He would feel how the air had that corrugated stillness that only occurred when the population of a given room consisted of decaying corpses. He would see the windowless Jeep with its green swirled armor and its rear-mounted M249 and his curiosity would overcome his common sense.

He would want it. If he could pick a lock, he would be pushing aside Jillybean's cushions in a minute and seconds later, he would be gazing greedily at the iPad monitors and the buttons.

The very worst case of all the scenarios was him then pressing the red button. If he did, he'd be dead three seconds later.

Chapter 14

Chris Turner

Not only was he not used to the zombie outfit, he was also not used to being told he was doing something wrong. Even when Chris was being passed from foster home to foster home, things had been relatively easy for him. He had only been held back in the third grade because he hadn't cared one whit about school, not because it had been difficult.

Jillybean's criticism had ground on him like glass in a blender, and as he made his way around the back of the houses, walking in a pretty fair imitation of a zombie whenever one was around, he grumbled: "What does she know? No stinking zombie can tell the difference."

He went on moving very quickly, but very quietly. There was an unnatural sneakiness about him. Without really thinking about it, he slipped into shadows and slunk beneath the boughs of trees and sprinted down fence lines or behind rows of shrubs. For the most part, he went about unseen, but when he was forced to move into the open, he went slower using his new zombie disguise.

It was strange to let the beasts get so close, and yet, like the little girl, he had no fear of the zombies whatsoever. It was like being afraid of a turtle. Even if they saw through his disguise, which he doubted they would, he knew they would never catch him; he was far too agile and far too quick.

The way to the next yard was blocked by a seven foot fence. He was over it in a blink, and with a grunt, he landed in the midst of three very large zombies. As fence climbing was a human action, they immediately turned on him, cornering him.

Still, Chris wasn't afraid. It didn't matter that they were all a foot taller than him and had long arms ending in diseased claws.

They were slow and he was fast. They were stupid and he was clever.

Taking one step forward, standing at the full extent of his five feet, two inch inches in order to keep their attention at the right level, he suddenly spurted forward, dropping into a dive roll right between two of the beasts.

Almost as if they were moving in slow motion, they reached down to grab him, but he was already past and sprinting for a pine tree at the far side of the yard. He sprinted instead of jogged as he usually would have because there were more of the creatures rushing out from the house and from the bushes that lined the back of the yard.

Despite being surrounded, he was unfazed almost to the point of being blasé about the danger. He leapt into the lower branches of the pine tree before climbing fifteen feet straight up, moving with such ease he might have been going up a ladder. When he was high enough, he worked his way to the trunk and then from there he stepped out onto a limb that hung over the next fence. It wasn't the biggest of limbs or the sturdiest. It groaned and creaked beneath his weight and the further he went out on it, the further it narrowed and bent.

By the time he was near the tip, he was shimmying along and the branch was no longer horizontal. It was bowed so far that when he released his feet and dangled only by his callused hands, he was over the fence and only eight feet above the ground.

Softly, he dropped to the muddy earth as behind him the zombies attacked the fence in a confused manner. Their meal had been so close, but had now disappeared.

Chris paused in a crouch as he let his senses inform him of the dangers and opportunities around him. There were always opportunities if one knew where to look. The tree on the other side of the fence was one example, just like the mud he had dropped into was another.

His disguise had been dubbed "too new" by Jillybean. The critique, accurate as it was, galled him and he'd been looking for a chance at a quick fix.

"I'll take care of that, no problem." From a boy's point of view, the mud at his feet was the good kind of mud. It wasn't corpse mud; the kind of mud found in a culvert where a decomposing body had turned everything nasty. And it wasn't bog mud, which was black and stank of hell and feces.

No, this was "clean" mud, a simple mixture of rain water and dirt. He rubbed it into his zombie disguise, even dabbing some onto his face in imitation of the girl. She had looked utterly filthy and yet, she hadn't smelled that way regardless of what he had said.

He knew he couldn't say the same about his own odor—she'd been right about that, too. When his last bath had been, he didn't know, although he did remember the last time he had changed his clothes; it had been after the last snowfall had melted, two weeks before.

Feeling somewhat embarrassed, he jogged to the house: another of the many rundown sixties style ranches that made up most of the town. This one had a *lingerer* in the kitchen, staring at him through an inch of glass. It was a woman zombie that was almost six feet in height and already getting agitated as he drew near. Chris might have looked like a zombie, but he certainly wasn't acting like one, especially when he slid back the door.

It attacked as they always did, reaching out for him with its arms outstretched. He had seen the shadow of the thing and thus wasn't surprised and he certainly wasn't afraid. Calmly, he grabbed the woman by the left wrist and used his hold to turn her to the right so that for a moment she was facing away from him. As he did, he slid his hunting knife out of its sheath and drove it into the gap at the base of the zombie's skull.

Before it knew it, the thing was dead though it took a few moments for its body to get the message as it flopped around on the floor. Chris stepped over it, moving silently into the kitchen, his ears perked for more danger, feeling the air of the house on his skin. The air was silent and dead.

"Just the one, then," he whispered, as he used a dish towel that had little smiling pumpkins stitched all over it to clean his knife. When it shone like silver once more, he stuck it away and headed deeper into the house looking for the master bathroom, where he gave a quick glance at his deodorant choices. They weren't many: something in a pink container that smelled like a meadow and another in a black plastic tube that was richer, hardier.

He chose the black tube and, lifting up the two shirts he wore, rubbed the gel all over his body, concentrating on his armpits. After he gave himself two coats of the deodorant, he said: "Not bad. Let's see her complain now. She'll be eating her words, soon." He was just stepping over the dead zombie in the kitchen when he realized he was letting the girl get into his head. "Not that I care what she thinks. I just don't want to smell is all," he told himself.

Doing his best to keep his thoughts from straying to the girl, he left the house, hopped two more fences and found himself on Bare Avenue, just a few blocks from where the town officially died, turning into farm country and empty nothing. To the north were the railway yards.

Chris had been to them many times in the last three weeks, scrounging through the cars and the warehouses, hoping to come across something "good." There wasn't much to find except a lot of useless junk that nobody wanted—mostly industrial items as well as carload after carload of coal. If coal still had any value, he'd be a rich boy.

Moving with a touch more than his usual caution, he crossed the frontage road, slithered under a fence and crawled across the first set of tracks and under the train sitting on the second set. Here he paused, once more focusing his attention on his keen senses; he even tried to sniff past his own deodorant infused aroma but the wet air held nothing out of the ordinary. Mostly he smelled what he always smelled: rusting metal and the earthy, natural chemical scent of coal.

"I'm not close enough," he whispered, crawling to the next set of tracks and ducking under a train car loaded with boxes of PVC piping. He moved onto the next, angling towards the warehouses in the eastern section of the yard. When the girl had come to town, he had heard the Jeep, recognizing the muffled sound of its steel-encased engine from the day before. He had triangulated the sound and knew that it was parked somewhere in the railroad yard.

The eastern warehouses were closest to town and the most likely spot to have hidden the Jeep, so he checked them first. It wasn't there. "Okay, they're too cagey for that...good." He tried to think beyond the obvious and picked out another building, this one smaller and set apart from the others. Other than the junk he had already pawed over the week before, it was empty, making him curse.

There were thirty-two other buildings in the railway yard and he didn't want to bother checking each. It was time consuming, annoying and, depending on whom the little girl had with her, possibly dangerous. He guessed that it was this Granny-person she had mentioned and thus wasn't overly anxious.

Stepping back outside into the drizzle, he saw his own shoe print in the mud; it gave him an idea.

"A Jeep makes tracks. I just got to find them." One way was to wander around with his nose to the ground. Another, smarter way, was to climb as high as he could and search them out from the air. The highest perch in the area was the *Golden Spike Tower*, a tall tower with a viewing platform for tourists who

125

were interested in seeing the world famous Bailey Yard. Not that Chris cared, but North Platte was the home of the largest railroad yard in the world, which at one point serviced 14,000 cars a day.

He had no idea what sort of person would want to tour a railroad yard, even a big one such as this. It looked dreadfully dull by any standard he could think of. Still, the tall, gold-capped tower dominated the area and on the observation deck were viewing scopes which were basically heavy duty binoculars with which Chris was able to pick out the Jeep's tracks without a problem.

They were the only fresh tracks in the yard. Strangely, they zigzagged all over the place before heading into an open warehouse that sat huddled among others. "Bingo. Time to surprise ol' Granny Annie or whoever it is in there."

He slipped down into the yard, angling toward the warehouse, using other trains and buildings as cover. When he got close, he studied the building for a good ten minutes, listening and watching, checking for any sign of humanity, and was surprised that he wasn't sensing any.

When he was ready to move up, he pulled the gun from his waistband. It was a monster .44 caliber Magnum Research Desert Eagle and with its eight-round magazine fully loaded, it weighed in at five pounds. It was ridiculously big. He knew it and didn't care. It did its job. When necessary, it instilled fear in people, or put big holes in them when the fear didn't work. It could knock down a zombie at close range and, although it had a hard kick, he was a fine shot with it.

Killing with the Desert Eagle was easy, but he didn't like to use it unless he absolutely had to. In his world, he was the good guy. When he let his imagination go, and he frequently did, he was the lone hero, ready to save the day. Of course, he was also just a boy. Experience had taught him not to trust anyone, even a seemingly harmless little girl.

She had her secrets and, judging by the pains she went through to keep them hidden, they were likely big ones. "Such as who's her secret friend? There's no way she's here by herself and she certainly didn't drive by herself." He couldn't think of anything so preposterous.

Chris waited, watched, listened, but all in vain; there was no sign of the girl's accomplice. Moving deftly and silently, Chris eased up to the open warehouse door and leaned over just enough to see inside. The dim, cavernous building was lined with industrial shelving that stretched forty feet to the ceiling, while in the middle stood a series of heavy-duty cranes that could lift a railroad car straight into the air.

Next to one of the cranes sat the odd, metal-covered Jeep, looking cold and lifeless. "They could be sleeping," he whispered.

Again, displaying patience beyond his years, Chris waited and watched. Nothing moved and the air did not stir. Still, he didn't approach the Jeep. He made a circuit of the entire building looking for any evidence that a second person had been there, but discovered only the faded tracks of the little girl's Keds.

His concentration was so centered on the Jeep and the warehouse that he was shocked to discover he was being watched.

On some level he knew it even before he heard the tiny sound behind him. He stopped in mid-step, his heart suddenly pounding. His mind had instantly deciphered the sound as the click of gravel bouncing off one of the steel tracks. It had also pinpointed the direction.

Turning quick as a cat, he brought the pistol up and pointed it across the yard at the nearest train. At first there was nothing to aim at exactly, but as he scanned down the length of the train he caught the barest sight of a blue eye and a few strands of fly away brown hair.

Chapter 15

Chris Turner

It was the girl!

And here he was caught out in the open, flat against the side of a warehouse. As quick as only he could be, he threw himself around the side of the open bay doors and flattened himself against the inner wall, where he faded into the gloom of the shadows.

He had the gun in both hands, the barrel just touching his lips, the smell of old powder in his nostrils. He was a coiled spring, ready to fight or flee at the first hint of danger.

"Hello?" Jillybean called out. "Hello, it's just me. I'm all alone, so it's okay. Sorry about spooking you like that. I didn't mean to scare you."

"You didn't scare me," he hissed, lowering the gun slightly. As far as he could tell she was alone, which had him completely perplexed. "How the hell did you get out of that rope?" He was sure he had cinched the rope down tight. In fact she had winced at how tight he'd made it.

She eased out from behind the wheels far enough so he could see her shrug. "Well, the rope wasn't so tight," she said, "and I have real skinny arms. And anyways, I told you that nobody was here and look, it's all empty. A-sides that Jeep is dangerous all by itself. I wasn't joking about the bombs and all. You coulda blowed yourself sky high."

"I wasn't going to blow myself up," he said, his eyes rolling —they seemed to do that a lot around the little girl. The fear and danger seemed to dissipate, so he stuck the heavy gun back into the waistband of his jeans before waving the girl over. She scrambled from beneath the train and, smiling pleasantly as if he hadn't just left her tied up in a house surrounded by zombies, she skipped over to him.

"Come on," she said, pulling on his shirt. "Let me show you all the modifications on the Jeep. It's pretty cool if you ask me."

"I didn't ask you," he replied, still not letting his guard down. Her cutesy act wasn't fooling him. There was more to her than she was letting on, that he knew for certain. Whenever she turned away, her smile dimmed and her innocent eyes grew sharp and hard. He didn't know what she was after, or what she was planning, but she had an agenda.

She ignored his icy manner, saying, "It's only an expression, like: *easy as pie*. People say that though it isn't always true, cuz making pies is tricky when you don't have all the right ingredients. But in this case, it is true, about the Jeep that is. It's cool and it works. It's like, been battle tested. See those marks on the side. They're from bullets."

The way she said it, he figured that he was supposed to be impressed—which he was, but he wasn't going to let her know. "What? Did you shoot your own Jeep?" he asked derisively.

"No, but I did do some testing on the armor. I had to see if…I mean the lady, um, Granny Annie, let me test the armor to see how well it worked. But all those marks were from bad guys. They were trying to get me and they were very mean, but I don't want to talk about them."

Chris gave the marks a close look. He was pretty sure that she wasn't lying; they had been made by bullets. The sight of them gave him a moment of unease. "Open the door," he said, taking out the .44 caliber pistol once more and bringing it up.

She didn't hesitate and after opening the door, she pointed inside. "See? There's no one in there, like I said. Here take a look." It was empty—she really was alone.

Although he was also alone, it just seemed extra weird that she would be as well. It was almost as if the universe or fate or God had made a mistake with her. She wasn't fast or strong or even lucky. She should have been dead. Chris glanced at her and whatever secrets she was hiding were buried so deeply that all he saw was a kid grinning up at him.

"That's where I sit," she said, pointing in at the cramped cockpit. "And that's all my stuff." The interior of the Jeep was dark as a cave and crammed with boxes of ammo and food and many strange odds and ends: wiring, magnets, string, thin coils of metal and an array of books.

Books bored him and carrying them around made little sense since you could get them anywhere. He barely gave them a thought, especially since the Jeep itself was so interesting.

"How do you see out of it without windows?" he asked, forgetting completely how only a minute before he'd been on the verge of shooting her with his hand cannon.

From the outside the Jeep didn't look all that much like a Jeep. It had the vague shape of one of the larger four-door varieties, but there was so much painted metal welded to the structure that to Chris, it mostly looked like an ugly box.

Jillybean pulled him back and pointed at a little gizmo attached beneath the roof rack. "That's a camera. There are six of them: two in front, two in back and one on each side. I have them on a direct feed and that's what means they play on the screens inside in front of the steering wheel."

"Interesting," he grunted. A second later, he was onto the next strange aspect of the vehicle. From the bottom of the armor hung three overlapping curtains of chains. "What's all this for?"

Before answering, she ran her hand along them, making them jingle, which at first made her smile, but it was short lived. "They make a lot of noise, don't they? I'm gonna have to fix that…Oh, right, the chains. It's just more armor. I had experimented with metal slabs, but they restricted the Jeep's ability to go up and down things, you know, like a steep hill or whatever. Oh hey, do you want to see the bomb dispenser? It's real cool."

First she dragged him back to the driver's seat and in an excited chirpy voice, she pointed out the buttons and monitors and the switches in the cab, explaining which did what. Then she tugged him to the rear of the Jeep, where she parted the chains and crawled beneath.

When he didn't follow right away, she said: "Come on, you gotta see this. Oh, hi. See that handle? Turn it, but be careful. Sometimes the bombs shift and they come popping out."

He had been all set not to believe her about any of this, but so far the Jeep had surpassed anything he could have imagined. Carefully, he turned the handle and out jumped a ten inch metal cylinder which he adroitly caught. It was heavy as if it was simply chalk full of explosives. "That really is a bomb, isn't it?"

"Oh yeah. It's called a pipe bomb and that's what mean you stick the blowing up part in a pipe to make it boomier…bigger I mean. You see the restriction in area for the expanding gas makes the corresponding explo…" She stopped suddenly, gave a little laugh, shrugged awkwardly from her back and then said: "It's loud. That's what I meant."

Chris caught the stumbled sentence, but thought nothing of it. He figured that she had been trying to show off by using big words, nothing he hadn't done on occasion when he was around new people. "What's that?" he asked, pointing to another latched box. This one was separated from the others and connected to the muffler by a metal chute that was obviously homemade.

"That's the smoke generator. You can open the door and see it if you wanna. It won't hurt you or go off at all. Oh, and it will definitely jump out on account of it being spring loaded."

"Spring loaded? Do you shoot it at people or something?"

She reached up, flicked the latch and out jumped what looked like a rectangular box made of aluminum foil. It sat on a simple construction of four *Hot Wheels* cars that had been soldered together with lengths of tin to form a small cart.

"The spring shoots it down here," she explained, "where it hits the muffler which is by-golly hot. That's what sets it alight and then...*poof*, it just starts to smoke like mad because on the inside is a bunch of chemicals: potassium nitrate and sodium bicarbonate, mostly, but there's also this yucky smelling yeast. What do you think? Pretty cool, right?"

Chris began nodding, It was more than cool, it was genius—bombs and armor and machine guns and smoke generators and cameras all on one, not very large vehicle. He had seen the giant trading vehicles and they had been impressive but this was a step above.

"And you say someone's grandmother made this thing?" he asked. The idea was crazy, but to Chris it was a million times more likely than a seven-year-old constructing it—that was so impossible it hadn't even crossed his mind.

The girl hadn't heard the question. Although she was staring at the housing of the smoke generator, her mind was clearly somewhere else. She began to frown and he asked: "What's wrong?"

"I'm thinking the smoke generator needs to be re-jiggered," she answered, speaking quickly, her eyes staring intently at the run of metal as it led from the box to the muffler. "The way it's all put together now makes it work only when the muffler is hot. What happens if we need it when the engine isn't on?"

He was a little lost by the speed at which she spoke, but he had heard at least one word that didn't belong with the rest. "What do you mean by 'we'? I never said I'm going anywhere with you. Man, you're crazy if you think so." He scrambled out from under the Jeep and then stood back, watching her as she followed him, thinking that it was a bad sign when she began to straighten her torn up outfit.

"You'd rather be all by yourself than come with me?" she asked. "That's silly if you ask me. What if something happens to you, like if you get hurt or something? You need people, you know."

"First off, I'm not gonna get hurt and even if I did, what would you do about it? Nothing, because you're just a kid. Now, drop it, okay? We should be talking trade right now. What do you want for the Jeep?" She had some nifty things, it was true, however none of it compared to the Jeep. He had begun lusting after it from the moment he poked his head inside. Now, he touched the armor with the tips of his fingers and then rapped it smartly with his knuckles. It was solid.

"I got some pretty choice items. Do you like chocolate milk? Cuz I got two things of that Nestle powder. You aren't gonna find that just anywhere."

She shook her head. "No, I don't think so. I doubt you have anything I want. I mean I'm sure you have stuff I want, but I need the Jeep. It's got to get me out to the Mississippi and I don't have time to buil…find another, I mean."

Although he had about a month's worth of food and a number of weapons and ninety rounds of ammo, the chocolate powder really was the only thing he could think of that the girl would want. "What's out at the Mississippi that you need?"

"Just some stuff," she lied. He knew it was a lie the second it left her false, smiling lips.

He wasn't all that upset. People lied all the time. It paid to be careful when giving away information. Deciding to make another bid at getting a hold of the Jeep, he said: "There are other cars around, you know and I have more than just the chocolate powder. Hey, why don't you come to my hideout and take a look?" He said this with all the charm he could muster.

Her claim of not having a crush didn't hold up as she grinned, happily and gushed: "Sure, that sounds nice. I can make lunch if you want. How 'bout we take the Jeep? Let me just move some stuff so you can get in."

In his mind it was proper and natural for an older boy to drive, so he went to the driver's side, stopping at the sight of the cramped cockpit and the raised pedals he hadn't noticed before. "What is this? Did that Granny lady put these in here? Do they come off?" He gave the long shaft of the gas pedal a shake but it didn't budge. Under his breath he wondered: "How the heck am I supposed to drive with the pedals so high?"

She came around to the driver's side and climbed up on her pillows; the pedals were perfectly suited for someone her size. "They can come off with a welding torch," she said, as if welding torches were just sitting around and everyone knew how to use them. "Or you can use a hacksaw, though it would take awhile. But I don't need to change out the pedals just yet. I think I grew an inch or two over the winter but I'm still good. Okay, get in."

Like Jillybean, Chris was a self-taught driver and wasn't bad, but he had to wonder how he would fare behind the wheel of the Jeep. He had never been claustrophobic, however once the doors were shut, the cramped passenger seat seemed to shrink in on him—in fact, he felt as though he had been suddenly plunged underground and the weight of the world was pressing in on the Jeep from all sides.

It got so bad, so quickly, that he had to open the door and take a deep breath. "Sorry, I just, uh, just needed to…I thought I heard something," he said, making a show of looking around. After a second deeper than normal breath, he shut the door once more.

After a pause, he was happy to find that the feeling had passed. Back to his old self, he leaned over the console to look at the four screens. He whistled as she punched in the security codes, turning each on. The driver's seat looked as though it was part of some sort of spaceship. Chris felt his craving for the Jeep like a hunger. "Wow, that's pretty high-tech," he said, in an awed whisper.

Jillybean grinned. "Thanks. I…Granny had to add secondary cameras." She touched the main screen and suddenly the angle changed slightly. "This one is higher up just in case the first one gets covered in monster guts or something. And this is the gun camera in back."

The view from the rear camera changed so they could peer right down the barrel of the M249. "Freaking awesome!" Chris cried. "Oh, I kinda wish we had some bad guys on our tail just to see that thing go."

"It's only okay. I wanted something bigger, but because of the room and the noise I stuck with an M249. It doesn't tear things up like a .50 cal does. There was this time that I…uh, never mind. Where's your place?"

Again he was so engrossed that he missed the improper pronouns used by the girl.

As he didn't know the name of the street he was currently living on, he had to direct her by leaning over the console and pointing out the landmarks as they appeared on the screen. From this angle, he was able to see the one major drawback of the Jeep: it's restricted viewing capability. In his eyes, this was a minor limitation compared to the power of the vehicle and the longer he was around it, the more he wanted it.

Chris was stuck in North Platte simply because the roads were too dangerous to travel on. Since Christmas, he'd been a part of three different groups—they had all been ambushed by bandits. Twice he had managed to get away in all the chaos. The other instance had been horrible. Five of the people in his group had been killed outright, while one had lingered in death at the edge of the bandits' camp as the women were raped.

Just because he was a boy hadn't saved him from a similar fate as the women. Two of the men had taken him away from the camp and had used him like a girl. Thankfully, a pack of zombies had ended the rape and he only just got away.

A shiver swept him as he pushed aside the memory. He forced himself never to think about it and this was no different. He let his vibrant imagination take over. "You know what would be cool?" he asked. "A roof mounted .50 cal. Think about that. We could get one on a swiveling thing so it could point wherever you wanted, and just blast the bad guys."

Jillybean looked to take the idea seriously. She glanced up at the ceiling of the Jeep and made a noise in her throat. "Hmmmm, maybe. It would be cool but there would be a problem with the ammunition. You ever see it in real life? It's like very, very heavy and bulky. And wanna know what's worse? You just don't come across a lot of that…sort…of…" She trailed off her eyes going out of focus. The Jeep began to slow.

"Hey, you okay?" he asked, reaching out a finger and poking her in the shoulder.

"Yeah, I'm fine." She tried to smile, but once more, it was all a lie. "Just a memory, or a part of one, really."

Once again, he didn't call her on her lie, mostly because he didn't care. He pointed her to the house he'd been staying in for the last three weeks. She said, "Hmmm," to this as well.

"What?" he demanded, feeling as though he was being judged, which was doubly bad since he was being judged by a little girl.

"Huh? Nothing, nothing. I was just wondering where I was going to put the Jeep. I can't have it sitting out. That's what means someone will try to take it." He suggested the garage but she didn't take him up on the very sensible idea. Instead she pulled around the block and parked the Jeep in the garage of a house that backed up to his. "Just to be safe," she said.

Now it was his turn to grunt in a judgmental fashion and her turn to pretend he hadn't. In his way of thinking, there wasn't anything to be afraid of in North Platte except for a few zombies. Her extra precaution was only extra silly.

When she had grabbed a few provisions, they made their way through the back yard to the fence, which Chris hopped without breaking stride.

She took a little longer to get over but once on the other side, and through a small backyard, he showed her into the house—it was trashed with old clothes and old cans and old everything lying in great heaps, and for the first time he noticed the smell of old socks. Her smile was once again a lie.

"The people who lived here before were kind of sloppy," he said, pushing aside a pile of empty cans that had been sitting on the kitchen table. One clanked to the floor, making a sour note. He caught it after it bounced once and set it back with the others. "That's why I chose the place. I could blend in and no one would notice."

"I…yes, I get it, I think. Smart thinking."

She wasn't buying it and couldn't hide the judgment lingering on her face. It made him grumpy. "Here. Take a look at all this." He showed her to the garage where he had accumulated a town's worth of goods. All the stuff he had collected was in brown boxes and here, at least, he had arranged things in a coherent manner so that the ammo was in one spot and the food in another. "So, what do you want for the Jeep?"

Perhaps just to make him feel as though he hadn't wasted his time bringing her there, she looked around, poking into different boxes and making a noise in her throat that simulated interest. Every once in a while she would pull something out and set it aside. When she was done, she had collected a few batteries, some .38 caliber ammo and a radio scanner.

"There's not really enough here for the Jeep, but I could use this stuff if you want to trade. I'll give you a good price." When his face fell, she asked: "Where do you want to go? Maybe I can drive you."

He shrugged, sullenly which caused her downy brows to crease. "Isn't the Jeep somewhat worthless without a destination in mind?" she asked.

"No," he shot back. "I could go anywhere and I wouldn't have to be afr...I mean, I wouldn't have to worry about the bandits. They'd have to worry about me." He laughed, picturing in his mind letting loose with the M249. "You know what the Jeep really is to me? It's freedom, something I haven't had since..." He didn't know the last time he could call himself free. It certainly wasn't when he was in the foster care system.

"I don't know when," he finished, lamely.

His honesty sparked something in Jillybean. She stepped back and reevaluated the Jeep. "I think I know what you mean. Before I had this, I had this KIA...no before this was Mister Neil's Jeep."

Her eyes went out of focus again and when she spoke it was in a softer tone as if she were talking in her sleep: "But we left that in Davenport. I remember that just fine. Then we had the pontoon that had to be modified. And what was after that? A truck...no, it was a 4Runner that we left on the other side of the river. No...I remember it just fine!"

This last came out as a snarl.

"I never said you didn't," Chris said, eyeing the girl closely.

Beneath the mud on her face, she turned red. "No, I wasn't talking to you. I...I just...it's nothing. Just a memory I've been trying to nail down. You know how they can sit on the tip of your tongue?"

"Sure," he answered, still giving the girl a keen look. "But this seemed more than that. Like you were talking to yourself."

The red in her cheeks deepened as she said: "I was really just mad at myself, you know, for forgetting. But that's not important. We were talking about the Jeep. I have an idea. Maybe I could give it to you."

He was no fool. "What would I have to do?"

"Nothing much. Just come with me on an adventure. It'll be fun."

Chapter 16

Jillybean

She was thoroughly exhausted by the time she left Chris two hours later. It wasn't just that she was drained from her long drive the night before and the stress of being tied up at gunpoint. What was far more taxing was pretending to be stupid. She had to watch every word and every action.

And she wasn't very good at it. Chris—she finally got his name out of him after she had threatened to call him, not *Kid X*, but *Kid Silly*—seemed to catch her every time she slipped up. She knew that if she ever wanted to be taken for a normal girl, she had to get better. She had to get smarter at being average.

"Still, he agreed to come with me," she said. "And that's something." It was something, she just didn't know what that something was, nor did she know the "why" behind the something. She really didn't know why she wanted him to come along so badly. Yes, she didn't like being alone all the time and he did seem to be capable in certain regards.

"He's really extraordinary and that's what means he's special, like me." Mister Neil had called her "one of a kind" saying that she was probably the only six-year-old girl to have lived through the apocalypse on her own. Jillybean figured that Chris had been the only eight-year-old boy to make it on his own.

"Now, I just need him to take a bath," she said, yawning. "But not until tonight." She slept in the Jeep, not out of any fear that he would take it. If he wanted to, he could have taken the Jeep at any point. Although only a year and a half older that she was, he was much bigger and faster. "Almost like a man."

This wasn't really a compliment. Other than a select few, Jillybean was not overly impressed with the men she had encountered since leaving the emptiness of her home a year before. For the most part, they were brutes who had epitomized "survival of the fittest," not survival of the kindest or the survival of the most moral.

Women fared no better in her judgment. So many seemed to use their physical weakness as an excuse to display the extremes of cowardice. The thousands of sex slaves across the country were the most guilty. Jillybean's role models were the strongest of women: Deanna, who had practically led a revolt against the Colonel, Sadie, who had the courage of men twice her size, and, finally, Sarah Rivers, who had stood in front of Jillybean, shielding the girl from an assassin with her own body.

Jillybean fell asleep thinking of Sarah and in no time she was dreaming of the battle for New Eden. It was a slow, grainy, dark picture show in her mind. It played out just as it had in real life: Neil Martin's love for Sarah had driven him to extremes and against his better judgment, he had unleashed Jillybean on the Believers and their evil prophet.

Don't, Ipes warned. *You won't be able to control it.*

No one had listened and the death that followed had been horrific. And it hadn't stopped there. *Remember Gunner?* Ipes asked from the passenger seat of the Jeep.

"Oh yeah," Jillybean said, smiling at her little friend. "Remember that truck I drove? I was the worst, most terrible driver ever." Suddenly she was no longer in the Jeep. She was in a beastly, rusted-out truck that was careening all over the road. She fought the wheel back to center as, ahead of her, a boarded-over grocery store loomed.

"We're going to crash," she said and stomped on the gas.

Beside her Ipes screamed and slid off the seat to land on the floor, he asked: *How did you get here?*

She woke, sitting straight up, and suddenly the memory that she had been searching for was tantalizingly close— snapping pictures formed: a box, a boat, a car. But what they had to do with each other or the memory, she didn't know. The answer was just out of reach but fading quickly as her mind switched to Ipes' question.

How had she gotten in that truck?

"I was left behind by Captain Grey and he needed my help." That was simple enough—but why had he needed her help? "Because he was rescuing Neil and Sadie from Gunner."

And who else?

She jumped in her seat, gazing around. That had been Ipes' voice and it hadn't come from a dream. It felt as though he was there in the Jeep, his beady black eyes looking at her from within the piles of knickknacks she had stuffed into the back seat. Goosebumps spread across her flesh. This wasn't right. She knew where the ghosts around her lived; they lived in her mind.

So what was one doing out in the world? And what would it do to her?

With a little scream, she scrambled for the door handle and jumped out of the Jeep as fast as she could, finding herself in a dusty garage that was, for a moment, strange to her. She wanted to scream out: *You're not real!* only she didn't know if that was true or not.

What she did know was that the ghost had asked a question and as much as she wanted to ignore both the question and the questioner, she knew she would end up dwelling on both if she didn't spit out the answer.

"Amy Gates," Jillybean said, breathlessly. "She was Shawn and Clara's daughter and she had been captured by Gunner's bandits and held hostage..." Jillybean paused, her eyes darting all around, fearing the return of the voice. She was prepared to go on. She had a very clear memory of Fred Trigg coming forward with a gun in his hand, fully prepared to execute Clara. He said...

A thump directly behind her nearly caused her to scream. She leapt around, barely holding in the shriek, and came face to face with a monster standing just on the other side of the door that led to the backyard. It was another big one, the top of its head higher than the door and its shoulders so broad that it would have to turn to get in.

Only the dusty pane of glass on the door separated it from Jillybean, and that wasn't for long. With a roar and a crash, it reached a gigantic hand through the glass. Shocked, Jillybean was slow in backing up and the long-armed beast managed to snag a handful of her flyaway hair.

Immediately her hand went for her .38, only it wasn't in her pocket! She had never gotten it back from Chris and now she was being dragged to the door's window. The pain of being pulled by the roots of her hair was terrific, but she knew it was nothing compared to what was coming next: she would be dragged over the jagged edges of glass embedded in the window frame, pulled out into the yard and eaten alive.

And there was almost no way to stop it. She lacked the strength to resist the monster's pull; she wasn't carrying a knife or any other weapon and there were none within reach, and she had no time to dig out one of her hidden razor blades to cut away her hair.

139

She had only a fraction of a second to save herself. Her body's reaction was to pull back, pitting her measly fifty-three pounds against the monster's two-hundred and fifty. She also wanted to scream in useless hysterics. She did neither. In a blink, she let her knees buckle and she dropped, but so quickly was she being pulled by the beast that she didn't even hit the floor.

The side of her face slammed into the lower part of the door but that did not stop her. With her scalp on fire and her hair pulled tight, she drove sideways along the short length of the door. There was a sharp tearing sound that seemed extraordinarily loud as the crystalline edges of the glass sheared away her hair, freeing her.

She fell to the glass strewn floor, finally feeling the searing pain of her scalp and the thumping throb on the side of the face. Her head felt wobbly as she stood, just outside the reach of the creature.

Enraged, the monster threw down the useless handful of hair and attacked the door with wild strength. It seemed to come apart as though it were made of cardboard, leaving Jillybean little time to decide which way to turn. Jumping into the Jeep was clearly the smartest choice and she took a step towards it before she remembered the voice she had heard.

Her step faltered. What if there really was a ghost in the machine? She didn't want to find out, at least not just then with a monster coming through the door. She'd be trapped.

She turned from the Jeep and ran to the door that led to the house. It was locked. This struck her as incomprehensible and she wasted three seconds rattling the knob in a useless gesture. She had been so smitten with Chris Turner that she had forgotten the basics of safety, the primary ones being: always have more than one escape route and never let yourself get cornered.

With only one option left, she hurried to the garage door, bent at the waist and heaved with her legs, lifting it only high enough for her to scamper under. She dropped and rolled just as the monster burst through the back door.

He charged the garage door, recklessly throwing himself at it like a bull and bending the metal as if it were an aluminum can. "Ho-lee mo-lee," Jillybean whispered, as its bleeding hands gripped the bottom and heaved upwards. The hinged door shot up with another crash as the right side of the door came off its rollers and fell onto the top of the Jeep.

Jillybean ran. Her Keds slapped wet pavement as she booked it around the side of the house to the backyard, heading straight for the fence that separated the property from Chris's house. She wanted her gun, but didn't think she was going to make it. The monster was fast. It didn't lumber like so many of the ones who were missing feet or toes or great hunks from their bodies. This monster was entirely whole and entirely bent on eating the little girl.

The skin and bones Jillybean of the year before would have been caught, but her heavy protein diet and her new exercise program had built stringy, lean muscles onto her arms and legs. She was at the fence in three seconds flat and over it just as the monster launched himself square into the wooden planks.

From the long wet grass, Jillybean watched as the fencepost nearest to her snapped at its base and the entire line of fence yawed over with the monster still heaving its bulk against it.

She hopped up, realizing she had been wrong to run to Chris's house. If she went inside, the thing would tear the place apart. "Better go out the side gate," she said and ran, but faltered as she caught sight of someone coming from the house.

Chris came flying across the yard towards her. In one hand he held a long, glittering knife and in the other was the giant pistol he had threatened Jillybean with. "That stupid thing is killing my fence," he said to her as he kept walking past her.

"No! Run!" she screamed. The pistol might have been big, but the monster was so massive that a round from a .50 cal might not stop it. Chris didn't run. He rolled his eyes at the suggestion and, much to Jillybean's amazement, began to walk *towards* the monster!

The fence was now so far over that it was more of a ramp that the monster used to gain access to Chris's yard. It charged, it's dead eyes alight in a rage of fury. Chris didn't even blink. Calmly, he began to jog forward.

"Chris," Jillybean said in a whisper. She had meant to yell his name, but she lacked the strength. Her muscles went slack and she could only watch as the two came together. She was sure Chris would be torn limb from limb right in front of her eyes, however just as the two should have crashed into each other in a festival of blood and screams, Chris juked, moving so easily to his right that he seemed made of light and fluid.

The beast, huge and nasty as it was, was also dim-witted and slow. As Chris passed, it reached out one giant paw but grasped nothing but air. Chris' left foot was substantial enough; he lashed out with it tripping the monster so it down into the wet grass, face first.

Faster than a striking cobra, Chris turned and went down on one knee, slashing with the wickedly sharp knife, cutting the tendons at the back of the monster's left leg. A second later, Chris was on his feet and backing away as the monster tried to stand. It couldn't. Its left leg was useless without the tendons connecting muscle to bone.

After a few futile attempts, it began to crawl at Chris who walked past a stunned Jillybean who had watched the short battle like a spectator. "Where are you going?" she asked. He had been heading towards a shed that sat against the side of the house.

"Can't leave him just sitting out here, can I? What would the neighbors think?" He chuckled at this, while Jillybean only gave him a weak smile. He missed it as he stuck his head into the shed. "Ha! This is better than I thought. I was hoping for some bricks but this will do." He drug out a ten-foot long length of decking. It was heavy and unwieldy and would have been useless to Jillybean, but Chris was strong enough to use it to crush in the skull of the monster. It took nine whacks before the thing stopped moving.

"Piece of cake," he said, tossing the board aside and heading back to his house. As he passed her, he added: "You're welcome, by the way."

"Thanks, I guess. I really was going to…" She stopped talking—she was alone in the backyard; he had gone inside. Angrily, she followed him in, ready to explain how she could have taken care of the creature on her own, however she stopped short as she noticed for the first time that he was clean.

His cheeks were rosy-pink and his dark hair was no longer the wild mane it had been. It fell to his shoulders as long as a girl's. Even his clothes, save for a patch of mud on one knee, smelled fresh and looked clean. Just like that, the anger left her to be replaced with a sudden anxiety over how she looked. Self-consciously, she touched her hair where she had used shards of glass to tear off a big hunk to escape the monster.

"Uh…uh, can I have my gun back?" she asked. "Thanks and all for killing that monster. It was very brave that's for sure, but I could've killed it if I had my gun."

"Monster? That was a zombie," he said, sitting down on a couch and picking up a discarded comic book. On the cover was a man dressed completely in red. His tights even covered his eyes—which was silly and at the same time familiar.

"Okay, it was a zombie. Can I have my gun back?"

He didn't look up as he pointed towards the kitchen counter. "It's over there by the sink. So when do we leave on this adventure? And what's it about? Really?" He had, of course asked this already, but as even she wasn't sure, she had dodged the question by answering: *We're on a quest.* He must have looked up the word "quest" since he added: "And don't tell me about this being some sort of quest. I want to know what we're gonna do and where we're going, exactly."

"Uh…uh, I can't tell you just yet. It's 'need to know,' only." This was a mysterious phrase that Captain Grey had used on occasion. It always sounded both cryptic and important. "We're going to start off by going to the Mississippi. I…I lost something that we need to find. From there, I'm not quite sure."

There was no way she could even explain where they were going and what they were after to herself as she only had two items to go on: a forgotten memory and the word *revenge.*

To keep him from dwelling on the vagueness of the quest, she put him to work. "We're going to need gas. While I get the Jeep ready, I'm gonna need you to scrounge as much as you can."

"Sorry, but there ain't nothing left to scrounge. You know that road you came in on? That's I-80. It's only like the biggest east-west road in the country. I bet a million people have come back and forth on that road since all this started and they took everything, gas included."

He went back to his comic book, possibly thinking that would dismiss the little girl.

His know-it-all attitude was infuriating, especially since he was wrong. She was close to balling her tiny fists and sticking them on her hips and putting him in his place, which, in her mind, was considerably beneath hers. But she couldn't. He had just saved her life and, what was more, she couldn't appear to be his mental superior without him getting suspicious.

She watched him flipping the pages, slowly eyeing each frame, perfectly content in that way boys seemed to have. There was an utter lack of urgency about him—it grated on Jillybean, who felt time slipping away. The long lonely winter was over and people would be moving again. Some would be looking for a better place to live. Some would be putting their plans for revenge into action.

"Actually, there is a secret way to get gas," she said, "and if you're going to own the Jeep, you're gonna have to know it sooner or later." He eased the comic down so that his hazel eyes appeared, but he didn't say anything. "Granny Annie showed me how and I'll show you."

Chapter 17

Jillybean

With a weary sigh as if it was *he* who had been traveling for days, Chris left the garage with the drill in one of his large hands and a broom handle slung on the other shoulder. Three empty jerrycans dangled from the end of the broom, tied there with shoe laces. He looked like something out of an old-time picture.

As soon as he was gone, Jillybean hurried to fetch water for a bath—there was plenty to be found in a town where two rivers collided. Once she had enough to fill half a bathtub, she began to heat clean river stones using two of her homemade sterno cans. When she dropped the stone in the water, they hissed like snakes and bubbled like champagne. One actually split in two upon hitting the water, which caused her to jump like a cat.

While she waited for the water to be the proper temperature, she took a long look at herself in the mirror.

The reflection wasn't pretty. Her hair, hacked off on one side, was atrocious. She had dark circles under her eyes which only made the extreme pallor of her skin all the more distasteful. She looked sick.

"I need the sun," she said to herself as she turned her cheeks this way and that. The summer before she had been crazy as a June-bug, but at least she'd had a healthy tan. Now, she was white as a corpse. The long winter had given way to a wet spring and that had been pleasant compared to the seemingly endless nights of driving and the scampering out of sight as soon as the sun cracked the horizon.

"Chris is lucky being as tan as he is," she said, easing herself into the steaming water. She had made it as hot as she could bear, hoping to boil away her filth. On the trip she had only taken what Captain Grey had once referred to as a "whore's bath." She had normally filled a basin or a bucket and had cleaned her face, her, hair and her "underneath."

Now, she sighed, contentedly and took her time washing every inch of her. Then, simply because she could, she laid back, the steam wrapping around the ceiling, the room lit with the last of the sun and a single candle.

I could fall asleep like this, she thought to herself. Without much enthusiasm, one way or the other, she added: *I hope I don't drown*. It was hard to care when she was so relaxed. The warmth coupled with the lack of sleep sent her right into a stupor and she was sure she was fully asleep minutes later when someone spoke to her.

And then what happened?

Jillybean jumped and shrieked, sending up a fountain of water as she scrambled to the end of the tub to see who had spoken. The sun had set and the candle was drenched, letting out a small hiss. The bathroom was cast in shadows, but where it was darkest was in the doorway—somehow the door was open. She had made sure the door had been locked before she had climbed in the tub. She had even rattled the knob to make sure.

But now the door was open and there was someone in the hall. *And then what happened?* the ghostly figure asked again.

Happened to what, or when, or to whom? She had no idea what the person was asking. "Go away," she hissed. The naked girl edged far down in the tub so that only from her eyes upward was visible. It was a foolish and weak position. If the voice was coming from a real person, then hiding in the tub like that would be seen as childish.

It wasn't real, however and she knew it. "Go away!" she hissed louder. "Sadie said that I'm healing, so go away!"

You've forgotten something very...

"Jill? Hello?" It was Chris calling from the front door. "You in here? I got the gas like you asked."

The voice disappeared and the fear in the room abated in a flash, and at first Jillybean went limp with relief, but then she heard his soft steps coming down the hall. She leapt up sending cascades of water pouring over her clothes as she grabbed her towel and slung it around her skinny little body. "I'm here. I'm okay. Just don't come back here...I'm not dressed."

Being wet and naked was the ultimate in vulnerability and she scrambled for her pistol. "Do you hear me," she asked, pointing the gun at the doorway. "Don't come back here."

He must have heard the fear in her voice and he stopped, saying: "I won't, don't get in a tizzy. I was just getting worried. It's getting late."

Late? For the first time she noticed that the room was more than just shadowy. She picked up her watch, wiped away what looked like a film of oil and saw that it was after nine in the evening. "Whoa," she whispered. How had it got so late?

"I-I was just doing some stuff for the trip. Give me a few more minutes, okay?" He agreed, answering in a mumble as his soft steps retreated. She took a breath to steady herself and then bent to grab her clothes, only they were soaking wet and didn't smell all that good.

Only her trusty Keds were still serviceable. She slipped them on and, wrapped only in her towel, tip-toed through the house to the garage, where she had an extra set of clothing.

"Better," she said, once she was dry and in a fresh set of clothes: soft, brown corduroy pants and a yellow shirt with a big pink heart stitched on the front. It was better, but it wasn't the best. She still had to do something with her hair. There was no way she could face Chris, or anyone for that matter, looking so pathetic. She went back to the bathroom, lit a half-dozen candles and gazed at her reflection, ignoring the pert nose, the pointy chin, the bruise on her cheek from where she had been smashed into the garage door, and the scrape on her forehead that hadn't been there the last time she looked in the mirror.

All she saw was her hair: a soft brown with golden highlights glinting in the candle light. When she bothered to "do something" with her hair, she combed it straight, parted it in the middle and put the back in a ponytail. She tried this again and nearly started crying at what she looked like.

"I'm so ugly," she whispered.

A voice behind her said: "You are not." She screamed and spun, trying to get her .38 out of her pocket. It was Chris. As quiet as a cat he had snuck up on her. "Why'd you do that to your hair?" he asked.

"Remember that big monster? He got me by the hair and I had to cut it away or he would have…you know."

"Hmm, yeah, I know. You know what you need to do? You got to cut it all off. You know, start over so it grows back even. Here, look." He turned her back to the mirror and took one of his strangely large hands and pulled back her hair so that she could see just the beginnings of her widow's peak.

With the bruise and the scrape and the dark circles under her eyes she looked like a boy. "No…maybe I can cut it into a mohawk and go Goth like Sadie."

Chris openly laughed at the idea. "You? Goth? Not hardly. Hey, I know!" He ran off suddenly. When he came back he carried one of his comic books. She recognized the *X-Men*; ten-year-old Joe Gates used to have a stack of them almost as tall as her chin.

"This is *Rogue*," he said, pointing to an odd looking woman. The front of her hair was long and white, while the rest was brown and thick and swept behind as if there was a wind that affected only it. "Her power is to steal other people's powers. Pretty cool, right?"

Jillybean was slow to answer. "Yes, I guess so, only I don't want white hair. That's what means you're old and I don't want to be old."

"Who wants to be old?" Chris agreed. "Being old is gross and it sucks. No, I was thinking that if you cut the other side of your hair so that it matches, it might look pretty good." He took a handful of her hair from the right side and tucked it up so that it approximated the left.

She saw what he was after. "Do it," she said without hesitation. "Cut it." He produced his long knife and stood behind her with it held perilously close to her face. "With scissors, I mean," she added, quickly.

"Relax, I was just kidding." He put away the knife while she opened the cabinet above the sink, finding a pair of scissors. Although there was rust on the metal like five-o'clock shadow, they were sharp and did the trick. He trimmed the long side, made a face and then trimmed the short side. "Just making them match, don't freak."

When he was done he smiled and nodded, saying: "Awesome." It wasn't exactly awesome in Jillybean's eyes, while at the same time, it wasn't bad. She'd had the same little-girl hair style for so long that she wasn't ready to decide whether she liked it or not.

It was different and just then, different was good. After all, she was trying not to be Jillybean and the haircut went a long way to making her look like someone else. "Thanks," she said, touching her hair and turning this way and that.

She allowed herself only another minute of staring at herself before she decided they had to get going before the owner of the voice returned. Though she wondered if it would. So far, it had only come when she was alone. But she didn't want to test the hypothesis and scare Chris off by talking to a wall or a shrub.

Sadly, she had decided that the voice wasn't real. "And that's what means I'm still at least a little crazy." On the subject of being crazy, Jillybean was an optimist—a little crazy was always preferable to being a lot crazy. "At least it's only a voice and at least it's only one voice."

"You say something?" Chris asked from on top of the Jeep. He was up there, hauling loads by hand. He had to store his belongings as well as the items from within the Jeep that he was displacing. Jillybean could have spent thirty seconds and set up a pulley and winch system using the pedal and gear system from an old bike, a length of rope and the exposed rafters, but that would have given away her brains.

Besides, Chris very much liked to show off. He sweated and grunted and kept up a display of strength that was more for his own benefit than it was for hers. Jillybean got the idea that he wanted to be needed.

"Just trying to make sure I haven't forgotten anything," she answered. That was almost a joke. If she was still crazy and there was a good chance that she was, then how would she know if she had forgotten anything—unless the voice came to her in a dream: *You've forgotten your umbrella. You know the one with the gold fishes on it? Yeah, that one, and it's verrry important.*

She giggled at her own crazy, but then sobered when she saw the pile of textbooks in the back seat. They would have to go. There would be no explaining them away. Chris was already getting skeptical about Granny Annie. She set them aside, but not without first jotting down the names of each on the off-chance she ever saw them again.

Once the packing was complete, Chris topped off the gas tank and they were ready to go. By then it was after midnight and a smiling sliver of moon had spun halfway across the sky. This left them with only six hours of driving until sunrise. Jillybean felt the time slipping past and with it came a sense of urgency that she had to actively fight against.

Time and again she would look from the main monitor and down at the speedometer to find that the Jeep was speeding faster and faster. With the roads so pitted and strewn with trees and trash and monsters, and of course, driving without headlights, anything over fifteen miles an hour was dangerous. Jillybean drove with sweaty palms, and her eyes anxiously staring into the monitor trying to pick out obstacles that seemed to loom up out of nowhere.

She was quickly vindicated in her sense of urgency—there were other people on the road. The weather had turned for the better and now humans began to creep out of their hiding spots, braving the night roads, stealing from cover to cover. Some were foolish and drove straight down I-80 with their headlights blaring for all to see.

"Those idiots," Jillybean said, when she saw the first headlights as tiny sparkles miles away.

Chris leaned over the console to see the monitor. "Oh yeah, they're gonna get caught. You better get off this road, quick."

She made her own exit ramp by knocking down the highway fence that separated the four lanes of asphalt from a rutted dirt frontage road. It wasn't much of a road and their speed dropped below ten for long stretches until Chris suggested they head north to take the Lincoln Highway that ran parallel to I-80 for nearly the entire length of the state of Nebraska.

This was a smart suggestion, but it didn't end the danger they were in as they weren't the only ones with the same idea. At just before three in the morning, Jillybean got the scare of her life as the front monitor was suddenly taken up by the front end of a truck that had been hurtling west at thirty miles an hour with its lights out.

The only thing that saved them from a head on collision was that the truck's driver chose that moment to light a cigarette. On Jillybean's low-light camera system, the light from the match had the intensity of a signal flare.

"Oh, my God!" she screamed as she turned hard to the right. The two vehicles passed within inches of each other.

Jillybean's heart was racing from the close call and her hands were shaking, but she couldn't pull over or even relax in the slightest. What if they were bad guys? Or what if they were being chased by bad guys?

Chris seemed to read her mind. "Get off at the next exit and go north. There's more roads that head east up there." He was so far over onto the console that he was practically perched there. It was the only position that would give him a clear view of the rear view mirror.

"Oh boy, they're bad guys alright," he said. Headlights had just flicked on behind them and now they were turning around, coming for the Jeep. "Let's get the machine gun warmed up."

"It doesn't need to be warmed up and 'asides, I'd rather not kill anyone if I can help it. We'll use the smoke."

"What? That's crazy. Smoke won't do us a lick of good. I say go with a bomb or the machine gun."

Jillybean knew what she was doing. The road was two lanes of potholes, litter, overturned cars and monsters. She just had to hope she got lucky with one of those four. She glanced one last time at the rear monitor and saw the headlights fast approaching; they were doing forty, while she was risking everything by speeding up to twenty-five.

"Drop a bomb! Hurry!" Chris cried, as the truck's headlights, looking like twin dragon eyes, quickly approached.

He had no clue about the delicate timing involved in using a bomb. Dropping one at random without knowing the speed and proximity of the target would be a waste and she only had a few bombs prepared. Instead, she flicked up the cover on the smoke button and pressed it. Seconds later, the view from the rear camera was obliterated by swirling grey clouds.

Afraid to be struck from behind, she gave the Jeep a touch more gas and leaned in towards the front monitor until her pert little nose was three inches away and her breath fogged it over every other second. The road whipped past the camera lens and for once it was empty; exactly what she didn't need.

Behind them the truck's lights could be seen slicing into the smoke, but how close it was Jillybean had no idea. Nor did she know how much smoke was pouring out from behind.

"You better get your seatbelt on," she said to Chris and then gave the Jeep even more gas.

One way or the other, there was going to be a crash.

Chapter 18

Jillybean

"I say drop a bomb," Chris said again. The truck was still on their tail. A second before, its headlights had cut out and they had both hoped the truck had given up the chase. Much to Jillybean's astonishment, Chris had opened his door and stood on the runner, his hair whipping all around as he looked back.

"They're still there," he said, as he climbed back in. "They're about forty feet back on the right. If they get ahead of us, we're gonna be in trouble. Try zigzagging a bit to spread out the smoke."

She wove the Jeep back and forth, enveloping the road, blinding them once more and probably angering them at the same time—someone in the truck started shooting a gun. They missed most of the time, but when they hit there was a fearful hammering on the back of the Jeep and both children hunkered down.

"If you won't drop a bomb, at least shoot back!" Chris cried. He was right. One of the bullets could get lucky and knock out the rear camera or it could slip between the chains and puncture a wheel. She switched the rear camera to the gun-mounted view and was just about to rattle off a string of shots when out of the corner of her eye she saw something large and strangely shaped take over the entire front screen.

By then, she was doing thirty-five miles an hour and with the truck racing up on her, she couldn't slam on the brakes or she'd be hit from behind. Her only choice was to lay the wheel over and hope to hit whatever it was a glancing blow.

A second later they struck something. The Jeep rattled and thumped and vibrated, while all around them erupted what sounded like the screams of a dozen terrified old crones. From their right came a terrific crash and then, before they could blink, they were past the obstacle. The front screen cleared of whatever they had driven through and showed that in front of them stood a barbed wire fence and an old wheat field beyond that.

Jillybean tried to brake, but she was nowhere close to being quick enough. They thudded through the fence with another screech, much like the last, and then they were in among the unharvested plants, gradually slowing.

"What did we hit back there?" she asked as she took the Jeep on a gently curving path back to the road.

Chris, true to his fearless nature, popped the door open once more and stood looking across the smoke-covered field. He laughed. "It was a downed tree. We passed through the branches and leaves and stuff, but that truck hit the trunk square on and flipped." He lifted a fisted and yelled, "Serves you right!"

"Get in here, please," Jillybean said and tugged him back inside. "Should we go back and see if they're okay?"

The idea shocked him. "What? I don't get you sometimes, not at all. We should go back and kill the survivors is what we should do."

This struck home. Jillybean had done that before, but she'd had her reasons...or rather her excuses. "No, we keep going," she said in a whisper. He only shrugged in a way that suggested he didn't care one way or the other, which was strange seeing as he had been outraged only a moment before.

When they reached a little two-lane black top, Jillybean kept both hands on the wheel to keep the fact that they were still shaking to herself. Chris didn't have fear to hide. As if nothing at all had just had happened, he leaned back with his hands behind his head and his big feet up on the dash and started talking about everything under the stars.

Unabashedly, he told her everything about himself. She found out that his real name was Christian and about how his dad had died in a car accident when he was four, and about how he had been in foster homes: eleven of them, and how a dead rat had infected his last foster-dad and how he had killed him with a butcher's knife and a garden gnome. Sometimes he bragged in the most outrageous fashion and sometimes he spoke in whispers of things that Jillybean didn't really want to know about.

This was especially true when he told her of the time he'd been raped by slavers. He didn't cry at the telling; she cried for both of them. He had been alone for a long time; she would say even before the apocalypse and she figured that all this talking was a form of therapy for him.

Jillybean found him to be a strange mixture of tough and soft, smart and ignorant, happy and sad. It was all woven into his being like the most intricate of braids.

He talked and talked until the sun started giving color to the sky ahead of them and in all that time Jillybean shared nothing. His stories were funny or upsetting or nostalgic, hers were, for the most part, murderous. She kept them hidden and tried to pretend that she was just Jill. Those other very bad stories had happened to someone else.

A little after sunrise, they cruised into the town of St. Paul, Nebraska. It was bordered by old farms and was laid out in a perfect square with the streets set out in a grid, forming little blocks, each a hundred and fifty feet on the side. The east-west streets were alphabetized: Adams Street, Baxter, Custer and so on, while the north-south streets were numbered.

The perfectionist in Jillybean found it all wonderfully perfect and she wanted to get out of the Jeep and walk the streets, perhaps to measure them. Unfortunately, there were too many monsters wandering around the town. They spent the day sleeping in the local high school, which had suffered some sort of calamity. The roof was missing from one of the buildings and the walls all along the southern end had come down.

Jillybean drove the Jeep right into the building and parked it in the cafeteria. Chris was the first out. He stood on one of the long tables with a smile on his handsome face. "I love it when a school gets it," he laughed. He then hopped down and started for a side door. "Gotta take a leak," he declared.

He did more than use the bathroom and didn't return for an hour. When he did he had two cans of soda, a bag of chips and an unopened pre-packaged sandwich that he had pulled from a vending machine; it was completely covered in a green and fuzzy mold.

"Should we open it?" he asked. His eyes were alight with impish glee. "It's not poisonous or nothing, right?"

"I don't know, but I know it won't be good smelling, so why would you want to?"

"Because it's fun? Duh. Here goes." He opened the plastic container and the tremendous, rancid smell that came from the little package was out of proportion to its size. It was worse than month-old milk. Chris groaned and made a face, while Jillybean backed away, covering her face with her yellow shirt. It didn't seem to help and her stomach started to heave.

"Get it...out of here," she begged, as she gagged. He ran to one of the exit doors from the cafeteria, banged it open and heaved it out in onto the hardtop, where the high-schoolers used to toe hackysacks into the air or stand around in little groups talking about the inconsequential things that seemed so important at the time: who liked whom, and which was better, rap or rock, and whose parents sucked the most. The run of asphalt was parade ground flat and, of course, perfectly square.

It was sadly empty.

Chris waved his hand in front of his face, shooing away the stench. Despite being green in the gills, he had a white smile. "Talk about gross! There was this time I found a body stuffed in a refrigerator. It was all swelled up and puffy like it was gonna explode, but even that thing didn't smell as bad as that sandwich."

Jillybean had been considering having a turned-around dinner at six in the morning but she was suddenly not hungry. She found a red, apple and cinnamon scented Christmas candle and quickly lit it. "Stupid boys," she grumbled under her breath.

"I heard that," he said, still smiling. "I told you I had the hearing of a hawk or something like that. And my eyesight is twenty—five. You know what that means, right?" She didn't. She'd heard the term: twenty-twenty before, but never knew what it meant.

After she shrugged, he let out a scoffing burst of fake laughter. "Who's stupid now? It means that I can see from twenty feet away what most people can see from five. The doctor said I could've been a fighter pilot. They had real good vision, too."

He went on bragging for some time until Jillybean started to yawn, at which point he abruptly left the cafeteria, saying something about exploring. Despite being big for his age, he was filled with little boy energy and it had to be used up before he could even think about sleeping.

While he was gone, Jillybean crept through the halls of the school, careful to watch where she was going. Every locker had been forced open and the halls were strewn with trash, books and paper mostly. She feared that the library would be in a similar state of disarray, however, other than a heavy coating of dust and an even heavier blanket of gloom hanging over everything, it was perfect.

"I guess there was nothing here to eat," she murmured. The words fell flat out of her mouth as if the mote-filled air had caught the sound waves and absorbed them. It was spooky and she was so absolutely certain that she would hear the voice again

155

that she said: "Yep, I forgot something important. By golly, I sure am dumb to forget something so important."

As she spoke, she walked quickly down the center aisle, her eyes scanning the shelves. She wished she had more time to browse, however the idea of the disembodied voice coming to visit her in such a spooky location caused her to snatch up the first book that interested her: *Inner Man*.

It was a heavy, picture-filled book detailing the many systems within the human body. A she scurried from the library, she flipped the pages until she found the chapter on the circulatory system. It was exactly what she needed for her "surgeoning"—a map of all the arteries and veins, that way she would know what to look out for when cutting into a person.

One of her monster patients had bled out when she had accidentally slit open its inferior vena cava—the thick vein that ran up the center of the body and empties into the right atrium of the heart. She had clamped it thinking she'd get back to it, but the next thing she knew it had swollen to the size of a bratwurst. Understandably, she had freaked out and released the clamp, only to flood the wound so she couldn't see a thing.

For over an hour, she was quite content to sit in the cafeteria, reading and cutting out pictures. When Chris came back, he moved so silently that he was able to sneak up on her despite the fact she was in an altogether silent environment. He laughed when she shrieked and scattered her pictures in a colorful storm.

"That wasn't nice!" she yelled. He only laughed some more, which sent her into a rage that was beyond her control. Before she knew it, she hucked the scissors she'd been using, right at his head, aiming for one of his smiling, hazel eyes.

He easily dodged the throw as if he knew it was coming. "Talk about not very nice. You coulda put an eye out." For some reason, he thought this was funny and laughed some more. Jillybean was far from laughing because he was right. What would have happened if he hadn't been so quick? What would have happened if the scissors had gone right into his eye?

She could stitch up a cut or maybe pull a bullet out of someone's leg if it only hit muscle, however she knew next to nothing about fixing eyeballs. If she had hit him, he would be half-blind for life. That was no laughing matter.

"I-I'm sorry," she said. "I didn't mean it and that's what means I just threw the scissors by accident."

His laughter turned into a chuckle. "Ah, you couldn't have hit me if I was glued to the floor. So, what's all this stuff you were cutting out? The hu-man circle-re-tory system? Huh? Why do you want that stuff for?"

"I was just curious," she said, going down on her knees to collect the pictures and diagrams. There was no way she could tell Chris about her wanting to be a doctor. He would just laugh at her and make her feel stupid for even trying. In that way, he was very much a boy. "Very much a jerk," she mumbled.

"Who's a jerk?" he asked. He had walked off across the room and had begun bouncing a tennis ball off the window, but somehow he had heard her. "You're the one who threw the scissors, not me. I got us soda and chips and two sleeping bags." He pointed towards the Jeep where he had set down the sleeping bags next to the wheel. "That's called taking care of business. My daddy used to say that."

"I-I didn't say jerk, I said jert...dirt. I have dirt under my nails. I'll be right back." She headed for the bathrooms, holding her hands in close to her chest to hide the fact that they were perfectly clean. She always kept hand sanitizer and a package of baby wipes in the glove compartment. Monsters were covered in monster-germs, after all.

There was only a single window in the girl's bathroom and it was covered in grime, so only a dull light made it into the room. As she was too short to see into any of the mirrors, it didn't really matter how little light there was. She went to the row of sinks and, out of habit, she turned on the hot water faucet.

A second later, she leapt back as the faucet let out an enormous burp. It was as though there were a giant on the other end of the pipe letting loose. The damp gas erupting from the faucet even stank like a burp. This sometimes happened when there was still pressure in the pipes, which was fairly common, and yet Jillybean was freaked out. Perhaps it was the spooky bathroom or the obscene smell or the way something in the walls began to vibrate and rattle. The final straw for her was when the faucet breathed out a long: *aaaahhhh*.

She thought for sure that some ghostly creature would begin speaking through the faucet. Before it could, she jumped forward and twisted the knob all the way over to the right.

Once more she backed away as the rattle in the walls built up. A long mirror on the far wall started to shake with such violence that her reflection blurred. She stared, suddenly seeing herself change. The two locks of hair that hung down, framing her face seemed to become downward pointing horns, and her twin blue eyes merged to become one huge eye that took up most of her face.

With a shriek, she turned and ran straight into Chris, who had, once more, come padding up on silent feet. His eyes were wide and his lips pulled back in a grimace of terror. The two of them ran from the bathroom into the cafeteria, where the light and smell of the apple cinnamon candle returned everything to normal so quickly that Chris began to laugh.

"Holy cow!" he cried. "That was scary. You shoulda seen your face. Ha-ha! I thought you were gonna wet yourself."

"But I didn't. And it was just the pipes," she said, mostly just to reassure herself. "And that's what means there was still some water in them…I think."

His nose crinkled. "But what kind of water? The smell coming from that faucet was like diseased or something. It was way worse than that moldy old sandwich. I wouldn't want try drinking it. You'd get diarrhea for sure. Hey, do you know the diarrhea song?" She didn't know if it was a song you sang when you had diarrhea or a song about diarrhea; either way she didn't want to know. This didn't stop Chris from singing: "*When you're sliding into first and you feel something burst: diarrhea! When you're heading off to second and your pants are full of foam, Diarrhea!*"

"Oh brother," Jillybean said. She walked away, which only made Chris sing all the louder. Secretly she was glad for the goofy song and for the casual, carefree way in which he sang it. Her fears were gone by the third verse. With him crooning in the background something about a 'squshy-tushie', she set four traps, a smoker and three noise alarms. "Don't leave the cafeteria," she told Chris when she came back.

She told him about the bombs, "another Granny Annie initiative," and then settled into the sleeping bag he had fetched for her. He unrolled his sleeping bag and fell asleep trying to compose new lines for his song. The last Jillybean heard was him mumbling: "When the smell is like a fart, but it comes out like a dart, diarrhea, diarrhea."

The two slept the rest of the day away and for the first time in weeks she slept full and completely. She was bright-eyed when she woke and didn't even mind that Chris had dreamed up three more verses for his song. "I'll get breakfast going if you'll get the water," she suggested."

"Water for what?"

"To, you know, clean up. Like for a bath, but a small one." She wasn't about to use the term: whore's bath. It was a crude saying that would guarantee a hearty laugh from Chris.

He grumbled about the need for a bath so soon after the last, but he fetched the water, nonetheless. Jillybean made soup with a side of protein bars for their evening meal. She then bathed, brushed out her hair before reforming it into the "new" look.

"I wonder what Sadie will say when she sees it?" She was sure that Neil would say only nice things though he would be secretly outraged. "Knowing him, he'll hint that I should change it back." At least she hoped so. It would mean he still cared about her.

"Are you talking to yourself again?" Chris asked. "That's not normal, you know."

Jillybean said nothing to this since there was no sense arguing with the truth. "I was just planning our trip," she lied. "We should be able to make it to Omaha by sunrise and from there it will be a day to get to Des Moines and another day to get to Davenport."

"And that's where our quest is?" he asked, his shrewd eyes watching her closely.

"Yes," she answered as honestly as she could. But in this, she was wrong. Their adventure started that night when they were forced to stop after six hours of driving when they ran into a monster horde that numbered in the hundreds of thousands.

At first, they thought it was only a few thousand and so they waited in the Jeep as the creatures washed over the two-lane road as if an ocean of corpses had flooded a levy and was washing over the land.

"There are more behind us," Chris said, pointing to the rear camera. Jillybean hated seeing the monsters in the grey light of the cameras; they seemed spectral, like ghosts or demons from hell. In her eyes, a demon was far worse than an infected person with their brains burned out.

They watched the monitors until the fear turned to boredom. Chris was the first to fall asleep and Jillybean soon followed. Her sleep was very deep and when she woke with the sound of voices outside the Jeep her mind was sluggish.

159

A glance to her right showed Chris' seat empty, which only added confusion to her torpid thinking. Next she glanced at the monitors, but they had switched to sleep mode. She was just reaching out to punch in the security code when there was a thump on the Jeep's door. It was a metallic thump as if the person was using the butt of a gun.

Too late, Jillybean looked over and saw that the door was unlocked. She scrambled to lock it, however just then the door opened and she found herself blinded by the early morning sun. She was blinking and squinting, trying to make sense of what was going on, when a man, hairy, wild, and evil, leaned around the door leveling a .357 magnum at her.

He must have been expecting someone other than a seven-year-old girl because his eyes went wide and he asked: "What the fuck?"

"That's a bad word," she answered, when she couldn't think of anything else that would suffice. Rhetorical questions were not easy for her straightforward mind.

That made him pause for a moment. "I know it's a bad word, so what? Get out of there!"

She started to climb down from her pillows but at the last second, she reached for the door and tried to yank it shut. If she could lock herself in, she stood a good chance of getting away— though if she did, she would have to leave Chris behind. Perhaps it was this thought weighing on her that slowed her hand enough for the man to grab the edge of the door.

He yanked it open, toppling her onto the pavement. At that moment, she was absolutely terrified and for the briefest moment she thought about going for the .38 in her pocket, however she saw all around her the boots and legs of men casting shadows as long as trees. She was in a forest of them.

"Well, what the fuck is this?" another man asked, coming forward to squat over Jillybean. He was bearded and stinky like the rest, however his blue eyes were sharp with intelligence. Those eyes roved over her, glanced up into the Jeep and then came back to her.

"I know you," he said. "You're Jillybean."

Chapter 19

Jillybean

She couldn't be Jillybean, especially not in Nebraska, the one-time kingdom of the Azael. She couldn't even be Jill; it was too close. "M-my name is Tr-Tristyn," she stammered. "F-from Scottsbluff."

"Oh, is that right? You're Tristyn from Scottsbluff?"

She nodded, hoping not to appear too eager. "Yes, sir. I'm looking for my mo....dad, I mean. His name is Jack and he's very strong and he's good with guns and he has lots of men with him."

The man stood, chuckling at Jillybean's pathetic lies. He was taller than the rest of them, and thicker. In a way, he reminded Jillybean of a bigger version of Neil Martin. He had a scar that ran down the left side of his face, making his dark beard jag oddly, and he was missing two fingers on his right hand.

"You know what?" he asked. "I think I killed some guy named Jack. Yeah, I killed him and all his men. That's too bad, isn't it? And you know what else is too bad?"

He actually paused, waiting for Jillybean to answer: "What is too bad?"

"I hate the name Tristyn. I mean I really hate it. I feel like killing everyone with that name." He squatted again, pulling out a deadly sharp Ka-bar and turning the point towards Jillybean. "You know what name I like?"

"Jillybean," she said, knowing what he was looking for. "Sorry, but I'm not her. But if you don't like Tristyn, you can call me Tris...or Chris." She couldn't help herself and when she said her friend's name, she glanced around, hoping to see his face peering out from the weathered cornfields that bordered the road on both sides.

Another laugh escaped him as he turned from her. He gazed at the Jeep for a moment before tapping the armor with the Ka-bar. "Huh," he grunted and stuck his head inside. "Are these... oh yeah, cameras, that's smart. What do these switches do?"

"The red one is for the back gun," she said. "The other two are to swivel the cameras." With the Jeep cold and unmoving, neither the smoke bomb or the pipe bomb releases would do anything, so a lie was easy.

He didn't press the buttons. In fact, he refrained from touching anything except the iPads she used as monitors for the camera feeds. "What's your passwords?" he asked, as the iPads went to the startup screens.

"I don't know," she said in a see-through lie.

The man gave her a sharp look and opened his mouth, but before he could say anything, someone yelled: "We got stiffs incoming. Looks like a couple of hundred, maybe more."

"Where?" someone else cried.

"South. In that field."

For the first time, Jillybean got a chance to look around and was surprised to see that these men weren't bandits, they were traders. Three of the huge, armored machines that they all seemed to use were parked just down the road from the Jeep. Jillybean quickly ducked her head down, hoping even more to lie her way out of the mess she had found herself in.

The last time she had come up against a group of traders, she had destroyed five of their vehicles and killed thirty-seven men. *But this is a different group, altogether*, she tried to tell herself.

The monsters were a hundred yards off and closing on the trucks, rapidly. "Alright, let's get buttoned up!" bawled the man who had guessed Jillybean's name. As the others hurried to the vehicles, he snatched the Jeep's keys from the ignition, slammed the door shut and lifted Jillybean by the collar of her yellow shirt; she bit back a cry of pain.

"Let's go talk in private," he said to her. He had an evil leer in his eye that sent a shiver through her and once more she stared hard into the overgrown field hoping to see Chris lurking. All she saw were the decaying stalks of corn.

The man led her into the last truck. It was the slave truck. The sketchy dimness of its interior, the stale smell, the pale, sickly women, all made Jillybean want to scream in terror and run, however the man had a firm hold on her shirt.

Most of the sex slaves cast furtive glances at Jillybean out of the corner of their eyes, but none said a word and neither did the three men in the truck. One raised an eyebrow, while the other two turned away, pretending not to see the little girl.

Once they stepped inside, the ramp was pulled up and the armored doors were shut fast with a heavy thud of metal. For a few moments, the interior was nearly pitch black and in that time, her captor's hand traced down her back almost to what her mom had always called her "behind."

Jillybean was now shaking so hard she thought that she would either vibrate herself into a thousand pieces and fall to the floor in an unrecognizable jumble or she would float away like a buzzing bee.

Then a candle was struck and she was propelled along the narrow center aisle until they reached the back of the truck, which opened up into a cave-like room that stank of feet and the ugly stench of beer-vomit. There were three worn couches positioned around a short, squat table where cards and poker chips were scattered among ashtrays and empty cans.

"Up there," the man said, pointing to a ladder in the corner of the room. He waited for her to go first and once more she considered going for the .38 in her pocket. *At the top,* she thought. She would get to the second floor and pull it out just as he stuck his head up through the hole. It was a fine plan except just as she mounted the ladder, her coat swung forward and the sound of metal on metal was unmistakable.

The man's dirty hands went up and down her body, finding the gun, a knife and the laser pointer she used to distract the monsters. For some reason, discovering these items actually caused the man to grin. "Not Jillybean!" he snorted before pushing her back towards the ladder.

She went up with a sinking feeling that was unlike any she'd ever had in her life. In all of her adventures, she had never been this defenseless with so few options left to her. She was utterly at the man's mercy and he didn't seem to possess all that much in the way of mercy.

"You don't remember me, do you?" he asked as he climbed beneath her. "I used to work for the River King, but then someone came around and blew up the bridge. Some people said it was commandos or Special Forces guys from the Colonel or the Valley, but there were others who remember a little girl ghosting out of the prison right before it blew. And I was there when we recaptured all the escapees. Remember the barge?"

Jillybean had made it to the top of the ladder and was shoved towards a room in the corner. Two of its walls were nothing but green blankets hanging from the ceiling. It was very dark and quiet on the second floor.

"That wasn't me," she said, without much hope.

"Oh yeah? It was definitely a girl who blew that fucker up and she was just about this tall." He stuck his hand on the top of her head. Another shudder wracked her. "That's what I thought," he said. "Either way, I thought the River King wasn't gonna last, so I headed west and met up with some of those Azael guys. I thought I could become a prince or something, but guess who showed up there as well?"

He pulled back the green blanket and pushed Jillybean into the room. She hit something at shin height and fell forward onto a mattress. She was panting in fear now and her mind was going mushy, unable to think past the terror growing within her. In a panic she scrambled herself into the corner of the room.

"You showed up," he said. "And what happened to ol' king what's his name and all his princes? A girl killed them. A little girl. The way I see it, she must be the most dangerous person in the world. A person to be feared. A person who is probably very valuable. Are you her? Are you Jillybean?"

"You're probably right. A girl like that would be very valuable," she answered, grasping at the proverbial straw he had extended. "There would be people willing to pay a lot for her. I know pe…"

Her tongue faltered as she heard the unmistakable sound of a zipper going down. Without thought, she launched herself towards the wall of blankets to her right. Like an actor trying to claw her way through the closing curtain, she found herself lost in the material when something hit her on the side of the face and spun her around.

Before she knew it, she was on the bed again and fighting to get up. The man swung a fist of iron and struck her in the tummy below her belly button. The pain was like fire and she gasped, unable to scream. Before she could do anything else he punched her again, this time on the cheek. The blow rocked her head back and she struck the side of the truck with a sound like a gong.

It echoed into her head as everything went deep, deep black.

Regaining consciousness was a slow affair. At some point she cracked a swollen eye, saw a ceiling with peeling paint and a wall of what looked like flowers, and then was out again. Sometime after that, the truck began to rock and her head lolled back and forth and with each motion there was a *clink* noise. She was dimly aware that she was chained by the neck. There was a firing port on the wall four feet above her head—it was dark out.

When she closed her eyes again, she slept in a dreamless state, however, nagging at her subconscious was the word: *revenge*. It echoed in her head for what felt like an eternity until a hand, gentle and soft, woke her.

She found herself staring into the peculiar green-brown eyes of Chris Turner. He put his index finger to her lips. There was blood under the nail. He whispered: "Don't say a word."

They were no longer moving and the truck, save for a few snores, was ghostly quiet. She feared that her chains would rattle, but she saw that the collar had been removed. "Huh?" The one, half-whispered word, was enough to send a jolt of pain along her jaw. It opened a floodgate of agony.

The side of her face, the back of her head, her stomach. Her tummy hurt so badly she could barely stand. When she did her legs trembled and she had to hold Chris' hand in as tight a grip as she could manage, which was such a light hold that he had to hold her by the elbow. There was more blood on his shirt.

"Everyone's asleep, so be quiet."

She had a thousand questions, maybe more, but she bit them back. They were escaping! A part of her wondered if she was still dreaming, however the blood splattered on Chris made her fear that it was a nightmare and that, at any moment, she'd be running from faceless men, her feet partially glued to the floor as she moved in slow motion, always just inches out of reach.

The darkness of the truck lent itself to the idea of a dream. Everything was murky and tinged with pain. Chris pulled her gently, but urgently along, passing curtained rooms until they were at the back of the truck and she realized that they were on the first floor and he expected her to climb.

He was five rungs up before he turned and saw that she was still at the bottom of the ladder, her hands holding weakly to the first rung, her lower lip going up and down.

"You can do it," he said, the words dropping on her with all the weight and importance of feathers. It took everything she had just to remain upright. She wished with all her heart to be able to go back to bed so that she could wake from the nightmare she was in.

He slid back down the ladder, leaping away from the final four feet to keep from hitting her. "Come on," he pleaded, fear seeping into his voice. He picked up her right foot and put it on a rung; her left came next. He was practically lifting each. Left then right, and then he had her weight on his shoulders and his hands were, unapologetically on her behind, thrusting her up.

Doggedly, she went up and up, hand over hand, until she gained the second floor and then she dragged herself along until only her legs dangled. Chris shoved her the rest of the way.

At some point, she passed out and woke to find herself being dragged along. "Okay," she said in a whisper.

"Come on!" Chris implored, frantically. She fought her way to her feet and allowed him to propel her along until they reached the ladder that led to roof.

Nothing had ever looked so high. She swayed staring up at it and her legs gave out at the thought. Once more Chris was at her side, begging: "Please try." He might have been as tall as a seventh grader but with the frightened quiver in his voice, he sounded like a first grader.

She couldn't make the climb. In all her short life, she had never felt so physically done in…so destroyed. The only way she was going up the next ladder was if she was carried. She couldn't even stand with the ladder as a prop. Slowly she sank down until she was sitting in front of the last rung, her strength gone. In three seconds, she went from "done in" to unconscious, her head resting on the cold steel.

A thud next to her had her blinking and when she could focus her eyes, Chris was kneeling next to her, fear and worry stamped on his face. She made an excuse why they couldn't go on: "We need the keys to the Jeep."

He looked around as if the keys would be just lying on the floor. "Who has them? That weird guy who took you?" She nodded and even that took an effort. "Stay here," he ordered.

Unerringly, he headed right for the back room. From a crumpled ball at the bottom of the ladder, she watched, her breath caught up in her throat, her eyes straining tears, one hand reaching out, pleading for him to come back, or to be careful or to kill the bastard. She didn't know which she wanted more. One thing she knew for certain was that she would never risk anything if it meant Chris going through the same pain she had. Revenge wasn't worth that much misery.

Her hand hung uselessly in the air until he had disappeared behind the green blankets, and then it dropped, slapping against her thigh in a dull, empty, sad sound of defeat. Stifling a groan and an agony-filled whimper, she struggled to her feet and forced her way, step by step to the blanketed room, afraid to find that Chris was even then waking the horrible man.

Fast as Chris was, he would be no match for the man who had hurt her. The man was gristle and grit and all muscle. He was an awful, horrible man in his primal worst and no little boy, no matter how tough or quick, would be able to stand against him.

Even though they didn't stand a chance, she wouldn't let him fight alone. She would do whatever she could, which likely meant biting him. Her pointy white teeth were her only true weapon.

But they weren't needed. She stumbled through the green blankets and found Chris rifling the man's pockets. He didn't mind because he was dead. Someone had slit his throat from ear to ear and then pinned him to the mattress with a Ka-bar. In splatters and pools, there was blood everywhere, but it was no longer warm. It was cold and tacky.

"I told you to stay put," Chris grumped. "You weren't supposed to see this." She wished she hadn't. It was too upsetting. Turning on her heel, she wobbled back to the ladder and began to climb. She wanted to escape, not just from the giant truck, but also from death. How many more bodies were behind her? How much blood?

She had to guide each foot onto the rungs and at first it wasn't a surprise to see that there was blood on her Keds. What surprised and shocked her was that it wasn't from the dead trader, it was coming from her. There was a dark stain running from the crotch of her jeans and down her right leg. The sight of it froze her in place.

"He ruptured me," she said. She'd been punched so hard that her insides were bleeding all over her outsides.

The blood was bad, but what truly scared her was trying to guess what had broken. The pain was low and deep. From her study of anatomy she knew the organs down there: the uterus, bladder, and colon. She didn't know which she hoped it was.

Chris appeared out of the murk and once more started pushing her on until she reached the top, where she had to turn a lever to unlock the trapdoor leading to the top of the truck. Cold, damp air washed over her when she opened the door, and above, the sky was heavy with dark clouds.

Everything was wet and slick. She wanted to ask when it had rained, but was afraid of the answer. What if she'd been knocked out for days or weeks? What if they were on the other side of the country? The three trucks were parked along the side of a road with forest on either side; that alone was far different from the endless prairies of Nebraska.

"Get going," Chris urged. "Like this, slide your feet. It makes you go quieter." The two made their way to the front, climbed down to the top of the cab, and from there, down to the ground. Jillybean followed after Chris, expecting him to head off into the forest. Instead he went to the back of the truck to where her Jeep was hitched in place by three chains.

"You're going to have to drive," she told him. Huddling in a ball and crying was all she was good for at the moment.

"No duh," he said, as he lifted her into the passenger seat. He was about to go unchain them when his eyes lit up in the dark. "Can I use one of the bombs?"

"You can use three," she answered, feeling a spark of something besides pain inside of her: it was the bitter hunger for revenge. The man who had hurt her was dead, but there were others who needed to die. As far as she was concerned, every one of the dirty men in those trucks should suffer the same fate.

They trafficked in human misery and if she had the strength, she would have figured out a way to free the rest of the slaves. But she was in too much pain.

"The bombs are here, somewhere," she said. The interior of the Jeep was trashed. Someone had gone through their belongings, but other than a few missing choice food items, it was all still there. Chris found the pipe bombs; he held them up with a big grin on his face. She pointed at the little piece of plastic taped into the slot. "They blow up when you remove that."

"Can I throw it like a grenade?"

"I don't know about that. You'd have to hold onto one end of the string and hope that when you throw it, the plastic doesn't come out. And asides, they're not super big bombs. They might not get past the metal outsides of the trucks."

His grin faded into a look of disappointment. "Well that sucks. Why did you go and make bombs that were so wimpy?"

"Because that was all the material I had to work...I mean Granny Annie had to work with. She thought it was better to have a lot of smaller bombs instead of one big one. And that's what means she's smart."

"You can stop lying now. There is no Granny Annie. You're Jillybean. I heard that guy you know."

Jillybean was suddenly afraid and darted her eyes over to Chris. "You're not going to leave me are you?"

"Why would I do that? Just cuz you're Jillybean? No way. I think it's cool. You're like world famous. Like Jesse James or something. I heard all the stories. In all the groups I been with, people talked about you, but I didn't think the stories were really true, not until I saw that guy's face when he was saying all that stuff you did. He *really* believed it."

Jillybean practically wilted in relief. She didn't think she would be able to make it on her own in the shape she was in. "Thanks so much for not leaving. I'll be good, okay?" That sounded weird, so she quickly changed the subject. "You can set the bombs in the underneath of the trucks like by the gas tank, and then run the string across the road to a tree and then we leave, we zip by and boom, boom, boom. Just don't do the slave truck like that. I don't want anyone who's innocent getting hurt."

His grin was back as he hurried to set the bombs. While he was gone, Jillybean turned on the cameras and the monitors. After a few minutes, she was able to see a ghostly image of Chris unhooking the chains from the front of the Jeep. For some reason, he appeared very small and vulnerable. She became anxious for him, afraid that someone would notice her missing and race out to find him.

No one did, however. The traders felt snug in their rolling fortresses. "Just like I did," she said, thinking that they were getting their just desserts, but not knowing exactly what that meant. "Dessert is a good thing, so why would…"

Chris opened the door. He was trying to suppress a giggle, but just couldn't hold it in. "Oh boy, this is gonna be so cool!" It took him some time to get himself situated. Because of the artificially raised pedals, he had to sit in the seat with his knees jutting up on either side of the steering wheel. He looked ridiculous and yet, he was able to drive almost as well as Jillybean.

Carefully, he backed up about a hundred yards and then charged the Jeep forward just as someone ran up to the top of the slave truck, carrying something a long tube of some sort.

"Oh, crap!" Chris cried. "What was that?"

He knew what it was, just as she did. Anti-tank rockets all looked pretty much the same.

Chapter 20

Jillybean

"What do I do?" Chris screamed, his foot coming off the gas. In a second, the angle on the front camera was too low and the man couldn't be seen.

"Don't slow down! We'll be a sitting down duck if you do." Other than hoping the man didn't know how to work the rocket or wasn't a good shot with it, there wasn't much they could do but drive as fast as they could and cut down the angle at which he could shoot, which meant: "Get as close as you can to the truck."

Of course, this also would mean getting as close as he could to the bombs he had set, and who knew what that would do to them.

Jillybean glanced over as the speedometer inched up over forty miles an hour and she just had time to wonder whether they could outrun a rocket when they passed the slaver truck. She watched it as it blurred past the left-side camera. The bomb on this truck was set all the way in front, which gave the man plenty of time to fire his rocket.

He fired it at the same moment the first pipe bomb detonated. The blast heaved the backend of the Jeep to the right just as a silver dart whipped past and exploded four feet from the front of the Jeep sending it into a wild spin.

The wet pavement and a gentle slope added to the effect and they spun in hard, gut-wrenching circles for seventy feet, thudded into the side of the next truck in line and drifted slowly backwards until Chris recovered enough to find the brake. They stopped parallel to the truck, just eight feet from the gas tank.

Before they could blink there was another explosion, this one fantastic in size. The Jeep lifted high up on Jillybean's side, but because of the weight of the armor it didn't tip. It came crashing down and as it did she saw the side camera monitor go from pure white to utter black, save for the words: *Signal Lost*.

The heat baking into the Jeep had Jillybean worrying that it was on fire or would be soon. "Punch it, Chewie!" she yelled.

"What?" Chris screamed back. There was a roar in the air surrounding them as if the Jeep wasn't just on fire, but *in* a fire.

"Go! Get us out of here." He turned the Jeep around and stabbed down on the gas, pinning them to their seats as they accelerated alongside of the next truck. As they drew abreast of the cab they both cringed.

This time, Chris eased as far to the right as he could and, with their momentum carrying them along, the last explosion did little more than knock them off the road. They clipped a tree and careened back again and then they were speeding away, the rear camera showing the night lit by geysering flames.

"Yes!" Chris cried out and slapped the Jeep's dash board. "Oh my God, that was too cool. Another Jillybean adventure, right?" He started laughing. "And I was part of this one."

Jillybean had to force out a smile. Her belly ached and her face hurt and her head rang from the explosions. "This wasn't a Jillybean adventure, this was a Chris adventure. You were the one who rescued me…thanks by the way. And you were the one who set the bombs and got us through all of this."

"I guess I did. Hey, do you think we're on fire?" She shrugged, to which he said: "Maybe we should check. What do you think?"

"Sure."

They were a good two miles beyond the burning trucks; it was still close enough that when they got out of the Jeep, they could see the light from the fires away to the west. Chris only glanced at it for a moment before turning to the vehicle.

"Ho-ly mo-ly. Look at this thing," he said. The Jeep was black and sooty all along the passenger side and there was a rent in one of the armor plates that went all the way to the original metal frame of the back door and dented it in. "This isn't the prize I thought it was going to be." He gave the armor a tap; it sounded fine to Jillybean.

"I think only the opposite," she said. "Jessica is proven and that's what means we know she can take it. She's tough."

"Jessica? You think this car looks like a Jessica? That's just crazy. I think it should be called something way more cool. Like *El Diablo*. That means the devil in Spanish. That's a cool name if you ask me."

With the burns and the dents and the bullet holes, it did have a certain sinister quality to it. She shrugged, all the emotion she could display at the moment. "It's your Jeep, so you can name it anything you want."

"Yeah, about that. Now that I know your secret identity, can you tell me what we're really after?"

"I guess I owe you that, though I don't think you're gonna like it cuz I don't like it." He leaned in, his interest piqued, his eyes eager. "What we're after is either a person or thing or a place that's real important. The only problem is I forgot what it is or why it's important."

The eager look vanished. "Wait, what? That doesn't make sense at all. So, all you know is that you forgot 'something important?' How do you even know that much?"

"I know that I know because my brain keeps telling me. It just won't tell me all of it, maybe because I can't be trusted to know, you know?"

"No!" he shouted. "How can I know anything when you don't know nothing? And what do you mean, 'you can't be trusted?' Are you crazy? People said you were crazy. They said you murdered a baby and a dog."

"A dog! Why would I kill a dog?"

"Why would you kill a baby?" His usual chipper disposition was long gone; ice had taken its place.

She sagged in defeat. Once more being Jillybean was hurting her. "I *was* crazy," she admitted. "I did things that were really bad, but I didn't mean none of them. It was this girl in my head. She was the bad one, but she's dead now and I'm much better. So you don't have to be ascared."

"I'm not afraid, especially of you," he snipped, as if the idea was preposterous.

"Good, cuz I really need you. Whatever we're after might could be dangerous and we have to find it before someone else does. My brain is ascared that someone who doesn't like me will find it first."

"Someone who doesn't like you? That doesn't narrow things down at all. There's a lot of someones who don't like you. Heck, *everyone* is after you."

This wasn't news to Jillybean. She put a hand to her face. It felt as though her jawbone had been softened by the punch. "I know," she said and then crawled back into the Jeep.

He joined her a second later. "Okay, you *were* crazy. I can deal with that. But how do we find this thing you're after? Do you have any clues?"

"Uh-uh. I was just gonna retrace my steps until I find it. That's why we're heading for Davenport. That's where the Colonel used to live."

Chris caught something in her voice. "Used to? The rumor is that there was a big battle on his island and that he disappeared. Do you know what really happened?"

She told him and as she spoke, his eyes got bigger and bigger. "And then what?" he asked, breathlessly. She told him about the River King and the traders and rescuing Sadie. "Wow, cool. You gotta teach me how to make bombs and we gotta get more of those heli-drones. I saw the one you have and I thought it was just a toy."

Jillybean only shook her aching head. She was tired and in pain, and more than anything she wanted to sleep and feel better, but she had a question of her own: "When those bad guys came and you got away, why didn't you take me with you? And where did you go? And how did you find me?" She expected him to jump right into his "boast-mode," however he went a little red in the ears.

"Well, when they came I was going number two. And I really was afraid they'd just grab you and go when all the zombies came but that leader guy was really interested in your Jeep. So they went and hid inside their trucks. While they did, I pretended to be a zombie like you did back in North Platte. That was scary, let me tell you."

He paused, smiling as if the memory was a good one. "If I hadn't just gone number two, I might have had an 'episode.' Ha-ah! But I didn't, and once I got the hang of being that close to them it was easy."

"Easy?" she asked. "What did you do?"

"Nothing, really. At least nothing at first. I went and hid under the last truck. There are all these cables and things under there and it was nothing to crawl up and, what's the word? Stowaway? Is that it? I think so. Either way, I hid until the zombies had taken off and the leader guy poked around in the Jeep. Then they took off and I tagged along. No big deal."

Hanging from the bottom of a moving truck seemed like a tremendous deal to Jillybean. "How long did you have to hang there?"

"Oh, just a few hours and then there were more zombies. It was kind of sporadic. We'd stop and go and stop all day long. It got pretty boring and I slept a lot so I'd be ready when it got dark." His hazel eyes glittered and a ghost of a smile turned up the corner of his lips. She thought he was going to go into stab-by-stab detail of what he had done, but the look left him and he only shrugged.

He ended with: "So that was that."

"Good," Jillybean said. "I mean, thanks. You were very brave and I…I…" She broke down, crying and wasn't sure what she was crying about. Yes, she was in pain and yes, she was in utter dread that she had been ruptured or hurt in some way that wouldn't be fixable, but this wasn't why she cried.

Chris reached out with his bloodied hand and gripped her shoulder. "Hey, it'll be okay. That guy is dead. I made sure of it. And you'll get better. You'll heal and be as good as new and nobody will have to know. Maybe this can be one of those things you forget on purpose."

She wished it was that easy, but the pain would be a constant reminder. "We should get going. Where are we?"

"Iowa. Those traders were heading in the same direction we were. There's a town called Ames coming up."

Instantly, she begged: "Please go around it. There'll be people there and we don't know what kind or if they have radios or if they'll try to catch us or what they'll do to us." Her voice shook with unexpected fear. First tears and now she was trembling over the mention of a town.

She didn't know what was wrong with herself. Chris put his hand back on her shoulder. "Hey, cool it. It'll be okay. You got me here and we got this badass Jeep and you are Jillybean. They'd be fools to mess with you. If they have radios, I bet they're saying: *hide, Jillybean's coming.*"

That seemed so unlikely that she laughed, which hurt, a lot. She asked for her medkit and took as much morphine as she thought her body could handle. The bottle warned about possible drowsiness as a side effect—she was out for twelve hours while Chris drove.

Eventually, Chris shook her awake and helped her out of the Jeep. They were outside the rear entrance of a brick building. She didn't have to ask what sort of building it was. The playground and the books and the broken remains of a child's desk a few feet away told her they were at another school. Chris led her inside to a sad, lonely classroom where he had already set up her sleeping bag and had a pot of water heating. The medkit was there, as well as a change of clothes.

"I'm gonna go hide the Jeep," he said. "It might take a few minutes."

He was leaving her alone for a reason. The crotch of her blue jeans was covered in old blood. She hesitated, afraid to take off her pants, worried that a part of her would be hanging out, or that she'd be swollen and turning purple. Her little hands shook as she eased her pants off.

She was stained with blood. It sat in crumbles in the folds of her flesh. She washed herself while looking up at the blackboard where math problems had been hand drawn in fading chalk. There were six problems, all long division.

As she cleaned herself, she stared off into nothing, her mind working out the math problems in her head. In the spur of the moment, she had decided that she wasn't going to look at where she had been punched. The idea was far too frightening. If she was ruptured; if her insides were torn up, she would die. That was all there was to it.

For all she knew, she was the closest thing to a surgeon between Iowa and the Colorado Rockies and she couldn't exactly cut herself open and poke around.

"I need more pills," she whispered. This time, in addition to the morphine, she added Amoxicillin, a fat pink pill that crawled its way down her throat. It was a "just in case" medicine to ward off any possible infection.

She then dressed herself. Despite moving slowly and carefully, she cried out on more than one occasion and there were tears in her blue eyes by the time she was put together. It could have been worse. Chris had chosen a white, long sleeve button up shirt, as well as a plaid skirt—both relatively easy to get on and off.

Exhausted by the work of bathing and dressing, she fell asleep curled in her sleeping bag. The day passed and when she woke, she was hungry, which she took for a good sign. Of course, as a doctor in training, the fact that she was no longer bleeding and that her temperature and pulse were normal, was more significant.

"Where are we?" she asked when Chris roused himself from his sleeping bag. He looked bleary and red-eyed, suggesting that taking care of her while crossing a land crawling with bandits and slavers was wearing on him.

"Ten miles north of Davenport," he said, scratching his head beneath a wild thicket of unruly dark hair. "Have you got your memory back? Do you know what we're after?"

175

Her first inclination was to shake her head, but decided that perhaps hidden memories didn't necessarily flash into a person's mind. Perhaps they had to be accessed, they had to be thought over. She ran over the particulars of her last trip eastward—and came away with nothing new. "Not yet."

His face fell. "So what do we do? The roads are getting crowded. Last night I passed three different groups. Luckily none of them turned on us."

Jillybean went with her old standby: "We have to get in close." She was always at her best when she was within knife fighting distance of a problem. It lent urgency to the situation, which seemed to kick her neurons into gear.

When the sun went down, they prepared to leave the school. Jillybean was stronger now and the pain in her tummy manageable. She took two Tylenol and another Amoxicillin and although she was stiff, she was good to go, taking a turn behind the wheel.

"Thank goodness," Chris said. "You don't know what it's like trying to drive like a frog."

"I can swim like a frog, or actually like a tadpole. That's what means a baby frog. When I was in swim lessons, I was a tadpole, which was pretty good, I think."

He gave her a look before rolling his eyes. "That's not something to brag about if you ask me. In real life, they just squiggle along. You should say you swim like a shark or something cool."

"But I can't," she said, as she started the engine and turned on her monitors and the gauges; everything was in the green. "Are we full up on ammo and bombs?"

"Yeah," he said, biting at his thumb nail. "I don't like getting this close to guys like the Colonel. I know he's dead and all, but whoever took over might be hot after you."

"It'll be okay. There's like a million ways into Davenport. They aren't all gonna be watched and even if they are, it's night out. They won't know who we are. We'll hide the Jeep somewhere in the city, go up by the river and check things out. It'll be okay, I'll get us there."

And she did. Jillybean was extra careful, taking the least traveled roads and moving at a snail's pace when anything felt in the least bit hinky. Knowing that she wasn't at a hundred percent, she eased the Jeep to within half a mile of the Mississippi.

From there, she and Chris turned themselves into passable monsters and walked slowly and somewhat stiffly, down to the river wall where she pulled a pair of binoculars from her pack. What once had been the Colonel's island had changed. No longer were there only rolls of concertina wire stacked up at the river's edge. Actual walls made up of cinderblocks ringed the island. This long wall was topped by barbed wire and guarded by fifty foot towers that ranged at intervals along the perimeter. There would be no sneaking back onto the island.

Although she hadn't known the scope of the change, Jillybean was prepared. "Can I have the heli-drone please?"

The drone sat under Chris's outer monster clothes. He shrugged it off his back and watched as Jillybean set it up for flight. "Can I fly it?" he asked, eagerly.

Since they were in a perilous situation and there was a lot riding on the flight of the little drone, she wanted to say, no, however he had saved her life and she owed him. "Just be careful, okay? Gentle moves, only. And don't feel the need to speed it all around. It's not a toy…alright, it kinda is one, but it's the only one I have left."

"I'll be careful. So, can we put a bomb on it?"

"No, jeeze. This is a 'look around' kind of mission. Those could be nice bad guys for all we know." Without a bomb on board, he was less enthusiastic about flying the drone. She pointed at the controls to the "up" key. "You're going to want to go straight up and then across the water. From there, I'll tell you what to do."

"Alright, sure." He pressed the key and the drone whisked upwards until it was lost in the dark. Then they both turned to the iPad to watch the footage from the onboard camera.

"Okay, you're high enough now. Go straight east. That's what means that way." She pointed across the water.

Exasperated, he snorted. "I know which way east is, jeeze. I can see the island right there."

"Sorry. Keep going." He actually had a fine touch with the drone and after a deep breath, she was able to relax and concentrate on the screen. She gave directions to the little harbor, where she saw the tiny figures of men scurrying around getting ready to launch a boat she didn't recognize. From above, all she could make of it was that it was a motorboat of some sort.

The harbor had also been modified. There was now a short wall of flat wooden boards blocking the entrance. Jillybean knew there had to be some way to move it, but the mechanism wasn't obvious with the dark and the sharp viewing angle.

Still, it didn't matter. There was no sneaking onto the island. The towers were manned and the guards seemed extra alert.

"You getting anything?" Chris asked.

"So far, uh-uh. Maybe if I retrace my steps. Head inland a bit. No, to your right. Not that far. Now back."

Chris groaned and pushed the controller into her hand. "It's not as much fun as I thought it would be. You do it."

She was happy to. Her concentration was much better as she seemed to will the drone along the exact path she had taken four months before: up the river wall and into the shadows along Rodman Avenue. She had slipped behind the manufacturing center, which had smelled overpoweringly of metal and oil, and climbed the fire escape to the roof.

From there she had guided Neil until he had been captured. Here, was her first memory break: she simply couldn't remember getting off the building or setting the bomb. For over a minute she sat there racking her brains, but the memory was gone. Had she suppressed it, or was it just so insignificant that it hadn't been worth remembering?

Eventually, she moved on, following her memory as she went to rescue Neil from the Colonel. She remembered going into his house with a hand grenade in one hand and a claymore mine strapped to her chest. "Only it was a fake mine," she whispered.

"Uh, Jillybean?" Chris asked.

"Hold on." They had then left the house to go pick up some ammunition. They were trying to fool the Colonel into thinking that was all they had been after to begin with. "But it didn't work...because he had discovered who Neil was."

Chris tugged on her arm. "Jillybean!" he hissed.

"Not yet," she hissed back. Her memory was getting jumbled. The trip to the armory was sketchy in her head. It kept getting mixed up with her telling Neil: *He knows who we are.* And then there was a flash of light and a body flopping...

This time Chris was more urgent. "They're coming for us!" The boat she'd seen earlier had cleared the harbor and was streaking right for them.

Chapter 21

Jillybean

She was pulled from her memory—it was like coming up out of a deep sleep. Chris yanked her around and pointed at the river. "They're coming! We have to go."

"But I was almost there," she said. She didn't know if that was true or not, however something about the trip from the Colonel's house seemed significant, but she just didn't know what. What occupied her mind was Ipes yammering into her head: *You're a good guy!*

Chris began hauling her along, away from the river, as behind them the sound of the motor boat grew louder. She wanted to tell him, *just a second*, but there were no seconds to waste—the boat's motor wasn't the only thing that could be heard. A car was coming as well.

Jillybean was yanked to her right as Chris changed direction; he wasn't going to let them get boxed in. If Jillybean had been more aware of what was going on around her she would have said that was smart, but she was still trying to piece together her memory of that night months before.

She was supposed to be a good guy. Ipes had been insistent about that and that was why she had tied up the guards the way she had. She had fooled them into thinking she had tied a hand grenade in with their ropes. *We don't kill innocent people*, Ipes had said over and over…or had he just said it once and she had let her mind dwell on it?

"Stop," Chris whispered, pulling her down. They were huddled next to a white painted wall that ran for another fifty yards. It was a barren stretch and he didn't look like he wanted to chance being so exposed. Chris had his head cocked, listening. After a few seconds, he turned them around.

"What are you doing?" she asked. She had been so far up in her own head that she was lost.

His answer was curt and frightening: "They're boxing us in." They hurried back the way they had come, but only for half a block and then Chris ducked into a building that, in her preoccupation, she hadn't noticed before.

It got her attention now. For a second, as she was caught between the confusion of her memories and the fear of the present, she thought they had stepped into a room filled with people. The dark forms stood in silence, or sat with books open on their knees, or huddled together in groups of two and three. And there were children—motionless children.

That was what clued her in. These were statues carved in stone, or cast in bronze and cement. There were hundreds, set around stone ponds or wooden tables or in circles like silent prayer groups. It would be easy to take seats next to them and hide in plain sight so to speak, but Chris pushed his way through them.

Drawn by his phenomenal instinct for survival, he headed out the back door where twenty feet away was a much larger building where the statues were manufactured. There were thousands of finished and half-finished stone people all over the place.

Once more it made sense to stop. Jillybean needed the rest. Her insides were hurting and she was tired and her head was in a spin. She felt as though she was missing something important and at the same time she knew the missing chunks of memory were not *the* memory that the voice in her head wanted her to remember.

Chris wouldn't stop. He marched through the building until they were on the other side, where he cracked a fire door that opened onto a loading dock, and listened to the night. "I think they're still in the showroom. Come on."

He led once more, stealing like a shadow into a residential neighborhood. They hadn't gone more than a block before there was a shout and the sound of a car speeding in their direction. Chris took off, running through a backyard with Jillybean straggling behind. He had to help her over a fence, but when she climbed down the other side, she found a monster charging.

The only thing she could do was pull her .38. "Don't," Chris said, from the other side of the fence. He had his eye to a crack in the boards. In the dark there seemed to be nothing to him but the eye and the voice. "They'll hear."

She didn't have a choice. She didn't have his speed or strength or his calm when a monster was crashing down on her. It took three shots to drop it and by the time it did, Chris was over the fence and pulling her along.

Jillybean didn't need his acute hearing to know that the bad guys had heard and were closing in once again. And they weren't the only ones. Monsters from all over were converging; Jillybean could hear them in the next street.

Chris struck out to their right, but she stopped him. Cutting that way would mean a string of fences to climb and she was nearing the end of her rope. "No, we'll blend in with the monsters. There's no way they'll think a couple of kids were spying on them."

This struck him as a good idea and they went into their moaning and stumbling about routine just as the side gate was destroyed and a pile of the beasts came charging in. On the way to the river, she had given Chris some pointers and he wasn't bad as a monster.

She was the weak link. She'd forgotten she was carrying the iPad and right away two of them turned towards her, forcing her to drop it. Afraid that it would get stepped on, she stood over it, watching the feed from the drone she had named, Matilda. In all the running around, it had drifted over the river and was dangerously low. If her course wasn't corrected, she would splash down in seconds. Luckily, just then a car pulled up and someone started ripping off a machine gun.

With the monster's attention diverted, she dropped down and stabbed the up arrow sending the drone shooting into the night sky. She also angled it towards them, but didn't get a chance to finish as Chris was once again yanking her along. There were more men and more guns in front and a single heavy banging from what sounded like a .50 cal coming from behind.

They had no choice but to go for the next yard. Once more, Jillybean needed to be boosted over. She staggered across the yard to the next fence, barely looking around. Chris stopped her before she put her hands on the mid board.

"Listen." Engines were revving and roaring away. There were three of them, now.

Jillybean knelt over her iPad, bringing the drone overhead. She could see the monsters milling around in confusion. The cars had gone in three different directions, but they didn't go far. They sped for only a few blocks and then men piled out of them spreading out creating a line that Chris and Jillybean would have to get past in order to escape.

Without Matilda, it would've been impossible.

With the drone feeding her information, she guided them first north and then east. They had only progressed a block before she saw the men moving again, racing for the cars. The bad guys couldn't have seen them and yet, she had a sinking feeling that they were coming their way.

She only had one Bumble Ball, but her gut told her to use it. They had been crouched against a car on a street that was relatively quiet. With bad guys coming, she needed the street crowded for them to escape. As though it were a strange bomb from out of a science fiction movie, she tossed it out into the street, where it danced and blinked.

In no time, there were monsters congregating all around them and more slouching in from all directions. The two children ducked into a house so that they wouldn't get accidentally shot when the men showed up. But it was an unnecessary move.

Almost immediately after throwing the Bumble Ball, the cars had stopped and now they were a few blocks away honking their horns.

"I don't get it," Chris said. "How did they know about the ball? There's no way they could see that thing from where they were. Do they have a spotter?" He went to the front window and peeked out from the corner. "But where is he? He has to be close because they caught us moving through that other yard."

A cold shiver went up Jillybean's spine as she realized what they were really up against. "They got a drone, too. That's the only explanation."

"Oh, boy, we're in trouble," Chris hissed, putting his cheek to the window and staring upwards, trying to pick out the drone against a black sky.

"You won't see it that way," Jillybean said. Instead of looking up, she was staring down, huddled over her iPad. She sent Matilda five hundred feet into the air, and centered it on the Bumble Ball. If she were working the bad guy's drone, that's where she would be.

At first she saw nothing and so she gradually dropped Matilda lower, as she did, she sent her eyes scanning back and forth across the face of the iPad, noting every pixel change.

Chris with his better than perfect eyesight saw the enemy drone before she did. "Right there, to the left and down. Do you see it?"

She didn't at first, but then she saw a tiny blinking light much further below her than she had expected. Grinning, she angled her quad-motored heli-drone at the enemy drone. This was her sort of battle. Muscle and might meant nothing compared to brains and quickness of reactions.

"Get it, Matilda!" Jillybean cried, as she dropped her drone smack-dab on top of the enemy drone and drove it towards the outstretched branches of a tree, fifty feet below them. The enemy drone reacted quicker than she expected and the image on her iPad went crazy for a second with stars shining upside down and the land way over on its side, but then she fought Matilda back to square and pushed it higher.

In this sort of battle, because of the bottom slung cameras, position was everything. Once more she drove Matilda down onto the enemy drone. This time she didn't try to send it crashing in one move. She banged it down and then lifted up. As expected, the enemy drone made some odd jerky movements and then righted itself.

"Ha! It doesn't know we're here yet," Jillybean laughed. The drone yawed left and then right. It then seesawed. "The pilot is testing its controls." It would try to go up next and so she settled directly above it.

When the two machines clashed, it was without sound and, really, without much in the way of excitement. Her video feed went blurry and showed only a dull grey as she pushed Matilda downward for all it was worth. It was hard to tell exactly where the two drones were in relation to the tree and, afraid that Matilda would get caught as well, she pulled up after a steady count of four.

The tree was a wide shadow twenty feet below, while the other drone was a grey fuzz shooting off to the right, jinking left and right. "Oops," Jillybean said, as she brought her drone up again.

"Oops?" Chris asked. "Why'd you say oops?"

"He knows we're here," she answered, tersely. The two drones were zipping in a near-silent *whirr* all over the sky. Like a hawk after a pigeon, she hounded it up and down, left and right until she was able to crash them together. Once more the feed went crazy as the two drones were locked, one on top of the other.

The other pilot tried everything to dislodge her drone, but she was flying more by feel than by sight. Her fingers danced over the controls, giving each just a touch in their turn. In this way she knew the exact position of Matilda in relationship to the horizon and she could feel where the enemy drone was by his response to the pressure.

Unfortunately for her enemy, his abilities were as stunted as his imagination. He tried rocking back and forth; he tried stopping in midair; he even attempted to drop out from beneath her and loop around. The drones were not built for that sort of maneuver and they became separated when the enemy drone pivoted so far that its blades no longer provided lift.

They were close to the ground when the drone turned on its side and plummeted. Perhaps the operator thought he was completing the loop because at the last second, the drone flopped over and crashed onto the roof of a house.

"Yes!" Jillybean cried, pumping her little fist at her victory. "That'll do, Matilda."

"Hmmm, nice," Chris said, without much enthusiasm over the anticlimactic end of the battle. "Too bad it didn't like, explode, you know? That would have been super cool. Hey, can you put a gun on it. Like the little, wimpy one you carry?"

She tried to picture how that would work; but after a time, she decided that it wasn't feasible. "I don't think that'll work, although a piece of string taped to the underside could be used to take out one of the propellers. If I was able to dip it right."

"String? Wow, exciting."

"Who says it has to be exciting?" she asked, watching her feed as the other drone twitched a bit, its blades spinning uselessly. "Winning is winning and now we can escape. There is that."

He nodded, again without enthusiasm. "We can escape, but to where? Are you gonna want us to go down to the new River King's city? I've heard rumors about that place and they aren't good. It's gonna be worse than this was."

"What sort of rumors?"

"I heard that ever since the old king died things have gotten bad. You know like battles in the streets and people fighting all the time. They got two groups, the east bridge guys and the west bridge guys. Each group wants control of the bridge."

It was astounding to Jillybean that she had somehow made things worse. "But it really isn't my fault," she said, mostly to herself. "And yeah, we're gonna have to go there, but we'll use Matilda again. From further away this time. It'll be okay."

"First we gotta get out of here," Chris said. "What happens if they have another drone?"

"It'll take them a few minutes to get it ready," she said. "And we'll be long gone by then." With trusty Matilda scouting the way, they made their way to the Jeep and fled from Davenport as fast as they could, taking a bewildering number of turns, and backtracking and setting traps just in case they were followed. However there was no indication that they were, and eventually they relaxed…slightly.

They were still deep into bandit country and each of the three hundred miles that they traveled had to be taken one at a time and with great caution.

It took them five days and every night they had at least one scare. Headlights would suddenly flick on behind them or they would run into a downed tree and an ambush, or trucks would come out of nowhere to try to cut them off in front or behind.

Each time a little smoke, or a blast from the M249 would do the trick and they would escape out into the night.

Although Jillybean grew stronger every day, the constant stress and fear of the ambushes made her feel like she was becoming an old woman by the time they saw a sign: *Cape Girardeau 10 Miles*. She was all too happy to get out of the Jeep and proceed on foot.

The lands around the bridge were simply crawling with monsters which was a relief, at least to her. Chris was never comfortable being so close to the creatures. He hated their smell and the way they looked and the stupid noises they made. Worst of all, he hated the dreadfully slow speed at which he was forced to move.

If he had his way, he would run all the way to Cape Girardeau. "I've been too cooped up. It's killing me."

"You'll be fine once we figure what all this is about and you'll love Estes Valley. You can run everywhere you want there."

"There you go again, thinking I'm gonna be going with you, which I'm not. You don't get a cool Jeep and then stick it up in the mountains where there's nothing to do but freeze and count sheep."

Jillybean hissed him into silence as a monster was angling towards them. It wasn't much of one, and in the dark, it didn't see where the sidewalk met the street and tripped onto its face where it struggled with only stumps where its hands had been.

Even with the danger behind them she didn't go back to their argument. In the last five days they'd had it more times than they had been ambushed and she couldn't believe how pig-headed he was about it.

She assumed that it was because he was a boy. He was *very* boyish in a way that was incomprehensible to her. Walls could not be walked around, they had to be climbed. Squirrels could not be allowed to peaceably gather their nuts; he had to throw rocks at them. He practiced burping his responses to her. He loved fire and explosions and found ripping off a fart the height of hilarity. Worst of all, he went out of his way to tease her on every subject.

It was infuriating, but she stayed with him partially because of the deal they had struck and partially because of the crush she had on him. It was a crush she denied both to herself and to him.

With the monster struggling to find its feet, she pointed them into the nearest building, which happened to be a bank. She locked the heavy glass door knowing that even the biggest of the new wave of giant monsters wasn't going to be able to get in. "I think we're close enough to launch Matilda," she said. When Chris didn't answer, she turned to see him going behind the teller stations to the vault.

"Look at this door," he said in awe, as he heaved it back. It was almost two feet thick and made a moaning noise as it opened. He knocked it with his knuckles and then grinned, shaking out his hand. "When I get a house, I'm gonna come back and get this door. Wouldn't that be cool?"

"Yeah. Hey, I'm gonna send Matilda out."

He only shrugged. "That's kinda your thing not mine. I'm gonna get all the money and pile it up. You wanna jump in it when Matilda gets back?"

It sounded like fun, however what she was doing was serious and the danger very real. With Chris around, the voice and its constant announcement of impending doom had been very quiet and yet she still felt the urgency. To her it was very real.

"Boys, sheesh," she muttered, turning from Chris and picking up the drone he had set down when they had walked in.

Matilda was starting to look worn. She had been with Jillybean since her days in Vinita and now there were scratches all over her and a tiny nick on one of her blades. There was also a small sticker on the lid to her battery compartment. Chris had put it there; a skull and crossed bones like on a pirate's flag.

"It signifies her first dogfight victory," he had said.

Jillybean had beamed at him for his consideration, to which he had rolled his eyes. "You be good and careful," she said to the drone as she flicked it on. She then went to the door and, after checking both directions, she darted out and set the drone in the street. She zipped back in and locked the door once more behind her.

"I'm sending her up," she yelled over to Chris.

"Okay, good," he called back.

Once more she complained: "Boys!" She thought that maybe she didn't want him coming back to the valley after all. If he teamed up with Joe Gates, the two of them would be the most irritating couple on the planet. "And that would suck," she said, pulling a chair over to the glass door.

She sat, folding her dress primly beneath her. She no longer wore the plaid skirt or the white shirt Chris had picked out. They had been too dull for her tastes. The white shirt had given way to a pink one—pink was her signature color. She had mentioned that to Chris once, which caused him to begin a fake gagging spell.

As she couldn't wear all pink, her dress was cowgirl themed: tan with carnations along the hem and the waist. Beneath it she wore blue jeans and her old Keds because there were still fences to climb, and monsters to run from and bad guys to battle.

With Chris cackling in the background, she sent Matilda out into the night. Perhaps, she thought, it was better he was preoccupied. Along with all the rest of his uber-boyishness, he had the tendency to talk too much. Sometimes, when she was feeling lonely or frightened, his blathering was good. This was not one of those times.

She needed to concentrate and it helped that he wouldn't be asking: "Do you remember, yet?" every few seconds. She was worried enough on her own because she had the distinct impression that there was nothing in Cape Girardeau for her.

Matilda floated over the sad and desolate city. It had shrunk. The double fence she had sent her monster army through had been abandoned and the original fencing had been reinforced. Despite this, it didn't appear as though the remaining people were crammed in on each other. The town seemed empty, except for the trash that is.

The place was a mess. Broken glass blanketed the city, while on every block there were overturned cars. Spent shell casings were cast about by the thousands and there were empty cans and discarded wrappers in the gutters.

And there were bodies decomposing in the streets. She could almost smell the stench through the video feed.

"This is my fault," she whispered. She had taken down an evil king only to have two even worse kings take his place. "If I had known, I...I...I wouldn't have changed anything," she said, speaking plainly. "The king needed to die. Probably these ones do too, but that's not my job. I mean I sure hope it's not. I don't want to do that anymore."

She sighed, remembering how she had planned on being a normal girl. "It's not working, is it?"

All of a sudden, she was overcome by a strange wave of loneliness. She missed her best friend: Ipes. If he hadn't died, he would have helped her understand what was going on and he would have helped her cope and he was always trying to get her to act "normal." He had wanted her to be normal from the very beginning.

"But he's gone."

Because of his crazy, bat-like hearing, she didn't add: *All I have is Christian.* Chris wasn't the best at helping her to be normal. He was helpful in the way boys were. If there was a monster to kill, he'd kill it, and if there was a fire in need of lighting, he would happily light it. For him, all of life's problems were very black and white.

He cared for her, but he didn't understand her. "You okay?" he asked, coming out of the vault as if her thoughts had summoned him.

"Yeah," she said, with a shrug. "I'm just sad and kinda tired. Cape Girardeau is as bad as you said and it's a little bit my fault."

"Not hardly. The city is full of bad guys doing bad things. Were you supposed to kill them all? Nope. Forget about them. Oh yeah, speaking of forgetting, did you remember what you were supposed to remember?"

"I don't think so." Other than the normal sporadic blank spots in her memory, she hadn't forgotten a thing about Cape

Girardeau and the bridge and the River King and all of the explosions.

Unexpectedly, Chris smiled. "Then we're done, right? And I get the Jeep? Don't worry, I won't leave you out here. I'll take you at least to the Kansas border."

"Sorry, but we're not done. What I forgotted must be on the other side of the river and that's what means we have to cross it, but don't worry, I crossed it lots of times. It's easy."

His smile faded and the sharp look was back in his eyes as he appraised her. After a moment, he made a face and grunted: "You're not lying. I kinda wish you were."

"I'm not a liar-person," she declared, an eyebrow raised and her lips pursed. The look of indignation lasted only a second and then her features drooped. "I wish I was done with this, too. I'm tired of bad guys and all that. And I'm tired of people dying."

The two were silent, each staring down at the iPad, which showed a dark and dead city as Matilda buzzed back to the bank.

Out of the blue, Chris said: "I miss dodge ball. I loved it."

Jillybean countered, saying: "I miss my mom and dad and my friends back in Philadelphia, Becky and Sue."

"I miss pizza and going to the movies." His white smile was back. "I used to sneak in to the movies and watch like six in a row."

"I miss being a kid, for reals," she said. "You know, like doing kid stuff and not having to be ascared all the time. And you know what I miss most of all? I miss my birthday."

Chris' smile broadened. "I can help you there. Close your eyes. This is no joke, close your eyes." When she did, he ran off, his steps barely discernible and when he came back, he was so silent that she smelled his earthy boyness before she heard him say: "Happy Birthday."

She opened her eyes and her mouth at the same time. She about to explain that she was a May-flower not a March-whatever, but then she saw what he held and her words got stuck in her throat. It was a silver necklace of white diamonds and the deepest, bluest sapphires she had ever seen.

"What do you think?" he asked, eagerly. "It's got to be worth a million, easy."

"I can't," she whispered. "I really, really like it, but I can't take it. It isn't yours to give to me."

He scoffed in that way of his that made her feel less like a genius and more like a seven-year-old girl. "It is mine. The old

189

owner is long gone. She probably died or was turned into a monster ages ago. And we are on a quest and when you're on a quest you get to keep any treasure you find. That is a fact. If we had defeated a dragon and found this, you'd be okay with keeping it. That's also true if we found a sunken pirate ship and this was in the chest of booty. Am I right?"

"Yeah, I guess so. Can you put it on me?" She turned and lifted up the thick ponytail that made up the majority of her hair. When he put the necklace on her, she could feel his breath and it gave her such an odd feeling that a shiver went up her spine.

"You look beautiful," he said.

Without saying a word, she dropped the iPad and ran to the bathroom. The room was black and yet the stalls loomed, looking like openings into some vast deep hell. She turned her back on them and, using her mini-Mag-lite, she stared into the mirror and saw that she was beautiful.

"Does he like me?" she asked. Her voice, small as it was, echoed and she shrank down in alarm afraid that he might have heard. She was pink-cheeked when she stood straight again. "Boy, if he heard that I'm gonna be so…"

Movement in the mirror froze her. There was something or someone in the middle stall. With the Mag-lite sending a diffused light around the room, she could see the ragged outlines of a person sitting on the toilet.

Her first thought was that it had been her imagination playing tricks. Then the body became somewhat clearer and she thought that someone had died in the bathroom months and months before and that this was their remains. Then, when it stood, she thought it was a monster coming for her.

A scream built up in her throat but got stuck in her windpipe, strangling her. She choked on nothing as the body spoke: *You've forgotten something very important.*

The scream burst out of her and rang on the tiles as her mind spun in horror and fear and confusion. The creature was impossibly big, its head higher than the walls of the stall. And worse, it was gruesomely dead. Its flesh fell away from it in moldy tatters while its innards poured out to splatter onto the floor.

You've forgotten something very important, it said again, advancing on the little girl who stood, frozen in shock. What she was seeing and hearing was impossible. This was no monster. This was an actual truly dead person talking and walking.

"How is this happening?" The only answer she could come up with was the worst one imaginable: "I'm still crazy," she said and with the thing looming over her, smelling like raw sewage and threatening to tear her to pieces, she calmly turned and walked out of the bathroom.

"You don't like it?" Chris asked, upon seeing her pale face.

For just a flash, she thought he was referring to her craziness. She began to nod her head but as she did, she felt the weight of the diamonds and sapphires upon her skin. "I actually love it. Thanks so much. But…"

"But we have to go?" he asked.

She glanced back at the bathroom before answering: "Yeah."

Chapter 22

Jillybean

The only adventure they had leaving the area was when they went to find Matilda. After Jillybean had dropped the iPad, Matilda had crashed. She was unresponsive and the video feed showed a steady shot of part of a highway with a strip of black behind it.

"That's the river," Jillybean said and, after looking over the map of the area, checking the drone's last known height, and factoring in a four mile-an-hour northwesterly wind, she led Chris right to the machine. It was stuck fifty feet in the air, far out on a tree branch.

"Hold my gun, I got this," Chris informed her and then launched himself at the tree.

He was twenty feet up the trunk before she could say: "There's an easier way….and a much less dangerous one," she added under her breath.

"What danger?" he asked. "Trees are our friends. They won't let you fall if you treat them right."

She smiled up at him instead of answering and made sure to keep her smile plastered on her face just in case he could hear that too. If she had her way, no one would have gone out on a dwindling limb five stories in the air to get a drone that could be replaced with just a little bit of searching. As much as she liked Matilda there were more just like her in most cities and large towns.

But he's getting the drone for me, she told herself and again the idea of a crush presented itself to her. It left her a little dizzy and confused. *If he likes me then why won't he come to Colorado with me?* She had no answer to that. As smart as she was, she just couldn't get into the head of a boy. Sometimes she considered them to almost be a separate species.

They were all crazy, but this boy was crazier than most. He went further and further onto the limb until it had bent far over and it wasn't long before first one foot slipped and then the second. He was hanging by his hands alone. Jillybean began to feel a pain in her stomach as instead of retreating back to the safety of the trunk, he went on until he was only two feet from the drone.

Then came a sharp crack as the branch broke. Matilda came free and dropped to the ground where three of her propellers broke. Jillybean couldn't have cared less. Her heart was in her throat as Chris held on to the branch as it swung down and towards the tree. Thankfully, the branch was a living thing and had not snapped straight off like a dead branch would have. The rough layer beneath the bark peeled back as the branch swung, but didn't tear away completely.

Chris hit the trunk with a jarring thud but managed to hold on. A moment later, he began laughing. He laughed so hard that he had trouble keeping his hold and ended up slumped over the broken branch. He laughed so hard that two monsters came lurching out of the gloom to eat him. Jillybean distracted them with the injured drone. It couldn't fly straight or really at all. It went up at an angle and buzzed in a strange curve, looking like a futuristic, mechanical frisbee. The monsters stared at it, engrossed while Chris climbed the rest of the way down.

"Ah well," was all he said about the broken drone. "Let's go." This was what Jillybean could not understand about him: he had foolishly risked his life for the little machine and now three seconds later it was as if the episode had never happened.

They made it back to the Jeep, where they took turns looking at the big map of America. She sighed over it, tired and glum. She had been all over the eastern part of the country: from New York to Georgia, up through Alabama and into Tennessee, Kentucky and southern Illinois. Her hidden memory had to be in one of the fourteen different eastern states she had traveled through—an immense area.

She wanted to give up, but even as that thought went through her head she heard an echo of the voice once more repeating the same aggravating message. She wouldn't be allowed to give up. "I guess I'll head towards the northeast. I should probably start in Philadelphia. That's where it all began. I'd understand if you don't want to come with me."

He shot her his: *are you crazy?* look. "Huh? Where else would I go? Besides this is a pretty fun adventure so far. It's a little light on the loot, but I don't know what I'd be doing otherwise. You know what I mean? North Platte sucked. I mean it really sucked donkey di…uh, sorry. That's what some of the guys in one of my groups used to say."

She was so happy that he was coming with her, that she glossed over the near-use of, not just a bad word, but a very ugly image. "Okay good, good," she gushed. "First thing we gotta do is build a boat that will hold the Jeep and get her across the river."

"What? Really? You can do that?"

She shrugged. "I think so. I turned this inflatable bounce house into a sailboat once. And asides, making a boat has got to be easier than building a new Jeep like Jessica…I mean El Diablo."

"That's okay. She can be Jessica for now. She isn't mine, yet. So, how the heck do we build a boat? And can we get a cannon on it?"

A laugh escaped her before she realized that he was being serious. "I think that would be a waste. It's just a short trip across the river. I don't think we have to worry about pirates." The crack about pirates was her idea of a joke and she started to laugh at it only just then her eyes fell on the open map of America.

It was crisscrossed with tan lines representing the highway system, but was also filled with little blue lines. "Rivers," she mumbled. Her tiny pointer finger began tracing one that ran from the Mississippi all the way to Pittsburgh. "That's most of the trip," she said, her mind buzzing with a new idea.

Four months before, she had travelled down the Mississippi on an unimpressive pontoon boat and it had been the safest part of her journey. "Maybe, just maybe," she whispered, her mind zipping along, jumping from idea to idea.

Chris interrupted her thinking: "We can get a cannon?"

"Huh? No…or maybe if we come across one. We will need something to protect us, that's for certain. And we'll need something more durable." Her initial vision had been of a simple affair: a basic, reinforced, flat rectangle built from looted wood from a hardware store. In order to buoy it she was going to use fifty rolls of bubble wrap caged beneath the boat by a light screen of mesh.

As motors were, for the most part, just lying around, she figured it would take a day to build the boat and another few hours to attach a motor. But that was for just a simple river crossing. A journey of a week or two would require something far more substantial, like a real river barge.

"And really, there are plenty of them," she said.

"Plenty of what?" Chris looked suspicious. "You aren't talking about cannons, I know it."

With the idea of traveling by boat planted firmly in her head, she switched on the Jeep's monitors and rumbled the engine into life as she said: "Of course not, silly. I'm talking about barges and that's what means a flat boat that goes on the river and carries stuff around."

"I know what barges are and I also know the old river king had them all destroyed. Everyone knows that, including you, so why are you bringing up barges?"

"Because they might not all be as destroyed as you think. You know how many boats used to be on this river? *A lot*. And do you know how many guys he had knocking holes in them? *A little*. And that's what means I bet they didn't do all that good of a job. I bet we can fix one pretty easy."

She put the Jeep in gear and went in search of a barge and by sunrise she discovered that there were fewer than expected. On the way south with Neil, so many months before, she had seen plenty of boats. Many had been half-drawn up on shore and others were tied to piers and some were hanging from davits as if the apocalypse had caught them in the process of being repaired.

The winter had changed things, drastically. The first thirty-two boats they came across were lolling, half-submerged in the muddy waters. Some were nose down, others had just a mast showing above the waterline, but most were keeled over on their sides, looking like the carcasses of whales.

"Maybe we should try looking somewhere different," Chris suggested. "I bet all the good boats are out in the ocean by now, halfway to Canada."

"Probably," Jillybean agreed. "What we need is a boat-selling place." In no time, they found a little house off the river road and, as the previous owners had been elderly, they had a stack of eight phone books in a hall closet, the oldest of them was three years older than Chris.

Jillybean went for the newest. "Okay-dokey. Here's a close place. Cairo Marine repairs. Good, it's a repairing place, too. It should have everything we need."

"You mean a bunch of already broken boats? I'm sorry, Jillybean, you may be smart or whatever, but do you know anything about boats? Or how to fix them?"

"How hard could it be?" she asked. "They float and the motor goes in the back. That's pretty much all we need to know for the most part." She guessed there would be more to it than that, however she wasn't going to waste her energy on worrying. Either solutions would present themselves to her or they wouldn't, and she guessed that they would.

As it was still night and they didn't want to give themselves away, they kept the lights off and drove at the same torpid pace they'd been using for days. Chris was tired of the pace. He drummed his fingers and sighed frequently and blew out in long gusts. Nothing he did would get Jillybean to go any faster and it was an hour and a half before they pulled into the Cairo lot.

"That sure is a lot of cranes," Chris said. He was leaned way over the console, his shoulder touching hers. "Movement on the right." He pointed at a shadow in one of the many buildings—there were seventeen of them, some big warehouses, some smaller storage buildings, all of them were rusting through their fading paint jobs.

Jillybean turned the Jeep in a slow circle while Chris practically sat in her lap, his eyes glued to the monitors. "I see three of them," he said, reaching with one hand for the door handle and with the other for his knife.

"Hold on for all goodness sakes. There's an easier way, you know. I could just run them down. You know squish them under the tires. It's icky and that's what means gross, but it's like real easy."

"Where's the fun in that?" he asked, tipped her a mischievous wink and then darted out.

"Oh golly!" she cried. She had yet to repair the passenger side camera, so she had no idea what the boy was doing. She couldn't even turn the Jeep in that direction for fear of running him over. "I could go the other way I suppose and circ…" Something struck the side of the Jeep.

It was too heavy to have been Chris. She almost opened her door, however a blur in the front monitor stopped her. The image was of mottled grey over grey and she couldn't tell exactly what it was except she knew it wasn't Chris.

Run it over! the thought struck her with a rich lustfulness. It wasn't a thought from outside her head or from another personality. It was her own idea. A part of her envied Chris and his physicality. He acted, while she considered. He hurled his body into every problem, while she hurled her intellect. He was primal and she was civilized in a world where the civilized were at a distinct disadvantage.

With a savage growl more befitting Eve the killer who had lived inside her head, she yanked the gear shifter down to drive and *almost* pulled her foot from the brake. Her mind got in the way once more. A thump on the side of the Jeep coupled with a monster in front could have few explanations.

"He's under the Jeep. Or he was." She didn't dare spurt forward now. Slowly, carefully, as though she were putting the pin back into a grenade, she shifted the car back into park. She sat there straining her ears and staring at the now blank monitors waiting for some sign that Chris was alive.

When a face, leering and grinning an awful, inhuman grin suddenly materialized in the front monitor she shrieked and jumped back. Chris' laughter seeped through the steel plates she had welded in place and she was within an inch of putting the Jeep in gear for real.

"For reals," she said to herself, her lips pursed in an angry pucker.

Her door opened a second later. The boy took one look at her pissy expression and broke down laughing so hard that he couldn't stand. He lay on the ground holding his belly as the sun crept into the sky. The monsters were dead, the tendons at the back of their knees cut and holes punched into their temples with the same knife.

"You shoulda seen your face. It was…" He couldn't go on, made weak by laughter. She stepped over him and wished she could have slammed the Jeep's door, but it was too heavy and she was too weak. It made a cranky, creaking noise as it shut and she had to settle for that.

Chapter 23

Jillybean

With the monsters dead, she had free reign of the yard and the buildings. Without waiting for Chris or even looking in his direction, she pulled on her backpack and marched to the closest building.

Metal had never stank in her nostrils before, however this thirty by forty-foot building had an ugly, industrial stench. There wasn't much inside except tons of rusting loops of cables stacked on heavy wooden shelving and a machine that she guessed was used to splice them together and another that wound them onto giant spools.

Nothing had been touched in the building, not since the last foreman had decided that going to work when there were zombies invading both coasts was a bad idea and that had been a year and a half before. After a grunt, she left.

The next building was a machine shop where there were enough tools for Jillybean to occupy herself for years. With the equipment in front of her, she could have fashioned, not just an entire boat, but a rocket to take her to the moon and back.

As time ticked away, she went to each station, her chin at the exact height of the tables, her eyes, four inches higher, running back and forth over the buttons and the steel and the gadgets and the many parts until she had categorized it all: lathe, miller, welder, grinder, drill press, electro plating, heat treater, etc.

"Wow," she whispered.

"It's all useless without electricity, you know," Chris said, making her jump. As always, he had snuck up behind her as silent as a cat.

"Electricity isn't the problem," she said. They were two miles from the Mississippi, which went on and on forever, and as long as it did, she would have all the electricity she would ever need. In her mind, she had already constructed an enormous water wheel that spun hundred pound magnets around a copper core the size of a city bus. If she had the time, she could make enough electricity to power a city.

"The problem is time," she said. To build the wheel would be the work of months, while a shuttle to the moon would take years to craft.

Chris blew the dust off of a gear grinder. "You're right about that. I feel like I aged ten years while you were oohing and aahing over this crap. Aren't we supposed to be finding a boat?"

"You're right," she admitted. With difficulty, she left the room, leaving tiny footprints in the dust as she went to the next building and then the next and the next.

There were boats and barges and odd vessels of great size parked all over the facility. They were all damaged in one way or another. The River King's men had found that the easiest method to destroy a boat was to either throw a Molotov cocktail into the engine compartment or to set the bunker tanks on fire.

Luckily for Jillybean, the engines without boats hadn't been touched and were just sitting around gathering dust. She just had to somehow find a barge that wasn't too bad off and mate it to an engine or two. By ten that morning she had an idea how she was going to accomplish this, but by then, she was yawning at a constant rate of a one yawn every thirty seconds and couldn't stay awake any longer.

Chris, who had tired of following around after her as she muttered to herself, was already asleep. He had hidden the Jeep in the cable house, but as the smell was enough to give them a headache, he had laid out their sleeping bags in a smaller, office building. Despite how tired she was, she set her usual alarms and traps.

Nothing untoward happened that day and they both woke up in different states of mind. Jillybean had work to do and so hopped up ready to go. Chris viewed what he would be doing as "slave labor," and so he laid in his sleeping bag for an hour until the sun was nearly set.

While he pretended to sleep, she found the right boat, though it wasn't easy. The boats in the yard were of every size, from fishing boats to awkward looking dredgers, to coal barges a hundred feet long. To conserve fuel, she would need a boat just big enough to carry Jessica Jeep. It had to be sturdy with a flat bottom since there was no telling how deep the Ohio River would be. And it had to be sound. Once she got it into the water, she couldn't have it sinking under her.

The boat she located that suited her the most was named *The Lilly*. It was a pretty name for what was basically thirty feet of rust. According to the work order found in the main office, *The Lilly* had been driven aground and was in to have its hull repaired.

With all the rust, the new welds and the new steel plating were the only parts of the hull that looked seaworthy. Still it was the best of a bad lot, so she took a hammer to it, tapping all around and found that the rust didn't go deep. It was more like orange lichen that she could scrape off with a putty knife.

Next she went below to the engine room and spun her light around at what looked like a prison cell on an alien world. Everything was black and twisted and very stinky. The room was cramped and so low that if she had been even an inch taller, she would have brushed her head against the soot-covered ceiling. Glass from a broken bottle crunched under foot and stuck like burnt slivers of diamonds into the rubber soles of her Keds.

The twin inboard engines were basically unrecognizable spasms of metal, but the two masses could be nothing else. She blew out of puffed cheeks at the sight. "Oh boy," she whispered, hugging herself to keep the soot off her clothes. "This is worserer than I thought."

On the point of giving up on *The Lilly*, she climbed out onto the deck and went to the pilot house and gave the wheel a turn. From somewhere below her, she heard a corresponding squeak. Quickly, she climbed down from the boat. It was set on a series of metal stands and she was easily able to duck underneath to inspect the twin rudders.

They were on a tension cable system that was independent of the engines. "And that's what means I can steer. I just need to make it go."

"It'll never happen," Chris said, suddenly squatting down across from her. "I'll bet you a million dollars."

"I'll bet you two million," she countered. She was just about to make it three million when she had a better idea. "I bet I can get her going and if I can, you have to come back to Estes with me."

This caused his smile to falter. He thought for a moment and added: "If you can do it by yourself in two days, you have a deal." He stuck out his big paw. Confidently, she put her tiny hand in his and gave it a shake.

"First things first," she said. "I need to get changed." She was too fond of her outfit to ruin it with dirt and oil and all the rest.

Chris laughed at this, but when she came out of the Jeep wearing his extra set of clothes, cinched at the waist and cut off at the arms and legs, he scowled. She only shrugged and went to work making a list of everything she would need and happily discovering that the repair yard really did have everything she would need to get *The Lilly* going again.

The first step was to charge four outboard engine batteries. She was a little surprised that they actually didn't sit in the engines themselves like a car battery. Of course this made them easier to get to and easier to pull out of their compartments. They weighed thirty-five pounds each, which was too much for her skinny arms, but was a piece of cake for the portable winch crane that she could roll around with ease.

Once the batteries were charging off the Jeep's alternator, she used a separate device: a pneumatic hoist, to haul seven outboard motors to where the barge sat. This would be the trickiest part as small engine repair wasn't something she knew much about.

In fact, the combustible engine was, for the most part, a mystery to her. She knew that gas went in and made the engine go, and she guessed, incorrectly, that the battery made the lights turn on and the horn honk, however after that she was relatively clueless as to what all the hoses and gizmos were all about. She had no idea what role the carburetor played, or what a crank shaft did or where the rods were or why there were so many dangerous looking spinning things going round and round.

Thankfully, it was a moot point. After feeding the engines some gas and hooking them up to the batteries, five of the engines started right up. Now it became simply a matter of mounting them to the back of the barge. Her mind went into overdrive picturing a myriad of ways of how to do this, but as she walked around the facility gathering the supplies she figured she would need, she encountered a stack of brown boxes clearly marked *Outboard Motor Transom Bracket Kit.*

"Ha!" she cried. Grinning, she went to pick one up. The grin morphed into a groany face—the boxes were heavy. "I'll just get the hoisty thing," she said.

By morning she had welded two of the mounts into place, the batteries were charged, and she had found four small fuel pumps and an installation instruction guide for them.

Exhausted, still covered in grease and rust, her pony tail sagging so that her hair ballooned out behind her like a brown Japanese lantern, she got into her sleeping bag. "I'm gonna win the bet," she said to Chris. He had spent the night roaming for miles, scrounging for gas and exploring the countryside. He was almost as tired as she was and only grunted as way of reply.

Although haunted by bad dreams, all of which centered on the man who had punched her in the down low, she slept like a dirty log for hours and didn't stir until three that afternoon. After hurrying through a breakfast of ramen and protein bars, she climbed back into the heavy welding gear she had found in one of the machine shops and went right to work.

By sundown the brackets were in place and she tested the welds by setting the engines in place using the hoist. They weighed in at over seven hundred pounds apiece and she was proud that only one weld, on the number four bracket, cracked. She was proud but also tired and cranky. "Oh for all goodness sakes," she cursed.

"You probably didn't let it set long enough," Chris said. "You know, like with glue? I did a model once and the instruction said to let it sit overnight."

Hoisting the motor out of the way, she said: "I don't have time for overnight, amember? 'Sides, this won't be all that hard to fix."

He climbed up onto the back of the barge and sat with his feet hanging over the edge. "I'm bored. This whole place is boring."

To Jillybean that was an amazing thing to say. If she wasn't on a deadline, she could have spent another month there, happily fooling around with all the gadgets and machinery. "Well, if you're really bored, you could put all our extra gas in the boat's tank. That could be fun."

"You'd think a genius would know the definition of the word fun," he grumbled as he dropped down and walked off to the Jeep.

Jillybean was actually having a pretty good time working on the barge. It kept her mind occupied so she didn't think about how her insides still hurt if she twisted around too far, or about the echoey voice in her head, or the impending feeling of doom that surrounded her.

Also, she liked mechanical things. She liked them even better than surgeoning because no one died if you made a mistake, and there usually wasn't a big time crunch like with a bleeding person. To her, the barge and all its pieces were like a jigsaw puzzle that had to be fitted together to make it go.

The Lilly launched an hour before sunrise. There was a nearby tributary to the Mississippi and a special machine that was used to haul the repaired boats, big or small to a launch point, but she couldn't get it to work and had to settle with using the Jeep and a rolling platform.

After the barge slid into the water, they both watched it as it bobbed at the end of its tether, each fearing that it would begin to sink. When it didn't, Jillybean crowed: "I win! Now you gotta come with me back to Colorado."

Technically, they weren't quite ready. The engines had to be synched to a single throttle controller which was a two hour long chore to set up, and then Jillybean felt the need to test the strength of the three foot high metal retaining wall that wrapped around all but the front of the barge. They could expect to be attacked and she had to know if the wall would offer protection.

"I'll do it," Chris said, excitedly. The fat .44 caliber rounds were the heaviest slug they had, so she agreed. When he fired it from a range of twenty feet, the *Krrannnng!* from the bullet hitting the metal wall was nearly as loud as the gunshot itself. They both hurried forward to see what sort of damage was done, which turned out to be nothing more than an odd dent and a marring of the rust.

"Let's try an M16 next," he suggested, excitedly.

She was firmly against wasting any more ammo, just as she was against getting the Jeep on board right just then. They wouldn't be leaving for another eleven hours and there was no sense letting their two most valuable assets sit out where someone could steal them in one quick move.

"But we don't have to wait. We can go now," Chris urged. "I'll drive. Come on, Jillybean, please." A part of her wanted to get moving as well. She felt that the idea of the boat had been a lucky stroke. It meant they could really zip around. Traps on the river would be hard to spring…and yet if they were sprung, what countermeasures did she possess?

"No, we can't, I'm sorry. I'm…" A huge yawn split her face and sleepy tears sprang from her eyes. "We can't leave until dark, and that's what means we'll be more safer. Especially if we set up some defensening stuff. But I'm too tired to stay awake."

He sighed, resigning himself to another day spent cooped up. Like a wolf, he paced for a while, before lying down. Jillybean barely heard. Within seconds of her zipping up her bag, she was asleep, once more in the same filthy clothes.

203

Just as the night before, she dreamt of the man who had attacked her, only now she wasn't being chased. Like the wolf, she stalked him, moving silently in the quiet traders' truck, her steps softer than the air that whistled through her clenched teeth, softer than the sleep-whimpers of the sex slaves, softer than the snores of the traders who slept deeply, unaware there was a monster loose in their midst.

She crept along without fear. Fear couldn't hold a candle to the bonfire of rage within her. It reminded her of the evil that was Eve, only this was more controlled, if just slightly. And there wasn't that sinister feel to it. The wolf wasn't hunting out of a lust to kill, but out of a hunger for justice. But it was not exactly a lone wolf. Jillybean was there staring out of its eyes as it went to the leader's room.

She had been there earlier, lying in a stupor, the world spinning from the blow to her chin, her down-below aching, aching, aching. It hurt to think about the pain and what had caused it and so she tossed it into the sewer of her mind where it gurgled and sank beneath the horrors and excesses she had endured.

Then, she found herself in the room with its green blanketed walls and its bloody mattress. She walked around it to the corner where she stooped to retrieve the knife that had been laughed at and cast aside. In the dream, the knife was hot in her hands.

Thankfully, she woke at that point, blinking in surprise as a late afternoon sunbeam shot through the western window, blinding her. Even though the dream was still fresh in her mind, haunting her, she listened for danger and did not twitch a muscle. Chris, asleep and sawing logs, the sad cry of a whippoorwill, and the dull moan of a monster somewhere in the yard, were the only sounds.

After a thirty-count she raised her sparkled, pink watch to her eyes and saw that it was already after four. Two hours and twenty minutes until sunset; plenty of time for work. With a sigh she sat up and nudged Chris. "We got stuff to do."

"No, five more minutes." After five minutes, in which she had rolled her filthy bag into a compact ball, and snuck into a corner to change back into her jeans/dress/pink shirt combo, she nudged him again, this time with her foot. He mumbled something that could have been "hotdog" or "hard fog."

It didn't matter and she kicked him this time. "Get up, for all darn it." This time he rolled over. One more kick got him sitting all the way up. "If you want a cannon on the ship, you got to get up."

He was up in a flash. "How?"

She had no idea. Cannons were monster guns in her mind, able to sink a boat with one shot. That wasn't going to happen with what she had on hand…but with the machine shop right there, she was sure she could fashion something. A catapult, a spring-fired thing-a-ma-jig, a bomb on a rope, towed behind the barge.

Only the last was in any way feasible in that it could be reeled in or detonated remotely when the time was perfect. The other ideas relied too much on chance and with her limited bomb supply that was like rolling the dice with her life on the line.

But there were some rudimentary things she could do to make *The Lilly* harder to be attacked. "There's all these thingies in that building behind the machine shop. It's glue in a tube. Can you get some of those and lots of glass," she asked him. His face twisted in confusion and she explained: "To line the wall. You know, just in case someone tries to climb up."

His handsome face lit with a sharp glee at the idea of bad guys cutting themselves as they tried to board. He rushed away to find what was needed, leaving Jillybean to figure out the rest of their defenses. A cannon was out of the question. It would take too much time to build one and she had only a vague notion concerning the power of expanding gasses as a propellant. Any plan would have to rely on the potential energy stored in springs or wound ropes or the kinetic energy of Chris's throwing arm.

Smoke would also be needed, however with the width of some rivers, attempting only rear-deployed smoke would be useless. It would be better to envelope the barge in smoke and shoot outward using her thermal scoped rifle.

She worked to place smoke charges around the boat. After that she set up firing stations, each with two Molotov cocktails and a gas mask.

"It's good enough, let's go," Chris kept saying, after he had finished gluing razor sharp glass all around the retaining wall. It made the barge look like an open mouth with jagged crystalline teeth.

She agreed that the defenses were as good as she could make them with their limited resources and, after driving the Jeep on board and tying her down, they slowly made their way down the canal to the Mississippi, where she allowed Chris to run the four engines at forty percent capacity.

For the most part, Chris piloted *The Lilly*. In spite of the dark, he had great vision and insanely fast reflexes and he looked beautiful standing at the wheel with his hair streaming out behind him and his hazel eyes locked on the river. He sort of looked like a man and Jillybean had to force her nose into a book to keep from staring.

The next couple of nights, first on the Mississippi, and then on the Ohio River, were the finest they'd had together. The openness of the barge with its wind and the stars overhead, were all in stark contrast to the musty, cave-like cab of the Jeep they had been stuck in for so long.

For a time, they felt free of the doom that had been hanging over them, but it did not last.

Each morning before sunrise, they would find a spot to hide the barge and sleep most of the day away. And each afternoon when they woke up, they would go out to scrounge for more gas. It was on that second day, with the sun still a hand's width over the horizon, that Jillybean was suddenly knocked for a loop by an unnerving case of deja vu.

She looked around in confusion. They were on a lonesome highway in the middle of flat land U.S.A. In the last couple of years, she had to have seen a million views just like this one and yet, she knew she had been there before. With her heart beginning to flutter, she climbed up onto the roof of a stalled out minivan and stared all around, trying to make sense of the feeling. Then it struck her. "Holy cow, this is I-71."

Chris was under the van drilling into the gas tank. His voice was muffled when he asked: "So? What's the big whoop?"

"I don't know if the whoop is big or not, I just know that I've been here before. We're really close to where I rescued Sadie."

"You mean where you blowed up those trucks?" When she answered in the affirmative, there was a rattle of metal on asphalt as he tossed aside the drill and climbed out from beneath the van. "Where?" he asked in excitement. "I gotta see those trucks."

He tried to pull her south, but she slipped out of his grip. "I don't know if I want to go." More than likely there would still be the bodies of the people she had killed in the wreckage. That wasn't something she wanted to see.

"Why?" he asked. "Because you made it all up?"

"No," she said in a whisper. "Because it's all true. You don't understand what it's like to be Jillybean. It's not fun and it's not easy. A lot of the time it hurts. And a lot of the…"

YOU'VE FORGOTTEN SOMETHING VERY IMPORTANT! The voice was no longer the echo she had grown accustomed to. It was like an explosion in her mind. Her eyes slid in different directions and she fell right over. Chris caught her before she broke her face on the highway.

"Jillybean! You okay? What happened? Did you have a stroke?" It took a moment for her to be able to focus on his face and when she did, she saw the concern etched into his features. Instead of being touched, she was mortified. Her cheeks blazed red and she struggled to her feet.

"I was just dizzy or light in the head is all. Sorry about that. Hey, let's go look at those trucks, okay?" She was so embarrassed that she couldn't look him in the face.

He held back. "Maybe I should go get the Jeep. You probably shouldn't be walking. Man, I never saw a person faint before. You just went all white and plopped right over."

"I'm fine and I didn't faint and the trucks are only a mile away and that's what means I can walk." She started south, saying over her shoulder, "Are you coming?"

Before she could blink, he had caught up. He seemed to have gotten the hint that she didn't want to talk about the fainting. Still he kept glancing at her with worry in his eyes.

"You ever have a fit before?" he asked. "I'm just asking because you're all sorts of pale."

It was true that she didn't feel like her normal self. The echo in her head had been replaced with a growing fear and with every step it built. She was walking closer and closer to the memory; she was sure of it. And it was very confusing. Her mind desperately wanted to forget what was ahead and at the same time it needed her to remember before it was too late.

She just didn't know what was too late for what.

They crossed a wide strip of land that was prairie and entered a forest. They were close. She had chosen the ambush site with the idea that the trucks wouldn't be able to maneuver because of the forest.

"Is that it?" Chris asked. It was a rhetorical question. Through the trees they could see three of the five mega-trucks she had destroyed. They looked like the burned out carcasses of

207

mechanical beasts. As Jillybean stared, the battle replayed itself in her mind—every single detail. She became white as a sheet, but this time Chris didn't notice. He was too focused on the destruction.

"Wow," Chris breathed. "You weren't lying. There's the rope you guys used to repel down onto the trucks. And there, those scorch marks are from the smoke bombs. And you can see where the rocket took out truck number four. That must have been awesome."

She shrugged. She hadn't seen the explosion. Mister Neil had saved her life by pulling her away from the blast of the launcher. The two of them wandered close and saw the first skeleton. A litter of bones were nestled in the spring grass next to the road. Further on there were more.

"Revenge," Jillybean whispered. Someone was after revenge. The voice had said so. "Or did it?" She tried to remember but the memory was vague in her mind as if revenge was a strong possibility but not a guarantee. "Knowing my luck, revenge is going to happen."

Chris raised an eyebrow, cleared his throat and then went around the truck, pretending not to have heard. "Is this the place for your memory? Because it may have been a waste of time coming out here. Everything that wasn't burnt was taken. You can tell people have gone through this thing. I can see footprints in the ash."

"This is the place," she replied. It was the place, so what was the memory? Nothing came to her. Raising her voice she called out: "So what is it? I'm here. Tell me what is so golly-darn important!"

There was no answer except silence, unless the feeling of doom blooming all around her like a cloud, was an answer. The terrible feeling was thick as fog, making her want to run to get away from it. She forced herself not to sprint, but walked slowly up the line to the next two trucks.

These two were not just burned, they were bent and twisted. They had been blown up by the mines she had set. She would never forget those explosions. Even then, months and months later, she felt the fearful thrill of them shake her spine. She walked on, thankful that the last two trucks were miles away. They would only add to the sadness filling the gaps in the fear.

"What's that?" Chris asked, pointing into the forest. At first she saw nothing. Chris started walking through the forest and she followed after. They were fifty yards in when she saw something gleaming among the greens and browns. It shone in the last light of the day.

"I don't know," she lied, in a whisper. But she did know. She remembered: with the trucks barreling down the road she had been busy setting up the ambush and had left it up to Neil to hide the 4Runner.

Once more, she began walking towards the truck, her mouth suddenly tasting like dirty pennies. Here was the real memory. Here was the cataclysmic danger. Here was what she had hid from herself because a part of her could not be trusted. It was the killer in her that this had been hidden from. She could blame Eve or Ipes or any of the voices that bounced around in her head, but the truth was, she was the real killer.

She got to the 4Runner and remembered what Ipes had taken to the grave.

Chapter 24

Neil Martin

It was late March, seven days after Jillybean walked through the forest off of I-71 and found the 4Runner sitting right where Neil had left it. While the rest of the northern hemisphere was beginning to warm up and green things were shooting up and flowers were blooming, the Estes Valley was only just throwing off the last of winter.

This change in seasons was marked by a dreary rain. Ten days before, Neil had called it persistent. He was an east coast man and knew his precipitation. The rain had been neither heavy or light; it was the kind of rain that would hang around for days. And it had.

"At least it's not snowing," one of the guards said.

"You got that right," another chimed in. "I remember there was a time that I used to like snow…and the rain." The winter had started off bitterly cold but relatively dry, but for the last three months the snow had built up higher and higher. Every day there seemed to be more fresh powder.

The valley had been a winter wonderland, only now it was wet and mucky. The rain was taking care of the snow, washing it all down the swollen Big Thompson River which was jumping its banks in places. Below them, Neil could see the water streaming across the highway. It had to be a foot deep and he was sure that if it continued it was going to undermine the highway. Another headache for Governor Martin.

There were six of them high up on the Red Gate, one of the two main fortified walls that defended the roads entering the valley. Neil was the only one of them not part of the night watch. His yellow slicker, zipped up over both a normal sweater and a sweater vest combo, made it obvious he didn't belong.

The dark couldn't hide the soldiers' furtive glances or the awkward smiles and Neil knew that the topic of the stuttering and forced conversation had turned to the weather mainly because few of the tall, young men really knew what to say or do around the stunted and somewhat hideous appearing governor. And it wasn't just the scars and the missing fingers, it was his reputation.

Everyone in the Valley had their stories. Each had been in harrowing situations: running out of ammo while surrounded by a raging horde, crawling through a foot-wide sewer pipe with a zombie scrambling after them, trapped in a tree for three days and drinking piss to stay alive.

But no amount of bragging could match the rumors that flew around Neil Martin, especially since the rumors were almost all true. Somehow, this little twerp had lived when so many had died, somehow, he always found a way. There was plenty of speculation and gossip and snide remarks swirling around the Valley concerning how he managed to get lucky time and again, but he never said yay or nay to any of them. Of course this stoicism seemed to confirm everything.

The latest rumors were as wild as anything the Valley had ever heard. It seemed preposterous, but the talk around the evening fires was that somehow Neil and the hell-child, Jillybean, had managed to break into the Colonel's fortified base, assassinate him, and make off with a boatload of weaponry.

As if that wasn't enough for them, they then headed south where they destroyed half of Cape Girardeau, rescued Captain Grey and killed the River King, ending his reign of terror once and for all. But the two of them weren't done even then. As if they did this sort of thing on a weekly basis, they then took on five of the armored trader trucks and freed a bunch of slaves before recrossing the country to arrive back at the Valley with a tanker filled with ten thousand gallons of gas.

The gas and the freed slaves—the Valley was chronically in short supply of women and anyone who brought more back with them was a hero in the eyes of the soldiers— and the grim look in Neil's baby blues seemed to have put an end to the machinations of Fred Trigg.

In Neil's absence, Fred had railed endlessly about Neil's lack of leadership skills and his misplaced trust in the now universally-feared Jillybean. However upon Neil's triumphant return, Fred had faded into the background, biding his time.

Neil had almost wanted a confrontation and was ready with a pre-arranged speech with the first ill-placed rumor that he could pin on Fred. He intended to call Fred down to the basement of the Stanley Hotel, where the boiler was always hissing and blowing steam like a squat metal dragon.

Next to the boiler, in a corner where no one could see them and where they could have a private conversation, and where the heat was more stifling than any jungle, were two folding chairs.

Neil would sit in the one closest to the door, blocking Fred, who would be already sweating through his shirt.

"Here's the deal, Fred," Neil would say. "If I hear one more lie come from your lips or if I hear one more rumor spread by your pathetic little gang, I'm going to instigate what is being called Plan Z."

"And what is that?" Fred would ask in his prissiest voice. "Something that's supposed to scare me?"

"It would scare me," Neil would admit. "Does the idea of someone finding your body hanging from a tree with a suicide note in your pocket scare you? Or maybe they find your twisted body at the bottom of a staircase, your neck broken. Or maybe there'll be a fire in your apartment or a freak carbon monoxide leak. Does that scare you?"

Fred would be stammering or blathering or threatening at this point and so Neil would reach into his pocket for the .25 caliber gun he had confiscated from Jillybean so long ago. "Or maybe I'll shoot you now and say that you got out of control and attacked me. I'd have to nick myself up a bit, but it would be for a good cause."

This would lead an outraged Fred to say something along the lines of: "You can't do this." Once Fred got talking he wouldn't likely stop and there would be more threats and blusterings. All the while, Neil would simply fix him with an icy stare.

"There you go, get it out of your system," Neil would say. "Get it out now, because if a rumor gets back to me that I threatened you, well my hands will be tied and Plan Z will go into effect. You won't know when or where but someone will get to you. Have a good night." Neil would leave because there would be nothing left to say.

Plan Z would have been only silly fantasy to the old Neil from New Jersey. That man had been weak and people had died because of his weakness. The new Neil already had a plan in place to deal with Fred. Up in the hills above Estes was a cabin and chained in that cabin was a zombie, a very large and hungry zombie.

It was a horrible, horrible thing to consider, however the division and distrust sown by Fred was already threatening the stability of the only democratically elected government on the planet. Fred was playing political games that could result in the loss of life.

Neil wasn't going to let that happen even if he had to drag Fred up to the cabin by himself, something that was a possibility if Captain Grey didn't make it back. "He'll make it back," Neil said, not caring that one of the guards had heard his mumble.

Grey and Sadie, as well as forty soldiers, had left on a trading/scrounging mission that had been meticulously planned out. They had been due back the night before and Neil had done his best to keep himself busy until midnight, at which point he went back to the little cottage he shared with Gayle Houghton, the ex-slave he had purchased months before so he could find out where Jillybean was.

Gayle had been very appreciative of what Neil had done for her and had bound herself to him in such an extremely forward and aggressive manner that for a while she was almost his personal slave. He had to declare her his girlfriend just to keep tongues from wagging. As far as girlfriends went, she was excellent. He had put on ten pounds, never went a week without being satisfied, and slept like a rock whenever she was in bed with him.

Deanna, mother of a little squiggle of a baby with huge blue eyes, hadn't slept much during Grey's absence and yet when she climbed the ladder to stand next to Neil, she managed to look even younger than ever.

"Who's watching Emily?" Neil asked. Sunrise was still an hour from turning the day from black to a dull grey, an odd time for the mother of a newborn to be standing on a wall in the rain. "You know he's fine. A little weather probably delayed them."

That was one explanation, but there were a dozen more that were just as possible and far more deadly and, if truth were told, which it wasn't going to be in front of Deanna, more likely.

"Yeah, maybe," she agreed, halfheartedly.

When he wasn't planning on turning a political rival into a zombie, Neil was naturally upbeat and optimistic. "They could have had a mechanical problem or they might have had to wait on a buyer to bring his goods, or hey, they might have come across a group with really bad teeth."

She smiled a perfunctory smile. The team had set out with little to trade beside four hundred pounds of deer meat, five thousand gallons of gas and a traveling hospital consisting of a nurse, a dental hygienist and Dr Hester, a surgeon who'd been pulling teeth in his spare time. He was getting pretty good at popping them out. Neil wished he would try filling some cavities but the doctor seemed to have no interest in it.

Deanna's smile was quickly washed away by the rain. "Have you considered getting a team together to go look for them? We know where they were going and what route they will take coming back on."

He had considered it and a three man squad was ready to go in the morning. Their job wasn't one of rescue but of scouting and possibly the beginning of diplomatic relations and perhaps even hostage negotiations. Though if it were the latter, the group that had done something to his daughter and his best friend would end up in a world of hurt.

Neil would race to Oklahoma and fetch Jillybean herself and set her upon his enemies with a venge…

His thoughts were interrupted as a distant rumble pierced the sound of the rain and the river rushing a few hundred yards to their right. Everyone on the wall stood as statues, unmindful of the water coursing over their bodies. Neil had to remind the sergeant of his duty.

"Call the ready team," he snapped. "What are you waiting for?"

Although Grey and his team were long overdue, there was no knowing if this was actually them and five soldiers, no matter how well trained, could not defend the wall against a determined attack by a large force. Any time engines were heard on the highway, they called up a twenty-person fighting unit who were always on call, just in case.

The five soldiers rushed to their battle stations and even Neil and Deanna went to stand behind mounted machine guns.

"I see them," one of the soldiers cried out. "It's…it's one of ours. It's a five ton." The truck pushed through the overflow of river water and stopped a hundred yards away. It flicked its lights in the prearranged pattern: short-long-short. Everyone relaxed and yet they did not step away from their weapons. Intense enough torture would have caused the toughest of men to divulge the simple code. The sergeant responded with three long flashes with a spotlight and the first truck pulled forward while the rest remained behind.

After enduring so much evil, the people of the Valley had become a touch paranoid.

The truck pulled up to the first barrier: a twenty foot deep moat, and a ragged, tired looking man climbed out of the cab. The sergeant turned the spotlight on him.

"Okay that's enough," Captain Grey called out, holding a hand in front of his face. He was scruffy but not haggard, tired but healthy. "Send a man out."

The soldiers, following protocol, sent one man to make sure that Grey's five ton, and the trucks behind his, were not filled with enemy soldiers.

Neither Neil or Deanna had any fear of a *Trojan Horse* style ruse. Even though it would have meant his death, it would have been the first thing out of Grey's mouth. They went with the soldier through the gate and waited while he lowered the drawbridge to cross the moat.

Grey stood on the other side, smiling at Deanna. Neil had received only a quick smile. "How's Emily," Grey asked. "Sleeping through the night, yet?"

She laughed. "You were only gone two weeks. Did you expect miracles? Oh, and by the way, she hasn't potty trained herself, either."

The bridge coming down made a shrill cry of rusting metal that could be heard for miles. The noise woke Sadie, who had been snoozing in the cab of the lead five-ton. She slid over to the driver's side, bipped the horn and started the truck forward, directed by the soldier.

"Oh, boy," Grey said. "We better get out of the way. She's not the best driver." The truck bounced and spasmed forward as she alternated giving too much pressure to the gas and then the brake. She got the truck across the moat without mishap, but had to take three tries at slipping the truck through the narrow gate. Back and forth she went, eventually pulling in the side mirror to keep it from hitting the wall.

"You can stop laughing any time," she hissed at Neil, who was having trouble controlling himself. "I've seen you drive. You're not any better."

He considered himself only marginally better and because of that, he wouldn't have tried to drive the truck through the gate, especially with people watching. Grey hugged Deanna fiercely and then helped her into the cab and climbed in after her. Neil was the last in, squishing up next to his friend.

"How was it?" he asked. "Did you sell off the fuel? What about the meat? Did you get good deals?"

"It was okay," Grey said. "The people down in the Springs were friendly and we did alright. But boy, there are some kooks in Pueblo. They're holed up in a correctional facility and you would have thought they were all ex-prisoners."

"Yeah," Sadie agreed. "They have a perfectly good river running right through town, but it didn't look like a single one of them had bathed in months. The good news for us was that, apparently they hadn't brushed their teeth in months, either. Dr. Hester really cleaned up. It's why we are late getting in. He was yanking teeth up until two days ago."

It had been Neil's idea to "pimp out" the doctor. Hester was to keep thirty percent of the gross from his work and the Valley would take seventy in return for providing transportation and security. Given the dangerous world they lived in, it was a fair deal.

"So what are we looking at?" Neil asked, hoping that his eagerness wasn't so obvious. Politically speaking, a lot had been riding on this first outing. He guessed it was why Fred Trigg had been so quiet for the last few weeks. Had the trading team been ambushed and Dr Hester killed or abducted, Neil's days as governor would have been numbered.

"About fourteen thousand rounds," Grey said, flashing his white teeth in a wide grin. "And we still have a thousand gallons of fuel left."

Neil sat back feeling both weak with relief and giddy. The future of the Valley had never looked so good. It even made him rethink putting the screws to Fred. "We should have a celebration," he said, sitting up and slapping the dash. "We should have a banquet for everyone who went on the expedition."

"But not tonight," Deanna said. "They're all beat and it's going to take a few days to put together."

They were quiet for a time as Sadie chugged the truck up over the last hills. When the Valley was spread out below them, dim but somehow still beautiful despite the rain and the dark, Sadie asked: "Where am I going with this thing? Up to the hotel?"

"I think so," Neil said. "We'll need to catalogue what you brought back. You know Fred, he's going to want to account for every bullet and ounce of gas."

Sadie's mouth gaped in a huge yawn. "When you said 'we'll' catalogue the stuff, you meant you're gonna do it, right?

Cuz I am beat. And so is Captain Grey, though he'll pretend he isn't."

"Yes, I'll take care of it," Neil said. "Don't worry…" They had just turned onto the hotel grounds and immediately he saw something out of place. The front doors were cracked open by about four inches, letting a long, thin rectangle of light fall out onto the white-painted porch. "Oh Jeeze," he said. "Who the hell left that open?"

Because of the ever-present zombie menace, the Valley practiced a strict no-light policy during the hours between sunset and sunrise. There was even a patrol that monitored and fined anyone not obeying this basic commonsense safety practice. Neil was mortified that the Stanley Hotel, the symbol as well as the seat of government within the Valley, was breaking such a fundamental rule.

Normally, a truck of this size would pull around to the back parking lot, however Neil pointed Sadie on to the front entrance. "Just don't hit…who is that? Miss Harvey?" It was just before six in the morning and the only people at the hotel were a skeleton crew of three people: a radio operator, the night maid, and a general purpose guard.

The Stanley was a big, beautiful old place that was a monument to stability, an iconic symbol that was the pride of the Valley and it was also a bitch to keep warm. Even inside, Neil had taken to wearing his sweater/sweater vest combination and still shivered half the day.

Because of this, no one lived there. During the day, the building buzzed with activity. Each of the council members had their offices in the Stanley and at any given time there could be a hundred people in the hotel. At six in the morning, the day crew of a few cooks and cleaning people was just coming on shift.

Neil rolled down his window as Tee Harvey glanced back at the looming truck. She was easily recognizable as she had mounds of dark hair that hadn't been cut since before the apocalypse.

"Hey, it's Neil," he said, figuring that, high up in the cab he wouldn't be as easily recognizable. "Can you do me a favor and find out who left that door open. I don't want to be a jerk about it but we should really set a standard."

"I was thinking the same thing," she replied. "It's probably that Cindy Monroe. Sometimes she can't remember to tie her shoes. I think the poor thing has a touch of post-traumatic if you know what I mean."

Neil thought that half the Valley had a touch of PTSD and it was no wonder after everything they had gone through. Cindy had been one of the sex-slaves that Jillybean had rescued on her way across country and she was a bit squirrelly. But it was still no excuse. "I do. Just ask around and let me know."

"Sure thing." Tee resumed walking up the gravel drive. There wasn't a lot of room and Sadie wouldn't chance running her over, so they stopped with a jerking motion.

"So?" Sadie asked, as they waited. "You gonna paddle that Cindy Monroe, Neil? I'm just asking because I know she's been giving you the eye."

"I'm with Gayle," he growled, "and you know that."

Sadie lifted a shoulder. "Whose idea was that? Everyone's been talking about how she adopted herself a sugar dad…"

She was cut off as Tee suddenly let out a cry. "Governor! Something's happened." She had mounted the steps of the front porch and was now inching forward towards the door.

Grey started to climb over Neil saying: "Tell her to keep away from there. I'll check it out."

As a survivor, Tee wasn't an idiot. She had stepped to the side of the door and was slunk low, peeking inside, ready to sprint out of there at the first hint of danger.

"Hey! Tee!" Neil hissed, reaching for the truck's door handle. "Get over here. We'll check it…" Her right arm suddenly jerked as if she were telling him to go away. Neil's first impulse was to become indignant. He was, after all the governor. Even in dangerous situations, it wasn't polite to shoo away the governor without explanation.

A split second later, he forgot his indignation as Tee's arm suddenly curled up so that the back of her hand was beneath her chin. She stared at it in horror, her eyes bugging, huge and glassy. She then turned to watch as her other arm pulled straight out and then twisted up and back. First the fingers on the hand curled inward, and then the hand bent to the wrist and the elbow twisted.

Neil heard the arm break like a snapping twig. Judging by the look of horror on her face, Tee heard it as well. Her mouth opened to scream in misery, but no sound came out and the mouth stretched open further and further until the skin split at the sides of her mouth.

"Oh God," Neil whispered, leaping from the truck and running for the porch stairs. He never made it, his right foot clipped the edge of one of the paving stones that led to the porch and he fell with Captain Grey falling over him.

The two of them scrambled to their feet as Tee fell with a thud onto the porch where she writhed like a caterpillar on a hot skillet. Her back bent and snapped and her legs stuck out, straight as lightning rods. Beyond her, seen through the crack of the door, were two bodies, both twisted into bizarre forms, their faces purple and unrecognizable.

Grey leapt forward, as always ready to tackle any problem, no matter how dangerous. Neil leapt forward and tackled Grey, grasping him around the knees and holding on tight.

"No!" Neil cried. He knew what was happening. It was horrible and terrifying and should have been impossible and yet with Jillybean nothing could be ruled out. Unlike her, he had not buried a single memory.

Four months before, with the five armored trucks rushing toward the ambush site, he had hidden the 4Runner in the forest. With time running out, it was the most he could do. He had raced back to the narrow road, and had climbed the rope into the tree, had fought and had done his duty in order to save his daughter.

The running battle had taken them miles away from the 4Runner and not for a moment did he suggest they do anything but go on. The 4Runner and what sat in the back was in the past. It was just a memory that he hoped Jillybean would forget. That was definitely a possibility. During their adventures, she'd had spells of what he called "psychotic amnesia" in which she blanked out on the worst atrocities she had committed.

Thankfully, she also forgot having forced the Colonel to carry with them a case of deadly VX nerve gas. On their trip down river, it had sat in the back of the pontoon, unmentioned and overlooked by Jillybean. To Neil, it was like riding with a nuclear bomb that was on a hair trigger. After the battle with the River King, Neil had been afraid to leave it behind and even more afraid to dump it into the river. He had put it into the cargo area of the 4Runner and could think of nothing better to do except lay a towel over it.

Jillybean never even glanced in its direction.

Then came the ambush and still she hadn't said a word. For her, it was as though the episode had never happened. Up until now.

Neil had envisioned the VX gas doing *something* to a person, but not this. This was horrible. Tee looked possessed.

"Get off me, damn it!" Grey seethed.

"No," Neil said, holding onto his friend with all of his might. "Look at her. What can do that to a person? And what can do that to more than one person?"

Just as he was about to fling Neil away, Grey paused. He studied Tee: soundlessly, she writhed, her face turning red as her diaphragm seized and her carotid arteries could be seen pulsing in tremendous waves along her neck.

"Nerve gas?" he asked and for the first time, Neil could hear a hint of fear in his voice.

"VX," Neil answered, speaking quietly and quickly. "Jillybean took a case of it from the Colonel, but she had one of her episodes and forgot we had it. I didn't know what to do with it, so I left it back in Illinois."

A dozen expressions seemed to cross Grey's face in a manner of seconds, before he settled on stern confusion. "Then how did it get here?" It was a rhetorical question. His eyes had shifted from Tee and were spying about, trying to pierce the shadows. "We should move back," he hissed.

As if a sniper was out in the dark, they scrabbled backwards, like lizards. Behind them, Sadie was half-out of the five-ton. "What's wrong?" she whispered. She had a perfect view of Tee and must have sensed the danger.

"Jillybean," Grey answered.

Sadie and Jillybean were apocalypse sisters and loved each other very much and yet, Sadie crouched down behind the half-open door of the five-ton. Just as Grey and Neil were doing, she stared all around because there was no telling what the little girl might do when she was out of her mind. Next to her, Deanna slunk low, so that only the top of her head could be seen.

It was ludicrous that four grown and armed adults could be so terrified of one seven-year-old child.

Chapter 25

Jillybean

The two children stood on a hill overlooking the Estes Valley as the rain came again, turning a cold, wet night into something that could only be endured, painfully. They were dressed as monsters, though with the rain on top of everything else, it sort of felt like a waste to Jillybean. After a frantic, seven day dash across the country, she wasn't sure what she looked like, but guessed she didn't look all that human.

"Huh, the Valley doesn't look all that great," Chris mumbled, gazing down. Rain coursed from his plastered hair, dripping from his chin. He seemed impervious to the weather, just as he seemed impervious to fatigue.

Jillybean was tired enough for both of them. She had pushed them on relentlessly. First on the river, taking *The Lilly* back down the Ohio to the Mississippi. From there they chugged north to St Louis, where they took the Missouri River hundreds of miles west.

The Missouri was small compared to the Mississippi and much more dangerous. Twice they were attacked by other boats, forcing Jillybean to set off the smokers, covering half the river in a man-made fog. After a few well-placed shots from her thermal-scoped rifle, they managed to escape both times.

Things grew hairy when they reached Omaha where the Platte River fed into the Missouri. Although the Jeep constituted an extremely light load for the barge, and it rode very high on the water, the Platte was frequently shallow, more of a large stream than a river.

Before the apocalypse, the flow of the river had been carefully controlled by dams and man-made runoffs, but now it was mostly up to nature. With all the snow melt and the spring rains, Jillybean thought the river would have been deeper, but there were times when they scraped the bottom or plowed into partially submerged logs.

The further west they went through Nebraska, the more frequent these groundings happened. In the dark, it was hard to tell depth and even Jillybean's genius failed her. She tried both infrared lights and spotlights, but both were utterly useless. Next she tried attaching glow sticks to arrows—both being plentiful in that area of the country—and firing them into the river ahead of the barge. It was such an inaccurate manner to gauge a river's depth that they got stuck on a sand bar and it took Chris three hours to dig them out.

Thankfully, other than the loss of a few layers of rust, the barge made it through these minor collisions without damage.

Exhausted from his digging on that fourth night, Chris refused to allow them to go on at night. Jillybean had to agree and at sunrise they continued their journey, but only after she had made a few more modifications to *The Lilly*. At a mall in Lincoln, she picked out a dozen manikins, makeup, wigs and clothing. These she dressed and set up around the boat, arranged in such a way so that the casual observer could mistake them for people crouched behind weapons.

As they weren't attacked on the Platte, there was no way to assess the efficacy of the manikins, however Jillybean liked to think they had something to do with their safe passage.

They were on the Platte for two days and with every passing mile, the river grew narrower and shallower until, just across the Colorado border, near a dust town called Julesburg, the river could no longer support a barge, even a bobbing one such as *The Lilly*.

Because Jillybean liked her so much, she took the time to hide the barge on a farm that was connected to the river by a canal. It was a tight fit and so shallow that she didn't dare use the motors, but instead dragged it along using the Jeep. Pulling it out of the canal and down a short road into a barn made a sickening screech that caused her tummy to ache in worry for her boat.

It also attracted every monster in the county right to them and they were forced to hide in the Jeep, and since they were still chained to the barge, they couldn't exactly drive away. They were stuck in the Jeep for almost four hours. Jillybean slept as long as she could, but her bladder was a bulge in her belly that had her squirming in her seat until she couldn't take it anymore.

"You could empty out that ammo box and pee in there," Chris suggested. "I won't look, I promise."

She glanced at the rectangular steel can and then at the cramped cab. There was no room in the back. She would have to put the ammo box on her chair and squat over it.

"Uh-uh. No way. Nope," she said and started the engine.

"Hold on," Chris said. "You're going to drive away while we're still attached to the boat? That's the stupidest…" He stopped in midsentence as she reached over and toggled the smoke release button. She then grinned at him. It was a painful smile, shaded by embarrassment. "You want me to unhook us, right?" he asked.

Her knees clenched while her ankles began to beat together. "Yeah, if you don't mind, that would be really good."

"Fine," he growled. "When I unhook you, just head back to the river to where those houses were. I'll catch up." He leaned over to look at the monitors. During the five days on the river, Jillybean had replaced the broken camera, changed out two of the tires, and had mended the armor that had been bent during their escape from the traders.

All of the monitors showed the same uniform grey color. Chris took a deep breath, cracked the door and slid into the maddening swirl of smoke where figures shuffled about and little could be seen except for a diseased hand with black, scabby nails, or the lower part of a jaw filled with broken teeth that were as sharp as a mouthful of glass shards.

Fearless as always, Chris went out among the undead. They were stirred up and confused, ready to bite the first thing that looked human. The boy threw his hair across his face, let his toned body droop and shambled like all the rest.

From the back of the Jeep there came a *thunk* and a *clank*, metallic sounds that suggested he had pulled off the heavy hook. Jillybean, her bladder close to bursting, waited, counting to thirty. At twenty-five, there was a thud on her door. She turned to the side monitor and saw Chris' hazel eye taking up most of the screen. He winked once and then faded back into the smoke.

She inched the Jeep slowly to the rear doors of the barn. Up close, they glowed as the sun cut through the slits between the boards. Using the front bumper, she gently pushed them open and then she gunned the engine as if an entire monster army was after her and raced back to the river where there were a few little houses sitting out in the open.

The Jeep, billowing smoke like a chimney, was going to stand out and be seen for miles—she didn't care. Her bladder was moments from either bursting or letting go. She ended up peeing in the kitchen sink of the little house. The front door was locked and she was too small to break it down.

She ran around to the back of the house and, had the back door not been open, she would have gone in the yard like a dog. The house was small and a thirty second search would have revealed the bathroom, but she didn't have thirty seconds. She had about three and she used them jumping up on the counter.

"This is indiclulous!" she hissed, as she peed for what felt like five minutes. Each one of those minutes was spent in dread that Chris would come in and catch her. When her tank was finally empty, she wiped with the paper towels that had been sitting just next to the sink. She tried "flushing" by running water, but nothing came from the faucet.

A knock at the front door, made her jump, guiltily as if she had done something wrong. It was Chris. "Jillybean? You okay?"

"I'll be right there." Her voice had been higher than usual, almost a squeak. "Okay, ready to go," she said as she walked out the front door. She couldn't look him in the eye and went right for the driver's side. The Jeep was layered in smoke, which was a plus in that she was sure her face was red right to the tips of her ears.

She remained quiet as they buzzed west on a I-76, the largest highway in northeast Colorado. "Are you sure you want to do this?" Chris asked. "I mean, drive right down the road in the middle of the day?"

"Sorry," she said, pulling to the side of the road. They turned back for Julesburg, found a truck stop and consulted a map. It wasn't good. Other than a few dirt roads that seemed only to follow property boundaries, I-76 was their one choice. Once they were in the mountains, things would only get worse. The roads were narrow, steep and dangerous. This time of year, they could expect, rock-slides, mud-slides and the occasional avalanche in the higher passes.

Worse for them was that possible ambush sites would be around every bend and Jillybean knew that there were a thousand bends on the straightest of roads to Estes.

"Maybe we don't have to go with the straightest road," Chris suggested. "Look at all these lines. Those are roads, right?"

"Not really. They're trails, like little dirt roads. And look, they don't even connect to each other, and that's what means there's probably a cliff right there or a mountain or something."

Chris *tsked* her. "Please, so what?" He slapped the dashboard. "You got a kick-ass Jeep. Mountains and cliffs are the sorts of things it was made for."

She was about to argue when she realized that he was right, so instead of arguing, she began planning. It was what she was good at. The first part of the plan was to get out of sight; they hid the Jeep in another barn, and like so many times before, they slept in the loft. With her alarms and traps it really wasn't necessary, but she did it out of a sense of nostalgia.

Neil had always set them up in barns when they were traveling, and wasn't she his daughter, now? Wasn't she Jillybean Martin? Thinking about him and Sadie and Mister Captain Grey and Deanna kept her tossing and turning and sleep was slow in coming.

At sundown they were off again, heading along county roads until they came to the town of Greeley, the last place of any size before the mountains, which loomed in the west. There she poked around in a computer store and the ever sought after RadioShacks, where she found two-way radios, a scanner, and three more drones which she speedily equipped with cameras.

"How fast are those things?" Chris asked, flipping through the instructions quickly before tossing them aside. He had proudly boasted at one point that: "I never read instructions." It was something Jillybean simply could not understand.

"Not very," she answered. Her simple plan was to send a drone ahead of them to scout possible ambush sites. With so many blind curves and other unknowns between them and the Valley, it was likely that they would need to keep one of the drones aloft the entire time.

"Maybe we should just chance it," Chris said. "Jessica is pretty fast and her armor is pretty good. I bet we'll be fine."

Jillybean would not hear of it. "We'll use the drones and this one's name is Michelle and she likes ponies." She leaned over her chair and dug through the stacks of goods until she got her sticker book. The twelfth page opened onto a section on horses and she peeled away four stickers, placing them on the plastic hubs that encased each of the four spinning blades.

"Look it's four horse power," she said, showing Chris.

He groaned. The next drone was named "Laurie," and Jillybean declared that she liked dragons. This sparked a little more interest in Chris, right up until he saw that the dragons in the sticker book were all rainbow colored.

When the drones were named and decorated, she pointed the Jeep to the west where the peaks were all white-capped and still very dangerous. Rain in the Estes Valley could mean white-out conditions five miles away on Prospect Mountain. There was no way to know what they would find past the first run of foothills.

Since he had the sharper eyes and the better reflexes, Chris drove, while Jillybean watched the drone's feed on her iPad. For hours that night, they slogged along muddy roads; even the paved roads were covered in a layer of dirt and debris.

They wound through the hills and canyons, slowly going higher and higher. They encountered only a few monsters on that first night and just one ambush. Jillybean had the drone at five hundred feet above the road, which gave her a broad but grainy view. From that height, she couldn't tell a monster from a man, however she could tell a running man from a stumbling monster.

They had entered the mountains on a canyon road that had appeared a far straighter and much more proper of a thoroughfare on the map. As quickly as they could, they left the canyon road and took to the winding trails, some of which turned out to be nothing more that extensive driveways leading to isolated mountain retreats while others were better suited for donkeys than for the Jeep.

It was on one of these that movement caught Jillybean's eye. "Hold on," she said, watching the feed from Laurie. "Those are people. Look." She brought the drone closer and saw grey figures hurrying down from a hilltop cabin.

There were six of them and they took up positions close to the road about eighty yards ahead of the Jeep, hiding behind boulders and trees.

"What do we do?" Chris asked. "Do we use the bombs?" His eagerness to kill bothered her.

"Is that your answer to everything? Blowing things up?" As soon as the words left her mouth, Jillybean felt an instant of regret. She didn't know the meaning of the word hypocrisy, but she understood the concept. "No, I don't wanna blow anything up. You know, cuz maybe it'll attract more bad guys or something. We'll go around. There was a turn off back there…"

His look stopped her. "Go around? You're the one who's in this silly hurry over nothing. So, someone stole all them vials of stuff. How do you know if they're gonna use them on your friends? Or if they're gonna use them at all?"

"I just do," she replied. Because of Eve, she understood the hate involved in revenge. "There's tons of people who would be after me or Neil or Sadie."

"Like who? Be honest, do you really think any of the old Azael would really chance coming into these mountains to let loose some nerve gas? They would have to be crazy to risk using that stuff. What would happen if the wind blew it back in their faces?"

She knew crazy as well as hate; the two tended to go hand-in-hand. "You would have to be crazy," she agreed. "And we fought some real crazy people. I told you about the loons from New Eden. Some of those guys would be crazy enough to do it."

He wasn't convinced. "Crazy enough to follow you all over the country? How many people knew it was you and Neil who took the VX to begin with? No one! And how many knew who was behind the attack at Cape Girardeau or the attacks on the trucks?"

"Only a few people," she admitted.

"Any of them from New Eden? They're not, right? You told me all of them were cowards, hiding underground and worshipping a false god. That doesn't sound like the kind of people who would chance crossing such dangerous country. Same with Yuri in New York or any of his bounty hunters. They would use a gun and you know it. So who does that leave?"

That last point was the clincher—anyone with any sense would use a gun or a bomb. "We should at least warn Mister Neil. I mean Mister Governor Neil. He's the leader and he would want to know. But we should keep it a secret. No one should know why we came."

"I don't think anyone should know we came at all," Chris said. "The last time you were here, they formed a mob."

She remembered and the memory was like sulfuric acid on a paper cut. "Yeah, I know. Can we go around these guys, please? I don't feel like killing anyone tonight."

They turned around and found a path that led up to an old hunting lodge. The door was wide open and all the windows were shattered leaving the curtains fluttering out at them. They didn't bother going in to scrounge. Behind the lodge, the trail pushed up towards a towering peak.

With Laurie leading the way, they went up the trail which eventually banked away from the peak and down into a valley that ran south towards Estes. It wasn't long before the trail petered away to nothing, forcing them to drive across country which began agreeably flat.

"Hey! We're in a bog," Chris said, when the Jeep suddenly began to lurch. In the dark, under the camera of the drone, the land appeared just as nice and even and inviting as they could want. Jillybean opened her door and saw that they were actually stopped in two feet of reed-covered water. They tried going left and right, however the bog seemed to go on in every direction for miles.

"We have to wait for morning," Chris said.

It was devastating news to Jillybean. They were only ten miles from the Valley. Ten miles from her family. Ten miles from safety. The Jeep was once again their place of refuge and, with the rain a constant drum, Jillybean slept deep and long.

She awoke in confusion: the camera on the west side showed the sun fading behind the cloud-covered mountains. "What the heck?" She sat up and checked her watch: it was after five in the afternoon. "How did that happen? Chris, we slept all da…" Chris wasn't in the Jeep.

Her first impulse was towards paranoia. The last time he had disappeared something very bad had happened to Jillybean. She quickly reached out and locked the doors. She then began checking the monitors. The gunsight monitor showed him forty yards away, peeing against a tree.

"Oh, um, sorry." She switched angles and then went about unplugging Laurie's batteries from the charger, waiting until Chris came into view on a different monitor before climbing out of the Jeep.

"You won't need that," he said. "I found a way into the Valley that doesn't need roads. Once we get past this marsh, we cross over that ridge." He pointed to a string of hills to their south that seemed impassable. "On the other side is Cow Creek and a trail that's called Cow Creek Trail. They spent a lot of time thinking that one up, ha-ha."

She crossed her arms. "Whoever named it that was from the before. It wasn't Neil."

"I never said it was. Either way, from there we thread through some great big craggy rocks that are called The Needles and wham, bam, thank you ma'am we're there. We could be there by midnight if you get your butt in gear."

Jillybean didn't care for the crude references but was so excited that she ignored them. "How did you do all that?"

"Laurie did most of the work, I just went without sleep. You're welcome." She tried to thank him, but he was bleary and full of yawns. "Whatever. I recorded the way on her camera. You can follow it while I get some sleep."

That was a dangerous way to travel and had they been anywhere else, she wouldn't have tried it. But they were close to the Valley on a scouted path. And what was more, Jessica Jeep was up to the challenge. She followed the recorded video. The reality of the world, as seen through her front monitor, was so completely different from the overhead view that at times she was forced to put her life on the line as she edged near steep drop offs and crossed through deep water bogs that would have submerged the heavy Jeep in seconds.

The path he had set out was neither straight nor true. It meandered for more than ten miles and yet at midnight they came out over a hill and there below them in a grey haze was the Estes Valley.

"We made it," she said, giving Chris a shake on the shoulder. When he sat up, scraping sleep buggers out of his eyes, she said. "There's a road right down there and I think it's MacGregor Ave. That runs right down next to the Stanley. We can be there in five minutes!"

"Not so fast," he said, putting out a hand to keep her from putting the Jeep in gear. "What about the mob and all that? Aren't you worried they're gonna do something if they catch you?"

"Mister Neil wouldn't. He adopted me. And neither would Sadie...Sadie Martin and that's what means she's my sister. And Captain Grey wouldn't because I saved him like a million times and Deanna..." She faltered at Deanna's name, because Deanna was afraid of her. And she must've had her baby by now and that would make her doubly afraid because...

Jillybean wasn't going to think about *that*. She shook her head to clear the image of her handing a baby a poisoned bottled, and tried on a smile that wasn't convincing in the least. "I should be okay. They are the good guys." All except Fred Trigg and his followers, she didn't add. Chris was acting flighty enough without mentioning Fred.

He seemed to sense there was more of an issue and said: "But to get on the safe side, let's hide the Jeep and go in extra sneaky. I'm sorry but that story of a mob coming after a little girl was nutty. People are weird, even the good guys."

Since Jillybean thought of herself as both weird and a good guy, she kept quiet. Laurie the drone led the way once more as the pair went into monster mode. It really wasn't the best disguise as they were the only monsters in the Valley.

"What if they just shoot us without even checking to see if we're even real or not?" Chris asked, in a mumble.

"They wouldn't waste any bullets on two small monsters like us," she said. "I think they'd just knock our brains in with a rock or a bat or maybe an axe. Did I ever tell you that Mister Neil uses…"

"An axe," Chris said, "I know. I think I'd rather be shot. Thankfully, there ain't anyone around to do any shooting or axing, or whatever." It was late and there wasn't a soul in sight. "Maybe we should slow down. You know, take the temperature of the town."

It was a strange thing to say. "I would guess it's around forty or so," she said. "It's cold but not freezing and that's what means it would be snowing."

"I mean, we should figure out what the mood is."

"We can ask Neil. He'll let us know. Don't worry, he is the nicest. His place isn't that far. You woulda thought he stayed at the hotel. That's where I would stay if I could, on account that it's all fancy. I bet they have big soft beds. Boy, I haven't been in a soft bed since Granny Annie's."

Chris was clearly on edge about meeting new people and he only gave a noncommittal grunt.

He will see, Jillybean thought, leading the way, glancing every once in a while at the drone's feed on the iPad. Only once on the way to Neil's apartment did it show anything except empty streets. A two person patrol crossed the street ahead of them, moving to the west and whispering to each other, unaware how close the two children were hiding.

Jillybean tracked them with the drone until she was satisfied they were well away. Three blocks later, she and Chris were across the street from the rundown motel Neil had been staying in the last time she had been in Estes. It was two levels of twin bedroom suites with outdated furniture and a roof that was in need of being re-shingled.

Suddenly nervous, she told Chris to "keep watch," though she wasn't at all afraid of an ambush. Her fear was of rejection. Yes, Neil had adopted her, but that was months ago and what if he had changed his mind? Or what if it had all been an act, maybe for Sadie's sake. What if he told her to leave and never come back? She didn't want Chris anywhere nearby if that was to happen. It would hurt too much.

With her nerves a jangle, she went to the fourth door and raised her little fist to knock only to hesitate. The motel was far too quiet. The last time she had been there most of the rooms had been occupied. Now, the building felt empty.

Even at night, people made noise. They snored, they got up to pee or to get a drink. By their very presence they disturbed the air around them. Jillybean stepped back and looked down the length of the dull, two story rectangular motel.

From outward appearances, the building looked well lived in. Most of the doors sported a welcome mat. Some had little folding chairs out front. A few had shoes neatly set to the side of the door, while a few had bags of trash set out.

Most of the windows had their shades drawn, which was perfectly normal; four of them did not. That was far from normal. Everyone drew their shades at night unless they were trying suggest to the world that no one lived there. That only made sense if you were traveling or being hunted.

Something was definitely worrisome about the motel, however Jillybean couldn't imagine a scenario in which she factored in at all. Nobody knew she was coming. She tapped gently on the door and was surprised when it swung in.

"Hello?" she called out. The suite was pitch black and she could not see more than a few feet in front of her. Warning bells began to go off in her head and her first impulse was to run, but she kept her feet in check. This was Neil and Sadie's place; there was no reason to be afraid.

But she was afraid. The smell of plastic wafted out to greet her. "Hello?" This time a whisper. When there was no response, she stepped inside, one hand reaching for the flashlight that sat in the side pocket of her backpack, the other hand going for her gun.

The smell of plastic was heavy and strange. There was even plastic on the floor. *Like a drop cloth. Maybe they're getting ready to paint.* This thought was comforting but untrue. Somehow she knew it. There were more clues as her eyes grew accustomed to the dark. She could see a few feet in front of her, where a coffee table sat. On it were plants, including a cactus of some sort. Just like everything else they were also covered in plastic, but she knew it was a cactus by the needles poking through.

The obvious thought struck her: *Who would cover their plants when they were about to begin painting? Why weren't they placed outside or in another room? Only an extremely lazy person would do that...or someone in a hurry.*

Neil wasn't lazy. He would have moved the plants. And what was the rush? He wouldn't have rushed, which meant that either this wasn't his room anymore or Jillybean had walked into something that she hadn't prepared for. It could only be the latter.

Almost at the same instant, she heard the scrape of a shoe on cement behind her and the crinkle of plastic to her left. She was trapped half-in and half-out of the room. Dropping into a crouch to make herself as tiny a target as possible, she went for her gun once more, digging frantically.

"Stop!" a muffled voice demanded, as a light transfixed her. She tried to squint past the light, but what she saw didn't make sense. The man with the light was dressed like some sort of astronaut; he had on a bulky mask and was encased in a plastic suit.

"You are under arrest for murder, Jillybean."

Chapter 26

Sadie Martin

She had been in denial. She hadn't wanted to believe it was possible. For the previous twenty-four hours, ever since she had watched Tee twitch and writhe her way to a horrible death, Sadie had argued louder than anyone that Jillybean couldn't have been involved.

"She's in Oklahoma for goodness sakes! You have no proof otherwise! We should be scouring the Valley for spies and assassins, that's what we should be doing." The louder she got, however, the more she felt a worm of fear in her gut that she was just lying to herself.

"And who should we be looking for?" Neil asked, his baby blue eyes hooded by weariness and grief. "Someone with a history of violence and murder? Someone who has been known to have had psychotic episodes? Or maybe we should be looking for someone who knew where I had left the VX gas. I wish it wasn't so, but Jillybean is all three."

Sadie had glared, feeling the need to leap up and run from the room. She hadn't. She had simply told herself to trust in the fact that Jillybean was far away, and that she was a changed girl and that she had an innocent soul—but then Jillybean had been captured and was currently locked away in the Estes Valley jail under a heavy guard.

The little girl had been stripped of everything, including her clothes and the bits of odd metal she had tied into the back of her hair. There would be no escape for her this time.

All through the night she had been interrogated, first by Neil, who had see-sawed back and forth from nice guy to stern father figure, and then by Grey, who had tried to reason with her as if they were both adults. Fred Trigg was next and he wasted no time and jumped right in as the "bad cop," yelling and screaming and making threats until Jillybean was in tears and cowering in the corner of her cell.

Sadie had put an end to that. Fred was bigger than her, but not bigger than the softball bat she had picked up from the chief's office. She would have broken his face open if he hadn't left as fast as he had.

And that left the two sisters alone to talk while the sun crept up. During their long conversation, Sadie had learned much about Jillybean's trip, but not who had been with her or where the rest of the VX gas was.

She knew there was an accomplice since the little girl slipped up and frequently used the pronoun *we*. "Who is it? Please Jillybean, you have to tell me who was with you. Please tell me or…or they'll blame you for what happened."

"What will they do to me?" she had asked in a tiny voice.

There was no way Sadie was going to answer that question with the truth. If Jillybean had turned murderer, yet again, Neil would have no choice but to kill her. If he didn't, there really would be a mob after her, a lynch mob.

The people of Estes were terrified. The council was terrified. Hell, Sadie was terrified. Over the last couple of years, she had faced many bullets and bombs, and countless zombies, but nothing had made her skin crawl like the idea of nerve gas, especially after having seen its effects first hand.

Neil had tried to keep the attack a secret but he felt he had to tell the council and, before long, word got out. People refused to get within two-hundred yards of the Stanley and when the wind shifted to the south, there had been a panic. With that had come a mood of anger and revenge, and even before Jillybean had crept down out of the hills, she was everyone's prime suspect.

The Valley was turned upside down searching for her. Practically everyone, including Sadie, was out, going from door to door. Unlike the others, Sadie had gone to find Jillybean in order to protect her.

One of the few who remained behind was Neil. "They won't catch her," he had said. "She's too smart. The only way to catch her is to bait a trap. And I am the bait. Jillybean knows me and I think we can assume that the gas attack had been meant for me. I'm usually the first person through those doors every morning."

"Bait? You can't go back there," Deanna had said. She was draped under a nursing blanket; Emily was having her dinner. "We don't know the half-life of that gas. It could be years before anyone can go into the Stanley."

"I know," Neil answered. "And so does Jillybean. She'll come for me, in my home. Probably not tonight, but it will happen eventually." They had captured her twelve hours later breaking into his place with a gun in her hand.

At midday, the full council sat to discuss what to do with her and even before a word was said, it was obvious that the vote would be seven to zero in favor of immediate execution. Sadie wasn't on the council. Neil had brought her forward out of a sense of fairness because she was the only person who could speak on Jillybean's behalf.

Grey and Deanna had volunteered, but as council members, Neil wouldn't let them.

Quietly, without interruption, they listened to Sadie spin the story of Jillybean's odyssey across the country, however it was a waste of breath; conclusions had already been drawn. When she finished, the seven nodded and thanked her and then asked her to leave. Sadie refused to budge, her hands gripping the armrests of her chair. "I wasted my time, didn't I? You're going to kill her even though it could have been someone else."

"Who could it have been?" Neil asked. Once more the others nodded. Sadie was in a fury. It was bad enough that her father wasn't siding with her, though she understood: he was the governor and sometimes he couldn't vote exactly how he felt. But Grey and Deanna didn't have that excuse, and Fred Trigg's smug face was making her want to puke.

"There could be others," she said, her voice so high it was almost a screech. "You of all people, Neil, know how many enemies we've made."

"Occam's razor," Neil answered. When Sadie only shrugged at this strange response, he explained: "In brief, Occam's Razor states that the simplest answer is almost always the correct one."

"Exactly," Sadie cried. "*Almost* always. Yes, it looks bad for her, but where's the rest of the poison gas? She didn't have it on her. Why use it once? She could have just chucked it through the door of our apartment and got out of there. And…and I believe her, about all of it. She came here to warn us."

They were in the conference room of the municipal building, sitting around a long table. Across from her was Fred. As though he were a prosecuting attorney, he steepled his fingers beneath his chin and asked: "And what do you base this belief on? And please don't say that you looked into her eyes and just knew she was telling the truth. We all know that *Jillybean* may have been telling the truth, but what about the other people living in her head?"

"There aren't any," Sadie snapped back. "She let Ipes die. Do you know what a big step that was?"

Captain Grey ran a hand though his hair, which because of the gas mask he'd been wearing for half the night, stuck up in every direction like the quills of a porcupine. "That was a big step, but I think it was also semi-dependent on her being able to stay with that old woman, and when she died, well, perhaps a part of Jillybean…that part of her that was mending…maybe it just broke."

Deanna raised a hand. "Also, by her own admission, she was hearing voices telling her to seek out the gas. I'm sorry, Sadie, she isn't fixed, far from it."

"But she stopped hearing the voices once she found the 4Runner. She says she's been completely sane for the last week. Right now, it's her word against a bunch of circumstantial evidence. What if you're wrong? There's no way you should k-kill her unless you have some sort of hard evidence. That was a law, you know."

"Yeaaah," Fred breathed out. "Look, I know you're just a kid and you think you know everything, but you're wrong. There have been many executions based on circumstantial evidence alone. I don't like it, Sadie. I don't like it one bit, but those are the facts."

It looked to her as though he actually didn't mind it one bit. In a barely controlled fury, she stood aggressively, making Fred flinch back in his chair. Sadie's eyebrows arched and she grinned, maliciously at his timidity. "Oh, so you like facts now? Give me one fact that directly links Jillybean to the attack."

Neil reached over and patted her hand. "I'm sorry, Sadie, but we have enough information to find her guilty. What we don't have are *any* facts that suggest anything other than she's in the middle of another dangerous psychotic episode. Talk to her again. Find out who her co-conspirator is. Find that Jeep. Find the VX. Find us some extenuating circumstances, please."

"Extenuating circumstances?" Fred asked, incredulously. "You mean you want her to find an excuse so that you won't have to make the hard decision. Tell me, Neil, what kind of leadership is that?" The room went silent as there was a sudden and unexpected paradigm shift.

Neil was being seen as weak and not even Captain Grey stood up for his friend. "He may be right on this one, Neil."

Emboldened, Fred glanced towards the window, where a crowd of hundreds had gathered in the street, waiting to find out what was going to happen to Jillybean. He went on in a louder voice as if he were speaking to them: "This is an extreme situation and we are living in extreme times. I think we need to consider extreme measures." He paused to gauge how this vague proclamation would go over. Only Sadie was outraged, which further fueled her outrage.

"Are you talking about torture?" she demanded. "She's only seven!"

"And how old was poor Tee?" Fred asked in a cold voice. "Or Richard Glassmeyer? Or Nathan Truby? Are you suggesting that just because Jillybean is a *young* dangerous, insane killer that we should ignore common sense?"

Neil tried to interrupt. "Fred, please."

Fred rounded on him. "What? Do you disagree? I want it on record that I am willing to take extreme measures to protect my people."

Everyone looked at Neil, who slowly nodded his head. "Okay. Let the record state that should some sort of torture be needed, Fred Trigg has volunteered." Fred grew pissy, while Sadie grew desperate.

She stepped between them. "Stop, please. Torture doesn't even work. Right Captain Grey? They water-boarded all them guys in Iraq and they got nothing, right?"

A pained look spread across his rugged features. He shook his head. "I'm sorry, but it does work. A lot of valuable information was attained through water-boarding and a lot of lives were saved." At this, the members of the council shuffled uncomfortably in their seats, looking anywhere but at Sadie.

"So, that's it?" she asked. "You're going to torture A LITTLE GIRL and then kill her?"

Fred straightened, squaring his chin. "She is a danger to everyone in this valley. I vote that we use the proven enhanced interrogation techniques to discover the truth behind these attacks. A show of hands…"

"No," Neil said, in just above a whisper. "I want to give Sadie one more chance with Jillybean." He turned to her, his scarred face filled with misery. "Please, get her to talk."

"Can I promise her some sort of deal?" Sadie asked, grasping at a single, limp straw. "You know, an immunity deal if she turns over who she's been working with. I'm not saying we should let her go free. We could keep her locked up where she won't hurt anyone."

This was such a civilized alternative that everyone except for Fred looked to Neil with a glimmer of hope. Neil dashed the hope by asking: "For how long? Do we keep her locked up forever? Or until she gets better? What if that never happens? Or what if she figures a way to escape before then? My problem with all of this, is that it doesn't really matter who her accomplice is. Jillybean, or…or some part of her was behind the attack and it proves, that despite everything she has done for you and me and Grey and all of us, she's still a danger."

"So, you're going to kill her no matter what?" Sadie asked.

"I never said that. I said get us some information. Get me something." He didn't mention what it was Jillybean could possibly say that would save her life, probably, Sadie thought, because there wasn't anything she could say.

Chapter 27

Sadie Martin

In silence, the meeting broke up. Sadie was the first out the door, heading straight away to the only occupied holding cell. With the council members watching in a huddle on the other side of the heavily barred door that led to the cellblock, she went to Jillybean's cage, but did not say a word. Jillybean was just a blanket-swaddled lump beneath the cot. She had crawled there to hide from the world and had fallen asleep.

Seeing her not as a murderer, but as a child, Sadie broke down crying, hanging onto the bars to keep from falling to her knees. Jillybean was likely guilty of three more murders, but in Sadie's mind, the little girl would always be innocent. It was the world that was guilty. It was humanity that had made her a monster.

She sniffled back the running snot, and when she did, she saw the blanket quiver just the slightest. It meant that Jillybean was awake and listening, and probably knew exactly who was at the bars. "Jillybean? I know you're awake."

The blankets didn't move. "You're crying. That's not good. That's what means they're gonna want to kill me again, right?"

Sadie had to swallow her misery and squeeze her eyes shut to stop the tears. "Yeah, but maybe if you help me, they won't. You have to tell me who was helping you."

"Why should I? You'll want to kill him, too. But you can't because you would never catch him. He's too quick."

"Is he faster than me?"

Jillybean poked her head from the blanket and shook it. "No, he's not faster, but he is quicker. You know, like his reactions. So even you wouldn't be able to catch him, I bet."

She had accidentally given a touch more information and Sadie jumped on it. "Is he young?" At the question, Jillybean's face went purposefully blank, which meant that Sadie was on the right track. "How young? He can't be younger than you, right?"

"No, he's older."

Sadie could tell that she wanted to say more, but was afraid. She had to be eased into it. Sadie tried switching things up and said: "I didn't tell you before that I like your new hairdo. It's pretty cool. Maybe I'll grow mine out a little and do that, too."

239

Jillybean touched the side of her head where her hair was the shortest. "It was mostly on an accident because a monster almost got me by grabbing my hair right through this door. It was a little scary and I had to cut my hair with glass to escape and then Chris…" Realizing her mistake, she clammed up and partially hid her face behind the blanket.

Sadie only shrugged, as if knowing the name wasn't any big deal. "So what if you said his name? We don't know a Chris, at least I don't. Was he with the Azael?"

"No, he was on his own. Like an orphan, same as me."

"Did he take care of you?"

"He saved me once from some slavers. They were very bad and had it coming, and you shoulda seen what happened to Jessica. Jessica is what means our Jeep and she got all banged up because of the 'splosions, but Chris got us out of there and helped to get me better. He watched over me and got me food and water and stuff."

Sadie was slowly getting closer to the truth. "So how did he know you? Had you met him before or maybe his family? Had they ever heard of you?"

"Chris didn't have a family. Even in the before he didn't have a family. And he didn't have any people on account they kept getting captured and all. But no one could capture him. Like I said, he's super quick and he can hear a mouse fart from a hundred yards. He said that once, but I don't know if it was true since I never was able to get a mouse to test it. But he could hear me every time I whispered anything, even when I wasn't talking to him."

"He sounds like quite a guy."

"He's no guy. He's a kid. Like nine or nine and a half or three quarters. But he's pretty good, you know. I just hope he doesn't try to rescue me because he might hurt someone or he might get hurt or something."

The two were quiet for a while, Sadie trying to figure out the right question to get her to open up completely, and Jillybean simply staring down at her bare toes. Jillybean spoke first. "I can trust you, right?"

"You can trust me with your life."

Shyly, Jillybean leaned forward and looked down the hall to where Neil and Captain Grey were watching through the gated door. "Do you trust me with *your* life?"

The answer was an immediate an emphatic: "Yes." Four months before, Sadie had been staring down the barrel of life as a sex slave, which to her was a fate worse than death. Jillybean had risked her life to save her.

She inched closer to the bars, looking as though she would dash back beneath the cot if anyone came through the door. "I'll tell you where I left the Jeep, but only you can go. Chris is very careful. He'll know if you're alone or not. Oh, and you can't bring any weapons, because he'll know that, too." She came right up to the bars and stuck out her hand with a tiny pinky thrust up. "Promise me." When Sadie hesitated, Jillybean said: "You'll never be able to talk to him unless you listen to me. I taught him too much for you to catch him."

Slowly, Sadie stuck out her pinky and when it was hooked, Jillybean gave her the exact directions to the Jeep. "And bring a white flag," she added. "He'll know what it means."

Sadie did exactly as Jillybean instructed. After she gave Neil an excuse about needing to find a toy for Jillybean that she claimed would definitely get her talking, she walked with her head down and the rain running from her shoulders into the old touristy part of town where there were still knickknack stores. Picking one at random, she went into it, crossed through to the back door and hurried back out into the rain. In the old days, a shrill alarm would have rung, but now there was nothing but the *splish* of her black, high-top Converse sneakers.

Behind the building was an ugly little alley that no tourist was ever supposed to see. She hurried along it, squeezed past a flatbed truck that stretched almost as wide as the alley and hurried on to the next street. From there, she began to make her way to the northwest, crossing through backyards and through open fields. She spent almost as much time glancing backwards to make sure she wasn't being followed as she did watching where she was going.

There were houses along the way and most were occupied, but a few were burned-out relics or in such terrible shape that they were fit only for badgers and owls. She ducked into one of these, her hand on the Glock she wore at her hip, her nerves running high. The place sat crooked on its foundation and was just as dark, dank and musty as a house could get—the perfect spot to find a misplaced zombie or some crazy fiend with a dozen vials of VX nerve gas.

"Hello?"

241

The air remained still and she relaxed the slightest as she crossed down a hall that ran at just enough of an angle to make Sadie worry that her weight would cause the whole place to tip all the way onto its side. Just in case, she walked on the high side of the hall. When she opened the hall closet, a pile of sheets came tumbling out; she snagged a white pillow case and then went to the kitchen and poked around for a broom.

After that, it was just a matter of forcing herself to leave behind her gun. She pulled it out and set it on the kitchen table, but for some reason it didn't feel right leaving it out in the open. Next, she stuck it in a drawer, but couldn't bring herself to walk away. With a groan, she fished out the Glock.

Yes, she had promised Jillybean but going about unarmed wasn't smart, especially when you were supposed to meet someone who may or may not be a murderer.

"I'll carry it, but I just won't let him see it." As slim as she was, hiding the gun on her body was impossible. It created an obvious bulge anywhere she put it. After exhausting the limited places available to carry it on her person, an idea came to her. "Maybe I don't carry it in the normal way."

It took only a little hunting around the crooked house to find a role of scotch tape, and she went through it all in order to plaster the heavy Glock to the handle of the broom. She then covered it with the pillowcase and set out into the rain on a two mile hike, following an old overgrown trail before branching off to cut her own path through a saddle between two small peaks. The Jeep was hidden in a copse of trees right where Jillybean said it would be.

Sadie resisted the urge to slink into the woods and come at the Jeep from a less obvious angle, but she had been warned: Chris would "know" and he would vanish. Feeling as though she had a rifle scope trained on her, Sadie walked through the steady rain straight to the Jeep, her eyes flicking all over the sparse forest seeing nothing beyond the grey mist and the drab trunks of pine and the boulders that looked as if they were either erupting from the earth or stubbed down into it like the forgotten butts of cigarettes.

Stopping fifty feet from the Jeep—and she only knew it was a Jeep because Jillybean had called it that—she waved the flag, which now resembled a sodden dishrag. It swung heavily back and forth and even she could see the impression of the Glock against the wet material.

"Just keep waving," she mumbled, feeling stupid. Five minutes of feeling stupid passed before she ventured: "Hello? Hi? Anyone here? Uh, Jillybean sent me. I'm Sadie. She might have mentioned me? I'm her sister." The rain pattering on the leaves was her only answer.

"Okay," she said, and waved the flag for another few minutes even though it felt like a cold and dull waste of time. Finally, when her arms began to ache, she cursed under her breath and tugged at the not-so-hidden Glock. The tape proved annoyingly strong. It took a great deal of pulling and twisting to free it.

"Alright, you win!" she cried out. "Look!" She jacked back the slide and expertly caught the chambered round in midair. She brandished it before poking it into her pocket. Then she thumbed out the magazine. She lifted it up in her right hand while she held the Glock in her left for all the trees and the nervous chipmunks to see.

With a flourish, she threw the magazine into the woods to her right and the Glock to her left, noting the landing place of each, just in case. If anyone had taught her the meaning of "just in case" it was Jillybean.

As if throwing away her gun wasn't enough, she pulled the pillowcase off the broom, hefted it like a spear and threw that away too so that she only had a soggy piece of linen to ward off the dangers of the world. For fifteen minutes, she swung the pillowcase around until she was too pissed off to bother.

"Fine! Fine, be that way, Chris. I'm just going to check out the Jeep if you don't mind." She took one step toward the odd vehicle before she thought: *Maybe he's in there.* Jillybean had mentioned the cameras, so she stood directly in front of the Jeep and slowly spun with her hands in the air.

Taking deliberate steps, she went in a wide circle around the Jeep. It was an ugly thing, covered in slabs of steel that were marked by fire and pitted by bullets. It had clearly survived more punishment than any ordinary car could have and, despite the lack of sweep or fine lines, Sadie thought it was an impressive ride. Because of the armor, she had to really bang on the side door with her fist until her hand hurt.

She then stood back for half a minute and then she rolled her eyes. "Oh, come on," she grumbled, as she reached for the door, yanked it open and ducked behind it, not knowing what to expect. Slowly, she poked her head around the door. The Jeep was empty. Or rather sort of empty.

It was empty of people, but crammed in a very Jillybean-esque manner: A pink tutu sat neatly folded on top of a box of dynamite scrounged from a mining company. There was a set of two-way radios charging on a shoebox filled with batteries. In one cup holder was a bottle of ThunderBird marked: *Do Not Drink!* And in another, a bottle of Pepto.

There were a variety of guns and a smattering of bullets and Jillybean's M79, though it only had smoke for ordinance. Sadie gazed at the monitors and the machine gun and the homemade switches, superglued to the dash. "It's a frickin' death machine."

But among all the odds and ends, there wasn't a boy with hazel eyes and little sign that there had ever been one. She found only a single set of boy clothes folded in the back seat under a pile of boxes. That they appeared untouched wasn't the biggest surprise to Sadie. In her world view boys weren't the cleanest of creatures.

What caught Sadie's attention and held her mentally hostage was the rather large stash of food, some of which was of an "exotic" nature: potato chips, Doritos, and Fig Newtons among other things. "Oh boy," she whispered, swallowing a sudden rush of saliva. She had lived off beans and venison, and poorly ground wheat for so long that this unattended stash was impossible to pass up. She reached back and grabbed the Doritos.

"Cool Ranch," she called out. "Gonna eat 'em if you don't stop me, Chris." He didn't stop her. He remained annoyingly aloof, if he was out there at all. "He's like friggin' Bigfoot," she muttered. Almost daring him, she climbed up onto the hood of the Jeep with the bag in hand. She then leaned back against the armored windshield, her legs stretched out and her feet crossed.

When she had crunched the last crumb, she groaned, balled the bag and threw it. "Chris! Hey, Chris! Jillybean sent me." Were it not for the rain, her voice would have echoed for miles. Still, if he was listening, he would have heard. "Which means he's not listening. So does that mean he's not around or that he doesn't exist?"

With Jillybean there was no way of knowing what was playing like a movie in her head and what was real. "I know the poison gas is real." She had seen that with her own eyes and the memory still turned her stomach. Thinking about the gas made her feel as though she was sitting on a bomb.

"Wouldn't be the first time," she said and grinned her rakish, lopsided grin. Climbing down she opened the back door and stood looking in at the stacks of "crazy-girl." Like an archeologist, she started at the top, under the drones and gradually unearthed a layer of welding equipment, a layer of magnets and copper wire, a layer of potassium nitrate, a layer of car batteries, a layer of Barbie Dolls and so on. When she had dug down to the bottom, she made a noise that wasn't quite a word: "Whaaa?"

There weren't any vials whatsoever. There was a single gas mask, but no plastic suits or MOPP gear or anything protective. Nor had there been any room for any of that or for the suitcase that Neil had described. "Unless Chris carried it in on his lap. But who in their right mind would do that. You know what? I don't think she did it."

Bursting with sudden happiness, she collected her gun and bullets, before running all the way into town. Breathless and streaming rain, she barged into the police station. "They're next door," the guard watching over Jillybean said. He was only half watching her; most of his attention was on a middle-school level word search. He couldn't seem to find the word "freckle."

Sadie thanked him, glanced through the doorway to the cells and saw that Jillybean was sleeping again, once more under the cot. "Good," she murmured and left, sprinting to the next building and brushing past a guard who tried to stop her. Considering it was their "City Hall," it was a squat and dull, and the offices were cramped.

The council was once again meeting, their argument loud enough to be heard out in the corridor. Fred was trying to get them to move up the water boarding. He was trying to sound confident, but there was a touch of fear in his voice. "You know they're going to come after us next. It could be happening right now."

"It's a 'they' now?" Neil asked. "Don't you think we would notice a mob of masked villains running around the Valley?"

Before Fred could answer, Sadie opened the door all the way and strode in stating: "I found the Jeep."

Fred's eyes were alight with fear and excitement. "And?" When Sadie only smirked, enjoying watching him squirm like a worm on a hook, he added: "Well? What about the VX?"

"There was no sign of it," she said, looking and feeling smug. "What's more, I don't think there had ever been any poisonous gas in it. I searched it top to bottom and…"

Grey's eyes shot wide in shock. "Sadie! What the hell? You searched it without protection?"

She was in such a giddy mood that she started cracking up over the question and no matter what she did, she couldn't control the gales of laughter geysering out of her.

Neil looked relieved…at first. "Sadie, hold on, I don't know if you've proved all that much. What about the person who was with her? Where is he? Did you even consider that he might have the case with him?"

Like a five year old, Sadie stomped her foot in fury. "You don't get it! Jillybean didn't do this. Come on, I'll show you." She turned on her heel and walked straight out of the room with the members of the council hurrying to catch up. Grey was the quickest and stopped her before she made it out into the rain.

"Protection, first." This time she didn't laugh. She only glared as he ordered one of his men to fetch plastic painting overalls. Next, Grey gathered a squad of men and two deuce-and-a-halfs. All of this wasted an hour and during that time, Sadie paced like a caged tiger, afraid that even then Chris was hiding the Jeep in some dark vale of which there were thousands surrounding the Valley.

Once everyone had climbed aboard one of the trucks, they chugged up into the hills. Amazingly the Jeep was still there and none of the gear and gadgets and gizmos that Sadie had pulled out had been touched. Not even the weapons were missing.

There were only two gas masks between them. Grey pulled on his mask and handed the other to Sadie, who started to shake her head.

"Get it on!" he barked. "And the rest of you stay back." He turned away to position his squad and when he did, Sadie tossed aside her mask and walked over to the Jeep.

"You see all of this stuff? It was crammed in the back and up on the roof. The only place you could fit anything the size of the suitcase was on the passenger's lap and who would ride across country with people shooting at you and trying to blow you up with *that* on your lap? You wouldn't. No one would."

Fred, who had picked up the discarded mask and had put it on, came up to the Jeep and glanced around, swinging his head in exaggerated motions because of the frog-eye lenses. "It could have fit up there easily," he said, pointing at the roof rack.

"Oh really?" Sadie asked, gesturing up at the Jeep. "Do you see that netting? When I got here, it was tied down, holding everything in place and no, there wasn't room for a suitcase."

"And we're just supposed to take your word for that?" Fred asked. Sadie turned on him in an instant and before she knew what she was doing, she had launched herself at him. His eyes went huge behind the mask, but only for a second and then her fist crashed into the side of his face.

In a flash, the mask was turned around on the side of his head with the buggy eye pieces pointing away to the west. He was blind and flailing, and didn't see the arm of a root arched up out of the ground as he frantically backed away. Down he went with Sadie on top of him. She was in a fury and after punching him twice more, tore the mask off of him. He gobbled out a cry and tried to hold his breath against the possibility of poisonous gas, however Sadie was planted squarely on top of him and she began punching him again until he was forced to breathe.

"Since you won't take my word for it, you can just suck it. There ain't no gas, Fred and there never was." She jumped up and stalked around the Jeep, breathing in exaggerated gasps to show it was safe. Oddly, it helped to calm her. "Take off that silly mask, Grey, and look at all of this stuff." She waved at the stash and then went to the sleeve of Fig Newtons, tore it open and casually ate one.

Neil was the first to come forward. He looked uncomfortable trying to breathe "normally," as he circled the Jeep. "All of this stuff fit in there? That's a lot of crap."

With an angry sigh, Grey took off his mask and gazed at the mess. "None of this is crap, except for maybe those Barbie Dolls. For the most part, Jillybean knows what's important. Batteries, guns, gas, food. She's got it all covered."

"Now do you believe me," Sadie asked.

It was a shock to her that it was Deanna who said, "Not necessarily. I'm sorry, Sadie, but you're missing something obvious. What if there isn't a Chris at all? What if she made him up?"

Sadie snorted, shaking her head as if what was being suggested was ludicrous. Neil snuck a careful look at Sadie before saying: "Think about it, sweetie. What are the chances that a lost and lonely seven year old would just happen to stumble across a similarly lost and lonely nine year old?"

"Okay, okay, what about the boy clothes?" she asked. "Why would she invent an entire person and then dress him in real clothes? That doesn't make any sense."

"Crazy doesn't have to make sense," Neil said. "If it did, I don't think we would call it crazy."

"Do the batteries make sense?" Sadie asked. "Yes they do. And do the radios make sense. And the Pepto? And the ThunderBird? Well, maybe the ThunderBird doesn't make sense, but you get what I'm saying. Jillybean was perfectly rational when it came to all that, but you're thinking she just made up a person?"

Deanna gaped at Sadie. "Are you forgetting about Ipes? And what about Eve? They were very real to her."

Of course Sadie hadn't forgotten about them. "Okay, let's say Chris is imaginary, it still doesn't point to Jillybean's guilt. It points in the opposite direction. When Eve was in her, Jillybean was terrified because Eve was evil. But she isn't afraid of Chris. She likes him. He is a good guy to her. He's a hero and in her world, heroes don't go around murdering innocent people."

"You're right," Deanna said. Neil and Grey both agreed.

Fred, who was clutching the mask to his chest, wore a pinched look as if his outrage was loosening his bowels and he was fighting to keep everything inside. "Seriously? You guys are trying to put a box around Jillybean's psychosis? Okay, let's say Chris is a good guy running around inside her head. Isn't it possible that since she's inventing good guys she can invent a bad guy as well? Perhaps one she doesn't even know about?"

"Why would she do that?" Sadie asked.

He threw his hands in the air. "Why would she do any of it? She's crazy, that's why! Maybe she secretly holds a grudge against us for kicking her out of the Valley. Or maybe she wants the attention. Who knows?"

Captain Grey had been admiring the construction of the Jeep. He had stuck his head in the cab and now he popped out to say: "There's one way we might be able to find out who is real and who isn't. We can check out if there's anything recorded on these iPads. We just need the codes. Man, I gotta say this vehicle is genius. She didn't miss a trick. Bombs, smoke, a machine gun, low light cameras, drones. It's got everything, though I would have put in a roof hatch and better grade tires. These are okay, but…"

Neil held up a hand. "We're getting off topic. I'm sorry Sadie, none of what I see here precludes Jillybean from having the vials. She could have moved them to a smaller container or she could have re-situated what was on top before she left. Chris really isn't the issue here. The vials are the issue and we have to find them one way or the other."

"You're still going to torture her?" Sadie asked, her hand slipping up her thigh to where her Glock sat in its holster. With an act of will, she kept from taking the grip in hand and yanking it out. "Tell me Neil, if she doesn't have the vials, how can she possibly prove that she doesn't have them?"

He couldn't look at her when he answered: "Either she has them or Chris has them. Under extreme, ur, stress her other personality will come out. I'm sorry Sadie, it's either this or we just straight up execute her."

Chapter 28

Jillybean

She had been in her cell for hours now, long enough to know the rhythms and the sounds of the police station. She knew when Gus was having trouble finding a word in his puzzle book. He would tap his pencil over and over and mumble the hidden word to himself between curses.

And she knew when a meal was about to be served. The crowd outside would grow louder, saying things like: "Why waste food?" They wanted to kill her. It was why she hid under her cot—that and also because she didn't want people to see her loosening the springs and bits of metal she would need to escape.

The cell had been made and maintained with small-town problems in mind: drunks getting into fights, shoplifters nervously waiting for their parents to come and get them, and the occasional domestic violence case. Estes Park had been a tourist destination and Jillybean doubted if there had ever been a true "desperado" in the jail until she had arrived.

Already she had removed a spring that was bigger than her thumb. It was useless as a lock pick, so she was using it to detach other pieces of metal such as one of the little cross bars that were in each corner of the cot. They were held in place with two small hexagonal screws that could be loosened with either a screwdriver or a wrench.

The spring, with its curves, was a poor substitute for a wrench but with it, she hoped to be able to remove the small crossbars which could then be used to dismantle the sink and the toilet to find even more pieces. Eventually she was hoping to fashion a crude key for use in the cell door's lock.

She was optimistic despite the crowd buzzing about killing her and the pain in her fingers from the repetitious twisting of the spring. In her mind, things that were made by man could be unmade by a little girl if she had a strong enough will and enough time. Just then, time was her biggest enemy.

It was late afternoon before she was disturbed from her work by the sound of the outer door opening. "She okay, Gus?" she heard Neil ask.

Gus' chair creaked as he leaned back. "Yup. Been sleeping most of the day."

"I don't mean to be contradictory, but knowing her, I doubt it," Neil replied. She heard Gus open the gated door that led into the cellblock. A moment later Neil said, "Come on out of there, Jillybean. I'm pretty sure that you're not sleeping. We need to talk again."

She crawled out, still wrapped in her one blanket. The two stared at each other; Neil with a sad look on his face; Jillybean passively neutral as she noted the plastic bag he carried, a damp line on his sweater vest beneath his open raincoat, and the muddied boots.

"Sadie showed you my Jeep," she said. "But you didn't catch Chris and now you want the passwords to the iPads in that bag."

"Impressive as always," Neil said, bowing his head slightly. "It's impressive because you aren't guessing. You're like Sherlock Holmes. How'd you know?"

She had never heard of Sherlock Holmes, but the rest was easy. "You were out in the rain just long enough for the water to creep through your zipper and it woulda taken a lot longer to catch Chris. The lighter color mud on your boots is what means it comes from the hills, where it's usually drier and that was where the Jeep was. I can see the shape of the iPad in the bag and you have the same look in your eyes as you did last year when you were gonna kill me. I think if you had captured Chris, you would have a different look—like an apology look."

"Oh."

A silence settled between them but as Jillybean hadn't done anything wrong, it was only awkward for Neil. Eventually, Jillybean asked: "Who's Sherlock Holmes? If he's like me, why don't you have him in jail, too?"

"He was a character from a book who was very smart and could deduce things from the slightest clues. I wish I could do that. If I could, we would have been done with all of this by now."

Jillybean only gave him a little shrug, thinking that he was wrong. He'd be done with the Jillybean part but not with who really had the gas. With a sigh she said: "All of the iPads have the same password: 5636. I know what you're thinking but you're wrong."

"Oh, yeah? What am I thinking?"

"You think the iPads will show you the suitcase thingy which held the gas but it won't, and that you won't see Chris, but you will. You'll see Chris on the one that was with Laurie. She's the drone with the pony stickers."

"Okay, thanks." Neil stood for a moment looking as though he wanted to say something to her, but he didn't except for a quick "Goodbye." She only waved in response and then sighed again.

An hour after that, Gus brought her dinner; a watery, dull soup that had far too many carrots in it for Jillybean's liking. He brought with him two hardcover books. "The governor wanted me to find some Sherlock Holmes stuff but the library was out. This is Nancy Drew. It's pretty much the same."

Jillybean thanked him without coming out from beneath her cot. She read while she slurped at her soup with a plastic spoon. It had to be slurped because it was too hot to simply ingest in a straight forward manner. After eight chapters, Jillybean looked up from reading and noticed that it was full dark outside. She had been enjoying the book despite the fact that although the word mystery was used frequently the story was far from mysterious, and there was very little in the way of deducing going on. The writing felt dated and it reminded her of her *Little House on the Prairie* books.

When her soup was eaten, Gus retrieved the bowl and spoon and eyed her and the cell closely, but not close enough, and didn't notice the missing spring. When he left, she reluctantly set the book aside. She still had a lot of work to do before she could get the cross-piece off the cot.

An hour went by and the nuts holding the cross piece hadn't budged a millimeter. She pulled her sweaty head from beneath the blanket and sucked on her aching fingers, listening. There was a new sound coming from down the hall: an intermittent rumble. Gus was sleeping.

Beneath the snore was another sound, one so soft and sinister that it stole fear into Jillybean's heart. This was no monster who had just happened to wander into town, this was a person, more than likely one bent on revenge.

She was stuck with nowhere to run and nowhere to hide, and so she stood, trembling, waiting on whatever fate was coming to her as a shadowy figure slipped through the half-open doorway. The jail area was lit by a single propane lantern kept just out of reach near her cell. It seemed to make everything outside its white circle look darker and the figure coming towards her appeared just as black as night with coal for eyes.

But then it flashed a white smile. "Christian?" she whispered, hurrying to the bars. "You shouldn't be here."

"No, you shouldn't be here." He stopped just shy of the door to the jail cell and peered in at the lock. "I wish I had all that stuff you carry. I don't even have my knife. They got to the Jeep and took it. I saw one of them coming and I thought it was a trap. I didn't know what to do except run."

"You were smart to run and you should probably keep running. My friends…they're not thinking right and…and I'm in real trouble this time. They don't believe me about that nerve gas stuff. They think I took it and used it."

His handsome, boyish face was marred by lines of confusion as he asked: "Used it on who? Someone around here?"

"Yes, someone used the gas and killed three people and they won't believe that I didn't do it. And they won't believe you, neither. You…you should go. This could be a trap. Gus could be in on it. He might only be pretending to sleep. They could have people hiding all around the building."

"Don't you think I thought of that? I watched this place for hours. I know their routines better than they do. I…"

The outer door of the jail opened. It was a soft, secretive sound which didn't make sense to Jillybean. Other than Chris, who would want to sneak into the police station?

"Get in that cell and hide under the cot," Jillybean hissed, pointing to the cell across from hers. It wasn't the best hiding place, it was the *only* hiding place. As quick and silent as a fox, he whisked out of sight and as he did, the mystery of who had come in was revealed.

"Uh, Gus? Hey, sorry. I didn't mean to startle you. I'm here to see Jillybean. Council orders." It was Sadie, sounding tired and worrisomely sad. It didn't take a detective to figure out that bad news was coming. Although she didn't feel as though she had moved, Jillybean felt the cot at the back of her thigh and she sat, pulling the blanket up to her chin.

Even more than Chris had, the girl in black swept in looking like a shadow and it was not until she entered the glow of the lantern that Jillybean got a good look at her. Sadie's face was pale and her features were cast down. Even with a false smile, she looked sad. In her hand was the iPad that was usually synched with Laurie the drone.

253

"What is it?" Jillybean asked. She felt like a patient in a doctor's office who was about to be told she had cancer.

"It's about Christian. I..." Her strained smile dipped and her breath caught for a moment. "I, uh wanted to show you this. Neil actually wanted me to, but I did, also. Um, why don't you get a little closer. You can bring your blanket if you want."

Jillybean didn't want to get off the cot; she was afraid to. "Chris didn't do anything wrong. We didn't have any vials of nothing. You gotta believe me."

Sadie leaned her head against the bars and said: "I don't know what to believe. We found something on this iPad. Here, let me show you."

With one last furtive look towards where Chris was just a shadow in the shadows, Jillybean went to the bars and knelt opposite of her sister, who had the iPad. She swiped to turn it on and then punched in the password. A video started playing.

"That's the recording Chris made," Jillybean said, feeling a sudden wave of relief. "I already saw this. All it shows is how to get to Estes without being seen. Chris was nervous about people and we were ascared that the bad guys who had really taken the nerve gas had gotted here first."

Sadie's fake smile was back and for some reason it made Jillybean want to cry. Sadie pushed fast forward, saying: "Yeah, that's what you told me."

"I told you that because it's the truth." Sadie only nodded to this as the screen showed the forest trail and the path between The Needles. The shot went very high as the drone ascended, giving them a wide-angle view. First, it hovered over the Stanley and then went to hover over the motel in which Neil lived.

"See? There's nothing," Jillybean said, quickly, hoping that they were done. Sadie kept the feed going as the drone flew back to the Jeep. From high up in the air, the Jeep looked like a little square of black and next to it was a tiny person. It could only be a child, staring upwards, directing the drone lower and lower.

At two hundred feet, the child was a blur. When it got to a hundred feet, Jillybean's lips parted and yet the air in her lungs ceased to flow in and out. At fifty feet, she saw herself on the screen of the iPad getting bigger and bigger.

"No," she whispered, suddenly finding her breath. "This must be an older file. Or it got spliced somehow." *Or it's a trick*, she thought. *Perhaps Sadie was just trying to get her to reveal where Chris was.* She leaned over and looked past Sadie at the dark under the cot across the little corridor. Was Chris there curled deep into the corner?

"The only person who could have messed with the iPad is you, Jillybean. Did you mess with it?"

The little girl shook her head. "But Chris might have. He was the only one who knew the code." *Besides me*, her own voice said in her mind. She shook her head at the voice, because it couldn't be true. She was getting better. Her mind was supposed to be mending. That had been the plan. Her brain would heal and then she would be able to come back and be with her friends and family.

But if Chris wasn't real, then all of that was wrong. "Can I see that?"

Sadie handed the iPad through the bars and Jillybean watched the last thirty seconds, feeling hollow and disjointed like those times when Eve would take her over. She felt like a ghost haunting her own body. "But he is real," she whispered. "He's right over…"

For a brief second, the ghostly feeling gave way to anger and she hurled the iPad through the bars into the other cell. The light of its screen kicked up crazy shadows, including something small and frightened beneath the cot, but then it fell with a tinkle of broken glass landing on its screen and the cell was dark again.

"I understand, Jilly…"

"Please get that," she interrupted, pointing at the iPad. Sadie, looking emotionally wrung out, nodded and went to pick it up. The light of the screen illuminated the cell, and Jillybean saw Chris hiding under the cot, but only for a moment, and then he faded away into shadow.

A million goosebumps broke out across her body and once more her mind felt dislocated from her body and at the same time, she could feel the puke rising in the back of her throat. "No. How? How can he…" Her mouth stopped moving and her eyes lost their focus and her brain seemed to slip out of gear. She stood, tottering, her muscles no longer controlled.

She would have fallen except that Sadie reached through the bars and took hold of her shoulder. Jillybean looked up at her in puzzlement unsure about everything. "Was any of it real?" she whispered. "Was Granny Annie? What about that girl I operated on? Did she really die?"

"You operated on someone?" Sadie asked, leaning away from the bars as if the idea was repulsive.

255

Jillybean shrugged. "I don't know. I didn't tell you because I thought you'd be mad. But…but, did I even shoot her first? Was that practice? Was that real life?" She searched Sadie's face, looking for answers and not finding any.

"I don't know about that girl," Sadie said, "but Granny Annie was real and the Jeep was real, and so was the poison gas. Do you remember the poison gas that you took from the Colonel?"

She did, only she remembered it as if it were a dream. It was one of the key memories she had tried to hide from herself. "But normal people can't do that," she said, talking to herself. "They can't hide things from themselves. That's what means I'm crazy. If I forgotted that, what else am I forgetting?"

"The gas?" Sadie prompted. "Where is it?"

Jillybean turned away from her, picturing herself stepping through the forest south of the highway, south of the destroyed trader trucks, her feet crunching leaves and snapping twigs, while beside her Chris walked. "Soundlessly," she said. Christian always walked as if he were on a velvet carpet.

They stopped with the 4Runner twelve feet away. The back hatch was open and the cargo area was empty. What was strange was that at the time, she remembered remembering. She could hear the conversation that went on in the Colonel's armory as if it were coming to her from a scratchy radio:

"Mister Colonel, sir, what is Venomous Agent X?" she had yelled from down the row of shelves. *"Is that snake poison?"*

His eyes had widened for just a second and then a strained smile jumped onto his face as he tried to conceal his fear. *"It's bad news. Don't touch that, whatever you do. It's VX gas. It's a chemical weapon that could kill all of us in seconds if you release it by accident."*

"He's right. Don't touch it," Neil had warned. *"I read about that stuff. It could end up contaminating this entire island, killing everyone. You can have anything else, but not that."*

She then remembered arguing with Ipes. He was afraid of the gas, but was more afraid of her. "He was afraid that I would use it and be like Eve, only I would never do no such thing." Or had she? Or had she? Or had she? The question kept hammering into her head, but all she could think about was Chris.

That he wasn't real just wasn't possible.

"And that's what means I'm still crazy. And dangerous, I guess. I never did want to be dangerous. I just wanted not to be lonely." Tears poured down her face as she remembered the first time she had thought she had seen Chis. There had been just a blur in the corner of her eye, a shock of unexpected brown against the drab background of a dead world. It had moved silently. Had it been a raven or a boy? The idea that a boy her age was alive in the world and on his own, appealed to her and yet she hadn't acted. She had let it simmer in her mind.

She had been going to find a new family: Laura's family in Scottsbluff, only the house had been empty and her dream of being with a loving family and playing with Tristyn and…

Jillybean blew out, wearily, realizing she had gone to find Tristyn but when she found out the girl was dead she had made up Christian, the perfect boy: handsome, strong, fast, courageous —everything Jillybean wasn't.

Her memories of him began to dissolve: Chris sneaking around the train yard, Chris on *The Lilly* with his hair streaming, him driving the Jeep even though his knees jutted practically up to his chin. Chris rescuing her from the traders with the bombs exploding all around…

"Wait," Jillybean said, viciously ripping a sleeve across her nose to rid herself of the childish buggers. "He rescued me from the traders. That was real. Sadie that was real! I was chained in one of the stalls and he picked the lock…or I think he did. I was knocked out." She touched her head where the lump had been.

Sadie looked unconvinced. "He picked a lock? You know I picked a lock once. It took me three hours and my fingers were bleeding by the time I got it open. How long did it take Chris?"

"I don't know. I was knocked out like I said. This bad man, the leader of the traders had hit me in the stomach and then punched me in the face. I blacked out and the next thing I knew, there was Chris. He had to practically carry me out of the truck."

"You told me this before and I'm having trouble with this. A grown man punched you? Twice? Really? I'm sorry but you're so small, you'd think one punch would be enough."

Jillybean couldn't understand why that was so hard to believe. "He was very bad, worserer than Gunner or the Colonel. And he was big and scary and stinky of old sweat and his hands were very rough. They hurt like tree bark and his nails were long and scraggy and they hurt when he…"

A sudden image, a hidden image, a horrible image came to her: the leader of the traders on top of her, his rough, cruel hands pulling her naked thighs apart and there, stiff and as dreadful as a spear between her legs...

The picture in her mind was so shocking that it was a moment before she understood what had really happened in the trader's bedroom.

Chapter 29

Jillybean

"No!" Jillybean screamed, clutching her stomach way down low with both hands. She hadn't been punched, she had been raped. The image of it wouldn't stop and it didn't remain static but moved and shifted and she could hear her own screams in her head and feel the burning inside of her. She cast one terrified look as Sadie and then ran to the corner of her cell and buried herself in the blanket, crying so hard that she couldn't breathe normally. Her chest hitched as she panted like a dog.

"What's wrong, Jillybean?" her sister asked, her tone soft, the worry obvious.

"Nothing. I-I want Christian back," she bawled. "Please, bring him back. Please. He rescued me. He loved me. He would never hurt me. He is a good person."

A long sigh escaped Sadie. "I can't bring him back, because he isn't real. The only thing I can do is try to keep you from getting hurt anymore. Are you listening to me, Jillybean? Your life is in danger if you can't tell me where that gas is."

Jillybean was an emotional wreck. She was a lost and lonely girl, afraid of the world and everything in it. But she was a survivor, first and foremost. She went numb at Sadie's pronouncement and the tears dried in an instant.

In order to live through the next day, she had to force certain concepts into her reality, accept them and move on: the hated rapist was in the past and could no longer hurt her, and Chris was no more real than Eve had been. This was her reality, now.

Her towering intellect stood upon a crumbling base, but it had not fallen yet. "I don't know where the gas is," Jillybean whispered. "It was gone when we…I mean, when I got there. Sadie? What are they going to do to me?"

"Fred is demanding that we waterboard you. It's a form of torture where they basically drown you and then bring you back and drown you some more."

The numb sensation spread until she couldn't feel her fingers and toes. "Even Mister Neil wants to do this? And Mister Captain Grey?"

"Neither of them wants to do it, but the people are up in arms. They're going crazy over the idea that the gas is out there, maybe hooked to a bomb or something."

"And if I can find them the gas?" Jillybean asked. Sadie answered by lifting one shoulder, which only had one meaning. "They're gonna execute me, anyways?" Sadie's chin dropped and when she nodded, only the top of her head appeared to move. "Oh," Jillybean said. The numbness was so bad now that she had to actively push the air in and out of her lungs.

Her mind wanted to dwell on Chris and the rape and the torture and her execution but all that was a waste of time. She had to focus...or die.

She thought back to the day she had found the 4Runner. The back was open and so were all the doors. Around the truck were odds and ends, mostly clothes that had belonged to Neil and Jillybean, but there were also pearls scattered about. They had been Jillybean's. Months before, one of the ex-sex slaves had given them to her as a gift for rescuing them back in Oklahoma.

Whoever had taken the poison gas had wasted energy ripping the necklace apart and throwing the clothes. It could only be someone who hated Jillybean with a passion. It was strange to be that hated. *Eve hated me like that*, she thought. "But she's dead."

"Who?" Sadie asked, eagerly. "Who do you think is dead?"

"Eve...the bad Eve. She's the only one who could have done this, but I haven't felt a thing inside me, or heard anything or nothing. Sadie, tell me, are they going to give me time before they start with the watering thing?"

The older girl's lips momentarily drew into a flat line. "Just until morning. They sent me to try to get you to cooperate. Only Fred is pushing for this, but they're all scared. Really, it's the entire Valley. Everyone is very upset. They, we...all of us, had hoped to be finished with all of this war and death and they want something done."

Jillybean wanted to be done with death more than anyone but since when did she ever get a choice? "Just until morning," she whispered to herself. "That's not a long time. Can I see that iPad again?"

"You can watch the video if you want, but you can't keep it. The council's orders and mine, too. I really am sorry. Once I saw that it was just you working the drone..." She left off, perhaps not knowing how to finish without directly accusing the girl.

Jillybean took the iPad and immediately turned away. The glass face of the device was cracked and pieces were missing. As the video ran, she carefully worked at the shards, plucking out two of the largest pieces and sliding them into the front of her panties where the elastic held them against her skin.

The slivers were sharp and she made sure not to twist or bend for fear of cutting herself.

"I don't think I did nothing wrong, Miss Sadie," she said, handing the iPad back. In the dark, Sadie didn't notice the missing pieces. "But maybe I did. I don't know. I might could dream the answer." This was her way of trying to get Sadie to leave. She was afraid she would need more time than she had left.

"Please. Please do. For your sake and for mine. I might go crazy myself if anyone hurts you." She reached through the bars as if she wanted to hug Jillybean. A hug would have been wonderful, however as Jillybean was afraid of the shards, she only held her sister's hand for a moment.

"Try to stall them, okay?" she begged. Sadie said she would and then left, slowly, casting looks back at Jillybean who stood at the bars trying to will her sister to move faster.

When the outer door was finally closed with Gus heaving himself up to lock it behind Sadie, Jillybean stood there for a moment, searching her memories and her mind. She was still in shock to discover that Chris wasn't real. The realization that she had been raped made her feel filthy and slimy, and terribly. Compared with that, being told she was still crazy wasn't that big of a deal. It was a little depressing, but as much as she wanted to be "normal" she was sort of used to being crazy. What didn't make sense was the emptiness inside of her.

Chris was gone; no part of him remained. And the voice that had egged her on all through her trip was nowhere inside of her. Eve had been banished and Ipes had died a hero's death.

"Hello?" she whispered, her eyes canted up towards her forehead. No one and no thing answered. She was really and truly alone in the cell. "Unless whoever stolded those vials is hiding real deep." Having been forced to live there by Eve, she understood the concept of the subconscious perhaps better than anyone. "What if there's something even below that?"

What if there really was a bomb with the gas in it and what if only this something deep inside knew where it was? "Then torture won't work," she said. "Whoever's inside me will let me get tortured and won't feel a thing, for all darn it! That isn't fair. If Chris was here…"

But Chris wasn't there. In frustration and grief, she pulled the two long horns of hair that hung from the front of her head. Strands of it came screaming from her scalp and yet the pain was necessary. It centered her thinking. If she didn't want more pain *and* the even worse pain, she needed to find the monster inside of her. She needed to go down into the black of her soul, down where Eve used to send her.

The only problem was that she didn't know how to do that and she feared it would take longer than a few hours. And if she was still here when they came to drown her...a shudder twerked her shoulders.

She needed time and that meant she needed to escape.

Taking a deep breath, she analyzed her situation. The tools available to her were limited: a spring the size of her thumb, two shards of thin glass and the Nancy Drew novels. She also had the blanket and the cushion on the cot, and her clothes, minus her belt and the laces on her Keds. It wasn't much to work with even for her.

Regardless, she went right to work, starting with a new inspection of the little hexagonal nuts holding the corner pieces of the cot in place. They were thirty-three pages wide as measured with the Nancy Drew book. Using that as her guide, she placed the two shards of glass thirty-three pages apart in the exact center of the book, leaving only a couple of millimeters protruding.

This was her wrench. Holding the book tightly closed, she slid the shards on either side of the first nut. The fit was exact. Now, all she had to do was hold it as tight as possible and crank the book counter-clockwise to loosen the nut. Simple in concept, impossible in reality.

The glass was too brittle and with every turn, it would grind into flakes and crystalline dust. She persevered for an even dozen tries until she realized the attempt was useless. "But the idea is solid," she muttered. "If I had a different material or some way to bolster the strength of the glas..."

In the outer room, Gus yawned loud enough to startle her. "Beetle, beetle...where is that damn beetle? There's a 'B' but no double 'E', damn it."

Jillybean tuned him out, thinking about what she had to work with. The glass-edged wrench had been a good idea, however she was pitting the strength of the millimeter width glass against steel. It would never work without some sort of barrier to protect it.

One possible barrier sat in her hand: the book. She tried insulating the glass with twenty pages but the seal around the angles of the nut wasn't strong enough and slipped without turning it. She tried ten pages on either side of the glass and wedged the two pieces as close to the spine as possible.

Once more the glass broke and yet, the little nut had turned. "That'll do, donkey," she said, with a grin, and adjusted the remaining hunks of glass in the book. In seconds, she had the first nut off and went to work on the second. Half the glass had crumbled to nothing by the time she got the second nut off, but she didn't care, now she had a flat hunk of metal: half an inch wide and three inches long.

Quickly, she went to the sink. It and the toilet were set close to the wall with most of their plumbing hidden behind the wall by a steel plate. Again, screws affixed the plate in place, but this time her trick with the book wouldn't work. They weren't hexagonal like the others.

Fortunately, they were flat head screws and the little shim of metal was able to fit in the notch; unfortunately, Jillybean's hands were too weak and her flesh too soft to loosen the screw. She attempted to use the Nancy Drew book as a handle by setting the metal in it, however this time the heavier metal proved stronger.

What she needed was another of the little metal corner cross bars and since she could use the first piece of metal in place of one side of the glass, the second set of screws came out with more ease. With the remaining glass, she cut a long, thin strip from the blanket and then wrapped this around the two pieces of metal so that they formed a cross.

Setting one end into the screw, she used it just like a miniature tire wrench. It allowed her to use all the strength she had in both hands. The screw resisted; she had to stop three times to rest her hands, but on the fourth try, as she strained with gritted teeth, it made a little squeak of a noise and budged over.

Two minutes later, the screw was hidden under the cot. She was on to the next one when she heard the front door of the police station open. "Gus!" a strange man cried. "What the hell? How can you sleep with *her* in the cells? If she had got out, she'd cut your throat before you knew what was what."

"Sorry," Gus mumbled.

263

"Is she even still here for Christ's sake?"

Shadows bobbed through the bars of the door—they were coming! Quickly, she spun around looking at her cell, afraid that something was out of place. The only thing that didn't belong were the metal bits lashed together in her hand. She stuck them down the back of her panties and whisked up the blanket just as Gus and another guard came striding down the corridor between the cells.

Jillybean's fear got the best of her and she threw the blanket over her head and trembled beneath it. What if this was the man who was supposed to drown her? She was afraid she would pass out if she looked at such a man.

"Hey, Jillybean?" Gus asked. "You okay?" Gus was somewhat of a sad sack. He had a drooping face that suggested he'd lost a great deal of weight very quickly and he stood in a stoop as well, making it seem as though he were carrying the world's cares upon his sloped shoulders.

"I guess so," she answered. "I don't want any visitors, if you don't mind." Through the blanket, she could see their flashlights swishing back and forth looking like spotlights searching for an escaped convict.

"I'm not a visitor. My name is John and I'm taking over for Gus. And by the way, little girl, you will not be escaping on my watch. Stand up."

She wanted to refuse, but she ran the risk of him coming into her cell if she didn't. After discovering that she'd been raped, the thought of being trapped in a cage with a man was enough to make her hands begin to sweat and her breath to come ragged from her throat. Slowly, she stood, letting the blanket fall away. She was dressed in baggy blue jeans and a Christmas sweater that Sadie had found for her. It was striped red and green with a reindeer stitched across the front.

The new guard transfixed her with the beam of his flashlight. She dropped her head so they wouldn't see her face and she clutched herself feeling vulnerable. "You're scaring her," Gus said.

"Oh, I doubt that," John said. "This is Jillybean. I saw her after she killed General Johnston. She walked right out of the Stanley, under guard mind you, and she was just as cool as could be. They say she's a sociopath. She can kill without batting an eye because she doesn't have real feelings."

"They say she was forced to kill General Johnston. That's what Kay told me. They made her do it. Is that what happened, Jillybean?"

She nodded and then said: "Can I be alone now, please? I don't feel like talking just at the moment."

"Well, you better talk tomorrow," John said. "Because if you don't, well let's just say, it'll suck to be you."

"It already does," she whispered, dropping down into her blanket and covering herself once more. They left her in the semi-dark of the single lantern and she didn't wait even a second before scurrying back to work. It was an hour before she got all the screws off and in that time, John came back to check on her three times.

Each time she huddled beneath her blanket, no longer quite as afraid. She kept the screws set loosely in their holes now so that any casual inspection wouldn't reveal her plan.

What that plan was would depend on what she found behind the plate. She waited to look until John checked on her again. It was a half hour wait which she took to be a good sign. John was a pimple-faced nobody who had been living on the streets when the apocalypse hit. He wasn't smart or hard-charging and Jillybean guessed that he would check on her less and less.

After he checked on her that last time, she undid the loose screws and gently pulled on the backing plate far enough to see that she had wasted her time. The plumbing had been designed with a minimum of moving parts to ensure that nothing could be used to escape or as a weapon. The only thing in the space between the walls were the four-inch water and sewer lines which came up from beneath the floor.

"For all darn it," she whispered, sitting back on her heels. John was in the other room yawning every few minutes and the chants and angry mumbles from outside had ceased, at least for the night. It should have been the perfect time for an escape. "Or to be rescued," she said, thinking about Chris.

Just then, she desperately needed him to be real. "Chris," she pleaded in a quiet hiss. "Christian?" Nothing. He remained just a fading memory and in his place was the real memory of the trader on top of her and the pain in her down below and the feel of his hand clamped over her mouth as she screamed.

"No!" she snarled, hopping up and pacing. She wasn't going to spend the next three hours thinking about one torture just to endure another. "What are my options? I can't pick the lock…

but maybe I can disable it." She went to her little stash of screws and picked out the smallest ones that she had pulled from beneath the cot.

"This'll buy me some time," she said, as she reached through the bars and poked the screws into the lock of the door. Next, she took one of her metal shims and jabbed it in as well. The screws sounded like gravel in the lock and she wore an evil grin as she mashed them as deep as they could go.

"Now what?" she asked, turning back to the sink. Breaking the lock was only a stopgap measure. Somehow, she had to escape. "I can do this. I've done it before, lots of times. Even that time with Chris, that was really me." That memory came to her and she didn't impede it.

Her body bled and ached in a place she had never felt such pain before and yet, she barely acknowledged it because, at least for that time, she was Chris. She was a boy and boys didn't get raped. They were strong and fast and courageous—she was strong and fast and courageous. Ignoring the pain, she dug out the picks tied in the back of her hair and went to work on the lock holding her chained by the throat. When she had picked it, she set out for revenge because boys knew about revenge. They were good at it.

Chris moved through the quiet truck like a stalking tiger, silent and deadly. He went up the ladder to the second floor, ignoring the blood that dripped down his leg. Now, he was just feet away from the room where Jillybean had been raped and he went in knowing that he was on the verge of murder.

"Execution," he whispered, as he found the knife that had been so casually tossed aside. Its shining blade, honed to a razor's edge, made things equal between the boy and the trader. He died with his throat cut, looking straight into Chris' blue eyes.

"But he had hazel…never mind," she said. It didn't matter whose eyes it was, the trader had died because of the things he had done in the cold light of day. He hadn't been crazy and he hadn't been forced. He had *chosen* to do the things he had done.

"And that's what means there's a difference between him and me." For a moment, she conquered the greasy rape-feeling that, although it was weeks old at that point, still clung to her. "Stow it away," she said to herself. "Hide it if you can, if not stick it somewhere in the back of your mind and get to figuring a way out."

That was easier said than done and when she looked around again a sigh of defeat left her. Escape seemed impossible.

She went to the sink once more and pulled back on the steel wall plate and saw that there was a gap between the evenly spaced studs: sixteen inches wide and seven inches deep. "Maybe," she said, reaching her hand up into the gap. The jail cell was made of cinderblocks with a cement floor, however it was surrounded by a framed building and this was the one way to get behind the walls.

Although Jillybean was a tiny girl, the gap was frightfully narrow; she would barely fit, which begged the question of how she would climb once inside it? For her, the only choice was up. She had no idea why, but the darkness beneath the building was a thousand times more scary to her than the darkness above.

"And coming down would be a lot easier if it turns into a dead end." With this rationale buoying her, she went to the corner of the cell and arranged the blanket into a clump that could look as though there was a little girl beneath it, if that was what one was expecting to see.

To give herself as much of a head start as she could get, she didn't pull any further back on the steel covering, but instead squeezed through the gap she had made until she was in the tiny space between the walls.

She had never been claustrophobic before, possibly because she had never been in any space that was so dark and so tight around her. *Oh, God! I'm in a coffin. Oh, God! Oh, God!* The thought seized her muscles and she couldn't move up or down and she ended up backing out of the space in an ungainly manner that felt as though she were being born backwards, birthed from a mother made of steel and cement.

It took a minute for her heart rate to return to normal and another minute to talk herself into another attempt. What got her moving wasn't the dreadful words going through her head: *They're gonna drown me!* it was the face of Chris that suddenly came to her.

The idea struck her that she had invented him for a purpose. She hadn't imagined she was talking to another little girl or even a woman; she tended to assume that most females were weak. And she didn't invent a man; they were too dangerous and given to violence, immorality and general brutish and uncivilized behavior.

No, she had invented a boy. Sure, Chris had been frequently annoying in his boyisms, but he had also been everything that Jillybean wasn't. He would have looked up into that hole behind the wall with as much excitement as dread. He would have been drawn to the idea of exploration simply for the sake of discovery. Chances were he would have imagined that some long ago ex-prisoners had stashed a bag of gold in the ceiling.

Even without the fear of drowning hanging over his head, he would have crawled up there. "I can, too," she said and once more wiggled into the space, this time, pulling back on the steel plate until her toes were the only thing keeping her from falling into the gap.

Now, she was practically trapped and had no choice but to begin inching her way up. There was no ladder to climb and she could only move by pushing up with her elbows and knees an inch at a time. Still, it was only a single story climb and it was only a few minutes before she could find a grip above her. She pulled herself into a wide, but cramped area that was barely three feet in height.

The roof above was just high enough for her to stand with a pronounced kink in her spine. Feeling like Granny Annie, she gazed around and was happily surprised to find that the space was not utterly dark. There was a little square vent on each of the four walls. They weren't large enough to crawl through, but were big enough to let her see her dusty surroundings.

There wasn't much to see. The space ran the length and width of the building and was basically flat and featureless except for the long rectangle of aluminum that sat directly in the middle—it was a vent that ran upwards at the very back of the building.

It had to lead to the roof.

A quick inspection showed that the sections of the vent were held together by little nuts. "Perfect," she said and whipped out her little metal cross, only she had lost the strip of blanket that held it together and she had left the Nancy Drew book down below. She fretted that she would have to brave the space between the walls once again. It was such an unhappy prospect that she decided to give her little bits of metal a try first.

She sandwiched the little nut between the two pieces of metal and gave it a turn. To her delight, the nut spun easily. They all did and in moments, she was able to shove one section away. It made a metallic noise that was louder than she wished, but there was nothing she could do at this point. Time was running away from her.

Without thinking about the possibility of getting trapped, she crept into the vent and began to wiggle upwards, her feet making unfortunate thumping noises that seemed terribly loud. Whether she went fast or slow, they still thumped and so she hurried. It wasn't far before the vent arched over and she could tell she was on the roof! In front of her were the blades of a giant fan and to her right were the slats of an exterior vent cover—behind her, echoing up the shaft came the grumble: "What was that?"

This was followed by the sound of a chair scraping. Jillybean had to fight the panic welling in her. John would check her cell first and see the bundle of blankets and assume she was sleeping. He would then flick his flashlight around. Would he notice the gap where the steel plate was separated from the concrete wall? That was fifty-fifty. If he did, he would start calling her name even louder and when she didn't answer, he would move to unlock the door. And when that didn't work, he would raise the alarm.

Jillybean figured she had two minutes to get away. How far would that get her? A quarter of a mile? Three blocks? She would rush out into the rain without a coat or a car or a weapon or even food. If that wasn't bad enough, in no time, there would be soldiers combing the valley, going door to door, searching every hiding place she could think of.

If, by some miracle, she managed to elude them, she would have to walk fifty miles to get out of the mountains along easily watched roads and once on the plains she would be alone to face thousands of square miles of flat, empty land infested with monsters and slavers.

This chain of thoughts caused her to pause, a prayer on her lips that John would give only a perfunctory glance around.

"What the fuck?" he said, the words running straight up through the vent. "Jillybean! Hey, Jillybean!"

Her worst fears had been realized.

Chapter 30

Neil Martin

A heavy thumping at Neil's door woke him. In a flash he went from dead asleep to wide awake and reaching for the gun he kept on his nightstand. It was a fully loaded twenty-five year old Walther PPK; the same type of gun that James Bond used in the movies when Neil was growing up. He never failed to mention that when someone asked about the gun. Although that was an interesting fact, what he really liked about the compact weapon was that it was one of the few that fit his small hands.

Leaving Gayle, who could sleep through a tornado, he slid out of bed a second later and saw that Sadie with her much larger Glock was already at the door, looking through the peephole.

"It's Grey," she said, raising an eyebrow and unlatching the door, letting in the burly soldier.

The captain had a pinched look on his face and instead of a greeting, he threw up his hands. "She's escaped. Ten minutes ago. Fred is going to freak out. But if he gives me one more 'I told you so,' I'm going to punch him right in the nose."

A part of Neil wanted to see that and another part wanted to just stand there in awe of Jillybean's indomitable spirit, however the largest part of him felt a green streak of fear cut through him: there were going to be more attacks.

"Talk to me while I get dressed," he said, but then stuck a finger to his lips, tiptoed into his room so as not to wake Gayle, and crept back out with his arms filled. Once the bedroom door was shut, he asked: "Did she escape ten minutes ago or did we just find out ten minutes ago?" He threw a pair of jeans and a sweater on over his pajamas; it was going to be cold in the rain and he was sure he would be out for a while.

"The guard heard something in the vents; he went to check on Jillybean and thought she was all bundled up in the corner, but then saw that part of the wall was off. The toilet and sink are sort of embedded in the wall…"

Neil interrupted with a laugh. "To keep people from escaping?"

"Probably," Grey answered. "Either way he called me and I called the ready platoon and the sheriff and he called the patrols. They're setting up at watch points at different areas of the valley.

I told them to keep an eye out for little zombies as well as little girls."

"Just the one platoon?" Neil asked, looking up from tying his laces. "And a few guys on zombie watch? That seems a bit like 'under-kill' if you ask me. We'll be lucky to catch her if we had the entire population of the Valley looking for her."

Grey shrugged and then yawned. "I don't know about that. She might not even be out of the building yet. The guard said he didn't hear a thing after those first thumps. He thinks she's trapped up in the ducts."

"Oh yeah? Which genius is on shift, John or Gus? Never mind. It doesn't matter, they're both morons." Once more, Sadie was ready before him. She didn't look particularly tired, nor did she seem nervous that a killer was on the loose. "Did you do something to help her?" he asked Sadie.

"No. As much as I hate to say it, I think it's better for everyone if she's behind bars. She's still dangerous. But I think you guys made her more dangerous with your talk of waterboarding her. You made her desperate when she didn't really have a reason to be desperate. If there's a bad personality in her, maybe some time locked away from danger, safe and sound, would have helped."

As always, Neil didn't know what to think when it came to Jillybean. She was sweet and innocent and deadly and insane. It was a sad situation, especially since she had been making so much progress.

The little group walked out into the rain which was coming down in sheets. Grey's Humvee sat parked in three inches of mud. It flew in spatters when he gunned the vehicle out of there and raced the half mile into town, heading straight for the jail.

John the guard was outside the building, pacing back and forth under a poplar across the street. "What the hell are you doing?" Neil demanded as soon as they drove up.

"I got a great view of the building. I can see both sides just by shifting a bit back and forth. She's gotta still be in there." He looked cold, wet and scared that Neil would tear him a new one.

Neil didn't bother yelling at him. They had all seen the setup of the jail and no one had thought escape was possible. There had been two locked doors between Jillybean and the outside world. She'd been strip-searched just as all her visitors had been. Even the missing pieces of glass had been thought of as inconsequential.

In Neil's mind, they still were. The glass had been too thin and brittle to use for anything except suicide and he'd be lying if the thought hadn't crossed his mind that Jillybean might try to kill herself. It was horrible, but wasn't it preferable to being tortured before being summarily executed?

"I feel like a complete shit," he whispered. Grey heard and grunted in what sounded like agreement. He wasn't being mean, Neil knew. He felt the same way. They all did—all except Fred, who was trying to parlay the deaths of three people into more power. Neil almost didn't care at this point. He absolutely hated the idea of being the man in charge of ordering the death of the little girl he had adopted months before.

"Are you sure she didn't come out the front?" Grey asked the guard. "She didn't sneak around you when you weren't looking?"

"There's no way," John stated, showing more desperation. "I went in just like they showed me. I checked left and right before I went to her cell. Trust me, her sneaking past was what I was most afraid of."

Neil didn't trust him and nor did he blame him. "Let's go take a look. We'll go around the perimeter first. John, you can wait here." Neil, Grey and Sadie went around the jail house and when they got to the alley that separated it from the municipal building, they saw the tiny footprints in the mud. There were only a few and they led from a drainpipe on the side of the building and towards Main Street.

"Fred is going to have a field day with this," Neil said. "He's going to demand shoot on sight orders, I know it."

Sadie turned on him sharply, accusing him of being an evil tyrant simply in the way she stared through slitted eyes. "Are you going to give in to him?"

Grey's eyes went to Neil's face and then shifted away. Neil understood. More than likely, it would be his men facing a dangerous criminal who was in possession of a weapon of mass destruction. Just because the criminal happened to be a seven-year-old girl didn't make her less dangerous.

"No, there won't be a shoot on sight order," Neil said. "It's Jillybean. I can't do that to her. We will apprehend her and put her on trial in the fairest way possible. Now, how do we go about capturing her? Do we use discrete squads and try to keep this as quiet as possible or do we go full bore and call out the entire population?"

Sadie and Grey took completely different sides, making Neil groan. Grey had the worst-case scenario in mind, another poison gas attack, when he advocated going full bore and capturing her as soon as possible. Sadie lifted one shoulder in her usual half-shrug. "You might as well resign your governorship then. Fred will blame you and there's no one better at whipping up a fear-frenzy than him. And when you go, he'll force Grey, Deanna and Veronica out of the council. And he'll force me out of the Valley. I don't think I want to live anywhere he's in charge of."

"Boy, leadership would be easy if everyone agreed on everything," Neil said, "only that never happens. I think I'm going to have to go with Captain Grey. We go full bore. What happens to us is inconsequential compared to someone dying. Grey, I want you on point on this. Do what you have to do to capture her. Sadie, I want you to go find Jillybean. You were going to go look, regardless, so I might as well make it official."

Sadie was off like a shot, heading for Main Street, while Grey ran the opposite way, heading around the corner to City Hall, where Neil had set up his new seat of government.

After a long sigh, Neil went back to where they had left John. "She's gone. We found little kid tracks around the side of the building. Why don't you show me her cell?" The guard led the way, bleating the entire time about how none of this was his fault. The whining, combined with the stress Neil was under, was giving him a headache. "I know, I know. It's my fault, John. I figured that a windowless, concrete jail cell would hold her for longer than one night."

John was relieved, which only made him babble more. Neil had to hush him. "I need to concentrate and for that I need silence." A second later, the raid warning siren went off in a warbling, shrill noise that could be heard from one end of the Valley to the other.

"The dice have been rolled," Neil muttered to himself. Louder, he said: "Let's go check out her cell."

"We can't. She broke the door, somehow."

Neil had to fight from keeping his eyes from rolling. "She broke the door, too?"

The guard shrugged. "I guess I mean she broke the lock. My key won't work. Here, let me show you." They went to the last cell on the left and as John dug around in the lock with his key, Neil inspected the room. Jillybean's blanket was balled in the corner in such a way as to suggest there was a little girl beneath it. He had to refrain from calling her name just to be sure she wasn't. The wailing siren could attest that she wasn't.

"Hey!" John said with some excitement. "There was a screw in the lock." He held out a small screw for Neil to take. "Now why on earth would she try to hide the wall screws in the lock?"

It was obvious that she wasn't "hiding" the screws in the lock. And nor was the screw in John's hand from the wall; it was much too small. "Remember the silence I was looking for?" Neil asked. "How about you just wait in the other room?"

When he left, Neil picked up the lantern that sat in the hall and tried to piece together the escape. The explanation started with the word "somehow" and this was followed by a dozen more "somehows" before Neil said: "And then she climbed down a drainage pipe."

Walking back into the front of the station, he jerked a thumb towards the cell block. "Hey, can you work on that lock some more? If you get it open, do me a favor and stay out of the cell. It's a crime scene of sorts." He then splashed out into the rain, hurrying for his office in the next building. There were going to be many visitors that day.

The siren drew hundreds. They were supposed to be going to their "battle stations" but fear had turned many of the valley people into bleating sheep and they came flocking to the City Hall. Grey had anticipated this and had a crew re-directing the reluctant stragglers away from the building and back to where they were supposed to be assembling.

As expected, Fred was the first of the council members to show up. He came racing up in his personal Humvee, splashing mud and throwing his weight around. He strode through the glass doors and went right for Neil's office and seemed shocked to find the door locked.

"I'm busy," Neil called out. Of course, a few minutes later, he let Gayle in without question; she had Neil's breakfast.

Since Neil guessed that Fred was there simply to assign blame and deal out a large helping of "I told you so," he kept him cooling his heels in the outer office while he ate his breakfast and told Gayle what was going on.

"As much as I love Jillybean, it's a good thing I brought this," she said, opening what once had been a seven hundred dollar Michael Kors handbag and producing a Beretta.

Neil shook his head. "Yes, the council is a pretty obvious target, but we have guards for this sort of thing. You should probably keep away, at least for the time…"

She snorted as if what he had said was funny, sat back in the seat opposite his new desk, and casually crossed her legs. "No. I'll be staying." For the rest of the morning, she didn't budge from that chair and the Beretta remained sitting out in plain sight.

It was after ten before he got his first update from Captain Grey: five thousand people had gone from building to building, searching every room, closet, garage, crawl space, flower bed and shrubbery within a three mile radius—and had come up completely empty.

Only then would Neil talk to Fred and he did so in conjunction with a council meeting, mainly so he would have witnesses. In a flat voice, he explained the escape and the steps being taken to find Jillybean. It was all pretty cut and dried and after stating the facts there wasn't much more to say and yet, Fred wanted to drag it on.

He had droned on for five minutes, saying basically nothing, when Deanna stood and announced: "Sorry everyone, but Emily woke up with the crud. I'm going to take her over to the clinic to see if Dr. Hester can knock back the fever. I trust you can listen to Fred whine without me?"

"I'm not whining," Fred insisted, indignantly. "I just don't think Neil is actually listening or that he understands the danger of the situation. Everyone in this room is in danger. Jillybean hates the council and me especially."

"Maybe you should try to be less of a dick," Neil suggested. "I think we can all agree on that. Should we have a vote?"

Fred sneered: "Ha-ha. Do you really think that now is the time for jokes? People's lives are in danger, Neil. Man, I knew this was going to happen."

"Don't think of it as a joke, Fred. It was meant as constructive criticism. And if you knew Jillybean was going to escape, why didn't you tell anyone? Don't you think that sort of information would have been good to know yesterday?"

Fred's sneer deepened until it bordered on a glare of hate. "I didn't say anything because I knew you wouldn't have done anything about it, that's why. At the most you would have relied on Jillybean's 'better nature' and made a mess out of things. Or should I say a worse mess of things."

Neil was just about sick of Fred and if there hadn't been a crisis going on he would have seriously thought about implementing Plan Z. As it was, he would have to make sure to steer Grey's search parties away from the cabin with the chained up zombie.

He jotted down a reminder to himself and then said, "You seem to know a lot about the future, Fred. Would you care to make any predictions about what's going to happen next or would you rather just tell us once it's too late to do anything about it?"

The other council members began to smirk as Fred spluttered, "Is…is this the mature way to handle this? We have a killer on the loose and you're putting people down like some schoolyard bully."

That had been the first time Neil had ever been accused of being a bully. Strangely, he kind of liked it. "I wasn't putting people down, Fred, I was putting *you* down. And to be fair, you started it by blatantly accusing me of not listening, when I was, and for not understanding the situation, which I do."

This calm assessment turned Fred cold. "Okay, sure Neil. And your plan to capture Jillybean is what?"

That was the question. How was he going to out-think a genius? He didn't consider himself the smartest person in the world and yet, other than Captain Grey, Dr. Hester, maybe Deanna and a few others, he was brighter than the great majority in the Valley. And yet, what did that mean in comparison to Jillybean?

"Nothing," he muttered, staring out of the window where tired civilians, cold and sloppy wet, could be seen coming back from their searches. They were downcast and bedraggled, standing around in groups, shaking their heads. Neil could read the anger in their faces as they came up.

"We don't have a choice," he said. "We have to keep searching until we…"

He was interrupted by a new blast from the siren. It no longer seemed to warble as it had earlier that morning. It seemed to screech, setting Neil's nerves on edge. Almost at the same time his secretary began to hammer on his office door, calling out: "There's been another attack! Governor Neil? Can you hear me? Governor Neil!" She sounded like a frightened child.

Chapter 31

Deanna Russell

Normally Deanna didn't drive in the Valley. On good days she rode a bike that Grey had set up with an infant car seat welded in front. This wasn't a good day. It was wet and miserable out. What was worse than the weather was the child-sized killer running around loose.

She kept the doors to the Rav4 locked, her Sig Sauer P220 in her lap, and her eyes peeled as she drove to the Estes Park Medical Center. It was a surprisingly large and sprawling campus considering the small population of the Valley at the time of the apocalypse.

It was so large, that prior to the arrival of Dr. Hester, it was deemed a waste of space and a smaller building which had been a veterinarian's clinic was used. But Dr. Hester didn't care for arrangement and demanded the use of an actual hospital. The council agreed to let him use the emergency room where he and his assistant, Margaret Yuan and two CNAs ran what everyone just called "The Clinic."

On that morning, all four of them were busy rushing around —the lobby was packed with people. There were at least forty patients waiting to be seen. "Oh, man," Deanna whispered as she got in a ten-person line just to sign in.

Ten minutes went by and only one person had been triaged. With some justification, Lieutenant Governor Deanna Russell was about to pull rank when she was startled by a woman peering in Emily's car seat. She was middle-aged with mouse-brown hair and deep set eyes. Of all the people in the emergency room, she seemed the sickest.

"Do you mind," Deanna said, moving Emily to the side. "I'm sorry, but I can't risk exposing her to any more germs. She's pretty sick already."

"Oh…okay," the woman said, without looking into Deanna's face. "She sure is a pretty thing. I…I hope she makes it."

It was an odd thing to say and yet, after Deanna had lost her first baby, poisoned while still in the womb, it had some meaning to her. "Thanks. Children are precious." She was on the verge of asking the woman if she had any children, but it was obvious in the way she stared at Emily that she'd had children and that they were dead or missing.

"They really are," the woman said. She grinned, shrugged and said: "I really should go. It's probably not a good day to be here."

"It sure is busy. By the way, my name is Deanna. Can I ask what's wrong? I guess I do have some clout around here." She could tell by her look that the woman didn't recognize her. "I'm the Lieutenant Governor. Maybe I can get you seen early."

This lit a smile on the woman's face. "Oh no, I'm good, but you should definitely stay and be seen. Tell me is it true about you and Captain Grey? Is this his baby?"

"Yes. We were lucky and got pregnant probably the first time. He's been a great fath…"

She was interrupted by Margaret Yuan. "Deanna, is everything all right with Emily? Oh my, she's got a fever. Come on, let's get her away from this crowd. It's not good for her to be around so many people."

Deanna only had time to wave goodbye to the woman in line before Margaret pulled her away, pushing through the crowd. "Is it always like this?" Deanna asked, staring around feeling a little confused. Some of the patients looked more bored than sick.

"It's the Jillybean thing. That and the bad weather. People always come out in the bad weather. You can tell the slackers from the people who are really sick—the slackers never mind waiting, and they come prepared. See that guy?" She pointed at a soldier who was engrossed, playing a Game Boy. "Dr Hester is going to prescribe him an emetic."

"Okay, what's that?" Deanna asked.

"It's a med that makes you vomit. It's mostly used in case someone ingests poison, but I got to say it works wonders curing slacker-itis. And the best part? No chance of getting sued! Thank God some things aren't like the old days."

As Lieutenant Governor Deanna didn't know what to think about doctors *making* people sick. "Well, that's not us. Emily started getting croupy last night and it's only gotten worse. I'm sort of nervous that she might have gotten a whiff of that gas. She's so tiny that even a little bit might hurt her."

"I really doubt it," Margaret assured, as she peeked behind a drawn curtain, apologized to someone, and moved on to the next exam room. After three tries, she flagged one of the CNAs. "Mandy! Do we have *any* beds open?"

"Uh-uh, all filled up," Mandy said, before she ducked into one of the rooms.

Deanna dreaded the idea of taking Emily back into the waiting room where there were, more than likely, actual sick people among the slackers. Margaret read the desperation on her face and pulled her into a room marked *No Admittance*. It was a private office with a heavy oak desk, a leather couch and a private bathroom. Even the view was fancy: a wide panorama of the eastern peaks. You had to look beyond the mostly barren and weedy parking lot to see the view, but it was still nice.

"Make yourself comfortable," Margaret said. "It might be a while, even for you. One of the soldiers who was out searching for Jillybean fell through the floor of some cabin. No broken bones, thank God, but he was cut up pretty badly."

Deanna was just sitting down on the couch with a sigh, when she heard a shout from somewhere in the emergency room. Then came a scream and before it was cut off, Deanna had her Sig Sauer in hand. More screams and then there was a crash of glass and metal. She was about to go to the door when movement out the window caught her eye. People were running...and then falling, and then contorting into ugly twisted versions of themselves.

It was the VX gas!

For a moment, Deanna froze, fear and loathing holding her rooted in place as she watched a dozen people die, not twenty feet from the window. Past the door behind her, the sounds of death crept around the cracks. What got her moving was the simple notion that if sound could get around the cracks of the door, the gas could, as well.

Next to the door was a coat stand with a ski jacket and two lab coats hanging from the ornate hooks. She grabbed the ski coat and laid it at the base of the door. Next, she picked up Emily's car seat and the two remaining lab coats and hurried into the bathroom, shutting the door behind her and laying the coats down at the base. It was a pathetic barrier, but better than nothing.

"Grey! This is Dee," she hissed into the radio she always kept on hand. Normally it was for mundane uses such as being summoned to a council meeting or for her to ask Grey to pick up diapers or to trade for a dozen eggs.

279

Grey didn't answer and so she switched to the channel reserved for the communications director for the Valley. "Hello? There's been an attack at the hospital! Come in!" she hissed into the radio, keeping her voice as low as possible. She had the irrational fear that Jillybean was out in the lobby standing among the dying, wearing a kid's size hazmat suit and perhaps stabbing her victims with a spear. The picture in her mind was ridiculous and she knew it, but that didn't stop it from taking over the rational part of her brain until she was afraid even to move.

"This is the communications office. Who is this? Over."

"This is Deanna Russell," she said in a whisper, covering her mouth with one hand. "I say again there's been a gas attack at the hospital." As much as she wanted to be rescued, and despite the fear roiling inside of her, she had a duty to the Valley that had to come first. "Call Captain Grey, we need to cordon off the area as soon as possible."

"Hold," he replied, leaving Deanna sitting on the closed toilet staring at the little radio.

Once the siren began wailing, she thumbed the mic: "I am currently trapped in the emergency room. There is no sign of Jillybean but she can't be far. Over." There was no response and so she repeated her message twice with the fear that she had been abandoned growing in her.

The radio only issued static so she switched back to Grey's channel. His first name was James, but she had never called him that. For some reason she couldn't put her finger on, it was awkward when she tried. "Grey. Come in, Grey." She paused and then begged: "Please pick up, please, please."

Finally, he answered, "Deanna, thank God you're okay. Where are you? The hospital has been attacked and I was worried sick."

"I'm at the hospital. Do you hear me? I'm trapped in the emergency room, in an office in the back. What do I do, Grey? Everyone's dead." The radio was silent for a long minute before he came back on, his voice raspy and filled with fear, asking about their daughter. "Emily is with me," she said, taking a peek under the soft, pink blanket. "She's sleeping right now. What do I do? How do I get out of here?"

"I don't know yet. This gas is worse than I thought. The military must have been experimenting with it, because it's far more virulent than normal VX."

That particular information wasn't exactly helpful. "Are you trying to make me cry?" she demanded. She was so afraid that she was on the verge of bawling. The only thing holding the hysteria back was the fear that she would lose control and breathe too hard. It was the one thing she couldn't do. Along with the hideous vision of Jillybean going among the twisted corpses was the idea, that above all, she couldn't disturb the air any more than she had to.

Death was literally in the air.

He came back on the radio, saying: "No, of course not. I was just talking nonsense, okay? Everything is going to be okay. I'm here, alright? I can see the Rav4 and the...and the hospital." She knew he had been about to say he could see the bodies and she was glad he hadn't.

"We're in a bathroom off the office. Ground floor though the ER. H-How do you get me out of here?"

His answer: "I'm going to work on that right now," was far from reassuring. What could he do from the outside? Even if he had special hazmat gear, which he did not, he couldn't exactly come waltzing through the emergency room and into the room with Deanna because he would end up bringing the toxins in with him. He would be fine, but she would be dead. And so would Emily.

Five minutes passed and the only good news was that Emily was still sleeping. "Hello? Grey?" she asked into the radio. "What's the plan?"

"Um...do you have anything blocking the crack of the door? Can you put down a towel or anything? Wet it if you can."

"That's it?" she asked, staring at the radio. "That's all you got?"

She hadn't thumbed the talk button and was startled when he answered: "We're working on it. Neil is here and so are Sadie and Veronica. We'll figure this out. Just sit tight."

Sit tight? "Where the hell would I go?" Time seemed to draw out. She spent it wetting the lab coats, searching through the drawers of the vanity, using the surgical tape she'd found in the top drawer to further insulate the room, feeding Emily, who woke just long enough to suckle, and, of course, she spent most of time being afraid.

She could imagine Fred Trigg out there right that moment demanding that all rescue efforts cease. He'd be afraid to let the toxins out into the air. "That would be his style except he'd be at home, radioing his demands. Too bad Jillybean has turned evil," she said. Deanna knew that if there was one person with the brains enough to save her, it would be Jillybean.

"Don't be like that," she chided herself. "Neil and Grey are smart guys, they'll come up with a plan…eventually. Of course, Jillybean would have figured out something by now."

Five minutes later, she felt the first odd jerk. A muscle in her forearm twitched—it made her heart buck in her chest. "Okay, that was just a case of nerves." Despite her brave words, she pulled off her jacket and laid it over the rocker, tucking in the edges to protect the baby as best as possible. She then sat perfectly still, barely breathing, waiting to see if the muscle would twitch again. It did, seconds later.

"Still could be nerves," she said, taking a wash cloth from the second drawer and placing it over her mouth. When the twitch came again, she laughed like a strangled turkey and bent over Emily, snugging the blanket down again, worrying over it until she had it so taut that she could have bounced a quarter off of it.

It would never be good enough and so she lifted the rocker and set it on the toilet tank while she sat on the edge of the sink, thinking that toxins had to be heavier than normal air. The muscle began to twitch as though it were dancing. It was joined moments later by one on her cheek that pulled the right side of her face into a half smile of misery.

She reached for the radio with a hand that was suddenly crooked into a claw, nearly knocking it onto the tiled floor. "Grey? Please hurry," she said, trying to hide the utter desperation she was feeling. It felt as though she were being slowly possessed by a demon, and one with a cruel sense of humor, one that wanted to make her into a cross between a roulette wheel and a stringed puppet.

"Why?" he almost screamed into the radio. "What's going on? Are you okay? Is it Emily?"

Was there a right way to tell him that the VX was somehow getting past her high-tech barriers of three coats and some splashed water? Should she tell him that the gas was just then beginning to turn her body into a soft pretzel? And if she did tell him, what would he do?

"He would drop everything and rush into the hospital," she mumbled, feeling her lower lip go numb. "And he will die."

Toggling the mic, she said: "We're good so far. Just scared is all. Sho hur-we" Deanna then put the radio on the sink and slurred around her numb lips: "Emery, I don't fink we're goin to make it."

Chapter 32

Captain Grey

It was crystal clear that Deanna was lying. The fear in her voice had come right through the radio and stitched nails into Grey's heart. She was dying. The poison was getting to her. It was seeping into the bathroom she had locked herself into and Grey could imagine that it was slowly twisting her and Emily into inhuman shapes. He could even imagine their screams.

Suddenly, he was unable to breathe. It was almost as if he were the one sucking in the VX. "Okay, this is good enough," he said, waving his hand at the assembled gear. At the moment, it didn't matter what they had, just then he would have rushed into the hospital with a paper bag on his head.

They were in the living room of a house two blocks from the hospital. On the floor were stacks of materials that had been rounded up. Neil walked around it, wearing a pinched look as he said: "Hold on, we only have two masks."

Although Grey had sent a squad of soldiers to look solely for gas masks, he doubted they would find more than the two they already had. The year before, the soldiers of the Valley had fought their way across half the continent, for the most part, fighting on foot. Early on they had tossed away any items that were deemed extraneous—such as their protective masks.

"We-we only need two," Grey declared. "I'll go without. Someone's going to have to check to see if the air is clean."

"No, that's just stupid," Neil said. "I have to insist that we either do this right or we don't do it at all."

Grey rounded on him. "You insist? What kind of crap is that? Right now you aren't the governor. You're either my friend who's going to help me save Deanna or someone who better get out of my way, or so help me." He pushed Neil aside and picked up one of the coveralls that were going to be used in place of an actual hazmat suit.

Neil took a steadying breath. "No. Sorry, about this but it's for your own good." He balled a fist and punched Grey right in the face—or that was the intent. Grey saw it coming from a mile away and simply leaned away from the punch, causing Neil to miss, wildly. Out of balance, the little man actually fell over.

"What the hell?" Grey cried.

"You're being reckless," Neil answered from the floor. "If it was anyone else there's no way you'd be considering going in this unprepared. Please, give it a few more minutes."

He answered simply: "No," and continued to struggle into the coveralls. They were painter's coveralls and the largest that had been located was a medium. Grey's shoulders threatened to split the thin material. Neil mumbled a weak curse and then began to pull his on as well. He'd only managed to get one foot in when Sadie raced up in a Humvee. She didn't bother with the driveway and parked the machine right on the front lawn.

"Alright, I got the third member of the team," she stated, speaking quickly as she burst through the front door. She stopped short seeing Neil sitting on the floor struggling to get his booted foot into the coveralls. "What is this?"

"I'm the third member of the team," Neil said. With the soldiers strung out all over the Valley looking for Jillybean or hunting down gas masks, volunteers who were willing to risk a horrible death were very few in number. "And really it's going to be a two person team. We only have two masks."

Sadie shrugged, said: "Is that so?" and then unexpectedly yanked the coveralls from Neil. He tried to get up, but she pushed him down again. "You're staying, end of story. Grey, give him a knock on the head if he tries to get up."

"Gladly," Grey answered. "So who's the other person? One of my soldiers? It's not Fred, that little weasel, I know that much." Fred wouldn't come within a mile of the hospital and was currently holed up in the mansion he had commandeered as his personal residence.

"Well…"

Neil looked shocked. "It is Fred? Did you tie him up? Ha, you did! Well, I guess you get to wear a mask after all, Grey."

Sadie grinned maliciously. "No, it's not Fred. I sort of wish it was, though. It's a chicken. Oh, by the way, Neil, we owe Mr. Meyers a chicken. I sorta stole one of his."

Neil nodded in a vague sort of way and said: "I should still go. I'm the dad and I am gover…" Sadie snapped her fingers at Grey, who promptly slapped Neil on the back of the head. "Hey!" he cried. "That wasn't very nice."

"Shut up. You're staying and that's it. Sadie and I, and the chicken, of course, can handle this." Once he had glared Neil into shutting his mouth, Grey picked up the radio. "Deanna? How are you doing? How's Emily?"

"W-we-re doin okay. B-but p-ease hur-ay." Her words were slurred and hitching. In the background, Emily was making a noise that was part cry, part cough, and part drowning gurgle. Tears were suddenly streaking down Grey's face.

"Okay honey, we're going in, but it's going to take a few minutes to get to you, so sit tight." He didn't bother wiping away the tears as he stooped to pick up the chainsaw and an armful of plastic draping that they had picked up in the paint section of the local hardware store. Sadie grabbed the stud-finder, three rolls of duct tape and the rest of the plastic.

They were halfway out the door when the emergency siren began to wail again, indicating another attack. Grey stopped for all of a second before he turned to Neil. "I don't care what that is. Ignore it. Have this place ready for when we get back."

He strode out and climbed into Sadie's Humvee. Around them the siren pierced the rain and further cemented the growing panic in the Valley. Inside the vehicle, it was quiet save for the nervous clucking of Mr. Myers' chicken. Sadie held the bird on her lap as she stared out the window. She had her game face on, stern and resolute.

Grey's face was set in grim lines of barely suppressed fury. The siren meant that Jillybean had struck again. It also meant that Grey was out of options. The next time he saw her, he vowed to shoot her before she could blink. She couldn't be allowed even a moment to say something cute, or to give an excuse. She had to be put down and the humane way was one shot between the eyes.

But what if he couldn't get to Deanna and Emily in time? Would it be just one shot? Or would it be a dozen killing her slowly?

The hospital came up fast, but instead of going to the emergency room entrance, he went to the other side of the building. Grey pulled out his mask and went to put it on, but Sadie stopped him. "Once it goes on it stays on," she said. "If anything happens…I mean if Deanna needs a mask, I'm giving her mine. No, don't! Don't look at me like that. I can't carry you or Deanna, but you can. I'm just saying, don't die for nothing."

Goosebumps ran across his skin. He understood the sacrifice she was offering and if he had even a moment to spare, he would have kissed her. But they didn't. They tugged on their masks and were out of the Humvee a second later carrying their loads to the doors.

Sadie lagged behind, slowed by the chicken. She had made a leash out of a piece of string which she had to give a yank every few steps to keep the bird moving. Its first test came when they entered through the glass doors of the rehabilitation service center.

"Deanna, we're in the hospital, over," he said into the radio as he watched the chicken. It seemed confused, which was just about normal.

"Her-ay," Deanna pleaded.

"I will. Hold on." His heart was racing as he looked around. Grey had been to the hospital many times during his long recovery the year before, but he had never been in this part of the building and wasn't exactly sure how to get to Deanna without simply charging through the emergency room.

He took a hallway to their left and angled through a series of cubicles until they came to a glass wall. "There's a map," Sadie said, pointing through the glass. The map showed the building's odd layout and had a "You Are Here" sticker that told them they still had to keep going to the left.

They crossed into the hallway, ignoring the sign and the arrow pointing them towards the emergency room. The air there was so toxic that death would come in seconds.

Instead, they crossed into the Multi-Specialty clinic, where proctologists had offices uncomfortably close to ear, nose and throat specialists.

The pair, and their chicken, were very close now. The doctor's bathroom backed up to one of the offices along the north wall but Grey didn't know which, and he couldn't start cutting holes in the walls for fear of flooding the clinic with VX gas.

"Deanna, I need you to make some noise," he said into the radio. "Bang on the wall or slam the toilet or..."

"Grey, look." Sadie was staring down at Mr. Myers' chicken. It was on its side spinning madly, its neck bent so far that its head was touching the middle of its back. Sadie looked like she was about to puke into her mask.

He turned her away from the chicken and was about to pull her into an office when they heard a soft thud. "This way," he said, yanking Sadie along. Into the radio, he yelled: "Keep going Deanna!" She didn't keep going. The thuds occurred twice more and then stopped.

"Deanna!" he screamed. They were outside the office of *Frank Marske, pediatrician,* according to the sign. He barged in and saw, just past a receptionists desk, was a restroom. That had to be it. "We'll tape the outer door. This office might still be somewhat clean. Then we'll start on the bathroom." It took only seconds to slash a rectangle of plastic tarp and slap it over the doorway with duct tape.

They entered an adjoining bathroom and, as Grey rattled the chainsaw into life, Sadie plied the bathroom door with more plastic. Neither knew if it would do them any good whatsoever. The bathroom could be filled with nerve gas and the moment they cut a hole into the next room it could flood in and kill Deanna and Emily outright. But they had no choice.

The stud finder was forgotten in Grey's haste; he simply blasted through the drywall until he could see into the next room. Deanna was on the ground moaning and twitching, while Emily was making a raspy sound beneath the pink blanket and Deanna's winter coat. "Deanna!" he cried. "We're here! Stay with me, okay. Keep breathing."

She didn't react in any way, which sent Grey into a hysteria-fueled rage. He tore the chainsaw into the wall, cutting through two studs and showering himself in sawdust. Rather than cutting any more, he grabbed the split studs and pulled the lower parts right through the wall making a big enough hole for him to reach through and grab, first the car seat and second, Deanna.

Sadie had barely finished taping up the door when Grey turned to her. The girl, barely eighteen years old, hesitated. Behind the round goggle-like eye-holes there were tears building.

"Please," Grey begged. "You can hold your breath in the hall. Just run right through."

"Okay," she said in a whisper. "I'll take Emily. I-I'll wrap her up. She'll be good." Sadie cut a square of plastic and placed the rocker in it and then wrapped it like it was a gift basket, wrapping duct tape at the top tight enough to seal the baby inside.

"There should be enough air for a few minutes," she said. "Are you ready?" Grey nodded and Sadie reached for her mask, but once again hesitated. "If something happens to me tell Neil I love him. And Jillybean, too." He hesitated and she grew stern. "Promise."

He nodded and said: "I promise. Now let's go."

Taking a deep breath, she took the mask off and gently placed it over Deanna's head.

Chapter 33

Sadie Martin

With her lips pressed tight together, Sadie grabbed the bundled baby and discovered how shockingly heavy a two-month old child and a little rocker could be. To make matters worse, the bag-rocker combo was also unwieldy. To keep Emily from spilling out of the rocker like so much pink goo, she had to hold the bag upright and out away from her body. She had always wondered why Deanna seemed to struggle everywhere when carrying the baby, and now she knew.

Sadie turned for the door only to remember the plastic. Setting the baby down, she tore at the plastic and then pulled the door inwards and held it to let Grey race by. "I'll be back for you," he said. Deanna was cradled in his arms, her head lolling and her hair a cascade of blonde.

Grey ran through the doctor's office and to the next plastic covered door. Unlike Sadie, he didn't need to set down his bundle. He grabbed the knob through the plastic and yanked open the door with vicious strength. The plastic tore along the seam and in wafted the poison air.

The first clue that Sadie was in trouble was the strange tingle along the right side of her face and neck. This tingle grew to a sharp, stinging sensation as if she had just walked face first through a vine of nettles. The pain was sharp enough that she cried out—and now the gas was in her lungs. She felt it immediately.

It was as if her lungs had been crushed in and she couldn't draw a full breath, only tiny sips as if the air couldn't get past the top of her chest. Panic set in as fast as the poison and she barely had the will to grab Emily before running…or rather, attempting to run away.

The entire right side of her body went limp within three steps. She fell, dropping Emily, as the weakness grew so bad she could only lift her arm with the greatest of effort. Her leg was slightly stronger and she forced herself up again and lurched on for another few steps before her hamstring unexpectedly bunched into a knot, pulling her calf all the way back.

She wanted to scream but the sips of air were enough only to form a squeak. The pain in her face and leg was nothing compared to the horror that she knew was coming. Earlier, she had driven past the emergency room and, in a disgustingly morbid state of mind, she had gazed at the bodies through a pair of binoculars.

All of the dead looked horrid, as if they had been spun through a blender, but one soldier stood out from the others. His head had been twisted all the way around on his shoulders, not once but twice so that his neck looked as though it was braided.

The horror of that pushed Sadie on. She snagged the bag Emily was in with her weak right hand, and using her still-strong left side, crawled on until she was a few feet from Mr. Meyers' chicken. It was now only an ugly pile of feathers with a chicken head sticking out. Sadie had never seen a chicken display any emotion, and yet that head with its beak frozen in mid-squawk looked as though it had died of fright.

Sadie tried to push past it, only her left side went from strong to utterly useless in seconds. The left side of her face went so flaccid that she found herself unable to control her eye. She could still see out of it, but it hung limp in its socket while her right eye could move normally. Though it wasn't moving exactly normally. It spun and spun as she fought to work what muscles were still under control.

Spastically, she inched along until she was a few feet from the door. At that point, she began to contort, her body twisting, uncontrollably. Her fingers became deformed, turning into the claws of a crow and there was a *snap* in her left arm as her humorous broke, and *thunk* from her right shoulder as her arm twisted itself right out of its socket.

As bad as this was, it was nothing compared to what happened next: her head started turning on its own. Inside, she wailed: *Noooo*, as she fought back with every muscle left to her, only she didn't have enough and as her head kept twisting, she felt the strain on her spinal column and on her barely functioning windpipe and on her carotid arteries.

Her head cranked over until she had a perfect view of Emily's rocker. A little hand was stretched out from beneath the blankets and the coat that Deanna had given up. The hand was pressed against the plastic and the fingers were beautifully, perfectly formed; not at all twisted.

Sadie saw that she had done at least one thing right; the impromptu plastic bag was keeping the baby safe and that alone was worth the price of her death. It came quickly. Her diaphragm seized and she began to suffocate. It was horrible, like drowning but instead of being submerged, she was drowning in an ocean of air. Desperately, she tried to draw a breath, fighting to suck in the smallest amount of air.

"Sadie!" Grey cried, suddenly standing above her. She could see him with her one fully functioning eye. He looked like a giant, only not a human giant. The gas mask made him look alien. Alien or not, Sadie was beyond fear. The world was fading around her. It was cloudy at the edges and so she didn't see Grey grab Emily's bagged rocker.

He then took Sadie by the collar of her plastic coveralls and was dragging her out of the building though Sadie didn't know it. From her vantage, with her head turned so that her chin was perched on her own shoulder, she saw a series of walls and doors shifting across her vision as if they were moving and she was just lying on the floor. Then she was outside on the sidewalk in a cold lashing rain that she couldn't feel.

Grey pointed her face into rain and then bent over her. His mask was off now and as he came closer, she thought he was going to kiss her goodbye. His lips planted on hers and then he blew into her lungs in one great blast of hot air that seemed to fill her chest almost to the point of bursting.

He paused for a moment, staring into her one good eye and then repeated the breath. It was amazing. Like a god, he breathed life into her. Her vision came back into focus and she could feel the rain and for a moment she had hope. It was for a moment only. He was no god.

The rejuvenating power in his lungs was a temporary force and the moment he disappeared from her sight, her neck began to crank over again and the terrifying feeling of suffocating was back.

Silently, she begged for him to return and kiss her once more. Eventually, he did come back, but it took so long that she had drifted into that beautiful dark area just before death took her. When he blew into her lungs, her eyes popped open.

"You're going to be okay," he yelled into her face. Then it felt as though she were floating. He had picked her up and put her in the front seat of the Humvee. Once more she drifted away only to be awakened by Neil leaning over her.

"Damn it, Neil!" Grey yelled. "Pinch her nose shut or no air will get to her lungs. Try it again. Easy, easy. Hey! You're not blowing up a balloon."

Her lungs had reached their limit and she felt strangely full when he sat back up. A moment later she belched like a kid in a burping contest.

Neil looked anxiously towards Grey who said: "That's normal when you blow too hard. Give her smaller breaths and check her pulse. And damn it, Neil watch her neck."

Once more, her head was beginning to twist around. She was able to see that they were in the same little house two blocks from the hospital. Naked as the day she was born, Deanna was laid out on a square of plastic with Grey hunched over her washing her from head to toe.

Off to the side, Emily was on her own square of plastic crying lustily. She was red in the face and there were...Neil gently turned Sadie's head back to square and blew once more into her lungs, this time with a touch more gentleness.

"I can't get a feel for what her pulse is," he told Grey. "It's jumping around too much. Going fast and slow and bounding or whatever." He sounded scared which Sadie took to mean she should be scared as well. Only she wasn't. She was tired and wanted to close her eyes and go back to that dark world where everything was soft and uncomplicated and where there wasn't any fear whatsoever.

"You're going to have to breathe for both of them," Grey said, grabbing his discarded gas mask. "I'll be back as fast as I can."

The next few minutes alternated between suffocation, brief moments of lucidity, and moments in the void between worlds. Sadie was partially awake when Grey returned. He stripped out of the coveralls in the rain and laid aside his mask in the shrub beside the door. When he came into the house, he had a bag of syringes, needles and bottles. He looked less than confident.

"I know I'm supposed to inject atropine and diazepam, but I don't know how much," he whispered to Neil. "And do I go IV or IM? Shit, I hate this. The one person I could ask is laying in a pool of his own piss back in the E.R."

"Use your best judgement. Trust it. It's gotten you this far. Start with Sadie. She's the worst off."

Grey decided to go with intravenously and slid an IV into Sadie's forearm. She didn't feel a thing and was only somewhat aware of Neil blowing air into her lungs every few seconds.

The first real clue that the meds were working was, unfortunately, the return of her ability to feel pain. It felt as though her joints were filled with ground glass and her broken arm screamed with fire and her dislocated shoulder thudded in time with her pulse. Grey slowly added more and more medicine to her IV until she began to cry.

It was only then that she realized her eyes were back in sync and that her fingers were hers again. Neil bent to blow air into her and jerked in surprise when she slurred: "No mo-rah." Her tongue and lips felt hugely fat and flappy. She tried again. "No mar. M-ore. No more, pease."

"Watch her!" Grey cried, excitedly and rushed to Deanna's side. Quickly she was hooked to an IV as well, and in minutes was blinking up at Grey. "You're going to be fine!" he yelled down at her as if her ears were as numb as the rest of her had been.

"Bay-gee," she muttered.

Grey glanced over at the baby, who didn't appear to need any of the atropine, whatsoever. "Emily's doing well. You did the right thing covering her in layers. I think the low dose you were subject to and the insulation saved her. Honey? Deanna?"

She had sunk into unconsciousness and Sadie quickly followed. This time she didn't visit that fine line between life and death. This time she succumbed to the heavy dose of diazepam Grey had given her. She had no idea how long she was out that first time but when she woke, her body was on fire and her arm ached like a dying tooth.

"Hurts," she said to Neil, who was sitting next to her in the back of a vehicle that was beyond her ability to describe internally. It might have been a truck or one of the flatbed Humvees. They were huddled under a tarp and rain beat down on it with steady force.

"Just a sec," he said. He reached for something and that was all she remembered until she woke sometime later, in the city hall building. The pain was still in her joints, but thankfully it was less intense. She didn't need to scream as she turned to look around, though she did grimace. Deanna was next to her but higher up on a leather couch. It was familiar and for some reason it was reassuring that it was familiar.

"Always the bravest of the brave," Deanna said, her voice croaky.

Sadie's eyes were heavy and when she lifted an arm to touch her own face, it moved toward her so slowly that it seemed she was watching a film in slow motion. "Is Grey okay?" she asked. "And Emily?"

"Emily is doing better than us, that's for sure. Grey is watching over her like a mother hen...or like a good father. He tells me that it was you who saved us."

Sadie tried to shrug in her usual one shouldered manner; she didn't scream, it was more of a pitiful yelp. She looked down at herself and saw her right arm was in a sling tied close to her body and her left arm was in a cast.

"Oh jeeze. How the heck am I going to use the bathroom or brush my teeth?

"You know Neil will do anything for you and so will I after what you did for me." Once more Sadie ignored the compliment. She never knew what to do or say when someone became too effusive. It made her uncomfortable. Deanna must have sensed this and switched the subject. "The gas did a number on you. Grey thinks you had the full whammy. You're lucky to be alive."

"I don't feel so lucky. I feel..." She felt as though she had never been closer to death and that it was still lurking nearby. The thought gave her the shivers which looked and felt like a short epileptic fit. "What time is it?" she asked to change the subject.

Deanna showed off her shrugging capabilities by giving a tired one. "Some time in the afternoon. I must have missed at least four feedings. My boobs are killing me." At Sadie's look of confusion, Deanna added: "I can't take the chance of breast feeding Emily. Some of the VX stuff may be in my milk."

"Oh." The one word reply began a period of awkward silence between the two women. They had covered all the important matters except one: Jillybean. Sadie was afraid to ask and the silence spun out so long that she fell asleep once more.

Grey woke her just as the sunlight beyond the window was beginning to fade. "Hey there, Sadie," he said, touching her softly on her cheek. When her eyes fluttered open, he asked how she was doing and where she was in pain, and how bad it was on a scale of one to ten, and if she could remember where she got the chicken and if she could count backwards from a hundred.

He stopped her when she reached seventy-nine and then he checked her reflexes and the strength in her right hand, and so on until he finally stood back. "You should heal normally. I bet you'll be up and about by tomorrow."

There was a heavy pause and Sadie knew what was coming next. He cleared his throat and began, "Deanna and I just want to…"

"Don't," Sadie said. "Just stop. You saved me before and Deanna saved you and Neil saved everyone and, well it's what we do. I bet that one day Emily will blow up a mountain to save us all." She had meant it as a joke, but Grey's face went stony and the smile on his lips was forced. Blowing things up was Jillybean territory. It was time for her to ask: "What about Jillybean?"

"We don't know," he said and then sighed wearily, looking exhausted. "Do you remember the siren right before we left for the hospital? Jillybean went after Fred Trigg at his house. He was just holding one of his stupid: 'Meet the candidate' rallies which, as we all know, is just a reason to bitch about Neil. Either way, he had just begun when Jillybean chucked one of those damned vials at him."

Sadie felt herself wilt slightly so that she was laid out like an old piece of lettuce that had been left on the counter all day. It took her two tries to ask: "How—how many died?"

"None, thankfully. The vial landed in the mud and didn't break. A couple of people did get hurt in the ensuing panic and the siren didn't help matters. We had people going in every direction."

"And Jillybean got away," Sadie said. There was no question of that. Jillybean was a perfect ghost when she wished to be.

"A clean get away," Grey muttered, angrily. "She's the reason why we're having an impromptu meeting of the council in a little while." He turned to Deanna and asked: "Neil was hoping that you would be strong enough to attend."

That did not bode well and Deanna and Sadie shared a look of alarm. "Why, what's going on?" Deanna asked. "Something more?"

Grey tried to dance around the subject, however neither woman would accept anything but a straight answer. "Things are very dicey out there right now. Neil's worried about how the council will vote. He's anxious that if Veronica and Steve go over to Fred's side, they will be able to push him out. And it could happen. That's how bad it is."

"So much of this is my fault," Sadie said, from her couch. "I've defended Jillybean over and over and I don't know if I can any more." It was a horrible thing to say, but she had seen and felt a great deal of horror that day and didn't think she could take much more. It would break her if she did.

The full seven-person council met an hour later in the lobby of City Hall. A couch had to be dragged in for Deanna who was carried to it by Grey. Fred had insisted on the odd location. Like a western gunfighter who was also a mobster, he carried a pair of pistols on his hips and refused to put his back to the glass front doors. He acted extra twitchy and swore that if he saw Jillybean he would shoot first and ask questions later.

Sadie wasn't allowed to attend but she wouldn't be shut away so easily. She tried to stand but ended up falling back on the couch, which caused pain to lightning through her limbs and along the break in her arm. For half a minute, she mewled in pain, wishing for the first time in months that her mother was alive and that she were there to take care of her as she used to when she was small.

Eventually, Sadie was able to get hold of the pain enough to try again. This time she trusted in the walls and planted her cheek against one, sticking to it like a wet sock. Slowly, she eased around the door frame and into the hall. The building was so quiet that she could hear the meeting as if she were sitting at the table.

"That's some tough talk," Neil said, in response to Fred's aggressive stance against a tiny seven-year-old. "I feel safer already."

"If you can't protect the people, Neil, *we* are going to have to protect ourselves." He emphasized the word "we" and pointed toward the door, where a few hundred armed and angry people milled about. A new lynch mob had formed under Fred's control and in truth they looked barely in control.

Every few seconds, one of them would bang on the doors and scream obscenities, demanding that "something" be done. Sadie guessed that it was the prevailing sentiment in the Valley, still it was a bit of shock to see the anger in their faces as she made it to the lobby. Afraid that Grey would carry her away, she didn't go all the way into the room. Using the door jam, she sank down to her knees and did her best not to cry out from the pain.

"The people need a man of action, Neil. They need a show of force in order to feel as though there's someone they can count on," Fred said, as one hand strayed to one of his pistols, caressing it gently. "Whether they know it or not, they need martial law."

"Slow down," Deanna said. "What's happening? I know about the latest attack, but no one was hurt, right?"

Fred raised an eyebrow towards Neil, who drummed his fingers for a moment before saying: "People are fleeing from the Valley. After what happened at the hospital, at least a hundred have simply packed up their cars and left. It's gotten worse since what happened to Fred."

"That's right," Fred agreed, with a twisted smile that was filled with smug, self-righteousness. "There's a hysteria sweeping over everyone. If you ask me, it clearly shows an utter lack of confidence in your leadership, Neil."

Neil stubbed the heel of one palm into the socket of his left eye and worked it around as he answered: "I have to agree with Fred. And, if I thought it would make the situation better, I would step down. But I have to look past this moment. Will a new leader be able to capture Jillybean and stem the flow of people fleeing the Valley? I think the answer lies not in who the leader is, but in his ideas. Whatever confidence you think you'll inspire, Fred, will vanish as soon as the next attack occurs if you don't have something new to offer."

"Oh, I have ideas. Trust me on that."

Fred's smugness reached an intolerable level and not just for Sadie. Unexpectedly, Veronica leapt up and threw her pen at Fred, missing his face by a few inches as it sailed across the room and bounced off of Sadie's black Converse.

"And how many people have to die before you tell us these ideas?" Veronica demanded. "Don't you have any clue what your role here is? It's not to be a colossal douchebag, it's to provide fucking *counsel* to the fucking governor so that he can make the best fucking decisions possible!"

Fred eyed her with cool anger. "Perhaps if he ever took my advice I would give it to him. Instead he mocks me at every turn. That's hardly leadership."

Other than Deanna, who was dull-eyed and weak, the people around the table began to bicker back and forth. Neil stopped it by doing nothing more than slowly getting to his feet. "Let's all be honest, Fred, is right. I do mock him and with some justification. Sorry Fred, normally, you do little besides Monday morning quarterbacking." Fred started to argue again, but Neil cut it off by slapping his hand on the table and yelling: "Stop it! Just stop it. I want to have a vote."

"On your standing as governor?" Fred asked.

Neil's lips pressed into straight lines as he answered: "No, not yet. We can all agree that my ideas haven't worked so far. Clearly, we need something different and I want to give you a chance. In fact, part of the reason I called this meeting is to force you to give up your ideas, now, before it's too late and more people die. *And*," he said forcefully, holding up his disfigured left hand as Fred started to interrupt, "and I want to officially give you credit for the ideas that the council implements."

Staring at Neil through slitted eyes, Fred leaned back in his chair taking a long time to answer: "When you say credit, you mean in an official capacity? As in giving me credit for capturing Jillybean?"

"Yes, if your ideas lead to her capture, that is. All in favor?" Neil asked, looking around the table.

"Anything to stop her," Grey said, and raised his hand. Deanna held hers up long enough to be counted and then she let it fall back to her side. A moment later, her eyes closed and her chin tilted to the side.

Around the table the votes were counted: seven to zero in favor. Veronica had been the slowest to raise her hand and now she said: "Alright, you won, so out with it, Fred. Let's hear these great ideas."

He stood, his right hand placed over his heart as though what he was about to say would be emotional and of great importance. "First, we need to declare martial law. It's imperative that the people know who's in charge. Next we need to restrict people from the streets; they can't be going around willy-nilly. And cars, too. Jillybean can only be getting around by car, otherwise she would have been seen by now. Next, we need to set up checkpoints around the Valley. They will need to be close enough so that each will be able to watch over the next."

Fred took a long pause as if to judge the reactions of the men and women around the table. It was a long enough moment for Neil to sigh, rub his forehead and say: "Sooo, you're suggesting martial law and check points? I really don't mean to be a jerk, but I guess I was hoping for more. Technically, we are under martial law already. And…" He gestured to the door, where soldiers could be seen standing at the corners beyond the protesters. "We already have checkpoints. And as for restricting movement, the only people moving around in the last few hours have been your rent-a-mob and the people hightailing it out of the Valley."

"As expected, once more you crap all over my ideas," Fred said. Sadie burned with anger to see him sit back, thump his feet up on the table, and cross them at the ankles. "So far you've done nothing for your people. Perhaps worse, you lack *presence*. At least I was out there among the people while you were doing, what? A job that should have been left for someone else. Your position demands more than running around putting out small fires when the entire Valley is about to go up in smoke."

Grey began to bristle at this, since Neil had been busy risking his life helping to save Deanna and Emily when no one else would. "Don't bother," Neil said to him. "Okay, a show of hands, who wants to enact any of Fred's ideas?"

Veronica gave a shrug. "The car thing is good, not that there are a lot of cars on the roads. Still, it would be good to stop them and give them a quick check."

"I'd go with the car thing, too," one of Fred's handpicked council members said. This earned him a glare. He knuckled under and added: "I mean all of it. The, uh martial law and the other stuff."

Neil was happy to see that only the car checks passed, but he wasn't ecstatic. He wanted real answers to a real problem. No one gave him any. Deanna had passed out and Grey was too preoccupied with her to really add anything. Veronica was a feisty ex-whore who was great under pressure as long as it didn't involve constructing complicated plans or trying to outthink Jillybean.

Fred's toadies were excellent at sucking up to him but were useless in any other situation. This left only Neil, who was harried, tired and uncertain of himself and Sadie, who wasn't supposed to be there at all and, who rarely had an original insightful idea. What she was good at was adapting and picking up the best and the worst of the people around her—and that included Jillybean, who did have insightful ideas.

"Maybe we can use drones," she said from the doorway, where she was slumped over, her slinged arms seemingly positioned in a strange self-hug. "Or we can set up stationary cameras. It'll keep the soldiers safer. Except that she isn't going after the soldiers." Sadie felt herself on the edge of an idea, one that was just out of reach. "Why isn't she?"

"Because she knows they would kill her," Grey said. "She may be insane, but she isn't stupid."

Sadie shook her head. "Since when is the crazy part of Jillybean worried about death? She attacked the Stanley, presumably to go after Neil. The attack on Fred was obvious, I think. Why did she attack the hospital? To go after Deanna? If so, how did she know she would be there?"

The lobby went stone quiet. "Do you think she's watching us?" Neil asked in a whisper, his head held perfectly still, his lips barely moving.

It hadn't been the tracks her train of thought had started on and yet it was one that would be smart to explore. "I don't know. You had people searching the entire Valley for Jillybean; did anyone search here?"

Neil started to shake his head when there was a sudden loud *crack* from the front doors. One of the protesters had thrown a rock. "Fred!" Neil snapped. "Do something about…" Another rock was thrown and this one left a star-shaped mark. "Ah jeeze!" he cursed in anger.

Grey stood, his Beretta already in hand. "Fred, either you fix this or my men will. I will not have this sort of…" It wasn't another thrown rock that stopped him; it was a scream of ultimate horror.

Sadie knew what it meant—Jillybean had struck again. The broken Goth girl pistoned out with her unsteady legs while bracing her back against the door frame, getting to her feet in time to see a man outside the front doors contorting and twisting into something that was only barely human in shape. There were a dozen more people on the ground writhing while the rest raced away into the rain.

"Oh God," Veronica mumbled, her face so slack-looking that for a moment Sadie feared the gas had already gotten into the building. They all had that same overpowering fear. Fred and his two toadies took off running for the back door, but Grey was quicker. He caught them two steps from the table and shoved the Beretta in their faces.

"Fucking cowards!" he seethed, the gun inches from Fred's left eye. "No one runs. We stay together. Fred and Steve help Sadie. Neil help Veronica with Deanna. I've got point. Dillon get our six and if any of you even thinks about running, I'll put a new hole in your head. We'll go out the rear in a controlled manner so that we can deal with any threat. Is that understood?"

Everyone nodded and under Grey's stern eye, they moved into the positions assigned to them.

Fear made Fred careless and uncaring to a greater extent than usual. He took Sadie by the arm—the broken arm, with more concern for himself than for her and when she cried out in pain, he only mumbled a perfunctory: "Sorry." Steve was more gentle, however he shook like a leaf and she was pretty sure that if someone yelled "Boo!" he would drop her and run.

This proved true twenty seconds later. Grey was leading them to the left, through the office section when a door opened as Sadie was jostled past. Jillybean stood there, framed in the doorway, looking tiny and pale. She said: "Stop," in a clear piping voice. It was a command that was utterly ignored.

Fred and Steve both squealed and dropped Sadie; Neil flung his arms out and threw himself in front of Deanna and Veronica; Dillon fled back towards the lobby as though a pack of demons had burst out of the office instead of the little girl. Captain Grey reacted in a manner true to his nature and training.

In a split second, he spun, brought his pistol up and fired from a range of twelve feet. He couldn't miss. Jillybean thumped back against the door and then slid down it as her legs buckled.

A moment later, she joined Sadie on the floor.

Chapter 34

Captain Grey

He could not miss a target as close and as stationary as Jillybean. Years of training had honed his reflexes so that he could react at nearly the same speed as he could think. The gun was up and sighted dead center on the girl's forehead before Sadie was halfway to the floor, before Neil could make his heroic and useless gesture and before Jillybean could finish uttering the single syllable word.

The trigger was three-quarters back in a blink, before Fred finished his frightened squawk and Dillon could take the first step in his panicked retreat. Grey fired just as he remembered the promise he had made to Sadie: *If anything happened to her, he was supposed to tell Jillybean that Sadie loved her.*

It was a stupid promise that hadn't made sense at the time and seemed equally silly just then with the Valley, the one stable and supposedly "good" society left on earth, crumbling because of this one child. One bullet could end their troubles and it was now too late to stop it.

And yet, he had made a promise. People missed targets all the time. It took only a single break in concentration or a slight weakness in the wrist or a twerk of the trigger finger. The twerk was the only thing a pro like Grey could emulate. It was just enough to send the bullet into the door a quarter inch from Jillybean's ear.

The little girl had been friends with Captain Grey for the better part of a year and must have seen her death in the muzzle flash from his gun. She went whiter than ever as her muscles twitched erratically. A moment later she fell to the ground, her chest heaving and her big blue eyes staring unblinkingly at a patch of carpet.

Then there was near silence in the building. The only thing that broke it was the sound of Dillon running to who knew where and Jillybean's breath as it ran in and out of her as though she were hyperventilating. The adults in the room stared at her in the same manner as they would stare at a bomb that was a fraction of a second away from exploding.

All, that is, save Captain Grey, who still aimed his pistol. This time there wouldn't be a twerk of his trigger finger. "Sadie loves you," he said before settling in behind the gun as he had a thousand times before.

"You're going to die," the little girl said.

The trigger started going back again. Neil stopped it, saying: "Not yet, Grey. At the moment, she's defenseless. She can't hurt us, so let's hear her out."

Jillybean was still staring at the patch of carpet in that blank, near-to-death way, but suddenly the right side of her mouth lifted in a smile. "When am I ever defenseless? You know me, Mister Neil, even now, I'm not defenseless. I could kill all of you if I wanted to."

"Why would you want to?" Neil asked, taking a step forward, his soft, but mangled hands held out. "Why did you do any of this?"

She began blinking rapidly, her eyes still fixated on the carpet. When she shook her head, they remained lasered in on that one spot. "I don't know, I really don't. I've been asking and asking myself the same question and I don't have any answers. I just know that if you guys go out the back door, you'll die. Ever since I runded away from the jail, that is the first thing that's made any sense."

Neil's mouth came open twice before he asked: "It does? How?"

Grey answered for her. "The attack in front was a diversion, wasn't it? You create a panic and then funnel us into a kill zone out back. That was your plan, correct?"

She shrugged. "I don't know what my plans are. Everyone says I'm an insane but I don't know. It used to not be like this. With Eve, she pushed me down inside the blackness and Chris was sort of like Ipes. He was a friend, but he did stuff for me while I was asleep, like kill that trader-man. But this is different. Things seem to be happening even when I'm awake."

"What sort of things?" Neil asked.

Another shrug. "Like right now. I don't remember throwing poison out front or setting up a trap out back, but it's happened anyway. That's what means everyone is right. I think…I think I need to be drownded." Her blue eyes were drowning in tears, but she did not look up from the faded green carpet, Nor did she wipe away the tears. One dropped onto her hand.

Fred, who had jumped into another office, eased himself back into the hall, guns in both hands. "She's right of course, but we should talk about this somewhere else. How do we get out of here safely, Jillybean?"

"I guess a window? Maybe? But can you trust me? If I say we can get out through a window, then *I* must have knowed I would say we could get out through a window and so there's no way we can use a window."

"Are you saying there's no safe way out of this building?" Fred demanded, his voice going high and squeaky.

Sadie, who had nudged herself to a sitting position with her back to the wall opposite from Jillybean, spoke in a quiet voice: "I think she's saying she doesn't know. We should pick an office as far from the front as possible and try to seal the door until we can figure this out."

"Unless," Neil said, "Jillybean knew we would pick one far from the front and booby trapped that one."

Everyone looked at the little girl, who sat up and said: "How should I know what I've been doing?"

"We're going in circles, damn it," Grey grumbled, holstering his gun. He stepped into the office Jillybean had exited from and glanced around, paying attention to the corners and edging. He even lifted up the carpet. "Okay, this one is clear. Let's get everyone in…get your ass back over here, Fred. You, Neil and Steve help the wounded. Veronica, go find Dillon." He assigned himself the task of searching Jillybean and relieving her of the many odds and ends she always managed to accumulate over time: batteries, string, paperclips, rubber bands, wire and more.

Next, once everyone was inside, he made sure the room was as airtight as could be. In the third drawer of the desk he discovered two rolls of mailing tape and, with Steve's help, he taped around the frames of the door and windows. Only then did he feel safe enough to talk.

"Now, Jillybean," he said, trying his best to control his emotion. There was no telling what sort of murderous surprises the little girl had cooked up around the Valley and he had to fight the impulse to pick her up and shake her until she talked. "Could you please tell us how you got out of the prison and what's been happening in the last day?"

With her chin on her chest and her eyes on her laceless Keds, she told them the details about the breakout which had Neil whispering in awe: "That's crazy."

"But I haven't got to the crazy part, yet," Jillybean said. "That was just normal stuff. I didn't get crazy until I got here."

"Can you tell us how you got here, then?" Neil asked. "The last time we saw your tracks, they were leading off toward Route 34."

She glanced up and there was guilt written across her face. *Here it comes*, Grey thought. He figured that Jillybean was about to open up and spill the beans; instead she said: "I didn't go nowheres, really. I squished in the mud pretty good so you'd see my feets prints going away and then I crept back in them and climbed up the jail building and then crossed on the old 'lectricity wires to this one and got in through the roof. All that mud got my shoes awful dirty."

Jillybean held one sneaker up for them to verify her veracity on the subject of muddy shoes. They were indeed caked with mud. The treads were all filled in, looking like old squeezed out mortar from between bricks.

She was about to put her foot down but Grey whipped a hand out and caught her heel. Jillybean flinched inward, afraid what the gruff old soldier would do to her. He simply flicked off a crust of the dried mud as though he were flicking a cockroach from a tabletop. "Go on," he said, letting her have her foot back. "What did you do next?"

"I don't know," she said, quietly. "I mean I thought I knew, but how do I really know what I know? I thought I stayed put, hiding in this office but I guess I wasn't. I thought…" She paused and her eyes grew haunted. "I went into the dark place where the whispers come from to see if there was a poisoner in there."

"Did you find anyone?"

She nodded, her eyes blank orbs as she remembered. "There's lots and lots of ghosts in there. They're all so hungry and they all want out. They came for me. They came to drown me in the blackness, but I ran and ran…and I found myself here. And now I don't know what's what."

Fred grumbled: "You're saying you were here the whole time having a seance or something. You're lying. This is my office and I've been in here twice since last night and I would have seen you."

"I don't think I'm lying," she replied, jerking as if coming awake. "Cuz I saw you Mister Fred. I guess you're not an observing person. Do you see that coat holder thing?" She pointed at his closet, where a black garment bag hung. "I took the coat out of that thing, cut a hole in the bottom and stood in it while you were in here. I picked this place because it was locked and that's what means I could hear you coming. You always jingle your keys before you come in and you never did nothing in here, so that worked out, too."

Fred's lip curled. "I was busy with the work of the people. Can we get back to the matter at hand? Where's the rest of the VX gas? And why did you come after me? And what about the people at the hospital? They were innocent and yet you killed them. Why? And don't say, I don't know."

Grey watched her tiny shoulders hunch further in and thought: *She'd crawl inside herself if she could.* He asked, "When you set off the gas in the Stanley were you trying to kill Mister Neil? Does a part of you hate him?"

She took a long time to answer. "No, It's kind of the opposite day with that. I love Mister Neil. I'm his daughter just like Sadie."

Grey nodded. "Okay, what about what happened at the hospital? Was there someone there who you didn't like? Deanna? Our baby, Emily? You did kill Eve because you were jealous of her. Were you jealous of Emily?"

Jillybean was quicker to answer this time. "I don't know Emily. I never even met her. And I like Miss Deanna. We were partners in blowing up the River King's bridge, amember?"

"I remember," Grey said. "And what about just now? You were trying to kill the council. Is it because we locked you away? Was it because we threatened to water board you?"

She looked lost and floundered into a guess: "It was because...because I was afraid?"

Sadie snorted: "Since when are you ever afraid? And if you were so afraid, why did you turn yourself in just now? You just asked to be drownded, remember?" Her voice softened. "You know what? I don't think you did any of this."

"What?" Fred cried. "She's already admitted it for pete's sake! Okay, this crap has gone on long enough. We all know 'Jillybean' didn't kill anyone. It was one of her psycho personalities and, as sad as that is, it doesn't change anything. We need to get out of this building and we need to get to the bottom of where the rest of the VX gas is."

"I don't think she did it, either," Grey said. Fred threw his hands in the air and was about to start another rant when he saw the hard look on Grey's face. He shut his mouth but wasn't happy about it. Grey turned to Jillybean. "You think you killed all those people? I want you to lay out the case against yourself. Start with why, what, where when and how."

It seemed like a somewhat cruel thing to ask of her as she looked around the room, perhaps for clues as to what her unbalanced mind had done and why. "I guess I did it cuz I'm crazy? That's what all of you said. That's what everyone says. I don't know why else. I can't seem to…I can't seem to find the evil thing inside of me, but when I do…"

"What?" Fred asked. "You'll stop it like you stopped Eve? Oh wait, you didn't stop Eve. She killed that baby with you looking on, didn't she?"

Jillybean was devastated by this horrific but utterly factual statement. More tears came now and a hitching started in her chest as her shame and guilt swamped her.

Neil stood up, aggressively, making a fist and a half; Although his right was fine, his left hand looked like a gnarly stunted root instead of a fist. "Those are my daughters you're blabbing on about and I don't appreciate your tone. I've forgiven Jillybean and I know Eve would have as well. What's more, I don't think she did this, either. None of this feels like my Jillybean."

Grey pulled Neil back. "Let me handle this. As you said, you're her father. You're too close to the situation. Jillybean, hey, Jillybean. Try to relax. Tell us a little something about the different voices in your head and tell me what they did for you."

Slowly she described Ipes and then Eve. Trying to explain Chris took longer since it was obvious that she was still coming to grips with the fact that he hadn't been real. Finally, she mentioned the "Dad" voice that came to her every once in a while, and the voice that warned her about the poison gas.

"And what do they all have in common?" he asked. When she couldn't answer, he did for her. "They were all there to protect you. Even Eve's goal was to keep you alive, no matter what. She was selfish and evil but made no bones about the fact that she was there to survive and she didn't much care for your bravery getting in the way of that. This is the exact opposite of what this new person in you is doing. Am I right?"

Before she could answer, Fred said, "Her insanity probably mutated. And isn't that the problem with the insane? They just aren't predictable and do you know why? Because they're insane, that's why!"

Grey put out his empty hands in a gesture of peace. "I agree, but let's look at some other points. As Neil alluded to, none of these attacks have that Jillybean feel. I know Eve was a bit brutish in her ways, but Jillybean, how far can you throw one of those vials?"

A new shrug. "I don't know, thirty feet? Is that good? I used to only be able to throw a crab apple across the street, but back in Oklahoma I was going to the gym to get stronger. I think I'm more like Sadie. That's what means I can run better than I can throw."

"That's what I was thinking, too. It made me wonder how you got close enough to throw the vial over at Fred's house or even out front here."

She scratched the side of her head where the hair was only an inch long and said: "Maybe I was sneaky. I can sneak real good."

"Can you sneak so good that your shoes don't get wet? That mud on your sneaker is dried. And your clothes are dry, too and so is your hair."

"I might could have used a drone."

Sadie sat in Fred's swivel chair, a sad smile working its way through the pain. "Or maybe you didn't do it at all. Maybe we jumped to conclusions since you just happened to show up at the same time the first attack happened. It's the only explanation."

"There are more explanations than just that," Fred said. "Maybe she does have a drone. We really haven't checked the building for one. Or maybe Chris is actually a real person. Or maybe you are all being fooled by Jillybean's innocent act one more time."

Grey and Sadie started to argue with Fred, but Neil stopped them. "Sorry to say, Fred may be correct. I believe that at the moment, we don't have enough evidence to convict Jillybean, but that does not preclude the fact that she might have an accomplice, or a drone or something. I personally don't believe it, and yet with so much on the line, we should be as thorough as possible."

"That's wise," Grey said. "We'll start by searching this room, but if there isn't any evidence then we really need to look for another suspect." They found nothing except Jillybean's stash of stolen goods: two water bottles, a can of french cut green beans, a John Grisham novel, a letter opener, paperclips bent into different shapes, a twenty foot section of homemade rope crafted from roughly cut strips of braided curtains, and a picture of a happy family of four that she had found in the trash can.

"It didn't belong there," she said, looking reproachfully at Fred.

When Fred started to get his back up like a house cat about to hiss in indignation, Neil angrily slapped his good hand down on the desk. "Enough! No more bickering. I think we've proven that Jillybean lacked the motive, the means or the opportunity to commit these crimes. In my book that makes her innocent, but to be on the safe side one of us will watch over her."

"I'll do it," Veronica said. "Anything to help us get out of this building. The back door is out of the question. Can we trust the windows?"

It didn't seem as though they really had a choice. Grey went to the office next door and inspected the window as closely as he could before he smashed it with a chair. He stood for a moment testing the air by taking small sips. It smelled like rain and other than getting a case of the shivers at the thought of being turned into the human version of a curly fry, nothing happened.

"We're good," he called to Neil. He climbed out first, gun in hand, eyes peeled, searching the dark. He was looking for a generic "bad guy" but his mind was on the poison gas. How far had the VX spread? Was the rain washing it away? Or was it still in the air and would a shift in the wind kill him in fifteen terrible seconds? He was so fixated on the horrifying death that awaited one wrong step, that he was slow to realize something else was wrong in the Valley.

There was too much movement for the night and too much light and too many cars and, seconds later, too many gunshots. The guns were going off everywhere. It wasn't a full-fledge battle. The shots were too sporadic and too spread out. They could mean only one thing: there were zombies in the Valley.

Chapter 35

Neil Martin

Captain Grey was on one knee, gun in hand, looking down the main strip running through the center of town when Neil came up. He had Sadie under one arm while Dillon had her by the other.

He was a little confused by the shooting and worried that in their fear of another poison gas attack, the people were shooting at each other. Then he saw the humanoid creatures shambling down the street. "Are those zombies?" It was a stupid question. Before Grey could give him that look of his reserved for the truly stupid, Neil added: "Right, of course they're zombies. I knew that."

"Then you should know enough to shut up," Grey growled.

Neil gave the "ok" sign and then glanced back to see the others straggling up. He found it somewhat humorous that Veronica had used the braided "rope" that Jillybean had made to put the little girl on a leash of sorts. What wasn't funny was how terribly worn and pale Sadie and Deanna were.

"The first thing we need to do is to find shelter," Neil said. "Any suggestions?"

"There's a bank right across that parking lot," Veronica said, pointing to their left. "I searched there yesterday for this little monkey." Jillybean had been peering through the rain at the zombies and now she was pulled back close to Veronica, who went on: "Its doors are intact. No zombie will get in there."

Neil pointed to Grey to lead the way. He went in first, crouched behind his gun while the others huddled in the rain, hoping that the dark night would keep the zombies from seeing them. With two of them unable to stand on their own, being attacked was the last thing they needed.

"Clear," Grey whispered, from the doorway a second later. "Let's move." They rushed in where it was dry but cold. Fred began to complain but only got a single word out before Grey grabbed him by the shirt and barked: "Shut up! You and Dillon get that back office ready. I want the windows covered and two couches brought in there. Steve and I will work on the conference room. It'll be our new command and control room."

"And I will get on the radio and call the ready platoon," Neil stated. "Um, first, does anyone have a radio? I left mine back in the other building." Deanna and Grey had lost theirs that morning during the cleanup from the gas exposure and no one else had one.

Jillybean held up a hand. "I have one in my Jeep. Her name is Jessica Jeep and I saw her parked right up by the jail. If you want, I can go get it."

"*We'll* go get it," Neil corrected. "You and Veronica and me. Everyone else stay here and listen to Grey. We'll be right back." He looked less than confident about going out into the night. Even after Grey handed over his Beretta, Neil's face was a light shade of green. There was no telling if the VX gas was floating around. They could walk right into a cloud of it and be dead just like that.

Fearless as always, Jillybean pushed forward, taking the lead, moving from bush to parked car, to the edge of this building or that. She only slowed as she came closer to the jail, where a number of zombies were crossing the parking lot. They were nearly out of sight when Neil accidentally kicked a rock. It skittered and then plunked loudly off the hubcap of an old Mercedes.

The zombies turned immediately towards the new sound and more emerged from around the side of the building. They weren't exactly in danger. Neil had a gun, only he couldn't use it as it would attract more of the beasts. There was also the option of running back to the bank. Unfortunately, they would then be trapped and would eventually have to fight their way out.

"I'll take care of this," Jillybean whispered. She wore a mischievous grin that made Neil nervous...more nervous, that is.

"No," Neil said, easing up over the fender of the Mercedes and counting the zombies; there were fifteen altogether and of course he had no idea how many bullets were in the gun. If there were only twelve things would get...

Jillybean interrupted his thoughts. "You two go on back to the bank. I'll be there in a minute."

"Wrong," Veronica hissed. She was a brave woman, but it had been a long time since she had to face zombies and she had never faced them empty handed. "We'll all go back and figure... hey! What? How did you do that?" Jillybean's grin was even wider as she held up the leash that she had been bound with. It was untied.

"Your knots aren't the best sorts of knots. I could teach you better ones later if you want. Even though I'm a girl and all, I read a Boy Scout book that showed some real doozies. Oh, I think they hear me so I better go."

Without looking back, she dashed away to the right where there was a line of cars that looked as though they had been there for years. Their paint jobs were fading or bubbling up and rust was beginning to show. They sat on crumbling flat tires, which made it that much easier for the little girl to climb right over one. Then she was off like a shot and Neil could barely keep up.

He had lost only a second in surprise before he had taken off after the girl, crying over his shoulder to Veronica: "I'll get her!" She was faster than she looked and faster than she had been the year before. "Hey, hold on," he yelled as all around him zombies closed in. "Wait for me!"

As she wasn't inoculated, she had a lot more to fear from the zombies and she didn't wait. She charged for the Jeep and jumped right in and shut the door in his face. He could hear the lock click. Now, he could only pray that the passenger side was open or there was a chance he could be eaten right there in the parking lot, and worse, Jillybean could get away.

He didn't know if he loved her or not, but he cared for her deeply and respected her immensely even when she was being crazy, like right at that moment. Her actions just then made him doubt his earlier declaration of belief in her innocence.

Two seconds later, he was scrabbling for the door handle, praying that it would open. "Ha!" he laughed when it did. He hopped in to the passenger seat, but his hubris was on display when he paused long enough to give Jillybean a look that said: *I made it*. That pause was long enough to allow one of the zombies to catch up and when Neil went to shut the door, it closed on a set of grey, scabby fingers that looked as though they belonged on something months dead and not on something still moving.

"Uh, Mister Neil? Maybe you should shut that better."

"I'm trying!" He hammered the door onto the fingers, watching in sick fascination as the bones broke and the nails snapped off. Finally, one of the fingers, a rotten sausage of a thing, popped right off to land in his lap and the door latched. For a moment, the finger wiggled like a worm, causing his late lunch to come crawling up the back of his throat and threaten to come spewing out of his mouth.

He swallowed it back down and then prissily flicked away the finger. "Are these zombies or lepers?" he asked, attempting a laugh but only able to produce a weak and very forced chuckle.

Jillybean, who had been digging around in the back seat, stopped to explain that: "Leopards are cats, Mister Neil. Everyone knows that. They got spots and everything. So, I'd say those things are monsters." She went back to digging in the stacks of this and that and everything else.

Neil stared around the Jeep as an unsettling feeling came over him. There were no windows and no light except for the dome light, and it wasn't the strongest. In the gloom he felt completely closed in, and instead of feeling secure or safe, he felt trapped.

"I don't have the keys, you know," he said, suddenly realizing that the feeling of being trapped was actually the *fact* of being trapped.

"Oh, really?" she mumbled. "Ah, that's too bad…ah, here we go!" She pulled out a slim black square that had Neil wagging his head. It was another iPad. "Last one. That was close. I was ascared you guys mighta tooked it."

He held up a finger—his own finger— the other was uncomfortably close to his left shoe. "Didn't you hear me? We don't have the keys, which means we're trapped."

"Ha-ha, that's a good one, Mister Neil." She handed him the iPad and opened the console between the seats. It looked to be a combination junk drawer and tool box. "Velcro, velcro, where's the velcro? Here's the scissors, but where is the Velcro?"

She popped her head out of the console and looked at Neil, her eyes somewhat out of focus. "I don't know where the velcro is," he said. "But I doubt it would really help to start the car. Maybe you should think about some wire snips and some electricians tape. You know…to hotwire the car?"

"Huh? You can't hotwire Jessica not unless you know the secret and nobody does. I switched the starter wire and the left turn signal wire. It was tricky and that's what means it wasn't easy. Oh, there's the velcro it was sticking to that mitten."

As Neil watched in confusion, she took a pair of scissors, cut the velcro, attached the sticky side to the iPad and then stuck it in place above the steering wheel. She flicked it on and punched in the four number code and sat back grinning.

"I'm so glad I'm not crazy," she said, her smile turning giddy. "I mean, I'm glad I'm not a bad sort of crazy, like using that poison gas and all. Or a killing people kind of crazy. That was making me sick to my stomach, you know?"

"Yeah, of course, so how do you go about starting the car?" She had shut the console where all the tools were kept and was just sitting there at the wheel.

"I mean, Chris wasn't real and that's crazy. I get that, now. But he was a nice sort of crazy. A good sort of crazy. I think I needed him so much that I made him out of nothing. You know, he was a little like Joe Gates. Hey, Joe is a real person, right? I didn't dream him up, too, did I?"

Before he could answer, there was a thud on the side of the Jeep, reminding him that they were still surrounded by zombies. *Just how good is this armor?* he wondered. Knowing Jillybean, it was probably strong enough to stop any zombie. That should have been reassuring but somehow it wasn't. If it was strong enough to keep things out, it might be strong enough to keep him in.

"He's real. He lives right down Elkhorn Drive with his sister and uncle. I'd take you to him if we can get this Jeep going."

Jillybean pooched out her lower lip. "I thought we were supposed to be getting a radio. You know I also have a scanner. We should bring that, too." She reached up a little hand and pressed the hazard signal, something that was all but useless in a world filled with zombies since there were hazards everywhere.

The engine rumbled into life and the thudding from the zombies became more frenzied. Jillybean didn't even seem to notice as she synced up the different external cameras to the iPad. She seemed to have recovered perfectly from the sad, depressed little girl of thirty minutes before, and Neil guessed that after everything she'd been through, a little VX gas, breaking out of jail, and being threatened with water boarding really was minor league for her.

Once they were ready to go, she dug in the back once more, handing over a package of batteries, a two-way radio, scanner, and something that looked like a large baked potato wrapped in foil.

"Smoke bomb," she explained. "I only got three left. Not including the one under us."

Neil felt his sphincter tighten at the idea of any bomb being under them. He tried not to let his anxiety show. "It's: I only *have* three left."

Jillybean smiled at the correction and that turned into a chuckle and then a full laugh. "I missed you correcting me. Chris used to talk like…" Bringing up the name sobered her slightly. "I mean, I guess I just missed it. And I missed you, too."

She switched the monitor view to the rear. What she saw caused her to frown. "It's gonna be bumpy."

It was bumpy and slightly squishy as they ground zombies beneath the big tires of the Jeep. After backing for a few yards, she eased out of the parking lot and was just about to turn left onto the main strip when Neil saw something in the monitor.

"What's that light?" It was the headlights of a Humvee flying down the road. Two more whooshed along behind it. "Son of a bitch! Those are from the barracks. What the hell channel is that? Five? Yeah, it's five. Hello? This is Governor Martin, is anyone on this net? Hello?"

As he tried to pick up someone from the barracks, Jillybean drove them around the corner to the bank. He was so engrossed in the radio that she had to shoo him out of the Jeep. "The monsters are right behind us, Mister Neil. Come on, let's get inside before they see us."

She just managed to get him inside. His first though was to get to Captain Grey, ready to burst in anger but the captain's smiling face stopped him. "I think we have a lead," Grey said. "I was saying that if it wasn't Jillybean doing this it's probably one of our old enemies like the Azael or one of the River King's henchmen. Veronica suggested we try looking into someone new to the Valley. She said that she did a tour for a new couple last week. She said that they spoke with a southern accent. Could be a Missouri accent."

"And where did they pick to live?" Neil asked, feeding off the excitement that was coming off Grey in waves.

The question had Grey nodding enthusiastically. "One of those places off of Dry Gulch Road." The homes in that part of the Valley were so secluded and far from town that they were barely considered part of the Valley at all.

"Okay, we need some men," Neil said, and then slapped his hands together in anger. "I forgot. Your men are deserting. We were almost hit by three Humvees coming down from the barracks. And I saw more headlights behind them."

"What?" Grey cried, before snatching the radio from Neil's hand. He started yelling into it. "Barracks one, Barracks One come in. Barracks One, this is Captain Grey, respond. Respond now, Barracks One. Shit! What's the frequency…never mind. Comm Central, this is Grey…"

He went on like that checking different frequencies until he got the ready platoon commander who had been summoned down to the Blue Gate ten minutes before. There was a lot of shooting from that direction.

"Are we under attack?" Grey asked. Everyone in the room went stock still as they waited for the answer. An attack just then, with no one answering their radios and men running away and zombies flooding down from the hills, and poison gas here and there around the Valley, would have been devastating.

"No sir," the reply came. "The gate guards were being overwhelmed by people trying to leave the Valley. We put a call into the communications team looking for direction, but they said the council had all been killed and that the Valley was being evacuated."

Neil stomped his foot and ordered: "Tell him it's not true."

Grey gave him a long look that could be read as: *Will you shut the fuck up? I got this.* "I was there, remember? I think I know what's true and what isn't. Listen Ready Leader, close the gate. Don't let anyone out. In fact, send whoever you have up to the US Bank just east of City Hall."

The ready platoon leader gave a soft, "Yes sir," and then cut out. Grey looked at the radio in disgust for a moment before mumbling: "He's not coming. Shit." He tried the Red Gate, and the barracks once more, and the communications team but without response.

When they looked out the front windows of the bank, there were more zombies and more headlights ranging down the roads. The land, the rocks, the swollen river—the Valley was still there, but the faith in its concept was crumbling, quickly.

Jillybean had been working the scanner and found a number of people desperately trying to reach someone to find out what was going on. Most wanted to know if it was time to run, a few wanted to know if it was time to fight. Grey directed them all to come to the bank.

"And see if any of them have any potassium chlorate or nitrate," Jillybean asked. "When they bring a horde of monsters down on us, we'll have to get out of here somehow," she said, in reply to Grey's quizzical look. He didn't ask and a frustrated Jillybean wandered away.

In twenty minutes, a small crowd had gathered in the bank and an even larger one gathered outside, moaning and banging on the heavy glass. "Maybe you should have asked about that potassium stuff," Neil said, seeing that they were basically trapped.

Everyone had weapons but no one liked the idea of using them. It would only draw more of the dreadful creatures and likely they would run out of bullets before they ran out of zombies.

Neil looked over the crowd. There were thirty people in the bank, however two of them were invalids, barely able to stay awake because of the diazepam Grey was sending through their IVs, and one was a known criminal. Every one of the newcomers kept away from the little girl and sent suspicious glances her way until Neil announced that she wasn't to blame for any of the VX attacks and that she had been instrumental in saving the council.

Because of the possibility of a chemical weapon attack many of them wore scarves or folded table cloths or linens soaked in vinegar across their faces. Despite this, he knew quite a few of them. Some were soldiers and some were his old traveling companions, people who knew the value of making a stand. Kay Gallagher with her big hair and her strange combination of courage and outright cowardice, William Gates, mostly covered but looking thick and bullish like his dead brother Michael, skinny, sallow-faced Travis Dunn who somehow kept surviving despite the fact that he looked like a gambler on a perpetual losing streak.

Gayle Houghton, the ex-sex slave Neil had bought and possibly the weakest person he knew, was also there. She might have been weak both physically and mentally, but she loved Neil and wouldn't leave his side in an emergency. She was also one of the few people in the building who had no fear of Jillybean. In fact, she trusted Jillybean with her life.

It was an odd group and unfortunately, a small one. There wasn't anywhere near enough of them for all the work that needed to be done, which meant chances would have to be taken.

"For the time being," Neil said, "this bank will be our headquarters. Veronica and Kay will stay and watch over Deanna and Sadie. They will also be in charge of communications. Fred, Steve and Dillon will pick five men each and go to the three gates. Red isn't answering, so Fred, I need you to go there and take charge. No one is to leave the Valley, is that clear?"

"And how do you suggest we stop them?" Fred asked.

Grey gestured to his slung pistols. "Those things you're carrying around are more than for just show. Use them if you have to."

This was an unsettling thought and many in the group looked uncomfortable at the idea of bloodshed. "He said, *only if you have to,*" Neil added. "I think your presence will stem the tide. I will take Jillybean, Nancy and William to start the generator and get the *Zevac* lights going, and Grey will take Travis, Lieutenant Hupp and PFC Hodges to check out the possible terrorists residing up on Dry Gulch Road."

The only person who looked happy about the terrible choice of assignments was Jillybean, who grinned up at her small team: William Gates, shrouded in his layers and Nancy Reyes, who was looking around trying to catch someone's eye, obviously hoping to make a trade, although there was little chance that anyone would want to. Not only was Jillybean on the team, a person who may or may not have been a dangerous killer, but Neil had also chosen the second most dangerous job. The *Zevac* was nearly the same set up Jillybean had created the year before during the war with the Azael. The lights had been modified for brightness and the walls built up so that there was little chance for any zombie to escape once they were funneled up into the mountains.

It was a dangerous job simply because it was the most expected move. "I'd use the gas and have a sniper up in the trees," Grey warned. "Listen to Jillybean and use that Jeep of hers, but don't expect it to keep you safe from the VX. We'll split the masks, one each." The only masks available to them were the ones they had used earlier. Although they had been cleaned, they were still suspect and yet, no one wanted to be without one when it came down to it.

Grey's team began to grumble, and for good reason. They were going to attack the root of the problem and it was almost a guarantee that the bad guys were going to use the gas if they found themselves cornered.

"One mask split between four men?" Lieutenant Hupp asked, his tone bordering on insolence. "You know they'll have masks. How the hell are we supposed to fight without masks?"

319

The captain looked as though he were about to bark into his subordinate's face when Jillybean piped up: "I have a mask. You can use that one if you want."

Gas masks were worth a hundred times their weight in gold and hearing Jillybean blithely offer one up caused Nancy's eyes to bug out and she made a noise in her throat as if she were choking on something. Neil glared at her. "We'll use hers," he said. "Grey's team will take the other two."

A familiar silence came between the two men. They had been down this road before: terrible odds, death in the air, their lives on the line.

Grey was the first to crack a smile. "Good luck and don't die."

"You keep your luck," Neil replied. "I'm starting to think I'm unkillable and someone throwing a bottled fart at me certainly won't be the thing that brings me down." The lopsided grin that came with this bravado was hard to keep in place. He had cried when Grey had brought back Sadie's twisted body, and what sleep he had managed to get the night before had been filled with haunted nightmares of a city filled with frozen, mutilated corpses, each reaching out to him with cold pleading hands.

"You can't think like that, Neil. You can die just like anyone else, so be careful and be smart." He leaned in closer. "And be lucky. That's what you're good at."

Chapter 36

Jillybean

"I'm better, I swear," she lied to Nancy Reyes. By no objective standard could she be considered better. She'd been hearing voices for months and had traveled with an imaginary person who had seemed as real as she was. That pretty much meant she was bonkers.

Not only that, ever since she had escaped from the jail, she'd had the distinct impression that she was being haunted. Things had been moving around her, and there had been whispers in her ear. But, since she wasn't killing people in an evil sort of way, she thought of the lie as one of those friendly "better than the truth" white lies.

To make the lie more palatable, she smiled her best smile. She had practiced her smile once a few months before after she had lost both of her front teeth, one after another, two weeks after moving in with Granny Annie. She had thought that the missing teeth had been fun and spent the next month hooting like a parrot or some sort of tropical bird.

Then her "big people" teeth had come in and she thought she looked like a rabbit and thus the smile practice. She found that the perfect combination was minimum teeth, maximum dimple and a slight tilt to the head.

Nancy looked far from convinced by this show of charm. There was a manic happiness in the little girl over not being the bad guy and not having to be tortured. It made her look a little crazed, more than usual that is, and Nancy's smile in return resembled the grimace a person normally reserved for a piss-smelling bum shaking a tin can with a few coins in the bottom rattling about.

William didn't seem to care one way or another. Always taciturn, he had become even quieter since the last time Jillybean had seen him mourning over the death of his brother. Also, he seemed bulkier, but that could have been the heavy wet-weather garments and the backpack he carried.

"Okay, so how do we know this isn't all an elaborate plot by…her," Nancy asked Neil, jutting her chin in Jillybean's direction. "Everyone knows she's trickier than the devil."

Neil had just come from kissing Sadie goodbye and his scarred and somewhat hideous face soured at the question. "Oh, stop it. Jillybean was always tricky with a purpose. Even her crazier aspects were formed for logical reasons: survival, loneliness, an emotional barrier against the cruelties of the world. These attacks aren't her style. They're too random. They're too…"

He was slow to think of a word and Nancy said: "Too perfect? This has only been going on for two days and already half the Valley is cowering like children under their beds and the other half is lighting out of here as fast as they can."

"If Jillybean had perpetrated these attacks I will guarantee you that half the Valley would be dead," he shot back. "The attacks have been far from perfect. If you ask me, I'd say the bad guys have gotten lucky. They stumble on VX which is the perfect terrorist's weapon and yet, without Jillybean showing up when she did, I doubt it would have gotten this far. Instead of searching all over kingdom come for a little girl, we would have been looking for the people who stood out or who were new, and we would have found them sooner rather than later and this would've been all over."

For a time, he was quiet and during this time, Jillybean kept smiling. Even though it hurt to hear her craziness discussed so openly, she was afraid that she would seem a bad sort of crazy if she looked angry or upset. Neil didn't notice the quiet desperation on her part; he was too busy blaming himself. "This was a failure of leadership. Like everyone else, I ignored everything good about Jillybean and only concentrated on the bad. I was suckered by the perfect scapegoat instead of…"

Grey interrupted, snapping: "Enough with this crap. We don't have time for it. We have jobs to do. First things first, we have to get out of here. Any ideas?" The bank was surrounded by the undead, those that weren't smearing slime on the glass were wandering around in the steady rain. There were too many to attack with knives or machetes, and a straight-up battle would waste too much ammo.

"I have my smoke bomb," Jillybean volunteered, holding up her foiled blob. At the sight of it, Nancy backed away. "It's just got smoke in it, no fooling." Jillybean gave it an exaggerated sniff to show that it wouldn't kill anyone. It was a poor demonstration since the potassium made her cough. Nancy wasn't the only one who backed further away. Only Neil, Grey and William Gates were brave enough to remain in place.

"May I?" Grey asked, holding out one of his big paws. When she gave it to him, he peeled back the layers and gave it a sniff. He coughed as well, but also nodded in satisfaction. "It's just a homemade smoke bomb, people. If there was VX in it, I'd be on the floor by now."

Nancy pointed at a part of the bomb that Grey hadn't inspected. There were wires leading from it. "What about that?"

"It's a thermal fuse and that's what means the thingy that starts the whole thing burning. I make them from the cigarette lighters you find in cars. My daddy used to always say that it didn't make any sen…"

A snap of Grey's fingers silenced her. "It's a smoke bomb. Let's leave it at that. We'll set it off in front. Neil's team will go first in the Jeep. It'll clear out most of the zombies. My team will go next. After that the Zs probably won't be much of a problem. Fred, you will be the last to leave. I expect you to be at the Red Gate ten minutes later. Everyone will radio in when they are in position. Is that clear?"

A volley of "Yes sirs," answered the question, however Jillybean wasn't listening. She had taken back her bomb, gave it a once over to make sure it was still intact, and then headed to the front door. It could either be remotely set or, with a little flick of a switch, manually triggered.

She waited until the first wisps of smoke began to trail upwards before she opened the door and tossed it out front. Everyone watched as it began to billow clouds out into the night. Soon, even the Jeep ten feet from the front door was hidden behind them.

Neil gathered his team by the front door of the bank. "There's not enough room inside, so you two," he pointed at William and Nancy, "will have to ride on top. Normally, I would ride on top but I think in this case it's probably best if I stay with Jillybean."

"Is she driving?" Nancy asked, her voice shrill with panic. "That doesn't make any sense. William should drive if anyone should. You can watch Jillybean from on top just as easily as you could from inside. This is probably favoritism or nepotism or something."

Her bugged eyes were wider than ever and although Neil tried on his least hideous smile in order to soothe her, she refused to be soothed. She was on the verge of refusing to go, when Gayle Houghton came up. "I'll switch places with you," she said. "I'm on Fred's team. They're going to the Red Gate. You could…"

"Yes, please," Nancy begged, backing away. "Thanks, thanks." Before Neil could say anything, Nancy, a young, fit, capable woman had been replaced by Gayle, a thirty-seven year old ex-sex slave who couldn't fight but who could form a delicious meatloaf out of a hundred different ingredients, none of which being actual meat.

Jillybean saw that she would die for Neil, but what wasn't certain was whether she could do anything else that could be construed as helpful. "Ok," Neil said, his smile strained at the edges, looking as though they would bend into a frown if his vigilance lapsed even for a moment. "This changes nothing. Our plan is the same. We head out to the generator. Get it working and then switch on the *Zevac* lights. Is that clear?"

Heads nodded, though William was so bundled it wasn't exactly obvious. Neil took his silence as a "yes," and went on. "If there's going to be a problem, a sniper or something like that, it'll be from one of those two churches across the street from the firehouse. My guess is it'll be from the Lutheran Church. It's got the best vantage point. Gayle and William, you two will position yourselves among the transformers and lay down cover fire if there's a problem."

"What do you want me to do?" Jillybean asked. She hadn't spent much time in the Valley and had only a vague notion of the generating station. It was a dun-colored, ugly box of a building that sat on the far western edge of Lake Estes. It was surrounded by the usual mysterious infrastructure common to power stations. None of which Jillybean knew a lick about.

"Does that M249 work on the Jeep?" Neil asked. Although she wanted to ask: *why have it if it didn't work?* she nodded instead. "Then, you'll cover me. But don't get too close. There could be VX gas all over that place."

"If there isn't, I could drop you off right in front," she said. "And that's what means nobody could shoot you from like, way away." She saw the question forming on his lips and answered: "Easy. There'll be monsters around and I bet they would die from the gas same as us. I have two Bumble Balls, you know."

He started snapping his fingers in excitement. "Okay, good. I remember those Bumble Balls. They're great, the zombies go right after them. Okay, we'll use the balls to lure the zombies in close. If they live, I'll let you drop me off closer where there'll be less of a threat."

"What about the zombies that'll be attracted by the bubble ball?" Gayle asked, the words squeaking out around her thumb. She was chewing the nail down to the quick.

"We'll kill them. It should be no problem. Any other questions?" Gayle, whose breathing was revving close to hyperventilation, looked as though she had a million on the tip of her tongue. But she didn't ask any and after a few moments in which no one did anything except look from face to face.

Neil pointed to the door where the smoke was dense and dreadfully eerie. Every few seconds a hand or a face would press against the glass and then disappear again. They would be plunging into a dreadful unknown where a scratch or a full scale attack could happen at any second.

"I guess we should go," Neil said. Gun in hand, he opened the door and in wafted an undulating cloud and one stumbling and confused monster. Before it knew it was actually inside, Captain Grey punched a hole in its temple with his Ka-bar.

The beast went right down and Jillybean nimbly jumped over it, heading out first. Because of her size and quickness, she wasn't afraid of the monsters. Gayle was, however. The older woman reached out a hand and snagged the little girl's shoulder, holding her close, almost like a shield. Her fear radiated out from those fingertips, which were like a hawk's talons on Jillybean's flesh.

A monster, huge and naked, loomed up out of the fog. Jillybean ducked away from it, leading Gayle to the right a few steps and then straight on, leaving the confused monster moaning and going in circles. A second later, just where she had expected, she found the Jeep.

In the dark, it seemed as big as a building. She crept along the side of it, ready at the first hint of danger to duck beneath. Thankfully, the monsters seemed to drift with the smoke as if it was dampening their usual hyper-aggression. Jillybean reached the back of the Jeep where the handholds were obvious and the climb up to the roof rack a piece of cake.

"Right here," Jillybean whispered when Gayle only clung to the Jeep and didn't immediately start climbing. "Go on, get up."

Gayle was a poor climber, going very slowly and making a whimpering noise as she went, until Neil rushed over, thrust his hand right up her hind end and started shoving. A second later, there was an ugly moan behind them; the monster was back, drawn by the noise. With the two humans, one atop the other, it couldn't tell what was what but it didn't really matter. It attacked.

Jillybean shot it square in the eye.

Unfortunately, all she had as a weapon was a laser pointer. Still it did the trick. The monster turned from the two struggling people and tried to grab the infuriating red light which splashed back and forth from one eye to the other. Enraged it tore at its own face, ripping out both of its eyes.

Although blind, it was still dangerous, able to track its prey by sound and Gayle was being loud. Her frightened breathing had picked up until Jillybean feared she would pass out and fall off of Neil's shoulders to split her head open on the asphalt.

"Hey, monster, over here," Jillybean said, in a quiet voice. The monster pulled its fingers out of its eye sockets and charged with its arms out, its bloody fingers reaching. Calmly, like the tiniest matador, she stepped aside at the last moment.

The ragged claws missed her by an inch and it blundered away into the swirling layers of grey. Attracted by the commotion, a second monster came rushing at her. Having not enjoyed watching someone tear out their own eyes, she danced the laser pointer on the smoke, jiggling it to the left. The monster attacked the smoke, ripping into it with its claws. Much to Jillybean's amusement, it even tried to bite it.

She had to hold in her giggles. It was strange to be this free and light in a time of danger. It was how Chris used to be—the thought didn't just sober her up, it also caused a zing of pain somewhere deep inside. The little girl forced herself to focus on leading the monster safely away. When she had, she dashed back to the Jeep, climbing in just as Neil was doing the same from the other side.

"Everyone on board?" she asked.

"Yes, get us out of here. Gayle is freaking out. Why on earth did she volunteer? She really isn't cut out for this sort of thing." Jillybean thought this funny coming from Neil Martin, the least imposing man left alive. He had the sturdiness of a slightly built seventh grader.

"She'll be okay, I bet," Jillybean said, as she started the engine and turned on her single iPad. The view was grey on grey and the only thermal camera was mounted on the rear gun. "I'm gonna have to drive backwards," she said to herself. "I'm not so good at that."

"If you want, I can work the wheel," Neil suggested. He leaned way over until he was practically on top of her. "You use the gas and brake and I'll steer. It'll be okay, the smoke can't stretch too far."

It was a fine arrangement, although she didn't end up using the gas at all. His instructions were either brake, more brake, or ease up on the brake.

Once they were clear of the parking lot and the smoke, Jillybean resumed her piloting, while Neil fished out his radio. "We are clear, Grey. You're next. Good luck. Okay, Jillybean, let's do this."

"Do you want to go to the hardware store first, Mister Neil?" Jillybean asked. "You know, for gloves and one of them painting suits? If there's some of that gas you'll need it."

"Oh, right. Good thinking."

"Yeah," she agreed. "I have some good thinkings. Hey, while you're in the store, can you pick me up a multi-tool? I like the SOG ones the best, but I'm not super-duper picky." He froze with the radio halfway to his mouth and she had to ask: "Uh, do you know what a multi-tool is? It's like a Swiss army man knife but better."

He laughed. "Sure, sure. I know what a multi-tool is."

Jillybean said: "Good. I figured you did." That was a bit of a lie, but it was a good lie. Like the lie she had told Nancy or the time she had told her mommy that the jeans she had on absolutely *didn't* make her look fat, or the time she had made up a boy named Chris and pretended that he was real. Chris had been a good lie.

At some point, while Jillybean had been sitting in the closet in Fred Trigg's office, she had decided that she had simply been lying to herself about Chris. And yes, she knew she was likely lying to herself about lying to herself, but either way, she missed him.

"Be right back," Neil said, when they pulled up to the hardware store. He was out of the Jeep before she really had a chance to check her monitors for danger. She punched through the video feeds as though she were flipping channels on a TV.

Luckily, there were only a few monsters shambling around. Two followed him into the store and she had a good laugh watching him run around with them chasing him. He really

327

wasn't in much danger. She would have helped him if he got in trouble. Her laughter dried up when she felt the Jeep shake and then a second later Gayle appeared in the frame, gun in hand.

When she fired it, the screen flashed momentarily white. After the two monsters were killed, Neil kissed the woman, smacked her on the rear end and pointed her back to the Jeep. "That's love, I guess," Jillybean said, thinking that no one ever patted her bottom anymore. Her mom used to but it was so long ago she barely remembered.

A sigh escaped her as Neil clambered back in. He had forgotten the multi-tool but that was okay. "I like Gayle," Jillybean mentioned. "She's nice."

"She sure is," Neil replied in a somewhat distracted manner. He was having trouble getting the plastic suit on in the cramped space and was already sweating.

"Are you going to marry her?"

He paused with the zipper halfway up his torso. "I think so. When we finally get a priest that is. But we need a new doctor first. Losing Dr. Hester was quite a blow. And I still don't understand it. Why did the bad guys go after the clinic? Just for the terror aspect or was there a different reason? If they had gone after one of the cafeterias, they might have killed three times as many people."

Jillybean could only shrug. At the moment, there were too many variables and too many clues in front of her. Which ones were pertinent and which were incidental? And did any of it matter? There were bad guys in the Valley. When she pictured them, she imagined the man as skulking and bearded, much like the trader who had raped her. The woman was a hideous witch with crooked teeth and a false smile.

She knew that they may not look like that at all. They could be in disguise, but what sort? "An army man outfit?" she muttered as she pulled back out onto the street. That seemed likely for the man, but not for the woman. With only six hundred or so women in the Valley, a strange woman would stick out. She'd be noticed as someone new. While Jillybean had been the main suspect that hadn't been important, but now it would be.

"Did you say something?" Neil asked.

"Just trying to figure this all out, but there are too many variables. Variables is a math sort of word…it doesn't matter though. Not right now." They were already just up the street from the power station and none of Jillybean's guesses would change what they would find inside. "Let me turn around so I can use the thermal camera."

"Sure," Neil said, his knee jumping up and down in a fit of nerves. She did a neat little K-turn and was able to scope the entire power station. There were a few heat signatures—monsters by the way they moved. "Darn it," Neil said. "I think I'd rather have seen someone lurking. We could have used the machine gun on him. Ha-ha." His laughter was forced and weak.

When she turned the monitor to the view in front, she caught sight of something strange: a long line of blinking lights coming down out of the surrounding hills. "There's how they gots all the monsters to come into the Valley. It's the same set up I used at New Eden." And really, it was the basis for the *Zevac* which would hopefully steer the monsters out of the Valley again.

"Someone is familiar with your work, Jillybean," Neil said.

For her it was just one more variable in a tower of them. Would it add to the confusion inside her or would it begin to narrow things down? It was possible that any of her enemies could have known about the details of the attack at New Eden. Possible, but not likely. The Believers of New Eden had been weak-willed and servile. They had run screaming from trouble. If she had to guess, it wasn't one of them.

Was it someone who knew them, perhaps? Or someone who had heard the story of the attack?

"It doesn't change anything," Neil said. "Let's move Gayle and William into position. Then drop me off. You'll stay in the Jeep and man the radio. If something happens call Captain Grey."

"Yes, sir." She trundled the Jeep slowly down the hill until they got to the edge of where the transformers were arrayed looking to Jillybean like the machinery inside of a robot's head. There were monsters around and none seemed to be acting the least bit wonky, which meant: no VX.

Neil climbed out, gun in hand and stood just inside the Jeep's armored door. He stared all around and when he wasn't immediately attacked, he breathed a sigh of relief and glanced up to the roof rack. "Okay, you two. Take up positions facing outward. Keep a special eye on those two buildings."

The camera in back was blurred as Gayle and William came down. Jillybean watched them take up positions among the odd hunks of machinery. Gayle scampered around, mouse-like, her fear obvious even in a thermal image. William didn't go far. He knelt behind the first obstruction.

Neil watched for a moment and then climbed back inside. Placing his pistol on the dash, he struggled Jillybean's gas mask over his head. "It's going to be okay," he tried to reassure the little girl, once the mask was in place.

She wasn't exactly scared. She would be locked away in an armored Jeep, able to tear out of there at any time. Her only fear was for Neil, who could be walking into a trap. "I'll turn her around so I can cover you," she told him. "Do you want to use one of the Bumble Balls?"

His voice came back to her muffled: "I think so. If there's a bad guy anywhere around here, it'll either be inside the station or up in those buildings and I would bet it's up there. It would be too easy to get cornered in the station."

"Yeah," was all she could think to say. Her fear for him was mounting and once he was inside, there would be little she could do to help him. She handed over a Bumble Ball and tried to smile, but it came out wrong; she could feel it on her face. "Please be careful."

His blue eyes twinkled behind the mask. "I'll be lucky. That's my thing. My dad always used to say it was better to be lucky than good. You can be the careful one. Stay in the Jeep no matter what. Fighting isn't your thing." He reached out a blue-gloved hand and she gave it a squeeze. "I'll be right back."

Once the door was shut, her world shrank to the dark, closed in cab. For the first time, it gave her the creeps. Flicking the iPad to the forward camera, she saw that Neil had thrown the Bumble Ball as far as he could towards the front door of the station. It dazzled the camera as the lights began flashing crazily. The monsters that had been wandering towards the windowless Jeep turned to watch the ball jump around.

A few went to stand over it amazed. It was ten feet from the door and they seemed unchanged. Neil climbed back in. "Get me as close as you can without disturbing them."

She let the Jeep creep forward, the tires crunching the wet gravel. The monsters didn't even seem to notice it not even when she pulled alongside of them. "Move back a good fifty feet and then call Grey," Neil whispered. "Tell him I'm going in."

He stepped out and very slowly inched his way past the group of monsters standing over the ball. When he reached the door, she put the car in reverse and pulled back, once more doing a K-turn so she could point her machine gun towards the door.

When he stepped in, she thumbed the radio: "Mister Captain Grey, this is Jillybean. Neil's just gone inside. So far, there's no sign of nothing, over."

His whispered voice came back. "We are almost ready to breach. So far, the house looks empty. Will keep you updated."

It was a second before she realized that his voice had been too clear. He wasn't wearing a mask. "Oh boy, Deanna is gonna be mad." She knew Grey well enough to picture him selflessly handing over the two masks and going without.

The wait became interminable and to pass the time, she flicked through her four camera angles, one after another. "Having just the one monitor sure does…"

"We're going in. Travis, be sharp. Go! Go! Go!" The radio spat out almost useless noise: thumps and bangs and odd thuds, all of which had Jillybean on the edge of her seat. Then came muffled voices: "Clear…clear…six is clear. Captain, we have a body in here. Hey, I know this guy. But that can't be."

Grey's voice came louder and clearer. "Who is it?" There was a pause before Grey yelled: "Everyone out! Jillybean be care…" Then there was only static followed by a rumbling noise that rolled down the valley. It was an explosion.

Jillybean's breath caught in her throat at the sound and her heart went into overdrive at she realized who was behind all of this. The lights down from the mountain, the clinic, the attack on Neil and Grey, and the body that was found. There was only one reason the body could be significant enough to warn Jillybean.

Chapter 37

Neil Martin

Starting the generator was harder than it looked, especially when Neil couldn't stop twitching his gun at every shadow and jumping at every sound, the great majority of which were sounds of his own making. He kept knocking into different machines and computers and even walls—he was surprised every time.

He blamed the mask, which was annoyingly tight, squeezing his face in its rubber grip. Worse, it had fogged over the moment he had put it on so that everything at the edges of his vision was blurred, making it seem that there were ghosts creeping around just beneath his chin or off to the sides of his face.

Of course, this just added to his fright which, in turn jacked up his already quick rate of breathing, which only added to the fog covering his lenses which made him even more afraid. It was a vicious cycle and if there had been an enemy within the power station, he would have been dead in the first thirty seconds.

He was slow coming to this conclusion and three minutes of frightened frustration went by as he blundered about in the gloomy building, trying, and failing miserably, to be quiet. And as for sneaky, only a kangaroo in scuba gear would have been less obvious.

By the time he reached the generator, his heart was racing, and the vein in his temple was the size of his pinky, and he was sweating so much in the mask that drops of condensation were dripping down the eye goggles. The generator was surrounded by pipes and columns and industrial fans and other mechanical doo-dads. There were enough hiding places to give cover to an entire squad of bad guys. And Neil would have to walk right into the center of the room to get the generator going.

"If you're going to shoot me, you might as well do it now," he said, giving up and flinging caution to the wind. Behind the mask, his face was cringed in expectation of a gunshot. Instead, he got an explosion that came through the walls as a low rumble.

His first reaction was to whisper: "Oh, Jillybean, what did you do?" His second was to turn and run back the way he had come. Once more he banged into a dozen objects, all of which were metal and unforgiving. The pain and the bruises went unnoticed—his people were dying.

He rushed through the station and out into the night in time to see Jillybean's Jeep, speeding backwards. Gunshots rang out and there was a scream. Strangely, this seemed to stop the Jeep. It sat there for a moment and then with a screech of tires, it came racing right at Neil who was standing perfectly dead center in the lane that stretched from the road to the power station.

"Oh jeeze!" he yelped and raised his pistol. He actually took the time to aim before he realized that the Jeep had been armored. Too late, he turned to run back into the station, only to run into a zombie. It was as confused as Neil. With the Bumble Ball bouncing and the explosion, and the gunshots and the Jeep roaring about, it had been going in circles.

Now, it and Neil fell together. Neil, who was more concerned with the Jeep than the zombie, couldn't see what was happening either. Right off the bat, the zombie had grabbed Neil's mask and tried to rip it off his head, however the mask was wedged on too tightly and the zombie only managed to twist it around so that Neil's nub of an ear was nestled in one of the fogged-over eye pieces and the straps were pulled sharply across his face.

Certain that he'd be crushed under the Jeep's tires any second, Neil shot the pistol twice using the sound of the creatures harsh breathing as an aiming point. The zombie jerked once, yanking the mask from Neil's head altogether and then fell back.

Too slowly, Neil turned to the Jeep which was plowing down on him. The gun was useless and he was out of time to run. This left him with the solo option of curling into a ball. The mewling sound he made was just an embarrassing bonus to cap off the last second of his life.

Through his slitted eyes, he saw the Jeep spin just as it came up so that he was presented with the right rear tire heading for his face. Amazingly, it stopped so close that he was splashed with rainwater and had pebbles bounce off his forehead. A second later, the passenger side door opened.

"Get in, Mister Neil!" Jillybean cried. She was in a state of wide-eyed shock and didn't seem to notice the gun pointed at her. "Don't forget the mask! We might need it."

Bewildered, he got in. "What the hell, Jillybean?"

"It's William…Shawn I mean. He broke the gun, Mister Neil. It doesn't work at all."

She began spinning the Jeep around in a tight circle. Neil grabbed the wheel. "Stop right now! What is going on? Who are you talking about? Who broke what gun?"

"Shawn Gates! That's not William, that's his brother Shawn. Do you understand?" Suddenly everything became clear and now he knew their enemies: Shawn and Clara Gates. The year before they had been banished from the group at Neil's suggestion. He had literally taken their children away from them and sent them out into the undead world with nothing. It had been a death sentence disguised as mercy.

If anyone had a reason for revenge it was them.

"And the explosion?" he asked, though he was afraid he already knew. The rumble hadn't been from anywhere close.

Jillybean's face broke in anguish. "It was a trap set for Captain Grey."

A picture formed in his mind: Jillybean and Grey radioing each other, spelling out their exact movements. "Oh, God," Neil whispered as the implications began to hit home. "What about Gayle?" He had left Shawn and Gayle together.

Jillybean was way ahead of him. She had the Jeep turned around in a second and was racing back the same way she had come. "I tried to shoot him with the machine gun, but it's not working. So, I'm gonna runded him over. If that's okay."

"I guess so. Can you see anything?"

"A little," she replied, squinting in at the monitor. Outside there was the bang of gun shots, followed by the thud/whine of bullets hitting the Jeep. Neil sat back in his chair, his nervous eyes flicking around, wondering when the armor would give way and the bullets would start finding their way inside.

"Oh no you don't!" Jillybean hissed turning the steering wheel in a wide arc. "He keeps running in circles for all darn it. Oh, farts, he's in among the towers and those box things."

Neil leaned over to see for himself but then he caught sight of Gayle's body. She was lying next to a transformer staring up into the rain. "Stop, please. We have to help Gayle. Pull up alongside of her so that the Jeep is blocking us from Shawn."

She was alive though probably wouldn't be for very long. There was blood bubbling out of her stomach and pulsating from her arm. Jillybean was on her in a flash. "Hi Miss Gayle, ma'am. Can you move your hand out of the way. Oh…okay, okay." She turned to Neil, her face as stricken as Gayle's. "I need my bag. My med bag. It's the blac…"

Two more bullets whizzed out of the dark. Jillybean fell across Gayle, while Neil ducked behind the Jeep. "Get her in the Jeep!" he ordered and then fired his gun. He'd had a clear enough target. Shawn was a hulking figure lurking out in the rainy night and although surrounded by plenty of cover, he was only crouching slightly.

Anyone else would have dropped him with the one shot but Neil had rushed it and missed by a good three feet, high and outside. Neil knew he was at a distinct disadvantage. He was just not a gun fighter. Everyone in the Valley knew it. When he picked up a gun, it was a running joke that he was just as much a danger to his friends as he was to his foes.

Shawn didn't seem to know his reputation and ducked behind a metal box. Neil found his own cover, squatting down behind a concrete platform where there was a puddle-filled rut. It was a good spot for someone with Neil's minimal skills. He had a stable firing platform, which also allowed him to remain almost completely out of sight.

Even better, the onus was on Shawn to press the attack because once Jillybean got Gayle into the Jeep, Neil would be able retreat inside as well, where they would be perfectly safe. "I just have to stay alive for a few minutes," he muttered and then fired off a shot, hitting the metal box dead center. Unfortunately, he was aiming for the edge, so it was another sad miss.

Shawn returned fire, clinking a bullet off the strut of the tower seven inches from Neil's head. "Jeeze!" Neil hissed and then rattled off three shots right in a row, only one of which hit the box. Smushing himself as deeply as he could go into the puddle, he cried: "Jillybean! Is she in the…" A bullet creased the skin of his good ear, splitting it.

Neil didn't feel pain or the blood trickling from his ear. He had gone instantly numb. Without aiming he fired twice, the second bullet just missed Shawn Gates, causing him to drop down.

"Is she in?" Neil begged.

"She's awful heavy, Mister Neil." With all the gun shots and Neil's heavy breathing, he hadn't heard Jillybean struggling to heave a woman who was twice her weight into the Jeep.

"You got to try, Jill…" Something came flying from behind the box. Neil's eyes tracked it as it headed right for him. It was a hand grenade, tumbling over and over in midair. An incoherent sound, something like, "Ghhh," escaped him as the grenade landed right in front of him, hitting the cement block and bouncing over him.

He plunged into the puddle, crushing his nose into the mud at the bottom as behind him the grenade went off with a noise like thunder. The echoes rang around the valley, while the fragments pinged off the different structures, some even hitting the Jeep.

"Mister Neil?" Jillybean's voice was a hysterical cry.

"I'm good," he called, though he really didn't know if he was or not. The numb sensation had deepened so that he hadn't even felt the kick of the Walther. His hands felt like they were made of wood and the rest of him like lead, which was positive in one regard: it kept him from jumping up and running to the Jeep.

At best, Jillybean could only be considered an amateur when it came to welding and it was a good bet that the armor on the Jeep wouldn't be able to withstand the blast from a grenade. In spite of the danger, he would have to stay where he was with only seven inches of cement covering one side of his body and the other side completely exposed.

"The best defense," he muttered and then came up firing, sending four shots towards the metal box, hitting it only once.

Again a grenade came flying. It looked like it was going to go long, missing the cement and landing just behind Neil, where it would explode, turning him into something that resembled Hamburger Helper. With no other choice, Neil started to plunge back into the puddle, but there was a noise *tunnng*! It was metal striking metal and then a second noise just like the first.

The grenade had struck one of the struts of the tower, bounced off another before bounding away. It went off ten feet from Neil with a noise that had his brain vibrating in its bone encasement and the numbness deepening. Luck, as well as the cement block had saved him once more, though it felt as though the repeated explosions were going to rattle his brain right out of his ears.

Jillybean called for him again, a frantic trill in her voice. He heard her, however it seemed as though she was calling from far away, or perhaps from down a deep hole.

Was it even worth answering? he wondered. The twin explosions had left him terribly lethargic, making it an effort to lift his head to see what Shawn was doing. Shawn had inched up over the metal box to assess what sort of damage his second grenade had done.

"Screw you, Shawn!" Neil yelled, his "Ss" slurring as though he were drunk. "We know who you are now and we'll get you." Just at the moment, that seemed a little farfetched and so he amended the statement: "Someone will get you."

In response, Shawn fired three shots, missing with all three, despite that Neil hadn't had the wit to duck. "You missed, ha-ha!" He cried and crunched down into his puddle once more. "I'll count to three then fire," he said to himself. "One…two…"

Just then the Jeep's door slammed shut and a second later the tires spun sending the vehicle flying, smoke pouring from the rear. "Shit," he whispered, thinking that the Jeep was on fire and that it would, more than likely, explode. It raced to the end of the lane and spun in a tight circle before heading back, pushing through the trail of grey it had left behind it.

Jillybean slammed on her brakes too late and screeched right past Neil. She paused for only a second and then reversed in the same frenzied, pedal to the metal, manner. Again she went too far and it was no wonder since the clouds of smoke from the Jeep had blanked the area.

"How the hell can she see…" It finally clicked in his slightly concussed mind that the smoke was from a smoke bomb and that she was giving him cover. The only problem was that there was now so much cover that she could accidentally run him over if he tried to use the cover to run for the Jeep.

The solution was to run past the smoke. He got to his feet in a wobbly sort of manner and ran through the clouds. He could hear the Jeep to his left heading back in his direction and so he spurted forward yelling: "I'm clear! I'm clear! I'm…"

BOOOM! Another explosion. An evil orange and black light lit the smoke and sent him stumbling down to the ground, his head ringing more than ever. Slowly, he got to his feet as his hands touched his chest, expecting to feel blood pumping from a dozen holes in him, but apart from his hearing being knocked out again he was unhurt.

A fuzzy static filled his ears and he had no idea if the Jeep had been hit by a grenade or what had happened. "Jillybean!" he screamed. Could she hear him? Was she even alive? And where was Gayle? And where in all that smoke was Shawn.

Afraid of being run over or exploded once more, he slowly backed away towards the road that led into town and in seconds found himself outside the smoke. It wasn't much of a relief. He was now standing out in the open where there was no cover whatsoever, exposed to the rain, the zombies, and grenades and who knew what else?

He was just looking around for something to hide behind when he saw, out of the corner of his right eye, what looked like the headlights of a Humvee heading towards the power station. His first excited thought was: *It's Captain Grey!* Then he remembered the bomb and all excitement left him to be replaced by a cold certainty that he wanted that Humvee to just keep going.

Chapter 38

Jillybean

She had kept her cool right up until the first grenade had gone off. Jillybean was absolutely certain that the Jeep could not handle a grenade, especially if it happened to run one over. She hadn't armored anything down there, not even the bomb compartment, something she was starting to think was a mistake.

After that first explosion spiked her blood with adrenaline, she did more than just urge poor Gayle into the Jeep. The woman had managed to get into a kneeling position but hadn't been able to pull herself into the Jeep.

Jillybean would have to do it for her. She jumped into the backseat and grabbed a coil of rope. Next she cinched it around Gayle's torso, just under her armpits. "Wait here," she said to the woman as she leaped into the cab, wrapped the long end of the rope around one of the gaps in the steering wheel and then hopped out the driver's side.

Without pause to see how the battle was progressing thirty feet away, she crawled under the Jeep and, as quick as possible, spun the remaining few feet of rope around the head of the drive shaft and tied it off. She didn't stop to second guess if this would work or not. The simple physics involved could not be denied.

"This might hurt, sorry," she said to Gayle as she stuck the Jeep into drive and released the brake. As the Jeep crawled forward and Gayle groaned in misery, the drive shaft spun, acting as a winch and pulling Gayle up onto the chair. She was bleeding like a stuck pig and crying sad, fat tears, but she was safe. Right then, that was all that counted.

The second grenade went off just as the little girl dropped out of the Jeep and crawled beneath it, knife in hand. Afraid that he was certainly dead, she yelled Neil's name—without answer. As she sheared away the rope from the driveshaft with the razor edge of the knife, she began to cry as well.

All of the people she loved were dead or dying. She was filled with a volcanic rage that was completely offset by a sorrow as deep as any ocean abyss. All she felt was a horrible, uncaring numbness that was practically an invitation for her insanity to come back, possibly on a permanent basis.

She could feel the crazy creeping up on her, looking over her shoulder at the terrible world. She felt haunted by it just as she had for all those hours hiding in Fred's closet. Within the haunted feeling, one idea kept pooling to the top: revenge.

If she gave in, it would be her turn to truly strike back. And it wouldn't end once she had Shawn and Clara tied to trees by the ropes of their own intestines. No. There would be more people made to pay. There was an entire world of bloodshed open to...

"Is he alive?" Gayle asked. She was bloody and wet, pale and weak, and terribly pitiful. She was so pitiful looking that Jillybean couldn't stop herself from pitying her.

"I don't know," she said, feeling the insanity creep back down into the pit of her soul. "Here, I can find out." She hit a button and dropped a smoke bomb down the shoot in the undercarriage, where it flared immediately sending out grey smoke. She then turned the Jeep around so that the rear thermal camera could pick out the humans from the surrounding wet background.

"I see Neil!" she cried. "He's moving. Oh, for all darn it, he's watching us instead of watch..." Almost too late, she realized that she was speeding forward completely blind. In a fraction of a second, she stamped the brake and hauled the wheel over. The scene on the one iPad shifted crazily as they spun.

Jillybean scrunched her eyes closed because she knew they were about to crash into the front doors of the power station. Her speed was too great and her momentum on the slippery surface unstoppable. But she had forgotten about the Bumble Ball and the pack of monsters. The back end of the Jeep plowed right into them. The vehicle stuttered and bounced but stopped with two monsters squished between the rear armored bumper and the door.

"That was a close one," Jillybean said as she switched to the front monitor. "Uh-oh."

She had used the smoke out of fear of Shawn and his grenades. Now, she saw she was going to have to drive right into it with Neil somewhere out there. If she veered to the left too far, she could run him over or drive straight into one of the towers. If she went to the right, she would run into the fence and could get caught up in it. She could creep along but then a grenade could get her or worse, it could get Neil.

"Oh Jeeze," she grumbled. With no good option, she'd have to make her own. Above the back seat, velcroed to the roof, was her fishing pole. For once not worried about tangling the lure, she yanked it down, snapped it in half and gave one side to Gayle.

"Yell if we go off the lane." Gayle started to question this, but Jillybean showed her. She cracked the door and stuck the pole out so that it poked down at the cement.

When she drove, it made a constant scraping sound. Gayle mimicked her and within seconds cried, "To the left!"

Jillybean swerved left, overcorrecting so that her pole went into the mud. She jerked to the right, causing Gayle to whimper in pain. There was no time for sorry. They had just come out of the smoke and had passed Neil. She skidded to a halt and for a moment was the world's biggest sitting duck.

She was convinced that Shawn was even then lobbing a grenade and so she yanked the Jeep into reverse and as she drove backwards, she changed to the rear thermal view. It was so much better than driving like a blind man with a cane.

When she neared the power station, she turned around for the third or fourth time. She had lost track. All that mattered was that once again she had the use of the rear camera. Compared to the dark background, Neil Martin stood out as a light figure hurrying across the road with his hands out in front of him.

Turning the Jeep slightly, she saw Shawn standing, his pistol, a glow of yellow in his hand. "We're going to get Neil, now," she said to Gayle. "He'll know what to do."

She drove backwards down the lane, watching the camera, constantly making little adjustments in steering. From above, the Jeep swiveled and snaked until it came to the entrance, where it turned, still going backwards in a plume of smoke. It was difficult driving especially when she turned and saw Neil standing right in the way.

At the last second, she turned and crashed into the perimeter fence. "Golly jeeze," she griped. She started to put the car in drive, when Neil hauled open the door, nearly spilling Gayle out onto the cement.

"Someone's coming!" he yelled and pointed.

Normally, someone coming would have been a good thing. After all, this was a valley filled with soldiers and good guys, or at least it had been at one time. As Neil helped Gayle over, Jillybean flicked on the side camera and caught sight of headlights heading their way. They were wide spaced, suggesting that it was a Humvee.

"But army mens use Humvees," she said to Neil, who had smushed in next to Gayle in the passenger seat. They were both small people, however with the blood splashed all across her front and the rope still pulled tight around her chest, Neil looked afraid to touch Gayle and was twisted in the chair so that his hind end was against the door.

"Everyone uses them now. Where's the radio?"

In all the excitement, Jillybean had forgotten about the radio. "It's here somewhere." She had no time to look for it. Shawn was behind her somewhere and Neil had given her a case of the creeps when it came to the Humvee. In her gut, she knew they had to get away from it.

And yet, she couldn't help thinking: *What if they're good guys? What if it was somehow Captain Grey? If so, we'd be saved!* She had to find out.

Jillybean struggled the Jeep away from the fence and turned up on the road but stopped sixty feet away. The rear camera had a good view through the smoke as the Humvee slowed near the entrance to the power station. "Still could be a good guy," Jillybean whispered.

Then she saw Shawn run up and climb into the passenger seat. "It's not a good guy!" she cried and switched the iPad to the front view, which was a mad swirl of smoke. She plowed right through it, knowing that it wouldn't be far until she was in the clear.

With the rain and the dark and the thousands of monsters, driving using only a seven by ten inch screen wasn't easy. It was like a video game set on "extreme" but, if you died, well, you really died.

"Head for the Red Gate," Neil directed. "If Fred's done his job, there will be soldiers there. Even if they're running away, they'll probably scare off Shawn. It'll give us time to…hey, I found the radio. Mayday! Mayday! Anyone there? This is Governor Martin, over."

He had to repeat this last twice before a haggard voice came back: "Neil? It's Deanna. Everything's going to shit. Grey… Grey…he's been blown up. He's dead."

It didn't sound like her. To Jillybean, it sounded like a ghost of Deanna. Although Neil knew Grey had been killed, he still took a moment to press the radio against his forehead, viciously hard, before he pulled it back to say: "I know. And I know who did it: Shawn and Clara Gates. I had them kicked out of the group before you arrived and they're back to get some revenge. They're after us."

Neil paused to see if Deanna would respond but there was only a crackling noise coming from the radio. He went on. "We're heading to the Red Gate. Call Fred and tell him. When we get there, I want these bastards to pay."

"No, not the Red Gate," Deanna whispered into the radio. "It's been attacked with more of the gas. It might have been a soldier working with Shawn. Someone in a Humvee threw some vials and took off. Neil, the Valley is falling apart. People are heading up into the mountains on foot to get away."

"We can still save..." A sudden crash from behind sent Neil and Gayle flying forward, while Jillybean was hard pressed to keep the Jeep on the road. She flicked to the rear camera in time to see that her smoke bomb had finally died out and, more importantly, she saw the Humvee coming up fast once more.

She tried to scream a warning but was too late. They were hit hard on the back quarter panel and suddenly the Jeep was spinning. It was a weird feeling to spin in a dark box, not knowing which way was forward or back. The camera was no help. The screen was a big blur until they thudded heavily and stopped altogether.

Gayle was sprawled across the console and Neil was in the footwell. Only Jillybean had managed to retain her position and that was mainly because she was wedged in so tightly. She flicked the camera over to the front view and really could not make heads or tails of which way she was pointed. There was a bush or part of a tree blocking her one view.

Acting with swift movements, she simultaneously stuck the Jeep in reverse and turned once more to the rear camera and saw that it was pointing up at the rain. There were edges of mountains in the lower part of the frame. They were in a ditch on the side of the road, just about as vulnerable as they could get. She roared the engine and the Jeep responded beautifully, practically leaping back out onto the road.

Other than a few monsters, the road behind them was empty. Which meant...she turned to the front view and saw the Humvee turning toward them. It must have been knocked sideways by the collision and now it was pointing at them once again.

Jillybean did not like her odds. The Jeep might have been armored, but compared to the powerful, wide-chassied Humvee it was top heavy and weak. Her one chance was to be faster and

343

more nimble. She surged forward acting as though she was going to ram her enemy, but at the last moment she tried to dart around. The Jeep wasn't fast enough and the two vehicles ground together with a terrific screech and a jolt that sent Gayle falling almost into Jillybean's lap.

The woman was now unconscious and dying right on the little girl who was trying desperately to get away. It wasn't possible. She was forced off the road and through a wooden fence that marked the boundary of what had once been a stable where fat horses hauled around fat tourists at a turtle's pace.

Neil was yelling something, however Jillybean didn't know what. The engine was screaming as she drove it through what had once been a field, but with all the rain was now practically a bog, as the Humvee hit them again and again. Jillybean was blind to where it was and with so many obstacles all around her, she couldn't chance switching to the rear view.

"What about the bombs?" Neil screamed into her face.

It would almost certainly be a waste. The Humvee was right on their tail, meaning the bomb would detonate well behind it and yet, what choice did she have? Armored as it was, the Jeep wasn't quick enough to get away and as it only had a quarter of a tank of gas left, it wasn't going to be able to outlast the Humvee.

She lifted the protective cover to the "1" button, pressed it and then cringed, expecting an explosion three seconds later. After five seconds she said: "I wonder what the prob…." The explosion cut her off.

Immediately, she switched to the rear view. At first, all she saw was a plume of orange taking over the thermal camera. It lasted only a second or two and then the Humvee formed and as expected it had survived. It probably hadn't taken any damage beyond a few scratches and yet the driver had slowed doing only about fifteen miles per hour to Jillybean's twenty-five. This was a perfect time to release another bomb.

"I'm dropping another!" Jillybean reached out and had just lifted the protective cover from the "2" button when the Jeep hit something.

Jillybean had accidentally spent two seconds too long staring at the rear monitor. The field had ended. They crashed through a fence which was alarming, but not so much as when the Jeep's nose pitched straight down only to bounce straight up again a second later.

Dazed and cross-eyed, Jillybean found herself in the backseat amidst all of her belongings which had been thrown around into a wild chaos. Neil was once again in the footwell and bleeding from a cut above his right eye. Gayle was draped across the console, with her blood dripping down the Jeep's instrument panel.

The good news was that the Jeep itself was still running. The bad was that the monitor was missing from the metal plate and the "2" bomb button's protective shield was still in the up position. Had it been pushed? Was there a pipe bomb sitting on the ground a few feet away with nothing but a tiny slip of plastic keeping the electrical series from engaging and blowing them sky high?

The worse news was that the Humvee could be heard growling to their left, its pitch changing slightly. Suddenly, Jillybean knew where the Jeep was—they had hit the ditch on the side of the road, bounced out and were now right smack in the middle of the road they had left fifteen seconds before. The Humvee's engine suddenly roared and Jillybean knew what that meant as well.

Once more they were a sitting duck. "Mister Neil! The gas! Hit the gas!" He tried, throwing himself over Gayle's body to reach the extended pedal, only he was too late and they were hit broadside with such force that the Jeep slewed around before rolling into the ditch.

Jillybean was buried under her own belongings. She panicked, afraid that she would suffocate or be stuck in the Jeep forever. With a gasping cry, she twisted like a cat, gasping for air, the fear spiking her heart rate over a hundred and forty.

Neil was much more fortunate and actually found himself standing where the passenger side window had once been with Gayle having slid into a tangle at his feet. Desperately, he climbed up the driver's side until he could thrust open the heavy door.

He came out firing his Walther. There was a burst of fire in response and then the revving of the Humvee's engine. Jillybean was frantic and screaming and twisting. A fraction of a second before they had been smashed into for the final time and now the Jeep was like a turtle, stranded on its back.

Jillybean found herself once again covered in her gear, only now it felt like she was drowning in it. Her fear was a monster inside of her right up until a familiar voice said: *Relax, it's just stuff. Look.* She tried to focus on the nearest thing and saw that it was one of Chris' comic books. *It can't hurt you.* Had the voice been Chris'?

"It can't hurt me," she said. Although the panic left her in a blink, she was unsure of herself and felt as jumbled in her head as the chaos inside of the Jeep.

Neil, who had already wiggled out, had to remind her of their situation. "Get Gayle!" he yelled and then disappeared firing his gun again.

With all the bullets smacking into the armor, outside seemed like a very unsafe place to be. She scrambled along the roof which was now the floor and then scooted out, butt first into a ditch that was filled with rain water and sucking mud. The air smelled strongly of gasoline and Jillybean wondered briefly if the Jeep would explode.

Neil didn't seem concerned with that possibility; he was crouched near the front, pointing his gun at the Humvee which was turned quarter on to them looking like a crouching metallic beast a moment from pouncing.

In the few seconds it took to look about, the Jeep had begun to settle into the muck and now the water began to flood in. Her fear was screaming along her nerves and the water only made it worse. What if Gayle drowns, she wondered. This thought was immediately followed by: What if I drown?

In two feet of water? a voice asked, within her. *Don't be stupid.* Like a knife, the voice cut through the bang of guns and the white noise of falling rain. It was remarkably clear and remarkably familiar. It was Eve.

"Shut up," Jillybean answered, in a furious hiss. She hadn't heard Eve's voice in months and hearing it now sent a cold shiver through her…and yet, Eve hadn't been wrong. Hauling Gayle out of the Jeep would be simple. All she had to do was wait until the water was deep enough to support most of Gayle's weight and then slide her out.

The water was up to her knee and she was just about to start pulling on Gayle when something green and round bounced off the under carriage of the Jeep, leapt over Jillybean and landed in the muddy field they had just driven through.

What the hell are you waiting for? It was Eve again, waking her up to the obvious. That hadn't been "something green and round" that had been another grenade. Without another thought, she dropped down over Gayle as above her the night was lit with a flash and a thunderclap of such proportions that it wobbled her head for a moment.

She was unhurt; the angle of the blast—three feet above her and five feet over—had been wrong.

Get up! Eve screamed. *You can't just lie there. We have to run away!*

There was another choice Eve hadn't thought of. Jillybean smacked herself in the face so hard that she fell down next to Gayle. "You're supposed to be dead," she said, her cheek throbbing red hot.

Idiot! I can't die. As long as you are alive, then I am alive. We're the same person.

"Then maybe it's time for me to die." She stood up, heading for the side of the Jeep. It wasn't a bluff. Death was preferable to having Eve inside her, making her do evil things. Eve seemed to know she had been beaten.

If you won't listen to me, maybe you'll listen to Ipes, she said.

"No," Jillybean said. "I won't listen to him either. He'll just tell me to run away and that isn't much of a choice." Running would require leaving the scant bit of cover they had. In all likelihood, she would be dead after twenty steps. Besides, it was the chicken way out. Sadie would not have run and Neil *hadn't* run even though he could have. He had stayed to protect the weak and the innocent.

"Chris would have stayed." It was practically an invitation for her make-believe friend to come back, but his voice was silent—all the voices in her were quiet which gave her a moment to think clearly. "I'll stay," she declared. To stay meant she'd have to fight.

Stepping away from the side of the Jeep, she looked into the partially flooded interior and saw only a mess. Where was the M79 and its two remaining rounds? Where was the Colt .44 that was way too big for her hands? Where was the M4 and the dynamite. Where were her last remaining smoke bombs?

The weapons must have been taken by whoever moved the vehicle to the Police Station and the last of the smoke bombs were: "Drownded," she whispered. Even if she found them, they'd be too soaked to work. So what did that leave? The two way radio which was ruined because of the water, Neil's mask which was floating next to Gayle's elbow and her electricity maker which was now as worthless and beautiful as modern art.

347

She was still staring at the mess when she heard a dreadful noise. It came from behind her; first there was the usual bang from Neil's gun and then a very loud *thunk*. It was a sound that had harrowing interpretations. She spun to see Neil staring at his gun; the slide was back and the chamber exposed.

"I'm out of ammo," he hissed. "Do you have a bomb or a gun or something?"

She shook her head. The only bombs left to her were in their spring-activated compartments on the under carriage of the Jeep which, just then, was a flat expanse with no cover whatsoever, at the exact same level that Shawn and Clara were shooting. If she went for one of the bombs, she would be the perfect target exposed for seven or eight seconds.

"Yes, but they're up there," she whispered pointing. Neil blanched at the thought. He then turned in a circle, his blue eyes very wide as he searched for some way out of their predicament. When one didn't present itself, he cursed, stuck his useless Walther PPK down the front of his jeans and with shaking hands started to climb.

He barely got his head over the edge when there was a smattering of gunfire. The tire next to his cheek blew and he ducked back so fast that he lost his footing and fell into the mud and water. When he came up, he was ghostly white. His face said it all: they were trapped, pinned down in a little ditch. The wall of the ditch behind them, though not very tall, was slick and muddy, not something they'd be able to climb up quickly. Beyond it was a field with zero cover, while to their left and right was open road.

"What do we do?" Jillybean asked.

Neil pointed along the ditch. "I'll distract them and you'll swim down this ditch and get away. Try to make it back to the bank."

It was a terrible thing to say to her; it left her feeling empty. She wanted to argue with him but there was no time. She wanted to go down fighting valiantly next to Neil, but they would only die ignominiously. She wanted to come up with a brilliant plan in the next twenty seconds before Shawn and Clara figured out that they were out of ammo, but that was impossible. She wanted to do anything besides running away.

You've done everything you can. It was Ipes, sounding terribly sad. *Go now, before it's too late.*

He was right and reasonable, but not omniscient. It was already too late. As Neil jumped out from the side of the Jeep and yelled, "Hey!" Jillybean splashed down into the muck on the other side, but only made it a few feet before the sound of the Humvee's engine kicked up.

For a moment Jillybean was confused since there was still shooting on the far side of the Jeep. Then it struck her as Ipes wailed: *We're trapped!* "And flanked," she added, as the Humvee rolled into view. Behind the wheel was mousey-haired Clara Gates holding a shotgun out across the passenger seat and pointing it out the window.

"Neil!" Jillybean screamed, a moment before Clara pulled the trigger. Flame leapt from the barrel and the thunder of the gun drowned out the little girl. It was so loud that Neil's cry of pain was muted. He was hit both in front and in back. The force of the bullets spun him in a tight circle before he fell into the ditch, landing next to Gayle, where his blood mixed with hers and together they turned the rainwater a dull pink.

Jillybean felt something break inside of her. It was such a familiar pain that she didn't cry. Turning back towards the Humvee and the sneering Clara Gates, the little girl only made a noise that was half laugh, half sob as the woman jacked back on the shotgun's forestock, spitting out the used shell and chambering a fresh one.

She was ten feet from the Humvee's passenger door and there wasn't a lick of cover except for the two feet of standing water she found herself in and that wasn't nearly deep enough to stop a blast from a shotgun. She expected to be shot right there and then, however Clara paused, even as she aimed down the barrel.

"You know who I am?" Clara asked without taking her sights off of her target.

Squinting into the darkened cab, Jillybean took two steps closer to the side of the Humvee; two steps closer to death. "You're Clara Gates and you're a bitch," she said. This was an extremely bad word. Jillybean knew it and didn't care. Someone needed to say it and she was sure that her father wouldn't be too mad at her when she got to heaven.

"I am a bitch," Clara said, and pulled the trigger with a deafening roar and a blast of fire.

Chapter 39

Captain Grey

It took a full minute for Captain Grey's eyes to focus and it was another before he knew where he was. It was a little longer before he pieced together what had occurred. Slowly the events came back to him as he sat up and brushed away pieces of wood and tile and charred flesh from his BDUs.

The four-person team had come at the house on Dry Gulch Road from two directions, moving from tree to tree, and boulder to jutting boulder, using every bit of natural cover. With the dark and the rain, Grey was sure they had made it to the edge of the property without being seen.

The pair of zombies near the garage door, standing like human toadstools in the rain, attested to that. It also suggested that the air around the property was breathable, which was a tremendous relief to Grey who was without a mask. Any commanding officer worth his salt wouldn't ask his men to face dangers that he shied away from. It would be unthinkable to him.

His bravery didn't make him foolish, however. He signaled Lieutenant Hupp and PFC Hodges to take out the zombies. They were not only masked, they were also dressed in coveralls. They didn't look very human to the zombies who stared uncomprehendingly until they received a Ka-bar through the temple.

Grey, who hadn't been watching, only heard the dull thuds of the bodies dropping to the ground. He'd had his Taurus trained on the house waiting for the least movement. Unfortunately, the house remained dark and silent which meant they would have to go in weapons free.

Once more the two masked soldiers took the lead, stepping up the porch stairs with their weapons trained—one towards the door, the other towards the bay window on the right. Grey had his gun aimed at the window on the left, while Travis hung back slightly, pointing his weapon out at the expanse of forest surrounding them.

"You ready?" Hupp asked Hodges. "On the count of three. One…"

Hodges nearly jumped out of his skin when Grey's radio crackled: "Mister Captain Grey, this is Jillybean, Neil's just went inside. So far there's no sign of nothing, over."

As he hurriedly turned down the volume on the radio, Grey apologized to the soldiers and then whispered to Jillybean: "We are almost ready to breach. So far the house looks empty. Will keep you updated."

"Now, on the count of three?" Hupp asked, after a sarcastic look at his superior officer. It was hard to convey sarcasm through the bug eyes of the mask, but somehow Hupp managed it.

"I'm not stopping you," Grey said, with a gesture towards the door. As Hupp counted down, Grey hissed partially to Jillybean and partially to Travis: "We're going in. Travis be sharp. Go! Go! Go!"

The door hadn't been locked and flew open with the two soldiers surging inside pointing their guns left and right, up the stairs and down the hall, as they rushed in. Grey knelt in the doorway, less worried about being shot than he was about breathing in VX gas.

He was taking only tiny sips of air and testing each one. It was ludicrous and he knew it, still he couldn't help himself.

Hupp led Hodges deep into the house yelling out: "Clear… clear…clear." after quickly inspecting every room.

From the doorway, Captain Grey yelled: "Your six is clear." He wasn't being chicken about going into the house, he was being cautious. If there was any gunplay he would charge in, but until then, he'd wait.

"Captain, we have a body in here," Hupp called. "Hey, I know this guy. But that can't be…It's William Gates."

"Who is it?" Grey yelled, feeling confused and scared, but not in equal measure. The flesh of his arms had suddenly broken out in a million goosebumps and his grip on both the radio and the Taurus was fiercely tight. The fear carried with it a premonition of doom, and although he didn't believe in that sort of thing, Grey actually took a step back away from the house.

Hupp's reply of "William Gates," was a mumble and yet in the heavy silence it carried easily. And it conveyed an obvious question: If the body was William Gates who then was currently with Neil and Jillybean?

Grey knew in an instant and bellowed: "Everyone out!" he turned and leapt down the porch stairs and as he landed in a crouch, he said into the radio: "Jillybean be care…"

It was all he had time for before the first floor of the house was eradicated in a terrific explosion. Hupp and Hodges were blasted apart along with every door, window and stick of furniture. Travis had his lucky streak end as he was flayed alive by a thousand razor sharp blades of glass.

He was a smoldering, fleshless lump that looked like a bloody pincushion when he landed next to Grey. The captain found himself blinking up at the rain and the smoke and a house on fire. He did not actually lose consciousness after the explosion. His head rang and his vision went in and out, and his limbs seemed unconnected to his body, and yet he remained awake. He wasn't lucid, but he was awake.

There was only one thing on his addled mind: he had to get to Jillybean and Neil before Shawn made his move.

It was a full minute before he could sit up and another before he felt he could stand without falling over. Once upright, he saw his gun sitting in the wet grass. "Craaaap," he whispered and then stretched out a hand. It took two tries for him to pick up the Taurus and then he was off in a stumbling run, feeling a desperate urgency, an unrelenting fury and an internal demand to save his friends that overcame everything else including his sense of direction.

He headed not for the Humvee that they had parked half a mile away around a bend in the road, but straight downhill for the town.

His head was thumping something fierce and it was safe to say that the explosion was still echoing through his cranium. It was a few minutes before he remembered the Humvee at all. He stopped and looked back, his chest heaving and his breath coming and going in uneven gusts, as he pictured running back up the mountain.

"Son of a bitch," he gasped and was just about to take off when he simultaneously heard a distant explosion and saw the headlights of a Humvee rushing along the road a quarter mile further down the mountain. If he hurried, he saw that he'd be able to cut it off and get a ride.

Grey practically threw himself down the steep slope running faster than his head or his legs could really control. In seconds, he was at the whim of fate and had he been three seconds slower, he would have run right out into the middle of the road and would have been run over.

Those three seconds should have been plenty for anyone to recognize the man in uniform as a human. The Humvee should have slowed down and picked Grey up. It did not. It raced past and down into town, heading for Lake Estes and the power station that was hidden from sight by a pall of smoke.

Every few seconds, the smoke flashed with gunfire and explosions. "Come on, Neil, you can do it," Grey said, as he started running again. This time he ran at a more measured pace, one that he could control. His mind was slowly coming back to him. The echoes of the explosion had dwindled and his brain no longer pulsed.

It allowed him to think clearly and when he saw the Jeep and the Humvee heading back he knew immediately that there was trouble. Yes, the shooting had stopped, however the erratic way in which the Jeep meandered all over the road meant Jillybean was driving and she was desperate.

Although they were heading for him, Grey saw that Jillybean wouldn't make it up the hill. The two vehicles were now bumper to bumper, fishtailing left and right, the Humvee hammering the rear of the Jeep. He was four hundred yards away when Jillybean let off the first bomb and three hundred when the Jeep was plowed upside down into the ditch.

By then, Grey had been sprinting full out for seven minutes and was nearly done in. Helplessly, from too far away to shoot his Taurus with any accuracy, he watched the Humvee pull behind the Jeep. There was a fiery blast from it and a small figure next to the front of the Jeep fell out of sight. It had to have been Neil Martin.

Grey's steps faltered and his ragged breathing took on a new tempo; unbelievably, he felt his chest begin to hitch. For a year now, Neil had been his best friend. They had fought and bled together. They had tried to build a better world together out of the ashes of the old one.

Neil, in his geeky, silly, sweater-vest wearing way, had been noble. And now he was dead in a ditch.

Grey barely had time to mourn his friend when he saw Jillybean stand up. Huddled in the water, she had been invisible to Grey, who was a hundred yards away now and panting on. "No," he said in a whisper. He lacked the lung power for anything more.

There was a pause and as he drew closer, he saw there was a woman in the Humvee. It could only be Clara Gates, a person with a single great reason to kill Jillybean. She was also a person with a track record of murder.

Clara, high up in her Humvee like some vengeful demigod looked down on the tiny girl who took a brave step forward. Clara looked down on her without mercy and when she fired her shotgun, Grey saw Clara's face frozen in the flash. It was the face of hate.

What happened next made no sense. Instead of flying backwards, her little body shredded by the blast, Jillybean dove *at* the Humvee. And then, instead of lying on the ground bleeding into the mud, dying there a few feet from her adoptive father, the little girl scurried forward.

"Impossible," Grey said in awe, seeing now the subtle move that had saved Jillybean. Clara had been too high up and when Jillybean had stepped closer, the angle at which the shotgun could shoot her had decreased so that there had been almost no margin of error. When Jillybean dove forward, she had been too close and too low to be hit by the flying buckshot.

She was still in trouble, especially as she had crawled beneath the Humvee. Clara only had to back up quickly and the girl would be smushed into so much pink goo. Clara did back up and Jillybean just missed getting crushed. She had saved herself but only for a second, Grey saw, because once Clara backed up enough to see where Jillybean was squatted down, a quick stomp of the gas would end the girl's futile gesture at clinging to life.

But Jillybean would not go down so easily. As the Humvee backed up, she grabbed the bumper as it passed and was dragged backwards, sliding along the rain-slicked road along with the Humvee.

Clara looked confused at not seeing Jillybean cast in the glow of her headlights and spurted back even further, only to see nothing but empty street. That's when Shawn, much to Grey's luck, showed himself. He stood up from the ditch across the road, not thirty yards in front of Grey and yelled: "She's in the front!"

Grey hadn't seen the man and would have run right past him if he hadn't stood. He was so surprised that he was slow to react and he was so tired from the run that his aim was poor. He missed with three straight shots. The first two were his fault. His chest was heaving and his feet were still stumbling to a halt on the wet sloping hill.

The third shot missed because Shawn was fresh, hyped up, and faster than he looked. In a blink, he dropped back into the ditch. A second later, he returned fire and Grey felt the bullets whip past as he stumbled for the ditch on the other side of the road, his legs like lead.

Once there, he let his training take over. Staying low, he splashed down the ditch towards the Jeep, pausing after twenty seconds to take a breath and to sneak a peek. He had almost taken too long. To his right, Clara was just climbing out of the Humvee with a shotgun in hand and to his left Shawn was standing, aiming his gun nowhere near where Grey now was.

The captain had a fraction of a second to pick a target. Shawn was the easier of the two to hit, but if Grey didn't take a shot at Clara, Jillybean would be dead in moments. She had not run into the forest as she should have, instead she had played ring around the rosy with a crazy woman holding a shotgun.

Grey owed it to Jillybean and he fired his Taurus at Clara who was mostly hidden by the heavy Humvee door. Once again, he missed, though he was able to frighten Clara back into the Humvee for the moment.

A fraction of a second later, a bullet cracking by his head sent him sprawling.

His instinct told him to move left, back the way he had come, however his need to protect Jillybean, and to reach Neil, drove him through the water until he reached his friend. Neil was covered in blood, lying half in the ditch and half out. Beyond him was Gayle. She stared up at the clouds, both hands on her belly, looking as though she were calmly waiting on death. Grey couldn't spare a moment to check on either of them.

He came up fast, gunning for Shawn Gates, hoping to catch him crouching again or moving from his position. Shawn was raised up with just his head visible. Grey snapped off a shot which blasted away his right ear. He had hoped for a kill, but the cursing from across the road told him that Shawn was only winged.

"He has grenades," Neil said, startling Grey. "No. I'm not dead. Pretty soon, I think."

Grey chanced a look at his friend, but with the dark and the rain, it was hard to tell what his injuries were exactly. A wound on his left thigh was bleeding in a gusher while his back was one large gory mess—being hit from a shotgun blast could do that to a person. Still, just the fact that he was conscious was good news.

"If he had grenades, he would have used them by now," Grey answered. In truth, he had no idea what Shawn would do, he just wanted Neil to remain positive and as alert as possible—their enemies had VX and weren't shy about using it.

He reached over and grabbed a strange copper contraption from next to the Jeep's open door. It was Jillybean's electricity maker, though just then, it looked more like a child's attempt at making a home-brewed ham radio. "Can you do something for me, Neil? When I say go, I want you to lift this up for Shawn to see and give it a little shake. He's going to shoot at you, but don't be afraid."

Neil seemed unconcerned. "I'm not afraid to die." He took the device with his mangled left hand which wasn't strong enough to hold it, so Grey shoved it into his right. Neil's eyes started to shut, so Grey pinched him on the calf. "Stay with me. We'll get through this. Remember, when I say, go." He hurriedly stepped over Gayle, whispering: "Hold on. I'll get you out of this."

Like Neil, she had a sleepy, uncaring look and her nod was set in slow motion. There was no time to wait for its completion. He got to the far end of the Jeep and edged up. A patch of pale forehead was all that was visible of Shawn. Of Clara, Grey thought he saw an elbow or the hump of a back which spelled all sorts of trouble—she was going for the VX.

Jillybean, tiny and vulnerable, squatted in front of the Humvee, holding a rock the size of a grapefruit. He wished she had run away; her presence made everything that much harder.

"Now," Grey hissed to Neil. With a deep breath, Neil raised the twisted copper, shook it once and then banged it against the side of the Jeep. When he raised it a second time, Shawn came up shooting. This time Grey was in a stable firing position, his breathing had slowed and he knew exactly where his target was.

He pulled the trigger once and watched Shawn drop out of sight. It was certain that he had hit Shawn, however it didn't feel exact, and so when he turned towards Clara, he did so with part of his awareness still to his left. It didn't really matter, Clara was inept with the shotgun, especially since it hadn't been sawed down and she was trying to wield it and remain in the safety of the Humvee. She ended up blasting the air fifteen feet to Grey's right.

Grey didn't even flinch. He moved to the right, aiming down the Taurus, ready for the next time she tried to anything at all. And if she didn't try anything, he'd get in a position in which she'd have to expose herself to use the gun and then pin her in the driver's seat.

The only problem with his plan was Shawn who wasn't quite dead. With every step, Grey became more and more certain that he had only nicked his enemy. Movement out of the corner of his eye confirmed this. As slick as he had ever been, Grey pivoted, his hands steady, his shoulders square, his breath held on the intake, his sharp eyes picking out the odd movement. It wasn't the moves of a man getting ready to shoot a gun, it was a man, shifting his weight back in preparation for a throw.

Shawn had at least one grenade left and Grey was an easy target standing out in the middle of the road and yet, he wasn't worried. He had thrown his share of grenades in his time and knew the mechanics and knew that in order to throw it properly he would have to expose himself right about...

He pulled the trigger a millisecond later this time catching Shawn dead center in the chest, blasting in his sternum and killing him instantaneously. He had been in mid-throw when he was shot and the grenade went basically straight up to land next to his dead body before it exploded.

Grey had followed the grenade's trajectory and had ducked away, making himself the smallest target possible, just in case. When he looked back towards Clara, she had changed position and was cursing: "Fucker! Fucker! You're gonna pay you, MOTHER FUCKER!"

She was going for the VX. Grey found himself in a terrible position. If he shot her while she was holding the vial, it would fall and break—and Jillybean was right there, still scrunched down at the front bumper. He could only hope for a lucky shot, catching Clara just right. Only she didn't cooperate.

Clara went through the Humvee and came out the passenger side, where Grey had no shot whatsoever.

Out of the dark and the rain, a vial landed right at his feet and broke open. Now he was the hunted. Clamping his lips shut, he turned to run, took two steps and stopped as another vial landed just in front of him, shattering and releasing its deadly gas.

357

He threw himself to the right, tripped as one leg went numb and tried to roll. He made it to the ditch, a strange stinging pain running up his leg and along his right arm. He couldn't feel the gun in his hand, and even if he could, he wouldn't have been able to lift it.

Grey could only turn over to see his death coming in the form of a woman with hell in her eyes. She had another vial in her raised right hand and was about to throw it when Jillybean screamed: "Stop!"

The little girl had gone for the shotgun. It looked ponderous in her scrawny arms, like the oar to a longboat. She had it aimed…somewhat at Clara who was teary-eyed and fierce. "No," was all she said and then threw the vial straight into Grey's chest.

He tried to throw himself back into the ditch but too late. The vial hit him and broke—the pain on his exposed skin was intense, but worse was the breath he took. It turned his lungs to shriveled raisins. He was as good as dead and so was Jillybean. The shotgun was simply too big for the seven year old. The effort to pull the trigger and aim at the same time was too much for her weak arms. The buckshot whizzed harmlessly past Clara.

The girl screamed, threw the gun away and ran.

That was all Grey saw. He had one good leg and it seemed possessed of a mind of its own as it kicked out twice and pushed his mostly paralyzed body right into the ditch where the water covered him over. It was the ice water of snow melt but in his death he didn't feel a thing.

Chapter 40

Jillybean

She didn't just throw away the shotgun as Grey supposed. Unfamiliar with this brand, she tried to kill Clara with it one more time, pulling the trigger, only it wouldn't budge. Normally, she would go down a checklist of possible problems and solutions except she had all of a second to discover the problem and enact a solution.

Besides, her shoulder ached and her right arm was numb. The gun was a full on adult-sized portable cannon and a part of her wanted to go back to using the rock she had picked as a weapon. It was more her speed.

With Clara bearing down on her, Jillybean tossed the gun aside and ran for the Humvee. If Clara went for the shotgun, which Jillybean suspected she would, the Humvee was the safest place to be. But Clara didn't go for the gun. Her heart was black with the lust for murder and she ran with her hands outstretched. Jillybean was fairly certain Clara wanted to strangle her to death.

The fear of it energized her flying legs as she ran in a circle around the Humvee, using her quickness to put some distance between the madwoman and herself. Had she wanted to, she could have circled the vehicle once more and then sped out into the forest, and likely, would have gotten away. Ipes was in her head begging for just that.

But Neil hadn't run away, and neither had Captain Grey. She wouldn't either—the decision seemed to sink Ipes back down into her and now it felt as though Chris was watching, rooting her on, making her feel as though she stood a good chance of defeating a woman twice her size and who possessed a strength only manic fury could bestow.

It was crazy, but then again, so was Jillybean, and so was Clara, who laughed in a shrill *I'm completely bonkers* sort of way when the little girl stooped to pick up the rock she had dropped earlier.

"This is all your fault, Fucky-bean!" she screeched, in a voice loud enough to be heard up and down the valley. "You did all of this by sticking your fucking nose where it didn't fucking belong!"

Jillybean didn't answer. She didn't have the endurance of an adult. Answering the crazy woman would be a waste of breath, both literally and figuratively. Instead she concentrated on her surroundings, looking for a better weapon or an edge in the unequal battle.

Two trips around the Humvee yielded nothing. There was a gas mask on the passenger seat of the vehicle, a few empty bottles in the foot well and a scattering of brass shell casings. The only real thing she discovered was the unsettling knowledge that Clara had been looking for a chance to kill her from the day she and Shawn had been banished.

"We were with the Azael when they attacked," Clara bragged in an eager way, as though she were remembering a great moment in her life. "When the Valley fell, Shawn was going to get the kids but I was coming for you, Jilly-fuck. I was going to stab your eyes out. I was going to fuck you with my hunting knife. What do you think of that?"

Jillybean thought it was crazy and when she looked back over her shoulder at the woman, who was only steps behind, she swore she was looking at some sort of brackish water demon instead of a woman.

Clara ripped a sleeve across her face, dashing aside the rain and hissed: "And when I heard the River King had Grey and was going to rip the flesh from his bones, we came rushing as fast as we could. We were coming to get you. I knew you'd show up and I knew you'd do something stupid."

The woman's voice grated out of her, thick and raspy and so filled with hate that it started to play on Jillybean's nerves. It was all she could do to concentrate on keeping out of reach.

"I just missed getting you. I was the one who found the River King's body and it was still warm. I knew you were close."

She is a demon, Jillybean thought. Once more her eyes were pulled back to stare in fright at the creature in human skin. She couldn't help it. The compunction to look back was overwhelming. It destroyed her concentration. Her feet tripped on themselves and she fell. Clara gave a shout, pouncing on her as though Jillybean were a baby gazelle and she a hungry lioness.

Still, Jillybean's fading energy was enough to save her. Just in time, she rolled under the high-seated Humvee and then began crawling for the rain and the darkness and the dubious safety of the wet night beyond.

Clara crawled after her, still yammering, the eagerness growing with every word. "I missed you there, but I almost got you in Vinita. There were rumors that a little girl was running around Oklahoma all on her own. A girl with flyaway hair. Somehow I missed you, but there were other rumors as well. Rumors up and down the Mississippi about a missing weapon. It didn't take much to put two and two together."

Jillybean pulled herself from beneath the Humvee, banged into the open passenger door and sprang backwards. She let her momentum carry her around the back end of the vehicle.

You've tried, Ipes' voice spoke into her ear. It was true. She had done her best to confront Clara and yet, half a minute had passed uselessly. Grey was probably drowned, Neil had likely bled out and Gayle had been going to die, anyway. *It's time to run,* the zebra said.

He isn't real, she told herself, but all the same, he was right. So far the only weapons she had seen in or out of the Humvee were the shotgun, which was practically useless to the little girl, and the VX which was even worse. Even if she could get one of the vials, Clara was always so close on her heels that the gas would end up getting them both and that sort of death scared Jillybean worse than being strangled.

But she wasn't ready to give up just yet. Clara was now out from beneath the Humvee and racing after her. Luckily, Jillybean had a lead of half a car length on her. This breathing room gave her an opportunity. Instead of going around the Humvee on the next pass, she went through it. She was small and nimble and darted across the seats and was out the other side in two seconds.

In those two seconds, she had seen the VX. Among other items associated with it, there were sixteen glass vials sitting in the fancy suitcase she had forced the Colonel to carry out of his armory. For a moment, she thought about grabbing one, however, they were in the backseat and just out of reach. Clara followed her in and then out again—her arms were longer and she came out grinning, holding up a vial in each hand.

"Who's the genius, now? I have the world's deadliest bio-weapon and all you got is a rock. What? Are you going to run?" Jillybean had been sidling along the back end of the Humvee, her feet taking over as her mind began to shut down out of fear.

"Go ahead and run. I'll even give you a head start. I'll count to three. One…"

Jillybean actually took two steps away from the Humvee before Chris' voice, speaking clear as day, said: *If you run, she'll be able to target you and not be hurt by the gas. Stay close.*

That seemed like the worst advice ever, except he was right. Just like always, she had to stay close and either create an opportunity or wait for one to occur. And she didn't have time to wait. She ran around the Humvee once more. This time, in her hubris, Clara only jogged and didn't do anything to stop Jillybean as she took a short cut through the vehicle a second time.

When the little girl got to the other side, she dropped to the ground, while Clara leaned in the driver's side and asked: "What's wrong, Jillybean? Did you drop your rock?"

Jillybean no longer had the rock. In her hand was the gas mask that had been sitting on the passenger seat. With her breath pent up in her lungs, she was desperately trying to fit the mask over her head and seal it tight. When Jillybean came back up again, Clara's face was frozen—frozen and twisted. She was only just then realizing that a rock in the hand of a genius is always so much more than just a rock.

On her way through the Humvee, the little girl had thrown her rock into the suitcase, where the tinkle of glass told her she had all of a second to get out and *maybe* another two to get the mask on.

Once it was in place, gripping her face in a pinch, she backed away as Clara warped into something hideous. Her features twisted, her front teeth snapped into pieces falling onto the driver's seat of the Humvee, her back arched until something cracked and yet she still stood, a hell-formed mannequin. Lastly, the two vials she carried burst and if the first whiff of VX gas filling the Humvee hadn't killed her, the contents of the vials escaping into the air around her certainly did.

Jillybean didn't stay to watch the rest, she had people to save. She ran for the gas-smelling Jeep to get her med bag.

As she came up, she saw Neil watching her through slitted eyes. "Hang on!" she screamed through her mask and then ducked into the Jeep. The medbag was the size of a piece of carry-on luggage and weighed over thirty pounds. It was half buried and should have been a struggle to free, however

Jillybean's blood was up. She heaved it out of the mess in one tremendous pull.

"Did we win?" Neil asked, in a tired whisper as she stood.

"Yes, sorta." At the moment, it didn't feel like Jillybean had won anything. In fact, it seemed to her as though she had failed completely—everything she held dear, her family, her friends, even the Valley itself, was dead or dying. And on top of that, she was going crazy again. *You never stopped being crazy, Jilly*, Eve said.

"I'll deal with you, later," Jillybean hissed. Neil's dim eyes grew confused and she was forced to smile. "No, I meant I'll be back for you, real quick."

She turned to run for Captain Grey, but stopped in midstep, suddenly afraid to move. Ipes was back yelling: *Stop! Remember the gas.*

"Right," she said, feeling turned around and shook up inside. At least four vials of VX gas had been broken open in the area and there was no telling where the invisible gas was or how far it extended or in what direction.

The closest shattered vial lay in the middle of the road, twenty feet away. It would be the height of stupidity to go rushing anywhere except over the ditch and across the field. Even with a mask on, the gas could get to her through her exposed skin; she could die just running over to Captain Grey.

She needed to be able to see the air and how it was moving in relation to the Jeep and the wounded. Some sort of smoke would have been perfect, only her bombs had been ruined. Her mind was going a mile a minute, trying to think of a way to save them all and not die in the process.

"If only Jessica hadn't been knocked about so bad…" She stopped as she could feel Chris' scorn: *There's no time for 'if onlys.' There's only time for 'what ifs,' such as…*

"Such as what if I can still use the Jeep?" In a flash, she fished out her lighter, flicked it open and produced a flame. "Sorry Jessica," she whispered and tossed the lighter onto the exposed and ruptured gas tank.

In seconds Jessica was engulfed in flames, belching out a heavy black smoke which drifted across the road at a slight diagonal, heading down the hill.

It was all Jillybean needed to see. In a full sprint, she raced along the edge of the ditch until she got to Grey. He had done the right thing by pushing himself into the water. Not only had it limited his exposure, the clean, running water must have washed away most of the VX—she hoped.

Better still, he was perfectly slanted head first into the water with his legs sticking up onto the bank. It was perfect because even if his lungs hadn't basically sealed themselves due to the gas, because of his angle, his nasal passages and throat were flooded but his lungs were dry—yes, he was dying, but he wasn't drowning.

Without pause, the girl splashed down next to him, grabbed him by the collar of his BDU shirt and heaved. It took all of her strength just to get his head and shoulders clear of the water. Then he was floating as she dragged him back upstream where the air was fresh and clean.

Still it was a risk when, in an all or nothing move, she threw off her mask, and sucked in a huge gulp of air. If there was VX, she would die if not there was a chance she could save her friend. She paused, waiting to feel the poison get her and when it didn't, she pinched Grey's nose shut and blew into him with all her might. His chest heaved once and then slowly settled.

By the time it did, she had her bag open and was digging through it, picking up rubber-stopped vials one at a time until: "Atropine, yes!" She had her own store of Atropine, though prior to the last few days she would have never thought to use it on a nerve gas victim. It was in her bag for cardiac emergencies which called for both Atropine and Epinephrine to be administered intravenously.

Only, there was no time for an IV. Moving as fast as she could, she sucked two milligrams into a syringe and then stabbed it straight into the fat vein in the crook of Grey's arm. To get the atropine to his heart faster, she took the arm and laid it on the bank above his head. When it tried to slide back down, she pinned it in place with her knee.

Without slowing down, she took another deep breath and blew once more, deep into Grey's lungs. "Hey! Mister Captain Grey!" He was unresponsive and for a moment hope left her. Had she chosen wrong? Was she wasting precious moments blowing into a corpse while Neil and Gayle bled to death behind her? Was she even then all alone, surrounded by corpses?

She looked back and found herself nearly blinded. Jessica Jeep was giving her all, turning night into day, casting a golden hue over the battlefield. She was a beacon that could be seen from one end of the Valley to the other.

"Someone will come," Jillybean said. She didn't want to be alone. She was afraid of it. "Someone's gotta come." She took another big breath and blew into Grey's lips. As the chest fell, she worked his arm back and forth, hoping to force the blood to his heart so the Atropine could start to work.

"Someone will come." She forced another breath into him and then snuck a peek down the slope, praying for headlights… and seeing them. "Oh God!" she cried, tears suddenly in her eyes. She went to blow once more into Grey's mouth but she caught him staring at her.

"They're coming!" she yelled in joy, hoping Neil was alive to hear her. She hopped up and ran towards the two sets of headlights before they could get too close. There was still VX gas to worry about.

Veronica and seven soldiers piled out of the two Humvees and at first they pointed their guns at Jillybean until she explained what had happened. Two of the soldiers refused to get near the gas, but the others followed the little girl along the ditch to where Grey was lying. His eyes were closed.

Jillybean was shocked; the grown-ups only stood there looking at each other, not knowing what to do. *Didn't they know anything about anything?* she wondered. Aloud, she asked: "Miss Veronica? Can you monitor him. Ya-know, his breathing and his pulse." Jillybean didn't wait for an answer. Neil needed her.

Like Grey he was half in and half out of the ditch and by the light of the burning Jeep, he looked to be dead. Where he wasn't splashed in blood, he was grey in color and the soldiers all cast their heads down. Jillybean knew better. Neil Martin had always been tougher than he looked.

And yet there was a limit to his toughness. He could barely open his eyes and when he spoke it was in a whisper. "Did we win?"

"Yes," Jillybean said, flashing him a smile before pulling out her pocket knife. As she cut away the clothes from around his wounds, she added: "Captain Grey is still alive and Veronica is here and she brought soldiers who'll help us."

In spite of her words, the soldiers still weren't helping. Once more they were staring around, uselessly. "The lady," she hissed at the closest one. "Get her out of the water. And you, sir, can I have your belt, please?" Neil's leg wound was still pumping blood, though at a slower rate, which meant there wasn't as much to pump.

Neil's head turned, moving slowly like a sun dial until he could see Gayle. Like him, there didn't seem that much to save. She lolled, lifelessly on the side of the road with two soldiers kneeling beside her. One took the initiative to check her pulse. "Fifty and kinda weak. She's got a belly wound. It doesn't look good."

"What about Mister Captain Grey?" Jillybean yelled, without looking up. She had wrapped the soldier's belt around Neil's thigh wound and now cinched it down as tight as it would —she needed it tighter. "Pull this as hard as you can," she said to the closest soldier.

"Grey's breathing is down, way down," Veronica called back. "And I can hardly feel his pulse."

Now that her hands were free, she reached into her medbag and got the Atropine out again. She handed it and the syringe to another soldier. "Give him one milligram of this right in one of his veins in his arm." She pointed at a little line on the syringe. "That's what means one milligram."

"Look at you," Neil said, a ghost of a smile on his lips. "I'm so proud of you, Jillybean. You really are a good one. Now go… go save her," he said. The effort to shift his eyes toward Gayle seemed to take the last of his energy.

"One sec," Jillybean replied, shoving him over to inspect the shotgun wound. It was bloody and nasty. His flesh was in ribbons and that was putting it nicely. The blast had caught him at an angle, a half second after he'd been hit by the 9 mm slug to the leg. She plugged her stethoscope into her ears and listened to his lungs, worried that one had been punctured and that he was even then drowning in his own blood.

Before she could get a read, however, he pushed himself over and repeated in a more forceful tone. "No. Save her. That is an order." He shifted, his eyes moving to the soldier who had a grip on the belt holding the artery in his thigh closed. "That is an order. Get her away from me." It would be his last order.

Epilogue

Sadie Martin

She stood on the crest of the last hill overlooking the Valley. Estes was a ghost town. Of the fifty-five hundred people who had called it home six weeks before, only a thousand remained and it wouldn't be long before they, too, were gone.

It was no longer the idyllic green-pastured, serene, Tolkien-esque hidden gem that it had once been. Now, it was death for the unwary. A sergeant in Bravo company—there were only three companies of soldiers now which was very sad—had wandered too close to the Stanley, hit a patch of VX and had died before his buddies even knew what was going on.

Three days of rain had taken care of most of the problems concerning the VX. Unfortunately it had created unforeseen problems as well; what people called the "downstream effect." For the most part, the VX had been diluted by the rains, but in some places, it had pooled to form a concentrate that was as deadly as drinking straight from the vial.

This was the main reason the Valley was being abandoned. The secondary reason was more arcane. Some people thought that Estes was cursed in some fashion, while others thought that Jillybean was cursed, feeling as though trouble followed her everywhere.

Sadie didn't believe in curses. She believed in the evil within men's hearts. If there was a curse it had been laid upon all of humanity, not on a single little girl.

She also believed in working out and had done so ever since she left the hospital three days after the attacks. Ever since then, she had run and jumped and lifted things until she was in tears.

The VX had done something to her. It felt as though her bones had been encased in sandpaper. Everything, her muscles, her tendons, her ligaments ground and grated against each other with every movement. It had been a tough six weeks, but gradually, with a lot of therapy and pain meds, the intense grating along her nerves had subsided, leaving behind only the desire to run again like she used to.

With a deep breath, Sadie took off down the hill, stretching her legs in long, bounding strides, the pack that held her weapons and water nestled firmly to her back, barely moving. This is what she needed on that particular day. Decisions were being made that would affect her small family and she hadn't been able to sit idly by while the new council debated.

The question before them was whether or not Jillybean would be allowed to accompany the group to Cheyenne. In her mind they would be fools to kick her out. A hundred times over, Jillybean had proven herself worthy.

"They govern out of fear," Grey had said when the question had been first raised. He had been grimacing through his own workout at the time. Like Sadie, he knew how important it was to be sharp and in shape. "And I, for one, won't be a part of an army led by cowards." Only a few dozen people had agreed with him, many of whom were people they had traveled with, meaning ex-whores whose fighting ability was suspect.

Sadie hoped it wouldn't come down to a split. There wasn't much in Cheyenne, and the winters were notoriously brutal, but it was better than being on their own again. If there was a split, they would head over the mountains to the west coast, where the name Jillybean might never have been heard of—or Sadie Martin for that matter.

She was still a wanted and hunted woman, after all. "They'll have to catch me first," she said, breathing easy, heading into town at a gallop. She ran down Highway 34 through the canyon of over turned cars until she reached the gap that headed to the southern portion of the Valley.

On the corner was a gas station where Jillybean spent a good amount of her time. Sadie ducked through the beads hanging from the door, and didn't bother trying to avoid the gravel that had been purposefully strewn on the floor. Jillybean didn't like being snuck up on and Sadie didn't like sneaking up on her. All too frequently, she would catch Jillybean in the middle of a conversation with an apparently empty room. Whenever this happened, Sadie pretended that she hadn't heard a peep.

Everyone in the Valley pretended that Jillybean wasn't crazy.

"Hey, squirt?" Sadie called as she made her way to the back bay. "You in here?" The place was dark and quiet and empty save for *Hank the Humvee*, Jillybean's replacement for *Jessica Jeep,* who was always referred to with great solemnity and sadness.

"She saved me a ton of times," Jillybean said of the Jeep. Despite this, she hadn't considered using another Jeep for a second. "Too underpowered and their center of gravity is too high. That's what means they can get turnded over by a Humvee."

Jillybean spent a part of everyday turning the Humvee into the perfect post-apocalyptic vehicle. Along with being bulletproof, it had a video system that was twice as extensive as the old Jeep's, self-sealing tires, remote detonated bombs, smoke dispensers that could be released without starting the engine, firing ports, a roof mounted M249 on a swivel that could also be fired from within, three exterior drone bays, armored fuel tank reserves, and a new sound system, complete with a library of books on tape.

It was a work of love.

When the little girl wasn't covering herself in grease, she was more than likely reading. She always had books with her and they always pertained to subjects dull enough to put Sadie into a coma such as chemistry, biology, anatomy, and pharmacological guides. Her current study was titled, without any nod to creativity: *Contemporary Oral and Maxillofacial Surgery*.

On nice days, she read these dusty tomes near the blue lake or in high mountain pastures. When it was chilly or wet, she read next to the fireplace in Captain Grey's cabin, which was, without a doubt, the coziest spot in the Valley. She liked to be near Emily, and Deanna liked to be able to nap knowing that someone was watching over her and her baby. Jillybean might have been crazy, but she was also fiercely loyal.

Sadie left the gas station, crossed the street and loped down Moccasin Drive towards the now abandoned hospital. The homes all around it were considered too close to the scene of the attack and had been deserted.

Jillybean had chosen one of these as her *laboratory*. She didn't call it that—everyone else did. The gossip in the Valley was that the little girl performed ghoulish experiments on the zombies she lured into the gated-off home. Sadie tried to tell people that Jillybean only practiced surgery on the zombies, but that was a lie that nobody believed.

It was true, the little girl did practice "surgeoning" on the living cadavers but she wasn't above satisfying her boundless curiosity.

"Hello?" Sadie called out softly as she let herself in through the tall gate. Although she thought that Jillybean's work was

369

important, she didn't like going to the laboratory in much the same way she liked sausage but didn't want to see how it was made.

Had she been there, Jillybean would have answered by now. Still, Sadie went on, pulling a flashlight from her pack and heading down into the basement. She was there to snoop, not because she didn't trust the little girl, but because the new council didn't trust her. One of the requirements allowing Jillybean to stay in the Valley this long was that she be monitored; a nice way to say spied upon.

"Hey Larry, Curly, Moe. How you guys doing?" Sadie said, to the first three zombies she found chained in the homemade cells on the left. These three were part of Jillybean's growth experiment. She had discovered that the zombies, even the adult ones, were still growing—now she was trying to discover if there was an upper range to how big they could get. It had been only five weeks and each was now over six and a half feet tall.

Sadie always made sure to walk as far from their outstretched hands as possible.

The two cells on the right held emaciated zombies, both as thin as sticks. These two were being deprived of food to see how long they would live. Listlessly they attacked the bars, trying to get at her. They had also been there for five weeks, without having eaten a thing.

Further on were different cells that had held different experimental creatures, but as they were empty, Sadie didn't bother to look into them. The final, and largest, cell was Jillybean's operating room, where the scent of bleach made Sadie's big brown eyes water.

There was a sad-looking zombie chained to a gurney. It bore hundreds of stitches, had tubes running everywhere, and was bandaged from here to tomorrow, and still it tried to tear itself to pieces to get at Sadie. She beamed her flashlight on its chains, satisfying herself that they were in no danger of slipping from its wrists or ankles.

"Good enough," she said, and left as quickly as she could, happy to breathe the clean mountain air once more.

As unsettling as the experiments and the "surgeoning" were, they were tolerated by the remaining people of the Valley. The seven year old was the closest thing to a doctor within five hundred miles and when she wasn't working on her Humvee, reading, babysitting, experimenting or surgeoning, Jillybean saw patients in the new hospital.

The new hospital was actually the old veterinarian clinic. It was hard to take anything seriously there since the walls were decorated with puppies and kitties, and the only doctor on call tended to wear a white tutu over a crushed velvet pink warm-up suit, grungy Keds, and a lab coat that had been sized down by Kay Gallagher. She also gave herself lollipops after a successful visit.

There was an obvious reason why Jillybean kept so busy—sadly, the voices had never left.

When Sadie got to the hospital, Jillybean was stitching up a soldier who claimed to have cut his hand open sharpening a hunting knife. "He really cut himself opening a can of Spaghetti O's," Jillybean said after she had finished up and was washing her hands, standing on a little stool. "I could tell because there was some sauce on his sleeve and some of the O's were on his pants and the cut had little curves in it."

Sadie grinned. "Nice detective work."

There was a heavy moment between the sisters as Jillybean dried her hands. "So?" she asked. "Have they come to a decision? Is that why you're here?"

"No, not yet. I just wanted to see how you were doing and how our patient was doing." Sadie felt a stab of guilt as she always did when she was reminded of the night of the attack. When the calls were coming in and the gas attacks were happening—there were actually three that night—she had done everything she could to get up and go with Veronica to rescue Neil, but she had been too slow and too wracked by the pain.

In vain, or so it seemed, she had crawled out the front door, only to be nearly run over seconds later by a midnight blue, pickup truck. The driver thought she was a zombie and had almost shot her; he had jumped and given little shriek when she demanded that he drive her. The shriek had reminded her of Neil and she had redoubled her efforts to stand.

When the soldier hesitated, Sadie had said: "Governor's orders!" That did the trick, and in seconds, she was racing up the winding roads to where a fire roared in the night. It was Jillybean's handiwork, Sadie knew it from a mile away. They got to the corpse-strewn road but the soldier wouldn't go further than where the other Humvees were parked. He didn't even want to get out of the pickup truck, but Sadie had hissed him into action.

As she couldn't walk, the soldier carried her and they were in time to watch Jillybean walk away from Neil's body, tears in her huge blue eyes. "What's going on?" Sadie had asked, fearing the worst.

When it was explained to her, she went over and stood by Jillybean as she examined Gayle's wound. "Can you save them both?"

Jillybean didn't look up. "No."

"Then save Neil, damn it. That's your father, Jillybean." Gayle had been staring up into the rain, slowly dying, but was still better off than Neil. It couldn't be denied, she had more color and unlike Neil, she was conscious.

"He probably won't make it. And…and he told me not to try."

Ignoring the pain in her broken arm, Sadie had taken Jillybean by the ponytail and yanked her to her feet. "You'll save your father and if you have time, we'll help Gayle." There hadn't been time for Gayle. It had taken every ounce of skill in the little girl to clamp off Neil's femoral artery and sow it up as he died beneath her knife. Then it had taken a miracle to revive him.

To keep him alive had taken four surgeries, a gallon of antibiotics and hours of prayers. Neil had been anything but happy to find himself alive.

"He's a little crabby," Jillybean warned.

"Yeah, I'm sorta used to it," Sadie said. There had been an edge between the father and daughter for weeks. "Why don't you come with me? He's always happier when you're around."

Jillybean grinned. "I'm his favorite, what can I say? You know what my secret is? I tell him he can't have all sorts of things and then I say: maybe a little. It makes me a hero."

"You're everyone's hero, especially mine. Come on, let's go see Mister Crabby Pants."

Neil was already out of bed, trying to dress himself. He grunted and groaned with every movement. "I should be at this meeting," he explained. "They don't understand. Cheyenne is a terrible idea. There's no barriers or…" He had to take a moment to catch his breath to finish his thought. "…or anything."

Jillybean gave Sadie a look suggesting Neil shouldn't do anything but get back into bed. Now it was Sadie's turn to be the hero. She helped Neil into his shirt and then slowly worked his pants on one leg at a time. He needed a break after that and by the time he was ready to get his shoes on, the sound of an engine coming stopped him.

It was the growl of a Humvee and it was coming straight to the hospital. It could only be Grey. The three waited in silence as the soldier's boots thumped down the hall. The sound of them caused Jillybean to back slowly into a corner. There was a finality to the steady tread. And it was worse when Grey came into the room. There were long lines drawing his face down into a grim frown.

Jillybean crumpled at the frown, her legs giving out. "They don't want me, do they?" Sadie could see a blanket of sadness cover the girl; she was being thrown out of the group.

"I'm staying with Jillybean," Sadie announced before Grey could say anything. "The group is a bunch of ingrates and they can go to Cheyenne and freeze to death for all I care. We'll head to California and work on our tans, what do you say? Just you and me, together." Jillybean gave her a shy smile.

"Slow down, you two," Grey said. "Some of us would like to go to California, as well. The new council made it obvious that none of the old council members would be welcome in Cheyenne. They especially think that you, Neil are an issue. They think you are a troublemaker."

Neil, who seemed a little woozy with all the excitement of getting out of bed, asked: "Me? They blame all this on me?"

"More or less," Grey admitted. "Either way, we're not wanted and neither are Deanna and Veronica and a few others. The main part of the group will be leaving in June. We have until then to make preparations. Thankfully, they are allotting us a share of the ammo and food based on the number of people going with us."

Neil sat back on his bed and gazed at the ceiling for a few moments. "And what about fuel?"

"Three hundred gallons," Grey said, the words coming out softly.

Neil's eyes went wide. "That's it? Oh, they are really screwing us, especially since it was Jillybean who got all that gas in the first place. Gah! How many people do you think will come with us?"

"Most of the women that Deanna led from the Island," Grey answered right away. "Each will have at least one man in tow. Some of my soldiers will come, but not that many, I'm afraid."

"What I'm afraid of is having too many. Jeeze! Three hundred gallons! If we have more than ten cars we'll never make it, and I get the feeling we're going to have more than ten. This new council strikes me as a little weak." Neil chewed on his lip as he considered things. "Okay, the first thing we need to find out is how many people will be coming with us. And, of course, we will need to figure out exactly where we'll be going. I suggest we look into San Francisco, L.A. and Seattle or the areas nearby. But with so little fuel we might find ourselves stranded."

"With so little fuel we can't afford for the entire group to be roaming up and down the coast," Grey warned. "We're going to need to sent scouts to find safe routes to the west ahead of the main body. I'm thinking three teams going to each of the three cities. I'll lead one."

"And I'll lead another," Sadie said. She took her sister's hand and lifted her to her feet. "And I'll take Jillybean with me. I know what you're going to say: it won't be safe, blah, blah, blah, but who do we have left that you trust more than me and Jillybean?"

Neil had been frowning; now he shrugged. "There's no one I trust more than you two. What do you think, Grey?"

The soldier was quiet for so long that Sadie wondered if he had heard the question. Finally, he answered, "There's going to be trouble no matter what, so…I guess it'll be okay. But you two are not going alone and you will do everything in your power to remain safe, got it?"

He had growled this last bit, which only made Sadie grin. "Don't worry, we'll be safe as cats."

Jillybean grinned. "Are cats really all that safe? I'd rather be safe as a safe. You know, the kind that holds jewels and stuff. They're called safes for a reason and what's in the west, anyways? Anything good?"

The answer was a complete unknown. No one knew what they would find over nearly eight hundred miles of mountains, desert and barren wasteland that crawled with millions of zombies and who knew what sort of people. The mystery of it was a lure to Sadie who wanted to get away from the Valley. She wanted to blaze new trails into a future where the possibilities wouldn't be limited by their past.

"There'll be something good," she said and then held out a pinky to Jillybean. "You and me?"

The little girl hooked it with her own, saying: "Always."

The End

Author's Note

Thank you so much for reading The Apocalypse Revenge. I certainly hope that you enjoyed it. If so, could you please leave a review? Reviews are the best way to help an independent author, so thanks in advance.

Now, to the question on your mind: yes, there is a book 10 and yes, it is out. **The Apocalypse Sacrifice: The Undead World 10** is not for the weak…

With people fleeing the valley in droves and Estes no longer the safe haven it had once been, Neil Martin must make some hard choices. His group has dwindled to seventy homeless refugees who have very little left to survive on. They desperately need to find a place to call home before their many enemies realize how defenseless they truly are.

Instead of risking everything on a blind thrust across the Rockies to the Pacific, Neil sends out three picked teams to not only find a safe passage through the mountains but to also find a community that will take them in. Captain Grey is the obvious choice to lead one team, but is Sadie really the person to take charge of another?

She is a capable leader, a survivor, and a veteran of dozens of battles, but can she control the schizophrenic eight-year-old who won't leave her side even when the blood starts to run and the voices scream in her head?

And what happens when their mission is balanced on the knife's edge with disaster on either side and Jillybean a second from going nuclear. Will Sadie be able to make the hardest of sacrifices for the sake of her family? Or will she let love get in the way?

What readers say about The Apocalypse Sacrifice:

"DO NOT pick this up until you are ready to commit to an all-night sleep-defying read!"

"WAY OUT WICKED"

"...full of suspense and intrigue, love, both innocent and romantic, hate, both blinding and unnatural, non-stop action, and a very real gripping and palpable fear."

A special thanks to my beta readers and my editors: My Mum-Elizabeth Meredith-your line editing is priceless, Joanna Niederer, you've been such a help on almost all the novels in this series, Brannon Estis, Tracy King, and Lauren Benton.

PS If you are interested in autographed copies of my books, souvenir posters of the covers, Apocalypse T-shirts and other awesome Swag, please visit my website at **https://www.petemeredith1.com**

Fictional works by Peter Meredith:

Made in the USA
Monee, IL
13 June 2020